Books by Jerrold Morgulas

The Accused
The Siege

THE
TORQUEMADA
PRINCIPLE

THE TORQUEMADA PRINCIPLE

a novel

Jerrold Morgulas

Rawson, Wade Publishers, Inc.
New York

Library of Congress Cataloging in Publication Data
Morgulas, Jerrold.
The Torquemada principle.
I. Title.
PZ4.M8524T   [PS3563.O87158]   813'.5'4   79–67639
ISBN 0–89256–124–6

Published simultaneously in Canada
by McClelland and Stewart, Ltd.
Manufactured in the United States of America by
R. R. Donnelley & Sons Co.,
Crawfordsville, Indiana
Designed by E. O'Connor
First Edition

*For my father
who early instructed me
in the moral ambiguities
of human behavior*

THE
TORQUEMADA
PRINCIPLE

September 7, 1938: Aspern Airfield, Vienna

The big three-motored Junkers lumbered blindly down through the rain, its landing lights winking, its pilot searching desperately for some sign of the Aspern Airport runway. The lower the plane dropped, the more intense the rain seemed to become. At seventy-five meters, the pilot could have sworn that he was at the bottom of the ocean.

"Blackbird to field control, Blackbird to field control . . . where are your lights? We can't see a damned thing."

"Field control to Blackbird. You cannot land, do you hear?" Static sputtered. The engines droned on. Then the voice came through again. "You cannot land, do you understand?"

"Field control, where are your landing lights?"

"The runways are full of transports. We can't move them because of the weather. Repeat. You cannot land here."

"Turn on the damned lights, field control. Turn them on, do you hear me?"

The co-pilot was pressed back against his seat, his face bloodless, his eyes closed. The pilot swore again but received only a burst of static from the radio.

The three lone passengers in the body of the almost empty transport caught only the sound but not the words, and leaned forward, trying to hear more clearly.

The Abwehr courier from Berlin, Lieutenant Bresner, fidgeted with the chain that held the dispatch pouch to his wrist. He noted with well-schooled satisfaction that the Security Service major sitting across from him was in a cold sweat and turning green. His fingers seemed welded to the iron-pipe framework of the seat, and his lips were moving rapidly. The only other passenger, a signal captain, was dozing with a copy of *Paris-Match* open over his face.

Bresner watched the SD* man's growing alarm. Hadn't he ever been in a plane before? And didn't he know the Viennese? This was at least the tenth time in the last few months that Bresner's plane hadn't been able to land because of some prob-

---

* Sicherheitsdienst—the SS Security Service.

3

lem or other on the field. Granted, things were worse now, what with near-mobilization crowding up every runway in the Reich, and the damned rain on top of everything else. Maybe the SD man was right to be afraid. Maybe they would crash this time. Well, if they did, Bresner would at least have the satisfaction of seeing one terrified SD swine go with him.

Through the open door to the cockpit came the distant, metallic radio voice again.

". . . you cannot land . . ."

"Blackbird to field control. Either you find us a place to come down or I set Iron Annie here down in the Prater, do you hear me?"

Then, over the radio came an odd exchange; the field control operator was talking to someone else. The voice, even through the static, sounded familiar. It sounded, in fact, like Bresner's immediate superior, Captain Henkl.

The operator's voice returned, alone.

"Field control to Blackbird . . . we will light magnesium flares on the north runway. There may be just enough space. Can you stay up for another ten minutes? It's the best we can do."

The pilot swore again. The cockpit door slammed shut as the plane banked sharply to the west.

The SD major blanched.

Bresner could not resist.

"An excellent flight, Herr Sturmbannführer,* yes? Very exciting, isn't it?"

The big Junkers wheeled again suddenly and started to climb. Bresner turned. Having an SD man aboard was no joke, even one who was petrified and airsick. He wondered whether Major Langbein had known about it. Of course he had. He had probably decided that it was safer, less likely to arouse suspicion that way. Or funnier. Langbein had an odd sense of humor.

Bresner looked out of the port window, just behind the door. As the plane banked again, he caught sight of a line of bright blue lights suddenly springing up out of the rain far below.

---

* SS equivalent of Major.

The engines' drone sank as the pilot cut the power. Lieutenant Bresner closed his eyes and sat up very straight in his seat, just as he had been taught to do, his head pressed against the back, his fingers tight on the arm rests.

The Junkers began to drop and the familiar sensation of landing panic swept over him. It was the worst moment. Always.

He opened one eye, very cautiously. The sky outside was a cold blue-white glare against which he could see each individual drop of rain. Then he could see the flares themselves, for only a second though, as the plane turned into its final approach.

He also saw that they were coming down in an alley formed by two ranks of closely packed military transports. The pilot would have less than five meters on each side by way of clearance. One bad gust of wind at the wrong second. . . .

Bresner swallowed hard; then, with a tremendous feeling of relief, he felt the wheels rake the ground. The tail began to settle and the plane came to a gentle, rolling stop.

The pilot came out of the cockpit, mopping his forehead.

"Did you see that?"

"A beautiful landing, Captain."

"Yes? Look outside." He kicked open the fuselage door. Bresner looked out into the magnesium glare and blanched. The port wingtip of the Junkers was less than a meter from the nose of a big Focke-Wulf Condor transport.

Lieutenant Bresner, somewhat shaken, climbed down as quickly as he could, not even looking back to enjoy the SD man's discomfort. He felt slightly sick and extremely grateful.

Squinting into the driving rain, he saw at once that he had been right. Klaus Henkl was standing there, waiting for him at the end of the improvised runway, silhouetted against the headlights of the idling car behind him, hands clasped together, not minding the rain at all.

"Lieutenant Bresner?"

"Sir . . ."

"You have the pouch, of course?"

"Of course, sir."

"Then get in, Lieutenant Bresner, do get in."

Bresner wondered what Henkl would have said if he'd

answered that he did not, in fact, have the pouch. The captain's tone certainly implied that if that had been the case he would have been left standing there out in the rain, to walk all the way back to Vienna.

They got into the front seat of Henkl's car. The SD man was just then coming down the iron ladder, still very unsteady.

Henkl saw him and frowned.

"You didn't talk to—*that*—on the trip down, did you?"

"Of course not, sir," Bresner said. "I think that Major Langbein must have known about him, sir."

"Most likely," said Henkl, still frowning. He kicked over the engine and started the wipers. It was teeming even worse now than it had been before.

"A moment, Lieutenant," Henkl said, and reached under the dashboard. There was a short-wave radio there, Bresner recalled, a special installation, all Henkl's own. The radio spit static for a second. Then, through it all, came the sound of organ music.

"Sir?" said Bresner, taken aback.

"Vatican Radio."

"I don't understand, sir."

"Frescobaldi. You don't have to understand Frescobaldi, Lieutenant."

Satisfied, Henkl stepped on the accelerator and the car moved down along the runway between the silent rows of Condors.

September 7, 8:25 P.M.: *Berlin*

It had stopped raining in Berlin around eight o'clock in the evening. The pavement before SD headquarters on the Prinz Albrechtstrasse glistened darkly, still wet enough to show clearly the tire imprints of those few cars that had passed that way since the downpour had abated. Steel-helmeted guards stood rigidly before the gates through which one had to pass in order to enter the building. A few lights burned in the upper windows. Downstairs, with the exception of Himmler's office —in which, whether he was there or not, a light almost always burned—all was dark.

Obersturmbannführer* Ulrich Schanz, SD, formerly of the Prussian state police, had always enjoyed walking just after a rain, and this evening was no exception. The air smelled fresh, the city felt clean and calm, if it could be said that anything these days could ever "feel" calm. He walked slowly, taking his time, though he knew that he was due at Standartenführer† Kepplinger's office at eight thirty sharp and that if he kept on at his present pace he would undoubtedly be late. He didn't care, not for rigid punctuality, not for the new rank titles and the uniforms. As far as he was concerned, Lieutenant Colonel would do nicely, just as it always had. And as for Kepplinger, whom he had detested since he first met him years ago, Colonel was not only good enough but far too good.

The summons had been too peremptory for his taste, though such curtness was clearly the fashion of the times. "Rudeness masquerading as efficiency," he had said to his son Helmut, warning the young man against the excessive arrogance of this new breed of para-military asses.

But Kepplinger was not a man to anger. He held too important a position and one had to be at least slightly careful. After all, no one, no matter who he was, dared trifle with one of Heydrich's protégés.

Schanz quickened his pace a little, rationalizing his acceleration as a reaction to the brisk air of the late summer's evening. Schanz was normally a man who prized punctuality, order, and schedule above almost all other things. His sense of detail and order had, in fact, been his making—as an expert on ancient records, bank documents, genealogy, and accounting, he had no equal. His most famous case, the Albrecht bank affair, was now textbook reading. It pained him, therefore, to be late, even deliberately late. Even when it was Kepplinger was was kept waiting.

Arriving at last at the SD building on Prinz Albrechtstrasse, he presented his papers to the guards and stared down their disapproving looks with some amusement. Schanz was a heavyset man, long past fifty, with a pair of iron gray mustaches of

---

* SS equivalent of Lieutenant Colonel.
† SS equivalent of Full Colonel.

a kind out of style since the war. Because of his size and shambling build, he avoided wearing a uniform whenever possible and dressed in a manner many of his superiors regarded as shockingly sloppy. This evening he was in a loose-fitting suit of English tweeds and wore a shapeless hat with a small Bavarian feather stuck in the band. No wonder the young guard had scowled; Schanz looked far more like an English tourist than an officer in the SD.

Standartenführer Ottakar Kepplinger was waiting for him in his upstairs office. The building was almost deserted. The few obligatory guards stood their ground at the landings and in distant rooms. Secretaries were busy pounding typewriters behind closed and perhaps locked doors. Kepplinger's own secretary looked up from a disordered dossier as Schanz entered. A large filing cabinet drawer hung open behind her.

"Obersturmbannführer Schanz?"

"Oberstleutnant* Schanz, Fraulein. You look surprised. Why?"

"You were expected at eight thirty," the woman said, in a vaguely surly tone.

"And it is now. . .?" Schanz lifted his wrist and glanced at his watch, "aha . . . eight thirty-four, is it not?"

"Yes, Herr Obersturmbannführer. Exactly."

The door to Kepplinger's office was partly open, and in the brief silence that followed, Kepplinger's voice could be heard concluding a phone conversation. The receiver was slammed down, too hard, whether in anger or in what Kepplinger regarded as brisk efficiency Schanz could not tell.

"Is that you, Schanz?"

"I was just having a pleasant chat with your secretary."

"Well, come in, come in. Frieda, you get back to work at once. And see that the outer door is closed."

Schanz smiled and went in. Kepplinger's office, precisely like the man, was nondescript, neither spartan—as was now the fashion with some—nor elaborately decorated as was the fashion with others. Kepplinger himself had hardly changed since the last time Schanz had seen him: a tall man, thin, with

---

* The army form for Lieutenant Colonel, as distinct from the SS.

sparse black hair combed flat back over a narrow skull, his eyes and nose always looking as though he had just gotten over a cold. There was something undeniably nasty about him, the way his mouth hardly ever moved, even when he was speaking rapidly. Like a ventriloquist's mouth. One could never be really sure whether that thin, hard voice was really coming from Kepplinger's throat or not.

"You're late," said Kepplinger, when the door had been closed.

"Precisely."

Kepplinger's eyebrows shot up.

"So as to remind you," said Schanz, "that you were once my subordinate and that now, even though you may outrank me, according to the rather peculiar order of things in our respective departments, we are at the very least—equal." Schanz paused to give Kepplinger time to reply. Kepplinger said nothing. Schanz smiled. "And what's more," he added, "I don't like being summoned so peremptorily."

"It was necessary."

"Really? I was taking my wife to the theatre. Whatever it is, couldn't it have waited until morning?"

"It was necessary," Kepplinger repeated dully, tapping his index finger on the ashtray. He seemed for a moment to ponder Schanz's attitude, then shrugged. Finally, with a touch of weariness and a flicker of a smile, he said, "Come now, sit down, Schanz. There's no need for unpleasantness."

"As you wish," Schanz replied—as if he'd had any intention of standing there whether Kepplinger wanted him to or not. He was at least ten years Kepplinger's senior and that, too, in the new order of things still counted for something.

Kepplinger tapped his cigarette out in a cut-glass ashtray.

"I see that you still remember," Schanz said. "That's good, very good, Ottakar. Now, if you don't mind . . . I'm puzzled. Why did you call for me, of all people?"

Kepplinger pushed a dog-eared dossier across his desk.

"I need you," he said, averting his glance.

Schanz smiled.

"Do you think you might open a window? That Turkish tobacco you smoke . . . awful, Ottakar, quite awful. . . ."

Kepplinger sighed and did as he had been asked.

A strained silence followed. Schanz stared at Kepplinger. It annoyed him that the man had hardly aged while he, Schanz, had put on at least twenty pounds since the days when Kepplinger had been an under-inspector in Schanz's division. Worse still, the trim black uniform looked exceedingly well on him while Schanz, in his rumpled tweeds, had all the military smartness of an ill-used taxidermist's model.

Finally Kepplinger spoke, measuring his words out with obvious care.

"We have a small problem that may require your—special abilities."

"Oh?"

"There are two persons . . . one in London, one in Graz. The exact identity of both is not known."

"My dear Kepplinger, there are nine million persons in London and perhaps one hundred and fifty thousand in Graz."

"Yes, yes, but there has been correspondence, you see, quite a lot of it. Between these two."

"But if you don't know who they are, then how . . .?"

Kepplinger cut him off. "The post office. Letters delivered to *poste-restante*. You know all about such things. We have descriptions, but that's all."

"Surveillance? Surely . . ."

"We have instituted surveillance, but since we did there have been no more letters."

"But why should any of this be of concern to you? People have relatives, friends, business contacts. There is no war as yet and, God willing, there won't be. What is the difficulty? Why can't the Graz police handle the matter, if it needs handling at all?"

"The Graz police are provincials. Clumsy. They can't be trusted and we have no established operation there as yet. It's too soon."

"But still, what difference should that make?"

Kepplinger sighed.

"There may be important persons in the government involved. The matter requires extreme tact."

"If so, I'd rather not be involved. I leave that kind of

infighting to those best equipped for it. Like yourself."

"And just what does that mean?" Kepplinger shot back, half rising. Schanz smiled pleasantly and rubbed his mustaches.

"Why, only that you don't want an old plodder like me involved in such a thing. One must be nimble, far quicker than I am at my age."

"Schanz, let's stop fencing, shall we? You're going to do it whether you like it or not. We both know that. Consider it an order. It *is* an order. Your superior has assigned you to me." He shoved a piece of paper across the desk. Schanz knew well enough his superior's looping signature.

"Now," said Kepplinger, "we have only this—that the letters have all been addressed to 'Frankenberger, *Poste-Restante*, Graz.' From London."

Schanz shrugged. "I would think that for you people nothing should be more simple. Just pick up every Frankenberger in Graz and . . ."

Kepplinger held up a hand. "Would I need you if it were that easy? Really, Schanz—"

"What then?"

"The problem is, there is not a single person named Frankenberger *in* Graz at the moment."

By the time another half hour had passed, Schanz had little more information than that. But he was beginning to feel distinctly uncomfortable. Every time he pressed for more details, Kepplinger grew surly—the old Freikorps belligerence breaking out again like measles. Schanz's job was simply to find out who this "Frankenberger" really was, and if it took rooting through every bank, birth, death, and marriage record back to the Thirty Years' War to do it, then it would simply have to be done.

"And with both tact and dispatch?" Schanz asked sarcastically.

"Exactly."

"A tall order."

"Not for the right man."

As Schanz was leaving, little clearer about Kepplinger's intentions than he had been upon entering, Kepplinger suddenly stood up.

11

"Oh, by the way. Give my regards to your charming wife, and to that fine young son of yours. He's still with General Hoepner's division?"

"Yes. On maneuvers at the moment, near the Czech border."

"Of course," said Kepplinger.

"Of course," echoed Schanz.

All of which simply added to those aspects of the exchange that Schanz did not like. Kepplinger barely knew his wife and had never even met his son.

With all of this, plus the distinct sense of urgency imparted by Kepplinger's tone on his mind, Schanz stumped along the empty corridor on his way out. Near the stairway landing he passed a man just coming up, as he himself had an hour before, and—again just as he had—looking at his watch. They almost collided.

The man excused himself and rushed on. Schanz looked after him; he had a definite recollection of the man's face but, for the moment, could not place him.

It was only after he had left the building and stood again out on the rain-slick street that the name came to him.

"Meinhard? Can that be old Meinhard from Linz?" And if it was, just why was he there? He had to have been on his way to see Kepplinger. There was no one else still at work on the upper floors.

"Sub-Inspector Meinhard of Linz," he thought, "a man who, like myself, has made his career as an expert on documents, forgeries, old wills, frauds, and the like."

Just what did Kepplinger want with Meinhard?

September 7, 9:00 P.M.: Vienna

For as far up the Mariahilferstrasse as Lieutenant General Tieck-Mitringer could see, almost all the way to the Westbanhoff, the roadway was filled with marching men. First came the black uniforms of the SS troops, their silver braid and insignia glittering in the torchlight. Behind them marched the men of Reichs-governor Seyss-Inquart's Storm Troopers, and after them the regulars of the Wehrmacht, looking by comparison almost disgruntled and unenthusiastic. The sky above the route of march, hemmed in as it was by low clouds, threatening but so far not delivering a drop of rain, looked like the sky above an iron foundry. The light of thousands of torches on either side of the mile-long route of the procession flickered and danced. The scarlet banners flapped in a brisk but still stiflingly hot breeze blowing up from the Danube and carrying with it a faint odor of refuse. The tramp of the marchers found its echo in the constant thud of kettledrums. A military band was playing the Horst Wessel song.

Unlike his direct superior in the Abwehr,* Admiral Canaris, who was always cold no matter what the weather, Lieutenant General Tieck-Mitringer was sweating profusely. Canaris wore his greatcoat even on the hottest summer day, whereas Tieck-Mitringer couldn't stand having it on even in winter and went about dressed only in his tunic when it was snowing, much to the distress of his aide-de-camp, Major Rudigier, and the division's senior physician, Dr. Zelzer. Making sure that all eyes were directed elsewhere, Tieck-Mitringer quickly ran his right index finger around the inside of his collar.

Damn September, damn parades and, most of all, damn Seyss-Inquart, who had insisted on the whole thing. Why one had to put up with such people, he simply could not understand.

Seeing the annoyed look on his superior's face, Major Rudigier thought it prudent to scowl.

"What's the matter, Major?"

"Nothing at all, Herr General," the surprised major replied, barely audible over the thud of drums. Now there was singing as well, a few thousand voices strong. A man had to be a lip reader to understand what anyone was saying.

"*Nothing* does not make one frown like that."

Rudigier could hardly explain that he had simply been imitating his commander and actually had no idea what it was that had made Tieck-Mitringer frown.

"With your permission," Rudigier attempted, finally see-

---

* Military Intelligence.

ing a way out. "Listen to what they're doing, Herr General."

The band was now playing "Deutschland, Deutschland, über alles" as the front rank of SS passed by the reviewing stands.

"It's disgusting," said the aide-de-camp. "If it was good enough for Haydn the way he wrote it, it should be good enough even for . . . ," he paused reflectively, as though to give Lieutenant General Tieck-Mitringer a chance to stop him if he felt it appropriate, then went on, "for . . . *them.*"

The band, unaware of the affront to Major Rudigier's musical sensibilities, continued thumping out the tune in the bastardized version current in Hitler's Reich.

Lieutenant General Tieck-Mitringer smiled wanly and continued to sweat. Major Rudigier seemed relieved. He was never quite sure just how far one was permitted to go in Tieck-Mitringer's presence.

"Otherwise," he added circumspectly, "it's quite a display."

Over the railroad station, powerful searchlights were playing, crisscrossing, and now and then catching the silhouette of one of the Junkers 52s that had been bringing in one SS detachment after another all week. Ever since the *Anschluss,* Aspern Airfield had been clogged with military transport. Only a few civilian flights a day had been even permitted, much less possible, because of the crowding.

"A display, all right," said Tieck-Mitringer in a low, obviously irritated voice, the tone of which seemed to invite agreement; he had been standing there in the sweltering heat for more than an hour in full uniform and was anxious to get to dinner. Colonel Hauseger had promised to bring along one of Vienna's reigning divas, a certain Vera Schalk, who was just then singing in a Kunecke "masterpiece" at the Theater-am-Wien. Tieck-Mitringer could not stand operetta but the woman was certainly a beauty, and the idea of bedding the producer of such magnificent sounds as Schalk was at least amusing.

He turned slightly and found himself staring into the floodlights. Why hadn't the Special Section people had more sense than to put the lights so close to the reviewing stands?

"A display, all right," he repeated, this time with even

more venom, as though daring Rudigier to respond.

"What, sir?"

"A display, I said. You chose your words well. A fine 'display.' If the intent of all this is to make our good Viennese hausfraus wet their pants, then it certainly is a fine 'display.' Otherwise it's absurd."

Major Rudigier looked around, hoping that no one else had heard. A few feet away stood Kropfreiter and three other staff officers whom he did not know. Below them, on the next level of the reviewing stand, were half a dozen others from OKW,* and to the left a battery of cameramen from Pathé and the Army News section. The important persons, Seyss-Inquart, Himmler, and the beefy, white-uniformed Goering, were in a boxlike stand by themselves on the other side of the street, well away from the heat of the floodlights, silhouetted against the Hapsburg pillars of the Kunsthistoriches Museum and row upon row of long red swastika banners. All of Vienna seemed covered with the red, white, and black banners. It was becoming difficult to find the names of the restaurants under all the bunting.

Major Rudigier stared across the heads of the marchers at the ranks of dignitaries, lined up like so many marzipan figures in the stands opposite him. He could not help thinking what perfect targets they made, stock-still there on their rostrum in the full glare of the camera lights. How easy it would be to machine gun the lot of them.

And what a pleasure.

He thought for a moment that he read a similar idea on Lieutenant General Tieck-Mitringer's scrubbed red face, but hesitated as much out of tact as out of fear to confirm his impression.

Just then the first of the marching Austrian SA passed below the stands, their expressions—to the man—absurdly fierce and rigid, the rhythm of their marching slightly off the beat.

"Good for street brawls and beating up old Jewish ladies. But for what else?" Tieck-Mitringer murmured as they passed. "We shall see."

---

* Oberkommando der Wehrmacht—High Command of the Armed Forces.

15

The march past continued for another twenty minutes. When the last of the regular troops had filed by, the search-lights over the railroad station at the head of the Mariahilferstrasse went off and the parade swung right onto the Opernring, then down the far narrower Kartnerstrasse where a shouting crowd of civilians was waiting to greet it. Many of those in the crowd still expected to see Hitler himself marching at the head of the procession, possibly in bright silver armor and on horseback as he had been depicted in a few of the more fanciful posters that had announced the parade. In fact, it had been stated that he would fly in specially for the rally and the parade that followed. However, according to the communiqué that had appeared in the late afternoon edition of the newspapers, the deepening Sudetenland crisis had required his personal attention. So he had sent "Fat Hermann" and "Black Heinrich" instead.

For a few moments the dignitaries, both military and civilian, remained in the reviewing stands, facing each other stiffly across the littered and now empty Mariahilferstrasse like so many waxwork figures. The generals, in particular, retained a strange, inexplicable rigidity, as though waiting for a special signal to release them from their frozen postures.

The crowd that had hailed the procession down from the railroad station flowed along the street, past the shop windows daubed, so many of them, with red paint—"JV": *"Jude Verrecke"*—across the Opernring, and down along the Kartnerstrasse.

At length, Lieutenant General Tieck-Mitringer and his ADC clambered down from the stands and stood about, sweating and trying to look proud and pleased. Of all the others of equivalent rank from the different services, Rudigier recognized only Arnstadt, the sole naval representative, Berg and Erlach of OKW, and Colonels Groensfeld and Lorch of the Luftwaffe delegation. All of them stood noticeably apart from their equal numbers from the SS. "Parvenus," Tieck-Mitringer always called them, "and with more than a bit of the gangster in them." That was what Baron Trcka said, too, and he was certainly right. There wasn't a one of the SS who understood

16

the slightest thing about responsibility, loyalty or, for that matter, patriotism.

"Where's the car?" Major Rudigier shouted, looking for his orderly.

"Never mind. We'll walk. The exercise will be good for you. It's only a little ways. My God, Rudigier, haven't you got the geography straight yet?" Tieck-Mitringer exclaimed. "Come on, the night air is pleasant enough."

The shouting of the crowd and the droning of the band had drifted off in the direction of the Danube Canal. Now it was even possible to hear the sound of gypsy violins leaking from the cafés on the side streets. Not everyone in Vienna had turned out to watch the display. It was a thought that Tieck-Mitringer found quite comforting. He could imagine Baron Trcka looking down on the city from the leaded-glass windows of his schloss just below the top of the Kahlenberg, watching the firefly procession finally disperse in the inner city, snuff out, and vanish. Then he would turn back to his viola and his dogs. How entertaining it would be if, somehow, it could be arranged that Canaris's wife should invite Baron Trcka to join the family for dinner on a night when Heydrich was coming over to play in their quartet. The thought of Trcka and Heydrich facing each other over their music stands, only a few feet apart, made him lick his lips—the baron with his viola and Heydrich with his fiddle.

"Come along, keep up, can't you? You need exercise? We can arrange for that, Rudigier, easily enough." The major, being much shorter than his superior, was having difficulty. He doubled his efforts, almost stumbling over the trolley tracks as they crossed the Opernring just behind a group of Luftwaffe officers.

A table had been reserved for the general in a back corner of the Hotel Sacher dining room and he had no intention of being late. Besides, he wanted to be ready and perfectly composed when Colonel Hauseger appeared with La Schalk in tow.

He glanced at his watch. It was just ten. The performance at the Theater-am-Wien would be ending in a few moments and, counting time for curtain calls and a change of clothes,

17

he could anticipate Vera Schalk's appearance at—yes, exactly ten thirty.

September 7, 10:00 P.M.: Berlin

By the time Kepplinger had reached Heydrich's office, he was suffering from nervous exhaustion. True, he had assembled all the pieces; true, he had obtained the best talents available for the task at hand. But to use such men, all of them of doubtful loyalty—especially Schanz—how could one possibly rely on such people? And particularly when none of them had even been given enough information to know what they were doing. What risks there were in proceeding in such a fashion. The whole business could turn into a disaster not only because of a deliberate betrayal but just as well by an innocent error. Even by the wrong question asked in the wrong place or at the wrong time.

But that was the way Obergruppenführer* Heydrich had wanted it and, as he had long ago learned, there was simply no point in arguing with the man. Merely to be thought argumentative had its dangers.

As Kepplinger entered Heydrich's office, the adjutant, Kulsky, stood up and snapped a salute far too brisk for the hour. Kepplinger looked around the empty room, beyond Kulsky, his neck red as always from too vigorous shaving, and tried to see into Heydrich's inner office. The door was open but the room seemed dark.

"No point in squinting," said the adjutant, with all the arrogance of a master's personal servant. "He's not there." No formal address, no "Herr Standartenführer," not even a "Herr Oberst." How Kepplinger detested the man.

"I don't understand, Kulsky. I was distinctly ordered to come up here after. . . ."

Kulsky, with his usual armored disrespect, smiled nastily.

"He's gone out. Three hours ago . . . *sir.*"

"And what, exactly, am I supposed to do?"

"Wait, Herr Standartenführer."

---

* SS equivalent of General.

Kepplinger swore. Now the titles, the mock respect. Only after the disrespect. Some day, he'd settle with Kulsky. In the meantime he considered the possible responses, and concluded that none were either appropriate or circumspect. He settled sullenly and silently into a corner of the leather couch that stood along the wall opposite Kulsky's desk.

"Damn the man," he thought. "Isn't it bad enough to have to answer to Heydrich without having to be kept waiting for him as well?" The worst of it was that Heydrich had probably done it on purpose. He was like that. Simply to assert his authority.

Kepplinger shut his eyes. Fatigue overwhelmed him at once. He fell into a half sleep in which, with disconcerting persistence, the faces of Schanz, Meinhard, and Inspector Weidele kept appearing, vanishing, and reappearing like bubbles. Vaguely, he heard Kulsky shuffling papers while a hidden clock ticked rhythmically from somewhere.

Suddenly, before Kepplinger had heard anything at all, Kulsky shot up from his desk with a clatter and a clicking of heels sharp as a rifle's report.

Kepplinger struggled out of his doze. Heydrich had just entered the room. He stood there for a moment, his tall, wide-hipped figure leaning slightly forward in the doorway, tense as a fencer. His face was slightly flushed, his eyes so narrowed that the whites were barely visible.

"Herr Obergruppenführer—" Kepplinger stammered.

"Oh, don't disturb yourself, Kepplinger."

"I didn't meant to doze off—the hour, it's very late and I hardly. . . ."

"I'm well aware of the hour, Kepplinger. Now just come into my office, will you?"

Not once during this exchange did Heydrich so much as look at Kepplinger. It was one of his peculiar and unnerving habits—he could talk to a man for an hour and not look at him once—and it was a habit that constantly and completely unstrung most of his subordinates. Kepplinger was positive that he cultivated it.

Kepplinger followed Heydrich into his office. Heydrich ordered him to shut the door and seat himself. His back turned toward Kepplinger, Heydrich then inquired whether he would care for a drink.

"I should not presume, Herr Obergruppenführer."

"As you like, Kepplinger," Heydrich said softly, and settled himself behind his broad desk. Kepplinger faced the desk with considerable hesitance. He knew that all sorts of weapons were built into the desks of the department heads. But he had no real idea just what, if indeed anything, Heydrich's desk contained. On the other hand, Heydrich was just as likely to slip poison into a man's drink—or at least to tell him that he had, as he'd done once already with poor Schellenberg.* Or to offer him a doped cigarette. Just being in the same room with Heydrich made Kepplinger sweat so badly that he was sure some day his fastidious superior was bound to notice.

In the light of the single lamp which Heydrich had just switched on, his face appeared unusually equine.

"Have you been waiting here for me long, Kepplinger?"

"It's of no account, sir."

"I've just been out to dinner. A most pleasant dinner. With Schellenberg."

"Again?" slipped out.

"Are you jealous, Kepplinger?" Heydrich said, with more than a suggestion of malice. "You needn't be. A charming man, of course, Schellenberg. A bit too charming, I'd say. He pays far too much attention to other people's wives. But such men have their uses. Speaking of which. . . ."

"It's all taken care of, Herr Obergruppenführer."

"Including Schanz?"

"Including Schanz, sir. He's reluctant, of course. That old pig's snout of his smells something, but he doesn't know what."

"Yet," said Heydrich.

"Yet," agreed Kepplinger.

"And if he does—sniff it out?"

"I'm not sure, sir. I've warned you—excuse me—*advised* you, I don't consider Schanz entirely reliable."

"Completely reliable men are also usually completely

---

* The young chief of the SD Foreign Branch.

20

without imagination. This project requires a certain amount of imagination, Kepplinger."

"Yes, Herr Obergruppenführer."

"Besides, unreliability, at least in the sense you mean, is just what I asked you to be sure of."

"In the event anything goes wrong," suggested Kepplinger cautiously.

"Nothing will go wrong. But in the event it does, it should be possible to point the finger in the right direction, shouldn't it, Kepplinger?"

"It certainly should, sir."

"So. You have sent Schanz off to Graz to dig out our phantom Frankenberger?"

Kepplinger nodded. His mouth was extremely dry. He disliked even saying the name, much less hearing it.

"And Inspector Meinhard, he will handle the research in Linz?"

"All the records will be obtained. He's been told to make an absolutely complete file. The documents we want will be so deeply buried in what he will assemble that he will never even notice it. Particularly if he simply has the records photostated as he's been told to do."

"He'd better not notice anything, Kepplinger. For your sake."

"I understand perfectly, Herr Obergruppenführer. You needn't . . . "

"Remind you? Oh, we all need reminding, Kepplinger. All the time. And Weidele?"

"He will be working with our people in London. That will be the simplest part of it all. We already know the answer there."

Heydrich touched the edge of the slim manila folder that lay on the desk before him. Kepplinger could see the little tab with the one word "Torquemada" typed on it. Heydrich's notion of a joke. What a grim sense of humor. But appropriate. One could hardly argue with *that*. Kepplinger's bowels went cold when he thought of all the possible consequences.

Heydrich's mouth turned slightly in what was, for him, a

21

reasonably broad if distinctly malicious smile.

"If we are successful, as we expect, Kepplinger, then no one, not Himmler, not Rosenberg, not anyone, *anyone* at all, will dare breathe one word more about Heydrich's 'Jewish' mother, no more about his father, 'Bruno Heydrich, born real name Süss,' will they?"

"No, Herr Obergruppenführer."

"We will be in a position where even to breathe such foulness, even to suggest by the merest tremor of a facial muscle that such a thought has crossed one's mind, will be to unleash the most unimaginable cataclysm on the nation, won't we, Kepplinger?"

"Yes, Herr Obergruppenführer," Kepplinger repeated, drymouthed.

"And as you know just how important this is to me—*personally*—you will, of course, succeed, won't you, Kepplinger?"

"Yes, Herr Obergruppenführer." Kepplinger felt the sweat pooling under his armpits. Twice, he knew, Heydrich had been forced into court to protect himself against racial slanders. Twice he had won a verdict exonerating him of any impurity of blood. But he could no longer risk even the faintest chance of such a scandal again. As matters now stood, with the struggle for power in the upper echelons of the administration intensifying every day, with no one, no matter how high and mighty, safe from the ax or a bullet in the back of the head, one had to take every possible step to protect oneself. Against everyone and anyone. Heydrich had certainly made *that* point clear enough.

"Is that all?" Kepplinger asked.

"For the moment. You will leave me now, Kepplinger. I count on you for the successful conclusion of this affair, do you understand?"

"Yes, Herr Obergruppenführer."

"You will report to me from time to time. At regular intervals. Every two days should be about right."

"Yes, Herr Obergruppenführer."

"And one other thing, Kepplinger—stop saying, 'Yes, Herr Obergruppenführer,' in that absurdly mechanical way. My

God, you sound like one of Himmler's automatons."

Kepplinger swallowed hard, saluted, and seeing that Heydrich was no longer looking even in his general direction, fled.

September 7, 10:15 P.M.: Vienna

Major Langbein had no sooner reached his office and turned on the light when Lieutenant Helmut Rost, the cipher officer, came in.

"It's not what we thought," Rost said.

"What, then?"

"Worse, possibly, sir."

Langbein's eyes narrowed. He had been living for days in constant dread of the London dispatch pouch, for what it might contain as much as what it might not. All the way back from the Mariahilferstrasse, he had been developing the alternatives.

Possibility: Von Kleist-Schmenzin's mission had failed.

Possibility: Von Kleist-Schmenzin had not even made contact.

Possibility: Von Kleist-Schmenzin had in fact had his interview with Churchill but had gotten no support.

Possibility: Von Kleist-Schmenzin had gotten support from Churchill but no assurance that the British government would react in the same way.

Possibility: the mission had been blown, and Canaris and the whole lot of them compromised.

The variations were endless, and Rost knew all of them. What then did he mean by that "It's not what we thought" of his?

Langbein took the dispatch and quickly scanned it.

"What in God's name are they talking about?"

Rost shrugged. "I only decoded it, sir."

"Where's Captain Henkl?"

"I'll go get him, sir."

Langbein paced about the almost bare room until he heard Henkl's instantly recognizable footsteps in the corridor. In addition to all his other peculiarities, Henkl had a slight and always audible limp that he'd brought back with him from Spain.

Henkl entered, saluted, and stood waiting for Langbein to say something.

"You're wet, Klaus," Langbein observed. "Why haven't you changed?"

"No time, Major. I was with Rost down in the cipher room."

"You've seen it, then?"

Henkl nodded his large, almost encephalitic head, with its fuzz of white-blond hair, bobbing like a pendulum.

"Well, what does it mean?"

Henkl shook his head again. "Beyond what it says?" He watched as Langbein took the decoded cipher, lit a match to it, and let it burn away to nothing in his ashtray. The smoke smelled disturbingly acrid.

"I'd say, sir," Henkl began, "that we shouldn't get too excited. After all, it could be anything."

"*Any* investigation that that swine Kepplinger institutes is bound to mean something unpleasant, Henkl. He does nothing unless Heydrich tells him to and that alone is cause enough to be worried." Langbein walked about the room, pausing for a moment under the framed photo of General Varela on the east wall, the sole decorative touch in the room.

"So. Kepplinger launches an investigation concerning a 'London contact' and . . . "

" . . . and 'an important personage' in our government."

"Just so. And that's all our people know."

"The information could have been planted deliberately, on a suspicion, to frighten us into giving him something real."

"But if that's so, then they already know at least *something* about what's going on. And, of course, the other possibility is that they know everything."

"I can't disagree with that, sir."

"Then would you care to revise your opinion? Would you agree that we should take countermeasures in any event?"

Henkl considered the major's question for a moment, chewing his lip all the while.

"I suppose there's no alternative. But we should still be extremely cautious."

24

Langbein sat down at his desk, fitted a key to the lock, and opened the drawer. He extracted a thin file envelope.

"Here, Klaus. I want an intercept on every one of these phones. Recordings. Every call. I'll listen to them all myself. Something may turn up."

Henkl took the file and glanced quickly down the list of names. They were all familiar enough. It was a list of every known SD agent, Gestapo informer, blackmailer, and information peddler in Vienna.

"Contact Count von Helldorf and see that the same precautions are taken in Berlin."

"It's done already," replied Henkl.

Langbein's eyebrows went up.

"On my own authority, Major. As soon as I saw—that." He pointed to the little pile of ashes in the ashtray.

"Then you were only testing me before?"

Henkl shook his head. "One doesn't have to agree in order to be careful. Measures are required in any event."

September 7. Graz, Austria

If anything, Schanz was even angrier as he prepared to leave for Graz than he'd been when he left Kepplinger's office.

The trip down, by train, at Kepplinger's insistence, would give him ample time to brood. Not only was he annoyed at having been yanked out of his customary routine and given an assignment which it seemed to him any idiot could carry out, but he'd gotten Ottakar Kepplinger as his nominal superior into the bargain. Worse yet, his wife was unhappy and he would miss seeing his son Helmut, who was supposed to be coming home that Friday on a weekend leave. Not that it really mattered, his not being there; the boy's leave would probably be cancelled anyhow because of the Czech uproar. But the idea that he might have missed him just because of that swine Kepplinger was enough to make him chew his mustaches all the way to Gratwein.

Nevertheless, as his superiors had always correctly assumed, even his anger did not prevent his immediately laying out a highly detailed order of investigation. In fact, it was precisely by doing this that he finally managed to calm himself down. If Schanz was nothing else, he was a thorough professional.

Yet Schanz's calm was not the total calm that he was accustomed to achieving once he'd gotten past the initial annoyance of being given a distasteful assignment. There had been something in Kepplinger's tone that had made him distinctly uneasy, a strong undercurrent of the paranoia that had spread like gangrene throughout the SS, the SD, the Wehrmacht, and every other official office right up to the Reichschancellery itself during the last few years. The "Night of the Long Knives" had started it all. The Von Fritsch homosexuality trial and the absurd Blomberg scandal had fueled the fire and created an atmosphere in which no one, no matter how steel-nerved, could function normally.

And Kepplinger had never been noted for his *sang-froid*.

By the time he had packed his valise, Schanz had already determined exactly what he would do and the precise order in which he would do it. It seemed that careful planning and an efficient execution was the only way to rid himself of the odious Kepplinger and get back to Berlin. Find this "Frankenberger" or whatever his name really was. Do the job. Get finished with it and go home for a bath, a glass of schnapps, and an hour with a good book, as he had always done after disposing of an investigation.

But where to start?

Obviously, the post office was the place. If the *poste-restante* clerk could give him any information, even a general description, he would at least have something to build on.

Next, the telephone exchange. All the old phone books, for at least ten years back. Then the registrar's office. Births, marriages, deaths, and changes of name. Somewhere along the line he would have to consult the regular police records, even though it seemed to him an utter waste of time. If there was anything there, Kepplinger would hardly have sent him down to find it.

Then there would be a visit to the Reichsfluchtsteuer Bureau, where Jews had to go to pay the exit tax, if they could afford it. There was always the possibility that this Frankenberger was a Jew and that he had left the country. Also, for the same reason, the Aryan Custody and Commercial Control office. And after that, he would go to the land records office. Then to the court, to search the wills registry.

Somewhere along the line, he would pick up a clue. A hint. That would be all he'd need:

And then he could go home.

September 8: Vienna

Henkl was just finishing a report on alternate troop dispositions along the Czech border when Major Langbein burst into his office. For the first time in days he was smiling.

"A piece of luck, Klaus. Von Helldorf called back." He stopped, suddenly remembering to look around to make sure Henkl had no visitors. But there was no one, as usual. Henkl was considered something of a hermit and, though respected, was not too well liked. Satisfied, Langbein went on: "It seems that this fellow came into his office yesterday. Absolutely insisted on seeing him. No appointment or anything, but mad as the devil. He'd been straight up the ladder. Everyone had turned him down. Von Helldorf was his last stop—"

"Major?"

"Yes, yes, get to the point? All right. Von Helldorf's visitor was an old chief inspector from the Prussian police criminal frauds department who'd gotten himself caught up in the reshuffling and had wound up in the SD. Which was bad enough for him, apparently, but now someone had transferred him from his regular desk and put him under our friend Kepplinger's command. He was furious, according to Helldorf. Absolutely livid. It seems he'd known Kepplinger in the old days. As a matter of fact, Kepplinger had served under him for a few years. He demanded to be let out. Von Helldorf said he'd do what he could, and when he began to ask around, he found out that the whole thing had started with Heydrich. He told the fellow that he couldn't help, sent him along, and called me."

"Who was the man? Do we know him?"

"The name is Ulrich Schanz. He has the rank of Lieutenant Colonel. I seem to recall someone by that name. But it's

27

not that uncommon, is it? It might have been someone else."

"Is that all? If so, I still don't understand."

"The point is that when Helldorf tried to get the man off, he wound up speaking to Kepplinger. Now, Helldorf's known Kepplinger for a long time and he swears that the man was frightened to death when he spoke to him. Very evasive, which isn't Kepplinger's style at all. Wouldn't say a word. Only that the orders were irrevocable. He wouldn't even discuss the matter."

"That's pretty slim, if you don't mind my saying so."

"If Himmler can rely on astrologers, we can rely on a little well-schooled intuition. Von Helldorf usually knows what he's talking about. And he says Kepplinger was scared out of his wits." Langbein paused to chew on the end of a pencil, a habit Henkl found impossible to understand, particularly in a man otherwise as intelligent and orderly as Langbein. "Oh yes, there's one other thing."

"Yes?"

"This Schanz person let fall that there was something about an 'English' contact of some kind involved, and demanded to know why such things weren't being handled by the IVA* office."

There was a pained silence. Neither man looked at the other. Finally, Henkl sighed. He knew what was coming.

"All right," he said. "Where has he been sent?"

"To Graz."

"To Graz? What in God's name for? It isn't even skiing season."

"This amuses you? Well, you'll have plenty of time to reconsider on your way down there. You leave in an hour. Your contact has been arranged. Major Eisenbach, who is in charge of the Strassengel encampment, will give you all the help you need."

September 8, 7:45 p.m.: Vienna

General Tieck-Mitringer tried to move his legs, but there was simply no room between the gilded chair and the front

---

* The section of the Gestapo in charge of Freemasons, emigrés, and Jews.

ledge of the box for a man of his size to stretch out. "Damned Austrians," he thought, "all midgets, dwarfs. Not a decent-sized man among them. No wonder they've been afraid to stand up for themselves."

The perfume emanating from the two nearly identical sisters in the box just to his left was so overpowering that even he, who had as great an appreciation of women as any man his age, found it almost impossible to bear. He looked back toward the stage and tried, not without some difficulty, to get a deep breath of air into his lungs.

The Staatsoper, normally closed until early October, had been ordered opened for a series of "gala" performances in honor of those high-ranking officers of the Wehrmacht who had found themselves marooned in the Vienna heat of this particularly dismal September. Given the choice between Richard Strauss, whom Tieck-Mitringer found insufferably boring both as a composer and a conversationalist, and Mozart, whose symphonies he could at least tolerate, he had opted for *Die Zauberflöte* as the easiest way of discharging his ceremonial responsibilities. His ADC, Major Rudigier, sat directly behind him, flushed with a pleasure that the general found utterly intolerable.

Domgraff-Fassbender, as Papageno, had just finished his "bird catcher" song. What a shame that Frau Schalk was not to sing Pamina. Tieck-Mitringer had hinted strongly to the intendant that such an event would be "greatly appreciated." After all, "guest" appearances were nothing new at the Staatsoper, and if opera singers could appear in operetta, why not the other way round too? The absurdity of such a question so little occurred to him that he was genuinely shocked to receive word back, through his chosen intermediary, that the conductor, Wilhelm Szymon, refused to hear of such a thing. The man had even had the effrontery to express himself in language which, if accurately reported, had been more appropriate for a ditch-digger than a musician.

What a shame Szymon wasn't a Jew of some degree or other or a communist or something like that; how easily the matter could have been dealt with then.

The general's chagrin at receiving such a negative response

had been aggravated considerably by the fact that Frau Schalk had gotten wind both of the request and of the response. It was said that she had laughed out loud for over fifteen minutes.

Well, time would tell. There would come a day—and it was not far off—when men like Wilhelm Szymon would regret their bad manners and their superior attitudes.

It was approximately at this point in his musings that Tieck-Mitringer noticed something he had not noticed before—Frau Schalk herself, sitting in all her blond splendor on the opposite side of the theatre next to an elegant-looking young Kriegsmarine officer.

The general seethed with indignation. But after a moment, he regained his composure. After all, what claim had he on the woman? Why shouldn't she do just as she pleased? Nevertheless . . .

He was also hungry and already looking forward to the buffet, though the first act had barely begun. The Staatsoper buffet was one of the finest in all Europe. At least he could console himself with open-face sandwiches and champagne, if not with the satisfaction of Frau Schalk's constancy.

The opera wore on. The stage was now filled with capering animals. Tamino was playing a jaunty little tune on something vaguely resembling a flute. Tieck-Mitringer began to fidget. There was no question about it; he much preferred Paul Lincke's operettas.

His gaze kept wandering back to Frau Schalk, whom he could just barely make out because of the recent darkening of the stage. Perhaps he would speak to this Herr Szymon himself. He simply had to find some way to compensate for the Kriegsmarine officer's youth. Rank obviously wasn't sufficient.

Just then the door at the rear of the general's box opened and a lieutenant in field gray slipped quickly in. He whispered something to Major Rudigier, who turned suddenly with a look of extreme annoyance on his face. The general noticed this with some satisfaction. He had been distinctly put out by the intensity of Rudigier's enjoyment and its implied superiority of taste. The interruption served the bastard right. It had not yet occurred to him that whatever it was the lieutenant wanted, it undoubtedly concerned him, not Rudigier.

The major leaned forward, his face a study in disappointment.

"Sir, you're wanted outside. It's urgent."

"Now?" Tieck-Mitringer spat out the word with such force that both the overly perfumed ladies in the next box turned to stare.

"*Now*, sir."

Tieck-Mitringer got up grudgingly. It didn't matter that he wasn't enjoying himself. What mattered was that his evening was being interrupted. Worse yet, if La Schalk noticed him leave, she might think he had left out of pique, and that, he fumed, would make him look impossibly ridiculous.

As he rose, he had a second thought; after all, why should he resent Rudigier's enjoyment so? He touched his ADC on the shoulder just as Rudigier started to follow him out.

"Stay here. I'll be back soon."

"You're certain, sir?" Rudigier's tone was that of a man reprieved only seconds before the trap is to be sprung.

"Sit."

It was clearly an order.

The general went out by the side entrance, following the lieutenant who had been sent to fetch him. A staff car was waiting. In the back seat was the disturbingly familiar figure of a tall officer smoking a long, thin, equally familiar cigar.

"Damn," thought Tieck-Mitringer, "it's that lunatic Langbein. What the devil does *he* want?" All his life he had been intimidated by men of Langbein's type—aristocratic, laconic, always seeming to be enjoying a secret joke at someone else's expense, infinitely superior in every way and maddeningly correct in their behavior toward *their* superiors. In short, utterly immune to criticism and, therefore, to retaliation.

The general got in and sat down. Major Langbein snapped his fingers as the car pulled away from the curb and out into the Ring.

"Well, what's it about this time, Langbein?"

"I've come to rescue you, General."

"From what, exactly?"

"Why, from Mozart, of course," drawled the major. "You don't like Mozart particularly, do you?"

"So your dossiers now go so far as to include your subject's taste in music, do they?"

"And in singers too, for that matter, General," the major replied amiably. "Vera Shalk? Really, General. . . ."

"Damn it, Langbein—" .

The car turned into the Parkring. A concert was in progress in the pavilion in the Stadtpark. The car stopped, maneuvering deftly so as to just barely avoid hitting a tramcar. Major Langbein started to get out. Tieck-Mitringer, baffled and growing angry, followed.

A large crowd had gathered on the lawn before the pavilion. There were hundreds of people there, some sitting on the grass, others on deckchairs, benches, or under trees. The orchestra was playing "Roses from the South."

"It seemed to me that this would be a far better place to talk, General. In the open. Not in our offices. Not in a car where we can be overheard by the driver, even *my* driver. Not —" he paused—"*anyplace* where it might possibly look suspicious. I've simply rescued you from a boring evening, that's all. What could be more natural? And here we are, chatting quite unconcernedly in the open. I will also invite you to take a light supper with me, if you'd be so disposed?"

"For the last time, Langbein. . . ."

The major's expression changed. His eyes narrowed, and the look of sardonic amusement left his face.

"Believe me, what I have to say to you is very serious. Don't let my little theatrical maneuverings deceive you."

The general knew that expression. The last time he'd seen it on the Abwehr man's face had been back in Berlin when Langbein told him that Admiral Canaris had proof positive the Gestapo charges of homosexuality against General Fritsch had been fabricated and that the evidence was secure in the Abwehr vault.

It was, in short, a look that Tieck-Mitringer respected.

"Go on," the general said, so softly that he could barely be heard over the swaying music.

"Two items. Which is the more important you'll have to decide for yourself. First, Operation Green is definitely on. The

32

exact date hasn't been decided yet, but it will be within six weeks at the most."

Tieck-Mitringer nodded solemnly. This he already knew. A memo from OKW lay on his desk. Final preparations for the invasion of Czechoslovakia had been under way for three days.

"And the second?"

"That Heydrich's lapdog, your friend Kepplinger, is up to something. A 'Special Investigation' is under way."

"Into what?"

"The only information we have so far is that it's supposed to involve a 'London contact' and 'an important personage.' Which may or may not be true. I thought that perhaps you might know something about it?"

Tieck-Mitringer shook his head and began to chew his lower lip angrily.

"How did you receive this information?"

"From a source that has provided us with very useful tidbits in the past."

"In short, the usual whores' gossip? Not very reliable, I'd say."

"Let me remind you, General, 'gossip' like this was precisely the kind that led to General Blomberg's disgrace. If a 'gossiper' hadn't recognized the prospective bride's name and looked it up in the police register, no one would ever have known that the good general was about to marry a prostitute—"

"Enough. I don't want to hear any more of this."

"You must take this information seriously, General."

Tieck-Mitringer paused to let applause punctuate the waltz. The orchestra, encouraged, immediately struck up another.

"All right, Langbein, but just what is it that I'm supposed to take seriously?"

"Consider; if we take this business of a London contact at face value, then there are a number of possibilities. First, it may be that Heydrich knows what General Beck and the rest of you are up to and is looking for a way to discredit you without letting the whole country know what's going on. One does wonder why, though. The SD has never hesitated to invent whatever evidence it needed before. It's also possible that they only

33

suspect something and have planted this information in an attempt to draw us out. And, as a third alternative, let me suggest that the term 'a London contact' may simply be a code phrase and that they're really after something else entirely. These people have rather Byzantine minds, after all."

"I don't know what the hell you're talking about, Langbein."

"Of course you don't, General. You rarely do."

The orchestra was by now playing the *Lagerlust* polka at full tilt. The general's face was flushed. He took out a handkerchief and mopped his mouth.

"I'm leaving now, Langbein, if that's all right with you."

The major smiled broadly.

"There's to be a 'club' meeting at Trcka's tomorrow evening. Around eight, General. You'll try to be prompt, won't you? I'm sure Frau Schalk won't miss you for one evening."

"Pig's fart," said Tieck-Mitringer. He turned quickly and trooped hastily back to the car.

The one thing he could not possibly afford was to let Langbein see how frightened he was.

September 9, 11:30 A.M.: *Graz*

The Berlin-Graz express rattled with a relieved gasp into Ostbanhoff. The day was bright and clear and oppressively warm. Schanz's woolen suit, ideal for the penetrating damp of Berlin's last two rainy weeks, was hardly appropriate. The heavy odor of sweat-soaked wool followed him wherever he went.

As he walked slowly along the platform, carrying a suitcase optimistically packed with only the barest essentials, he paused now and then to fan himself with his hat.

After checking into a small hotel not far from the police headquarters on the Paulisthorgasse, he went directly to the post office.

The clerk in charge of the *poste-restante* window, a small, unhealthy man called Bock, seemed totally unimpressed by Schanz's show of credentials. What could an SD colonel possibly want with him? He was indifferent. In fact, he seemed to treat the whole inquiry as a joke in rather poor taste.

Shortly, Schanz found out why.

They sat in a small musty room behind the mail-sorting area. A fan turned ineffectively overhead. In the next room someone was listening to a Bruckner symphony on the radio.

"If you'll excuse me, sir—it's a very odd question."

Schanz, disturbed by the man's tone, settled into a glower.

"And why might that be, Herr Bock?"

"Because there are no lists whatsoever."

"How is that possible, Herr Bock?"

"Because the clerks we have here are rotated daily. No one is ever at the *poste-restante* window for more than twenty-four hours.

"Which still leaves us with the question of why what I asked you is so odd."

Herr Bock allowed himself a disrespectful and faintly superior laugh.

"Why, if what I say is the case—and it certainly is—how could anyone notice that a particular person was getting an unusually large amount of mail from England? Unless he happened to come in each week on the very same day that a particular clerk was at the window. If you'd like, I can call them all in. There's Mueller, and Grossman, and Kruger, and . . . "

"That won't be required," snapped Schanz. "Just tell me, *if* you know, who it was who sent in the report. He, at least, must know something about this."

"You'll have to ask my superior. I really couldn't tell you, except to say—naturally—that it wasn't I."

A short conversation with the far more cowed chief clerk, Herr Wertheim, yielded no more information than Schanz had been able to extract from the diffident Bock. By the end of another half hour, Schanz was both hot and irritated.

No one in the post office, it seemed, had any idea who had sent in the report.

There was simply no information of any kind to be had there concerning Kepplinger's "English letters."

Schanz went to a nearby wine garden to cool off and brood. For a seasoned professional, he had made a signally bad start. He had allowed his irritation at having been assigned to Kepplinger's command to distract him completely. Kepplinger had given him almost nothing to go on, not even the name of the official from whom the initial report had come. That he could have neglected to insist on being given such a basic piece of information infuriated him. And calling Kepplinger was out of the question. He wouldn't dream of giving the man the satisfaction.

Deputy Inspector Gruner had been going about the daily routine of his office with his normal drowsy summer cheerfulness. The customary problems with tourists had waned considerably this year because, not unexpectedly, there were far fewer tourists. There remained the usual incidents, assaults, brawls, and the continual clean-up of homosexuals, nothing more.

Gruner had just settled down to read the newspaper and have a cup of coffee when Schanz erupted into his office. Gruner, a man of distinctly casual if not slovenly habits himself, could hardly believe that Schanz was a Standartenführer SD. Why, the man was even less prepossessing than Gruner himself. Hair uncombed. Generally unkempt appearance. Dirt under the nails. A fleck of tissue stuck to one side of his mustaches. Not at all the sort Gruner had been expecting.

Gruner called for his orderly to bring in another cup of coffee and the two men sat down facing each other across the deputy inspector's conspicuously barren desk.

"So. *You* are Schanz?"

"I had thought so until this morning."

"Oh? By which you mean exactly what?" Gruner replied, lazily and with good humor.

"That a person with my experience should not make the foolish mistakes I've already made."

"Ah, but we all make mistakes, Herr Schanz. I think often that the first we make is being born at all."

"Those are things over which we have no control."

"Indeed. And so, Herr Schanz?"

Schanz smiled; he had taken an immediate liking to Gruner. Lazy Austrians always inspired in him the pleasant kind of confidence that comes from a sure knowledge that one is dealing with a person of similar temperament.

"We play games with each other, Herr Schanz," Gruner said, after an interval of coffee sipping. "I enjoy games. So—we can play games as long as you like. Then you will tell me what I can do to help you, yes?" Gruner reached into a drawer and took out a small fold of paper. Schanz recognized at once the formal black heading of Kepplinger's office. "You have but to ask. We here in Graz would deny Prinz Albrechtstrasse nothing."

Schanz sipped his coffee before replying, pausing to note that the caffeine was working with remarkable rapidity. Also that the wine had done the same.

"Do tell me what I can do to help you find your non-existent Frankenberger, Herr Schanz," Gruner said amiably.

Schanz lowered his cup.

"This, then, Herr Deputy Inspector. I need, first of all, an assistant, a man who is good with documents and records. Perhaps a senior clerk of some sort."

"Done. I shall gave you Bernkassler, from my records department. He's not only exact, thorough, and careful, but he has an almost photographic memory."

"Next, I will need access to any records I choose, whether public or otherwise. Can this be arranged, without attracting attention? I would rather not display my identity papers."

"Your Colonel Kepplinger has cautioned discretion. Naturally we will do our best to comply." Gruner paused thoughtfully, then said, "You don't care to tell me what it is you're really after, do you?"

"Since Berlin has directed, the fewer people who know, the better."

As Gruner tossed back his head and laughed again, Schanz wondered whether he himself knew what he was doing. Two hours ago he had almost convinced himself that he did.

Now he was beginning to wonder again.

In the end it had proven impossible to refuse Gruner's invitation to dine that evening. Schanz knew the type, the perpetual superannuated bachelor who had either to badger one of his subordinates into going out with him or face a dismal meal grudgingly prepared by an equally dismal landlady at his lodgings.

They took dinner at an inconspicuous little *weinstube* on the narrow Sporgasse, not far from the police building. Soldiers from the adjacent barracks strolled by on their way to the Hauptplatz. The bells in the Franziskaner church tower banged relentlessly.

Gruner was in an expansive mood. Schanz, on the other hand, was tired and wanted nothing more than to go to bed after a good hot bath. For four hours that afternoon he had worked with the clerk, Bernkassler, outlining what was required and giving him lists of registers to be obtained, books to be borrowed, and records to be gathered up. Bernkassler had proven both efficient and accommodating, surprisingly unruffled by being so suddenly yanked out of his normal routine and set to tasks more befitting an antiquarian or an archeologist than a police file clerk. A small, wizened man of a kind who could not possibly be employed in a similar position in Berlin, Bernkassler went about his work humming and nodding like some clockwork toy set under a Christmas tree. Just watching him had been enough to tire Schanz out, accustomed as he was to exerting himself far more than most.

Gruner was pleasant enough company, though watching him eat was also something of a trial. Not once did he mention Schanz's task or ask any questions about it. Schanz took a glass of wine, a nice Liebfraumilch, then another and another. Gruner chatted on. What did Schanz think about the Czech situation? Was there really a chance that the English might step in, and if they did, what would happen then? He leaped from one subject to another with a disconcerting agility. Mundane police matters, variety *artistes* Schanz had never heard of, the latest French and American films.

At length, Schanz was almost compelled to turn the conversation back to precisely that subject Gruner was so fastidiously avoiding.

Schanz set his wine glass down carefully next to his by-now empty plate. "By the way, Gruner, who is the department IVA man here? I'd like to see him in the morning."

"Why, Schanz, don't you know? There is no IVA in Graz. Surely you knew that? The Gestapo simply hasn't gotten down here yet, at least not in any organized fashion. We are treated as a provincial backwater, even in such matters."

Schanz stared at him, trying not to let his surprise show. Gruner obviously did not know that Schanz was only SD by virtue of the recent amalgamation that had brought the Kripo* under the Security Service's control, nor that Schanz's entire career had been in the criminal, not the political, section. It was at that moment, too, that Schanz realized how unaware of things he himself was.

So the Gestapo had not yet established a IVA office in Graz. Enemies of the state went undetected, unsought. Just as he was about to ask another question, Gruner began again.

"You seem so surprised, Herr Schanz. Why, if I may ask?"

"If there is no IVA office here, then who handles the surveillance of mail and such functions?" Schanz leaned forward, then checked himself. He did not want to seem too anxious.

"Why, no one," said Gruner.

"No one? Not even your office?"

"Oh, on known criminals, of course. But that's all."

Schanz studied the man's face; no, he wasn't lying. Why should he? What he was saying was perfectly consistent with his questions that afternoon. The initial reports had not come from his office, obviously. Otherwise he would have known precisely what Schanz was after, having instigated the investigation to begin with.

But there was no IVA office in Graz. Who then had been checking the mail? Certainly not the postal officials. Not, at least, if Superintendent Wertheim was to be believed. And why in heaven's name would *he* lie?

Schanz took another sip of wine. Perhaps it would be better simply to do as he'd been ordered, get the job over with and get back to his wife and son. He glanced anxiously across the table. No, his concern had not communicated itself to Gruner.

---

* Criminal Police, division of the SD.

He was safe enough for the moment.

But he would have to watch himself every second. Very carefully.

Just then Gruner lifted his glass in the twentieth toast of the evening.

Schanz, without even hearing the object of Gruner's toast, followed suit automatically.

As things should be done.

September 9, 7:45 P.M.: Schloss Trcka, The Kahlenberg, Vienna

Melitta Trcka ran her hand quickly over her tightly coiffed black hair and peered through the little circle she had cleared on the window. The heat inside Schloss Trcka, combined with the centuries-old dampness, perpetually fogged the panes and turned the windows into a good facsimile of one-way glass.

"They're coming in now. There's Roon, and Tieck-Mitringer with him. August will be along any minute now."

Reichsgerichtsrat* Bernhard Michaelis leaned against the wall next to the window and sighed.

"What a shame. If only we had a few more minutes. . . ."

"Later, Bernhard. You'll stay the night, of course?"

"Of course."

She smiled quickly, glancing into a mirror to make sure that their few minutes alone together had left no visible traces. She could still feel the warmth of Michaelis's body on hers and the smell of the cologne he wore would linger in her nostrils for hours. It was at such moments that her sadness was at its deepest. They had been lovers for over two years now, yet each time they were together felt to her like both the first and the last. Her husband knew; there was no question about that. Not only did he tolerate the affair but it seemed at times he even encouraged it. Solely, she knew, because he understood how fond she really was of Michaelis. This placid understanding of his was the most intolerable aspect of the situation. Yet, she knew it was also August's best defense against losing her entirely.

---

* Judge.

Michaelis bent over and pressed his mouth against the back of her neck. She shivered, and instinctively reached to touch his cheek with her hand. Then she recovered, slowly and reluctantly.

"The guests, Bernhard."

"They'll be quite content for another few minutes. Fessler will see to it that they have plenty to drink. And the Führer has given them plenty to talk about."

"If only I could be as calm about all of this as you are."

"I only seem calm, my dearest. Actually, I'm terrified."

"Of failing?"

"Not nearly so much as of succeeding."

He adjusted his tie and smoothed his jacket. Tall, lean, and erect, he would have made a perfect staff officer. Once blond, his thin, now colorless hair hung loose and in a perpetual fringe over his high forehead. His mouth, she had told him once, was a bit too thin, too bloodless. Hers, he had replied, was too full, too insolent. They were, in fact, complete opposites in most ways. He pale, bleached, she dark and intense, unmistakably the daughter of her Hungarian mother and the exact opposite of Michaelis's blond, bland wife of a dozen years.

She took his hand

"Shall we face them together or go down separately?" she asked.

"It would be more discreet, of course—"

"Of course. *Discreet*. What a charming word. We should always be discreet, by all means."

"In everything, Melitta. We have no choice."

September 9, 8:30 P.M.: The Kahlenberg, Vienna

A large portion of the woods high up on the slopes just below the Kahlenberg had belonged to the Trcka family for more than two hundred years. The seventh Baron Trcka, Gustav Eugen, had hated the dense, gloomy pine forests and had begun to draw up plans to have them cleared, replacing them with formal gardens and vast expanses of rolling lawn. By a stroke of good luck, or so the present baron, August Trcka, had viewed it, the old man was carried off by an apoplectic seizure

41

before actually putting his plans into effect. He left behind him a much-relieved son who was far more attached to the woods than to his father, a wife who immediately decided to spend nine months of every year in her native Budapest, and a number of creditors, not least among whom was the landscape architect who had worked two long years drawing plan after plan for the forest's destruction.

August Trcka did not allow hunting in his woods, yet he himself always carried some form of firearm when he went walking among the pines. Often he would use the rifle as a walking stick, much to the disgust of his valet, Fessler, who had to spend long hours cleaning out the barrels and making sure that if the Herr Baron should take it into his mind to actually fire at something, he would not end by blowing his own head off instead.

The solitude of his beloved woods was one of Baron Trcka's few solaces. He could walk for hours in the woods without thinking of anything except where he was going to put his foot next. If he went to a concert, even to hear a piece he greatly loved, he could not pay attention. Within minutes he began to rehearse mentally all the ills that had recently beset him and his country. The same thing happened at the opera and at films. He could not stand the theater, and the boredom of dinner parties only served to open the floodgates of his mind that much wider. Inevitably, he would find himself drowned in unhappiness, scheming, plotting with himself, reviling those who had brought about Austria's present condition, damning them all for failing to prevent it, knowing in his heart that he was as guilty as they.

Only with his beloved viola or in the woods could he find peace.

His wife knew this and let him walk alone, forbidding the faithful Fessler to follow him or even go out to look for him, no matter how long he stayed away. Often he disappeared for as much as a day, returning with his clothes soaked through by the dew, his hat crumpled, his boots black with damp, looking like some sad, dark figure out of an ancient Teutonic myth.

This time, he had been in the woods for less than six hours. It was growing dark and the sky threatened rain. The air was hot and heavy. Insects leaped in the undergrowth and small animals scurried fearfully out of his way. Over his shoulder, he carried an English-made shotgun, double-barreled and beautifully engraved; it was one of the few such weapons he owned that he had not abused.

Through the trees at the head of the incline he could see the lights of Schloss Trcka. Standing on the front lawn, silhouetted against the even more distant lights at the top of the nearby Kahlenberg, was old Fessler, patiently waiting, standing like an ancient crane, motionless and faithful. August Trcka knew that he had been and would forever be a puzzle to the old man. For this he felt some regret. He had known Fessler almost all his life, and would have liked to have been understood.

He tramped wearily up the last incline, out of the edge of the forest and onto the lawn. The castle was ablaze with lights. He felt a curious impulse to lower the shotgun; it was, in fact, the first time in hours he had even been aware he was carrying it.

"My God, but you're becoming defensive," he chided himself, forcing a laugh. But his nervousness was genuine enough; and it mattered little whether its cause was unexpected guests, a houseful of his wife's English or Hungarian relatives, or a visit from the police. The end result was the same. Always there was a churning of the stomach, a distinct twitch on his right cheek, and a definite desire to turn and walk away.

"Fessler?"

"Is that you, Herr Baron?"

"Who else would it be? What's going on in there? We have guests? Who?"

"Your friends, Herr Baron," the old man replied, somewhat taken aback. "Surely the Herr Baron recalls when the Herr Reichsgerichtsrat Michaelis phoned just after the noon meal. . . . ?"

"Ah yes, yes. Of course. In the woods, Fessler, one tends to forget about such things. There is such peace here, such tranquility." He paused, a pained look on his face. "Well, we'll have to see what's gotten the hive so stirred up, won't we?"

"I'm afraid so, Herr Baron."

Trcka whistled for his dogs, turned, and began to walk toward the house. "How many have arrived already?"

"General Tieck-Mitringer has been there almost an hour. Also the gentleman from the Ministry of the Interior, Herr Roon."

"Melitta is at least keeping them occupied?" The baron sighed. How he dreaded these meetings. "There is plenty for them to drink, isn't there? We still have a few bottles of the special Rothschild for the General, yes?"

Fessler smiled, the smile alone speaking all that needed to be spoken. Fessler was, if nothing else, adept at his profession. Then, with a gentle, reassuring tone, as though offering the ultimate consolation, Fessler added, "Reichsgerichtsrat Michaelis is there too, Herr Baron. He arrived this afternoon, just after you left the house."

August Trcka simply nodded and took a deep breath. Of all the men with whom he had come in contact during the last few years as a result of his involvement in what had become known rather delicately as "the club," Bernhard Michaelis was the only one for whom he had developed a genuine warmth. There, the disillusioned Trcka had concluded, was a true kindred spirit, a man of breeding and intellect, soft-spoken, profound, gentle but firm. Such a man as he himself would have liked to have been. That his wife Melitta shared his opinion of the man only validated his own instincts.

He entered the castle with Fessler at his heels, the dogs far behind, loping over the lawn. The long, high-ceilinged corridors that led from the front of the house to the enormous living room were all hung with ancestral portraits. Every branch of the family was represented. As a child, he had known all of their names but now had to put on his glasses and squint at the brass nameplates in order to identify most of them. Only his father, with his proud Franz Josef mustache, was immediately recognizable and at that portrait, out of delicacy and a vague feeling of guilt, he refused to look.

A fire was blazing in the hearth. From above the mantle a huge boar's head glowered. Tieck-Mitringer seemed mesmerized by the animal and was standing near the end of the furthest sofa, staring into the animal's glass eyes. Trcka repressed a shudder. From the expression on Tieck-Mitringer's face it seemed the general was considering the possibility that his own head might soon be mounted over someone's fireplace, most likely in Heydrich's home in the Schlachtensee. A man like Mitringer simply couldn't be trusted. He did what he did not out of moral conviction but out of fear. Tieck-Mitringer, together with Beck, had been almost hysterical when they had heard of Hitler's plans. There was no way in the world, Tieck-Mitringer had argued bitterly, that the "thing" would not turn into a disaster. The troops under his command would be decimated. He himself would be ruined, humiliated. It was for this reason that he hated his masters. And it was this that in August Trcka's opinion made him extremely dangerous.

He entered the room. His wife caught sight of him and laughed good-naturedly. Surely he was a sight, standing there in his damp-stained knickers and boots, his rumpled hat which he had forgotten to take off, and still carrying the shotgun which Fessler was desperately trying to take from him.

"Melitta—always the perfect hostess," he said. "You never fail to compensate for my rudeness." He stood still, receiving. Tieck-Mitringer, the Abwehr major, Langbein, and Herbert Roon came across the room to meet him. Only Michaelis remained where he was, his slight frame almost swallowed whole by the wing chair in which he was sitting, his head lowered over a book he had open across his lap. At last he looked up, just as Trcka came over to him. Michaelis smiled, pushed a few unruly strands of hair out of his eyes, and extended his hand.

"An island of sanity in an ocean of madmen. I'm delighted to see you, Bernhard."

"If only the occasion were more pleasant, Herr Baron," the lawyer began. He closed the book and put it on a nearby table; he had been reading Von Chamisso's *Peter Schlemihls Wundersame Geschichte*.

"Let's hope *that's* not prophetic," Baron Trcka said, pointing toward the book.

"Not prophetic," said Major Langbein, who had wandered over, a glass of Tieck-Mitringer's favorite Lafitte-Rothschild in his hand. "Descriptive would be the better word. We've all sold our shadows to the devil a long time ago. And just like poor Peter, we're all floundering about trying to find a way to get them back."

Tieck-Mitringer looked pained. The massive, normally truculent Herbert Roon, formerly an officer of the Reichsbank, seemed merely confused.

Melitta Trcka, a look of apprehension on her face, moved in quickly between Langbein and Michaelis. Although they were in fact closer in outlook than any other two people in the room, the major's tart, sarcastic manner always seemed to irritate the judge and, conversely, the Reichsgerichtsrat's soft-spoken caution, which Langbein often mistook for weakness, never failed to annoy the major.

Both men, understanding the purpose of the baronin's move, immediately withdrew. She stood there alone for a moment, the absolute center of attention, knowing that she alone had the power to force these fierce, unruly men to behave themselves and at least be civil to one another. However pleased she might be by this, their refusal to let her participate in their dealings angered her intensely. Did August or Bernhard think for a moment that she didn't know exactly what they were all up to? Why couldn't they understand that she was as deeply committed to their goals as they were? Perhaps even more so. Couldn't they realize that she, with her Hungarian birth and breeding, her swarm of aristocratic relatives from London to Warsaw, could see the monster in the Reichschancellery with a clarity that no Austrian or German could ever achieve, that her horror of the man was deeper by far than theirs could ever be? Yet they insisted on keeping her on the periphery of the conspiracy. A hostess, nothing more. Just thinking about it made her burn with silent shame and anger.

"My dear," her husband began, forcing a smile, "you've done marvels here. As always, no? But I'm sure you understand."

She turned, trying to restrain herself. She knew exactly what he was about to say.

"A surprise that brings all these distinguished gentlemen running up here so unceremoniously certainly must involve—"

"Not another word," she replied, with a forced lightness. "The day that you have to *tell* me to leave, dear August, that will be the day that I really shall leave."

Michaelis threw her a sharp, cautionary glance and turned quickly away.

"Perhaps," August Trcka went on, without the slightest understanding that he had wounded his wife yet again, "perhaps in an hour or so you will join us again, yes? In the meantime it would be a good idea to see if Cook can find something decent to put before our guests."

When Melitta had gone out, Trcka motioned to Fessler, who was still standing at the threshold, the shotgun cradled in his arms.

"See that the doors are shut and the front door locked and bolted. I want no disturbances."

"Does the Baron wish a hot drink?"

He hesitated; he was chilled from his walk in the woods, no doubt about that, and normally would have had a glass of hot milk laced with cognac upon his return.

Langbein, with an unmistakable sense of urgency in his voice, solved his problem, advancing with a bottle of whiskey and two glasses.

"Thank you Fessler, but this will do nicely."

When Fessler had gone and the doors of the room had been shut tight, the five men disposed themselves in the chairs nearest to the crackling fire. Tieck-Mitringer tried not to look at the boar's head. Michaelis could not sit still and soon rose to stand by the hearth, jabbing at the logs with a long iron poker.

"All right. I can tell from your faces that this is no ordinary 'club' meeting. What's happened? Am I the only one here who doesn't know?"

Langbein handed the baron a tumbler of whiskey.

"Beck's resigned," he said.

"What? When did this happen?"

"This morning, while you were in the woods, apparently," put in Tieck-Mitringer. "I was there, of course. We were all summoned," he added with a special emphasis, meant to remind those present that he was, after all, a member of the General Staff. "I've only just gotten back from Berlin. It took a special act of charity from our friends in the Luftwaffe for me

47

to be here. Have you ever flown in a twoseater? Never again, I assure you."

Trcka's face sagged. Michaelis seemed ethereally unconcerned, resigned, as though there had been no doubt in his mind that exactly this would happen and he had long since come to terms with the event.

"I suppose I must hear just what happened."

"That's up to you, but let me tell you, it wasn't a pleasant experience. The man's a mystic, there's no doubt of it. The type that prefers to think and, if you wish, to dream, rather than to act."

"I'd say he's acted," put in Michaelis quietly.

"Yes, I suppose you'd say that, wouldn't you? Well, letting go of the tongs when the handle gets a bit hot is no way to pull the roast out of the fire, if you ask me. He stood there, with that damned pastor's face of his, and lectured us for almost an hour on morality and independence. Some of my colleagues thought that he was most profound. As far as I'm concerned, it was all shit and nothing more. The Pope could have done better."

"And no one, not a single one, resigned with him?" Trcka asked, incredulous.

Tieck-Mitringer took the question as an accusation. "You hardly expected *me* to follow suit, did you? A fine position we'd be in then."

Langbein sipped his whiskey. "Perhaps it's all for the best."

"How can that possibly be?"

Langbein smiled patronizingly, reminding Trcka how unpleasant it was to do business with people who always knew more than he did.

"They've put General Halder in his place," Roon said, his mellow, banker's voice filling the room. It was the first time he'd spoken since Trcka had come in. "I know Halder well, better than anyone here . . ."

"Except me," said Langbein.

"I mean personally," said Roon. "And let me tell you, gentlemen, you will find Franz Halder everything that Beck was not. He is motivated by a genuine hatred of our 'friend,' not merely by exaggerated notions of Christian ethics. He is an aggressive person, perhaps even irritatingly so. He will not shrink—"

Langbein seemed in agreement. Trcka could say nothing. He had never even met General Halder and knew him only by vague reputation. It seemed incredible to him that after accepting Beck's resignation, Hitler should have appointed someone of the same views and with an even more thorny personality.

"Is he capable of mobilizing a mass resignation of the General Staff?" he asked finally.

"The time for such tactics has passed, I'm afraid," said Tieck-Mitringer, his eyes glinting sharply, reflecting the firelight in tiny cat's points.

"What then?" Trcka's voice was sad, resigned.

"I told you, Halder's the more aggressive type."

"I simply don't want to think in those terms," Trcka shot back. "It's inconceivable."

"Whether you like it or not . . ."

"Gentlemen, gentlemen," interrupted Michaelis, "let's not fight among ourselves as—*they* do. Consider. Events sometimes have a way of preempting us. Really, it's a question of alternatives, pure and simple. We can only work with what we have."

"And what, exactly, is that?"

Langbein, who had remained silent up until now, spread his hands over his knees and stared off into space.

"Let us not beat about the bush. Oster has contacted certain people in Berlin, officers who will be willing to follow orders if Halder is the one who gives them. The Berlin Defense District is in agreement, as is the police. We have infantry, and an armored division at our disposal if necessary—"

" 'If necessary'? I'd say the question is 'if appropriate.' "

"*If*," Langbein went on, ignoring the baron's interruption, "*If* the madman actually goes ahead with it and starts Operation Green, then it will certainly be, as you put it, 'appropriate,' don't you think? Can you imagine a better moment? Even if they won't stir to help us, most of the old fossils on the General Staff won't make a move to stop us either. In their hearts, they all agree—Von Brauchitsch first among them."

"I can tell you this," Michaelis said quietly, "we shall have the necessary medical certifications ready. The trial will be quick and conclusive. The evidence—"

"One hardly needs better evidence than the catalyst itself," Tieck-Mitringer put in bitterly, laying his finger squarely on his own wound. "Can you imagine, propelling us as we are now, unprepared, improperly equipped, into a full-scale war with Britain and France and God knows who else? What an insupportable risk. Who but a madman . . . ?"

"Or a very shrewd manipulator," put in Michaelis.

Trcka lowered his eyes. That was precisely the problem. Everything that Hitler did was the result of an insanely brilliant insight into the weaknesses of others. Here they were, the lot of them, sitting before a fire, drinking whiskey and talking. The lunatic, however, was out there *acting*, doing things, taking advantage of everyone else's indecision. Soon it would be impossible to stop him short of taking his head off. With every tactical victory, his support grew stronger among the masses. He was rapidly acquiring the status of a latter-day prophet. As yet, he had not made a single mistake.

"When will Halder act?" asked Trcka and, even as he did so, was acutely aware that once again he was looking to someone else, someone this time he did not even know, to commit the act, to run the real risk.

"In my opinion," Tieck-Mitringer said, "and it is also the opinion of General Halder, with whom I've already spoken—"

"And of Colonel Oster as well," put in Langbein.

"Yes, of Oster too—we must wait until the exact moment that Hitler gives the order to attack the Czechs. Then there can be no question of our motives. We will certainly be understood."

Langbein stared hard at Tieck-Mitringer, wondering whether the general was going to say anything about the "investigation." Tieck-Mitringer, in turn, waited for Langbein to speak, and when he saw that the major had no intention of bringing the subject up, he continued outlining the rather hazy plans that were being formulated by the Abwehr cabal and the discontented generals. Langbein sat back and listened, hardly aware of what Tieck-Mitringer was saying. He kept thinking of the reports Bresner had brought back from London. Von Kleist-Schmenzin's mission was so far only a partial success, which meant that it had also been a partial failure, and that was dangerous enough. It was clear to Langbein that, whatever his personal reservations, they would be forced to act. The English were not about to pull the General Staff's chestnuts out of the fire by calling Hitler's bluff.

The risks involved were growing larger every day but, as Michaelis had said, what—really—were the alternatives?

September 10, 9:00 A.M.: Graz

Schanz had been provided with an unused office on the second floor of the north end of the police building. He half suspected that Gruner, proceeding from an inability to see why anyone would wish to work as hard as Schanz apparently planned to do, had given him a room with such a splendid view of the Schlossberg on purpose. To distract him, to bring him down to earth, to remind him of sun and sky and the pleasures of life.

"After all," Gruner had said, "if this Frankenberger of yours does not even exist, what harm can he have done? As for myself, I'm going for a ride up to the castle just before noon. To inspect the flowers and the young girls. Why don't you come along?"

Schanz had declined the invitation and had finally gotten down to work. Bernkassler had been waiting for him at seven thirty, already surrounded by piles of ledgers, land and tax record books, birth, death, and marriage registries and, in fact, almost all the source books Schanz had asked for the afternoon before. Schanz was amazed, Bernkassler appropriately modest.

"If one is on good personal terms with the proper people, Herr Obersturmbannführer, there is no special magic to all this."

Two enormous steel bookshelves were filled with massive musty volumes scavenged from all parts of the city. Schanz had coffee brought in, lowered the green window shades to cut off the distracting view of the Schlossberg bathed in bright

September sunlight, turned on the overhead fan, and got to work.

The telephone registers yielded no information at all. According to Kepplinger, they had already been examined for five years back. Schanz went through them for twenty years back, with the same results. One Frankenberger was located, in the 1915 listings, but he turned out to have been a pastor of a church in Strassengel who had died during the war, leaving no known relatives. The birth records were also barren of Frankenbergers save for the lonely pastor, Freidrich.

By eleven, Schanz had proceeded to the land registers. Surely there would be something there.

"Herr Bernkassler, where are the 'F' volumes?"

"There are no 'F' volumes," replied Bernkassler.

"They're missing?"

"They never were. The land records in Graz are not kept according to the transferor or the transferee but according to the parcel of land itself."

"There is no cross-indexing?" Schanz exclaimed, astonished.

"Graz is a small city. I regret, Herr Obersturmbannführer, we have never—until this day—thought it required."

It would be necessary, then, to go through every page of every volume. To find what? And to go back how far? To pick up something, some mention of another Frankenberger, from which a line might be dropped to locate descendants, cousins, collaterals. . . .

Schanz shook his head. It was simply too enormous a task. If it was to be done, it would be done last, after everything else had been tried.

"The imperial tax registry then, Herr Bernkassler?"

"As you desire. Where shall we start?"

"The year 1900 seems a good enough place. You go backwards, year by year; I will go forward."

But there was nothing. Bernkassler, to be sure, was slower, even more thorough than Schanz, but by the time the clerk had reached 1885 and Schanz had made his way forward to 1931, it seemed as though another tack might be more appropriate.

52

Just as Schanz was about to consider lunch, Bernkassler spoke up.

"These are only the tax records of individuals, Herr Obersturmbannführer. Have you considered those which deal with businesses?"

"How far back do they go? I'm no student of Austrian history, Bernkassler. Did the Emperor tax business profits? And since when?"

"In many ways, oh yes, he certainly did. There are records. All the way back. Much further back than these."

"Well, then, we shall have to look at them, won't we?"

"As you wish. But they are not here. You didn't ask for them so, of course, I brought only what you asked for."

Schanz sighed. Perhaps it was not so terrible after all. A little walk in the noon sunshine was not such a bad idea. The room had grown oppressively warm and Schanz was sweating heavily.

After lunch, Schanz accompanied Bernkassler to the vaults below the Rathaus. It seemed that Bernkassler knew everyone and it was not necessary even once for Schanz to show his disc.

The stone stairway down to the vaults passed two subcellars. By the time they reached the bottom, Schanz had no idea just how far below the surface they actually were. The air was cool but surprisingly dry, especially in view of the proximity of the Ufer River.

The clerk who had led them down handed Bernkassler a large iron ring of keys. They halted before a set of heavy double doors while Bernkassler fumbled with the ancient lock. They went in, and to Schanz's surprise, there were electric lights.

The vaults were enormous, more like the storage stacks of some huge library than anything else. Graz may have been a small city, but its history was long and well documented.

Bernkassler pulled up a little wooden table, turned on yet another overhead light, and bent to face Schanz.

"We shall start at 1900, as before?"

Schanz nodded.

"But this time," he said, "*you* work your way forward and

53

I shall go backwards. Even a crab may eventually reach his goal."

"Let us hope so, Herr Obersturmbannführer."

"Let us indeed, Herr Bernkassler."

Schanz put on his eyeglasses, blew his nose, and took off his suit jacket. The dust in the room was such as to inspire immediate and total respect.

It was mid-afternoon before it occurred to Schanz that he was hungry again. He had become so absorbed in the registers that he had not even noticed the time.

So many taxes. Iron tax, salt tax, cartage tax, storage tax, building tax—the Emperor's treasury department had been most inventive. The entries paraded by, year by year, this time alphabetically. He had only to check the "F" pages and, just to make sure, the "PH" sections as well.

Hunger, however, had surfaced and begun to gnaw. Bernkassler continued to work away, the clockwork gnome. But the sheets of notepaper at his elbow were as clean as they had been when he'd started.

As Schanz was about to call a halt in order to surface for food, his eye lit on a small entry at the bottom of the page. He might well have missed it, it was so small, but the hand-writing was markedly different from that on the rest of the page. And something about it struck him as distinctly odd.

"Here, Bernkassler. Can you make this out? My eyes aren't up to it."

They took the ledger over to the strongest of the available lamps.

"What a scrawl—here, what does it say? Isn't that—yes, it is 'Frankenberger' or something like that, isn't it?"

"Possibly. It's hard to say, Herr Obersturmbannführer."

"And after it? What is that?"

"A note that a tax has been paid to the Gemeine—the community organization," Bernkassler said softly.

"What community organization is that?"

"Why the community organization of the Jews, of course. Once, we had quite a few of them here. In those days they

were allowed their own little government, Herr Obersturmbannführer. Well, we've put a stop to all of that kind of thing,
haven't we?"

Schanz's eyes scanned the page, his glance rising again to
the very top of the book where the date had been entered:
1856. He had gone back that far without even realizing it.

But there it was, an entry—clearly, now that he looked
at it more closely through his second and stronger pair of
glasses, clearly and definitely "Frankenberger Verlag." And
next to it a note that this "Frankenberger Verlag" had paid a
fee of so many Kroner to the Jewish communal organization in
April of that year.

So. There *had* been another Frankenberger and this Frankenberger was a Jew.

At least in 1856.

Schanz had caught up with Gruner just as he was about to
leave. He was taking a woman friend to an open-air concert
that evening and, completely in contrast to his behavior the
night before, seemed anxious to be rid of Schanz. Who could
blame him? Gruner was dressed, pressed, and cologned like a
Frenchman, while Schanz looked like a coal miner after his
day in the Rathaus vaults.

"The Jewish communal records? Good God, you must be
joking, Schanz."

"It is quite important to me, Gruner." Then he added,
"And it could be to you too."

Gruner's expression darkened for a second. "Yes, yes, I can
understand you perfectly." He glanced at his watch. "Ah, well,
how long will it take?" He picked up the phone, and while
waiting to be connected, looked up and said, "There is one
man, of those still left here. One man who might know."

"And he is?"

"A Jew named Weissblum. He was a deputy under the
Emperor. Now we've got him working for us at the Reichsfluchtsteuer Bureau." He averted his gaze; someone was talking
to him on the phone. He spoke quickly, a little harshly. Schanz
was surprised by his tone, by the subtle change in it.

55

Gruner snapped the receiver down.

"He will be brought to you within the hour. If you care to wait in my office, I'll have some dinner sent in. Now," he looked again at his watch, "I really must go. Hedwig does not care to be kept waiting."

September 10, 10:00 A.M.: Graz

Schanz had just finished his kaiserschnitzel and was eyeing the linzertorte when he heard the tramp of boots in the corridor.

The door opened and a uniformed Orpo* man pushed in a small, emaciated creature wearing large, steel-rimmed eyeglasses, one lens of which had been broken and was held in place by tape.

"The Jew, Weissblum," said the Orpo man. "At your service, Herr Obersturmbannführer. Shall I wait?"

"If I need you, I'll call. The man is in my custody now."

"He is not under arrest, sir," said the Orpo man. "Not yet."

"I will call if I need you," repeated Schanz.

The door slammed. He looked across the desk at Weissblum who, in turn, was staring unbelievingly at him.

"You are a colonel?" Weissblum asked in a barely audible voice.

"Security Service," Schanz said, suddenly becoming aware of his grimy appearance again. "We don't all parade about in shiny black uniforms. Now, sit down, Herr Weissblum."

"Sit? Should I not stand?"

"Sit, Weissblum. We have things to discuss."

Weissblum sat. He clasped his hands in his lap, utterly baffled and very nervous. He began to swallow rapidly and to lick his lips.

"Have you eaten?" asked Schanz, noticing that Weissblum was staring at the empty plate on the desk.

"Not today, sir."

"Nothing? And you were at work?"

---

* *Ordnungspolizei*—The civil police.

"In the Reichsfluchtsteuer Bureau, sir. I am in charge of the records."

"Just so," said Schanz. "Here, have the linzertorte. I don't want it anyway."

"You want *me* to eat—your. . .?"

"Unless you're not hungry, Herr Weissblum."

Weissblum took the pastry and wolfed it down. Schanz averted his gaze; there was something embarrassing about watching the way the man ate. He felt distinctly uncomfortable.

When Weissblum had finished, Schanz began again.

"Now let us talk, Weissblum. No. Let me talk and you will answer, please."

"What is it that you want of me?"

"Inspector Gruner tells me that you are an authority on the records of the Jewish community organization—such as it is and such as they are."

Weissblum nodded.

"Good, then. How far back do those records go?"

"There was such a community in Graz—at least by 1820."

"Do the records still exist?"

"So much has been destroyed, sir. It is not our fault."

"Do they exist, Herr Weissblum?"

"It's possible. A year ago, the answer would have been absolutely yes. But today, how can I be sure? Can one man know all the things a hurricane will destroy?"

"I appreciate your philosophical observations, Herr Weissblum, and they are very well put. But the question is—the records?"

"I know where they should be. We shall have to look."

September 10, 10:30 P.M.: *Graz*

The gray Daimler drew up almost soundlessly before the deserted synagogue on the outskirts of the city. What windows were left were boarded up. The stone face of the building was streaked by great fingers of black smoke. Obscenities done in whitewash covered those areas not already disfigured by fire.

There was only one streetlamp on and that far distant, at

the very end of the street. As though even the municipal lighting system of the city of Graz were somehow ashamed of what had happened.

Schanz turned off the motor. Weissblum sat still, with his head sunk down onto his breastbone.

"Here?" asked Schanz.

Weissblum raised his head sufficiently to nod. Then, suddenly, he turned full face to Schanz.

"All the records were taken here when the Gemeine building was confiscated. Why they weren't burned then, who can say? Perhaps it was because of the men from the Racial Museum. They thought that the records might be useful someday. Amusing, they said. Evidence of our decadence, our special privileges." For a moment he was silent. Then, "Why do you want these records? Who do I destroy by helping you?"

"Let's go in, Herr Weissblum. The door is unlocked?"

Schanz switched on a flashlight and they went in. Weissblum went immediately to the light switch and turned on the lights in the ruined vestibule.

"You see, you have left us the light with which to see clearly our degradation—that, at least."

Schanz swung the beam of the flashlight around so that the light fell directly on Weissblum's face, and even though the electric light was on, he was blinded.

"Listen to me, Herr Weissblum. I don't care about you or about you Jews. To me it makes as little difference that you are a Jew as if you were a Moslem or Buddhist or a Lutheran. I am not responsible for what others do and I don't participate, do you understand? But there is work to be done and you will do as you are asked, without any more such remarks. Is that clear?" He switched off the flashlight and stood in the dull gloom of the dirt-spattered bulbs overhead. "I don't care to be made to feel guilty for something I neither did nor approve of. Now, if you please."

Weissblum sighed deeply. Schanz followed him into the synagogue proper. Such light as there was revealed an interior in shambles. The benches were splintered, there was broken glass everywhere—so much that it was impossible to understand where it had all come from. The ark had been burned out so

58

that all that remained was a charred shell. Scraps of torn prayer shawls and pages of holy books were everywhere. The place smelled of urine and dog feces and looked like a garbage heap.

Weissblum stood for a moment surveying the wreckage. He spoke, barely audible: "Once, this was a holy place."

"The records, Herr Weissblum?"

"Not in here. This was a place of prayer. I only wanted to see it once again. Come, follow me."

Weissblum led Schanz around the back of the room to a small door near where the ark had been. The door opened onto a large room that had been an office of some kind, perhaps the rabbi's study or the library.

Schanz swung his flashlight beam around until Weissblum found the light switch. Again, unaccountably, the lights still functioned.

The room was piled high with crates. Each crate bore a tag with a number scrawled in black ink and the seal of the Racial Museum.

"1903," said Weissblum, taking a tag in his hand.

"1877," said Schanz.

Weissblum let the tag fall and looked around the room. "They all seem to be here. But who can tell? A crate for each year. Inside, there will be ledgers, books of all kinds."

"In Hebrew or in Yiddish?"

"In German, Herr Obersturmbannführer," Weissblum said, an unexpected sharpness to his tone. "Excellent German. There was a time when the Jews of Graz considered themselves loyal subjects of the Emperor and were treated in kind."

Schanz stood there for a long time without answering. He would have liked to have felt anger, but the only sensation of which he was really aware was a nagging shame mingled with impatience.

Finally, he directed Weissblum to help him with the crates. He would start at 1865 and work backwards. Weissblum was to do nothing but hand him the ledgers. Schanz did not want to have to order the man's death or be in any way responsible for it, and if he found what he was looking for and Kepplinger, in turn, found out that the Jew had been involved, at the very least he would be on his way to Mauthausen within a day. If not shot out of hand.

"Which do you want first? The birth records or those for deaths?"

"Whichever. It hardly matters."

A gray rain-sodden dawn filtered in through the boarded windows. Schanz was bleary-eyed and feeling his age. In the street outside, trucks rumbled by. Auto horns honked like distant geese. Voices could be heard in ordinary, everyday conversation.

Schanz slumped against the remains of one of the benches, an open ledger in his lap, a pile of similar ledgers on the floor next to him. Weissblum, exhausted, was asleep on the floor.

It was there, all of it. Frankenberger, the name, the address, the whole family. All had been noted, registered, written down in every detail. Members of the community. Not a large community, less than one hundred at that time. But all meticulously recorded.

He had names now. Of sons and daughters, grandsons and granddaughters. Now, at least, he could work forward, not backwards. Forward from a point in time a hundred years in the past.

Another time, another universe, it seemed.

Schanz wrote the names down on some of the file cards he always kept in his pockets. He ached in every joint. If his wife could have seen him just then there would have been no end to the recriminations. Even his son Helmut would have been harsh.

A man of your age, Ulrich.

Perhaps, he thought, sometime in the future it would be necessary for him to be harsh on himself too.

He went over to the sleeping Weissblum and shook him awake.

"We go now, Herr Weissblum. Now, if you please."

September 11, 6:15 A.M.: Vienna

From the sitting room window of Michaelis's apartment on the fourth floor of a centuries-old building on the Dorotheergasse, both the spire of the Stephanskirche and the huge iron ring of the Prater ferris wheel could be clearly seen, the wheel and the spire superimposed one on the other like some ancient hieratical symbol whose meaning has been lost in antiquity. The sky to the east was lightening, a hazy gray that would soon be the silver of a clear, hot September morning.

Melitta Trcka, still seated on the cracked leather sofa as she had been since eleven the night before, narrowed her eyes against the sudden and unwanted light. She had not seen it come. There were many things, she thought, that she had not seen coming. Now they seemed all to have been as inevitable as that gray, unwelcome dawn. Still, one had to struggle. There was really nothing else to do.

She passed her hand through her hair, moved her legs under her, and felt her muscles protest. Thirty-eight was not old but it was not young enough, either, for the things she was trying to do.

"Bernhard?"

She kept her voice low, almost to a whisper, not actually wanting to wake him. As she looked over at him, she noticed the lines of strain still tight around his mouth, and thought how he had always, even when sleeping, had the power to move her deeply.

She could not even remember exactly when they had met but only that it seemed as if she had always known him. It was like trying to remember the precise moment of her birth. August had spoken of Bernhard Michaelis so often that when she finally came to meet him it had been like the renewal of an old acquaintance. Or like meeting someone with whom she had been corresponding for a long time.

She had dim memories of talking to him about politics over dinner, about art and music before the fire in the salon or in the foyer of the Staatsoper while her husband looked on, proud of her quick mind and a little amused. Those times had set the stage for what had happened later between them.

It had been on that cold, slate-gray day in early March of 1936 when German troops had marched back into the Rhineland. Michaelis, who had been in Vienna for the week, had appeared at the Kahlenberg just as it was getting light. His coat had been dark with rain. His thinning hair had hung in damp strands down over his forehead. His car had broken down a little north of Nussdorf and he had come the rest of the way on foot in a driving rain, wild-eyed and hardly able to contain himself.

He had come crashing into the large downstairs salon and stood there shivering until old Fessler, barely awake, had fetched her down. August had gone on business to Linz the day before. She had only a blanket thrown over her nightgown. When she saw him standing there in his rain-soaked clothes and mud-caked boots, she thought for a moment that he was being hunted and had come to her for refuge. She knew how despondent and angry he had become in the weeks since, like all the other judges and lawyers in the court system of the Third Reich, he had been forced to join the Nazi League of German Jurists, the N.S. Rechtswahrerbund. Having to give the Hitler salute in order to retain his place on the bench had sent him into a dark fury that lasted for weeks. For a moment, she feared that he had done something irredeemably foolish.

Then, in a torrent, he had told her why he had come, that the troops of General Blomberg were even then going back over the Rhine bridges and that the French were not making a move to stop them. He had gotten word less than an hour before from friends in the office of Abwehr, Berlin.

"And you dragged yourself all the way up here, at this hour? But why?"

"I had to tell you," he said quietly.

"What possible difference could it make whether August or I knows an hour or so before it's on the radio? August? He won't even understand. He'll wait for you to tell him what it all means."

"Don't say that. August is a good man."

"So are you, Bernhard."

"It was important to me that you hear it from me. Now that it's done, you're right—it doesn't seem so important any more."

"That isn't true," she said. "You were right. It was important."

She touched his cheek with her fingertips for a second, then took her hand away.

He shook his head and moved closer to the almost dead fire. The smell of ashes was strong and pungent in the room. Fessler had discreetly withdrawn.

She got him a brandy. The room was empty, dark. She prodded the embers in the hearth, and the fire stirred and flared up.

Michaelis continued to shiver; he was soaked through.

She threw her blanket over him, completely unconcerned that she was now almost naked in her thin gown. He held his head in his hands and spoke slowly, barely audible.

"They'll be cheering in the Reichstag this afternoon, you can be sure of that, those troglodytes. And then they will continue to cheer until they drown out the sound of the boots and the tragedy that will certainly overtake us if all this goes on."

She leaned over him and his head pressed against her breast. For a moment, foolishly, rather clumsily, they moved their hands over each other's bodies as though each was unsure of the other. Michaelis continued to shiver until she covered his mouth with hers, held him for a time, and then led him upstairs.

There was no hesitation. She had undressed him and taken him at once into bed, warming him with her own body until at last he had stopped shaking.

Then, without a word, they had made love.

It seemed to her, now, that it had always been that way, that they had been able to find each other only in moments of anguish or crisis and that, somehow, desperation had always been and would always be an indispensable part of their love. And silence. It had always been better when there were no words.

Now Michaelis lay like a discarded scarecrow, crumpled in sleep in a huge wing-backed chair by the crowded bookshelves. He stirred, always a nervous, light sleeper, even more so now.

"You're not really asleep, are you?"

He opened his eyes. "No, not really," he assented, his voice thickened by exhaustion. His face seemed gray, lined and old, his pale straw-colored hair almost white in the watery dawn light. A lamp was still lit on the reading table. The light gave the room a strange, out-of-time look.

She lit another cigarette, clumsily, striking three matches before it caught. The room was full of stale smoke. Between them, she and Michaelis had smoked over four full packs since midnight.

It was her habit to smoke constantly when she was angry and when she argued. He was the same way.

"One day," went their regular mutual warning, "we shall both immolate ourselves."

She had said it that evening. Michaelis had replied, "It will be more likely the ax, unless something is done."

She had shivered uncontrollably for ten minutes, and he had held her in his arms and comforted her like a child who has just awakened from a nightmare.

After that there had been no possibility of making love. Instead, they had argued all night long.

Now the light had grown stronger. One single beam of sunlight crept up over the rim of the Kahlenberg. Michaelis rose from his chair and brushed the ashes from his lap.

"A fine pair we are. A fine pair of fools."

She said nothing. Her eyes were heavy with sleep and she felt cold all over. Perhaps she should go into his kitchen and try to prepare some coffee. But if she waited, he would do it. She wasn't sure she could manage by herself.

"Have you changed your mind yet?" he asked suddenly.

"What do you mean, 'yet'?"

"I mean, of course, that you *will* change your mind, Melitta. You must." He started to move toward the corridor that led to the kitchen. "Coffee?"

She nodded, relieved, and followed him. He fumbled with the pot, spilling the grounds on the tile floor. She knelt, trying to sweep them up with a newspaper. The burner ring hissed. He leaned against the white tile wall. The kitchen had only one small window that looked onto an airshaft. It was almost as dark as night there.

"You simply must leave, Melitta," he said.

"Don't start again, please."

"I won't ever stop. Not until this is all over." He began searching in a bin for something to eat. How gaunt he looked, how haggard. If one night's lack of sleep could do that, she thought, what must the prisoners in the camps look like? Or the condemned, waiting for the headsman?

"It's simply out of the question for you to stay," he went on, at the same time struggling with the cap of a jar of preserves. "Have you any idea what those beasts might do to you if something were to go wrong and we were all to be arrested? They're no respecters of women, I assure you. Quite the contrary. They'd love to get their hands on you, Melitta."

"I'm not going to leave either of you," she said wearily. "You know that."

"I know only what's logical, what makes sense."

"None of this makes sense, Bernhard. It's all a nightmare."

"Nightmares, according to our friend Jochmann, are in fact simply a logical reordering of subliminally perceived fears. They make 'sense'—he says—out of natural disorder. They warn us. . . ."

"Bernhard, for God's sake."

He shrugged and carried the coffee pot back into the sitting room. Then he turned on the phonograph, the same record he had played at least a dozen times already the night before, the Variations on A Silesian Lullaby, Opus II, written by his father, the composer Karl Michaelis.

The music was for her a leitmotif of their exhaustion; she knew she would hear that simple, droning melody and the elder Michaelis's dense, Brucknerian chords for the rest of her life, however long that might be.

"Melitta, listen to me, please. And understand that there's simply nothing you can say that will convince me you are refusing because of—as you put it—because of 'us.' I want you to go. Ask your husband, he'll tell you the same thing. He understands. More than you give him credit for, I think." He began to pour the coffee. Slowly. She could see that his hand was trembling slightly. He noticed it too and grimaced, a quick, nervous tremor of the facial muscles, nothing more.

"Whether August wants me to go or not is beside the point. I won't leave him."

"The reason you won't leave has nothing to do with your husband. We both know that."

"Bernhard, I refuse—"

"You refuse to listen to sense, *that* is what you refuse to do, dear woman. You are either very very brave or very very foolish. Probably both. It makes little difference. It's a bad combination, believe me. Such people usually live short, violent lives."

"I'm thirty-eight, Bernhard."

"And I am forty-six. Shall we both try for another year or two?" He leaned forward. His eyes were bloodshot and watering. There was an unattractive grayish stubble on his cheeks and chin that she had never noticed before. "Forget this insane passion you have for being at the center of things, for being important no matter what the risk. You *are* important. To us, to August, to me. You have helped us a great deal. You can do even more for us by leaving the country now and staying away until this nasty business is finished one way or the other."

"I can do more for *you?* Even the way you say it—I'm to be kept out, of course. When it's convenient, I will be used."

"My God, the way you talk."

"It's true, isn't it? Why shouldn't I take the same risks you take? Don't you insist on being at the center of things, on taking the very same risks you warn me away from?"

"You *will* leave the country, Melitta. As soon as possible. Tomorrow, if I can arrange it."

"I will not take orders, Bernhard. From you or anyone else."

She rose, pushing the cup away with such violence that the coffee spilled. A look of unendurable sadness passed over Michaelis's face. He reached out to take her hand.

At that instant, there was a soft knock on the front door.

"Into the other room, at once."

He went to the door and spoke through a little grate. "Yes?"

"Ernst Langbein," came a voice as soft as the knock had been.

Michaelis turned, furious that Melitta had not moved.

"It's Major Langbein. He should not find you here."

"He's a policeman, isn't he? He'll know in a second that someone else is here. I've left my tracks all over the room."

Michaelis sighed and went to the door, opening it a crack. Langbein, in full uniform, stood balanced on one leg like a crane, his habitual stance.

"My God," he drawled. "You look awful, Bernhard. Are you ill?"

"Come in, please. Quickly, yes?"

As he crossed the threshold, Langbein saw Melitta. Without so much as a flicker of surprise, he bowed and greeted her.

"You see," said Michaelis, "nothing strikes the Major as unusual."

"We are all aware, Frau Baronin . . ."

"*All* of you? How droll."

"That is not to say—" the major flushed for a second.

"Oh, certainly. *Don't* say, please. But *do* sit down, Major."

"Michaelis, perhaps we should be alone?"

"Perhaps we should, but it is unlikely that the lady will permit us the luxury."

"Quite unlikely," Melitta confirmed.

Langbein appeared annoyed but sat down quickly, adjusting his trouser legs so as to avoid unnecessary creases.

"Let us come directly to business then, Bernhard. There is something I didn't bring up the other day that I think you should know. Tieck-Mitringer has already been informed and he dismisses it as a matter of no importance whatever. Like most things that puzzle him. I take a somewhat different view and, so, I thought. . . ."

"Your friend Kepplinger's investigation, is that it?"

"You know?"

Michaelis tried to smile. "Only that something is going on. Otherwise I'm as puzzled as you are."

"I hope that none of our 'associates' in Berlin has been indiscreet." A dark, suspicious look clouded Langbein's normally cheerful countenance.

"Consider, Major," Michaelis went on, "consider that the police presidents of both Berlin and Vienna are with us, that we also have on our side the head of the criminal police and the head of the foreign branch of the SD itself, and you have boundless opportunities for—indiscretions, as well as other things. We can hardly dismiss the possibility that something has leaked out. Considering that every subordinate of the gentlemen I've named, and every subordinate of their subordinates, is undoubtedly looking for a way to unseat his superior and that an accusation of high treason is an extremely good way to create a vacancy, I wouldn't be surprised at anything that might happen. Up to now, I can assure you, neither Von Helldorf nor Nebe* have done anything indiscreet. In fact, they've done nothing at all except let us know that they can be counted on."

"Which may in itself be a ruse. It would be far better if they'd compromised themselves in some way."

"And if they had, what would that prove? A double agent wouldn't hesitate to compromise himself to establish his credentials."

Langbein nodded. There was no denying the truth of what Michaelis said. One had to have a certain amount of faith.

Michaelis, at least, had exactly that faith and vouched for the character of all those involved. Langbein could do nothing but concur. He had met Count von Helldorf, the police president of Berlin, a number of times and had been very impressed. The man's credentials were impeccable. Iron Cross, first and second classes, a member of Rossbach's Freikorps, leader of the SA, and finally a deputy to the Reichstag. It was the same with all the others. They were all men of integrity and of accomplishment. And, to the man, they had realized, some earlier, some later, that they had been betrayed by a madman.

"I do have some information," Michaelis said.

"Yes?" Langbein's eyes lit up. Michaelis was obviously ahead of him. Under the circumstances he could not afford to be jealous.

"At least I know the names and the whereabouts of the people who were brought in to assist."

"That may give us a clue."

"I doubt it. They're not people known for anything in

---

* Arthur Nebe—Chief of the Criminal Police.

particular. Oskar Weidele, who comes from Graz and has been dispatched to prowl around London. We already have someone watching him. Meinhard, the second, he is a good administrator and something of a handwriting expert. He has remained at the Albrechtstrasse, so there's little to be done as far as he's concerned."

"Anyone else?"

"A man named Ulrich Schanz."

Langbein considered for a moment. "Yes, I know him. Five, six years ago, he was a detective inspector in the Prussian state police. Not at all a political man. They used him mostly on counterfeiting cases and stock frauds, that sort of thing. A good mind. Rather plodding, as I remember. What could they possibly want him for?"

"I suppose we're going to have to find out," said Michaelis. "Would you like some coffee? It's not very good but it's hot. We'd made it just before you rang. No pastry, I'm sorry."

Melitta scowled; she had always disliked the note of levity that inevitably crept into Bernhard's voice when others around him began to grow serious.

"Listen," said Langbein, ignoring the otter, "do you know where he is?"

"In Graz at the moment. Where Weidele, who comes from there, ought to be. Now what do you make of that?"

"If they're onto Oster and the rest of us, why would they send a man to Graz? Or to Linz, for that matter?"

"It may be that it's really what it appears to be—nothing more."

"Even so, how would you explain Graz?"

"I can't. I thought you might have a try."

"You're sure that's all you know?"

Michaelis did not answer.

Langbein knew the Reichsgerichtsrat too long and too well to press him further. He shrugged.

"We've put someone on it already. We have just the man. He's down in Graz now, and by tomorrow morning we should know just what our friend Schanz is up to."

He rose, turned to bow to Melitta, and saw that she had slumped back against the sofa with her eyes closed. Her face was flushed and patchy. A long ash hung from the end of her cigarette, threatening Michaelis's carpet.

Langbein went over without a sound and removed the cigarette from her hand, depositing it in an ashtray. Michaelis watched with a weary, apprehensive look on his face. Only when Langbein had reached the door did Melitta open her eyes.

"He's gone?"

"As you see." Michaelis began to pace, hunting at the same time for his cigarettes. She had picked up the packet while he was talking to Langbein and held it now against her skirt, hidden, faintly malicious, waiting to see what he would do.

"So . . . so . . ." He went to the window, came back, went again. She felt like screaming, watching him pace so. She was afraid, too. She had never seen him like this before, so visibly agitated.

"It is possible, probable, in fact," he went on. "They may be onto the whole business."

"*They?*"

"The SD. Heydrich. That whole filthy, degenerate lot. You heard Langbein. An investigation of 'an important personage.' An 'English connection.' What else could it possibly be? They must be aware of Von Kleist's meeting with Vansittart." He turned sharply and with an unconsciously but unmistakably prosecutorial gesture pointed suddenly at her. "So, you see? You absolutely *must* leave. At once, Melitta. Go to Paris. You have relatives there. Or go to your friends in London. You have an old admirer there, don't you? Go to Lord Cranwell, then. Is there a city in Europe where you don't have a relative or an old lover? You may have to try each one of them in turn if we don't stop that madman. Better begin testing the waters now."

"And you?"

"I must go to Nuremberg, to the Party rally. With Roon. We go together. The Britisher, Henderson, the Ambassador himself, he will be there. It's all arranged that we will speak to him."

"And *that*, I suppose, is not dangerous?"

"Of course it is. Everything we do now is dangerous."

70

"Then I stay right here, Bernhard."

"We are not going to discuss this further. You go to London tomorrow. Or to Paris. Or to your mother in Budapest. Anywhere. But away from this lunatic asylum."

"Bernhard—*no, no, no!* Don't you hear me?"

"Must I beg you? Do you want me to do that? Please, consider . . ."

"If you both stay, you and August, then so do I."

He drew a deep breath.

"I'll be back from the rally in four or five days. We'll talk about it again then."

"No, Bernhard. I will not go."

He reached angrily for her but she evaded him. His expression was wild, angry, his face so flushed that for a second she almost thought him comical, even grotesque.

Before he could say another word she had scooped up her jacket and bag and was out the apartment door.

He stood there for a moment listening to her heels rattling against the stone of the corridor. Out of the corner of his eye he caught sight of the obligatory photo of his wife that sat on the window ledge. *She* would never have had the courage to say no to him, about anything. Which was worse, a woman who never said no or one who said nothing else?

In the end, he knew, he could always speak to August Trcka himself. Melitta had to be made to understand, but if that was impossible, at least she could be made to obey. For all of their sakes, she had to leave.

September 11, 7:15 A.M.: Berlin

A light mist hung over the Tiergarten. The great lindens and chestnuts were barely discernible through the early morning haze. Statues and monuments loomed up now and then out of the mist like phantom vessels, vanishing almost instantly without so much as the echo of a leitmotif.

Admiral Canaris shivered, not so much from the early morning chill against which he had taken his usual heavy woolen precautions as from the strange presentments conjured up by those wraithlike figures. He allowed his mare an easy canter and sat lightly in the saddle, trying to concentrate on the black line of the bridle path that curved ahead through the carefully tended woods.

He had left his home in Schlachtensee very early, while his wife Erika was still in bed, his only company at breakfast his two dachshunds, Kaspar and Sabine. His orderly, Rossler, had driven him to the Tiergarten stables and then taken the Mercedes on into central Berlin, to the Abwehr offices at Tirpitz-ufer, leaving the "boss" to his solitary morning ride.

The bay was spirited and wanted her head. Canaris, lost in thought, restrained her. The horse resented the pressure and gave a rebellious neigh. The admiral patted her on the neck and allowed her a little more speed.

Thank God there was no one else on the path. It had taken great effort to rise early enough to ensure a little solitude before he met Oster. The events of the last few days had left him drained and exhausted, barely able to get out of bed. But the effort had been worth it, like that first heart-stopping plunge into an icy lake. If only he could bring himself now to the greater effort that would be needed in other, far more important matters.

This horse, his dogs, they were the only living creatures he could trust, who were certain not to betray him. The rest, with few exceptions, all seemed to him criminals of the worst kind. That he had come to realize the full extent of their criminality so late came perilously close to making him their accomplice. Perhaps he already was. Ever since he'd seen Hitler's preliminary plan for "Operation Green," the destruction of Czechoslovakia, he had been like a man haunted by a crime that he repeatedly commits in his dreams but has not yet committed in reality. The madman, this "Emil" as Colonel Oster had dubbed him, had actually contemplated staging a theatrical incident in order to give him an excuse to make war; he had actually thought to order the murder of the German minister in Prague by the Gestapo during a prearranged "anti-German" demonstration. What kind of a mind could conceive a plan like that? Only the most criminal mentality.

It grew lighter. The mists began to rise in the gradually warming forests. From a great distance, he heard the anguished roar of some poor caged beast in the Zoological Gardens. They were all caged, he reflected, not only the animals here but the generals and the admirals as well. After learning of Hitler's intentions, General Beck, the Chief of Staff, had twice sent detailed memoranda to General von Brauchitsch, to the Reischschancellor, urging him to abandon his schemes. To precipitate a general war—and that would be the inevitable result of an attack on the Czechs—could only bring disaster. Germany was not prepared, Beck had insisted. The Wehrmacht simply was not strong enough to take on the Czechs, the English, and the French all at once.

The memoranda had been read and then thrown into the trash.

On August 4, twenty of the highest-ranking generals in the Wehrmacht had met to consider the situation. All had agreed with General Beck's assessment of the situation.

None would act.

And so, in desperation, Canaris had let Colonel Oster and his circle have their head. He remained skeptical and told Oster as much. How could they possibly succeed? Who would follow them other than a handful of generals and intellectuals? But he would help as much as he could. Desperate times required desperate measures.

Hans Oster was that kind of man, given to vigorous action, to quick, even rash decisions—the personality, in short, of the archetypical cavalry officer. Which was exactly what he had been until a romantic entanglement with a senior officer's wife had gotten him cashiered.

Now, Canaris awaited Oster's appearance with an almost romantic urgency. He envied Oster his dash, his decisiveness, but he could not emulate the man. The most he could do or would do was to let Oster use the apparatus and personnel of the Abwehr to try to reach the goal that both of them desired.

The latest attempt involved Canaris's close friend, Ewald von Kleist-Schmenzin, who had been sent by Oster's group as an emissary to sound out the British and get some idea of what their reaction would be if a *putsch* were to take place. Canaris had supplied the false papers and the special permit under which Von Kleist had travelled.

Canaris rode slowly, waiting, killing time. Shortly he would have to return to the stables where Rossler would pick him up for the drive to Tirpitz-ufer and the beginning of his round of morning appointments. First on the list was the SD chief, Reinhard Heydrich, whom Canaris despised and distrusted. Something was up with Heydrich, and whatever it was, it was being kept a careful secret. Canaris was convinced that it might in some way involve Oster and his people. But thus far he had been unable to find out anything at all.

Suddenly a large blackbird flew across the path. Another rider approached at a gallop. It was Oster, sitting straight up in the saddle, his monocle in place, very much in possession of himself. At least a head taller than the admiral, the "little Levantine," as his subordinates good-naturedly called him, Oster had pale, wiry good looks that made him seem more like the filmmaker's conception of an intelligence officer than the typical, rather more dismal article.

"Sorry I'm late. This damned fog. It's like being at sea," Oster said, as their mounts took up a matching gait.

"I got used to being at sea a long time ago," said Canaris. "I suspect we'd all better get used to navigating in the fog now. So. Any news?"

"He's arrived—our friend Kleist. And he's seen Vansittart already."

"What of Churchill?"

"Today. He should be at Chartwell," Oster raised one hand theatrically to look at his wristwatch, "just about now."

"Let's hope the bulldog gives him what we need."

"A good, unofficial show of teeth? I wish it could be more."

"So do I. But it's the best we can hope for at the moment. From Chamberlain we'll have nothing but procrastinating and backwatering. Bendlerstrasse must be made to understand that the English will fight if our good 'Emil' sends the army against the Czechs."

"And if they don't?" Oster asked, his face going grim.

Canaris suddenly spurred his mount forward, leaning so

74

steeply over the pommel that for a second Oster thought he had been shot.

His voice came back, punctuated by the drumming of the mare's hooves.

"Then God help Germany, Hans. God help us all."

September 11, 8:00 A.M.: Strassengel, Outside Graz

Major Lutz Eisenbach, commander of the Strassengel cantonment, had put on a fresh uniform to meet the Abwehr man from Vienna. He waited before his office, his hands clasped behind his back, legs slightly apart, watching a somewhat stoop-shouldered, large-headed young man trudge down the gravel path between the pines. Not looking up. It was as though he were sleepwalking.

The Strassengel encampment was entirely hidden in the deep, fragrant woods, surrounded by heavy and enormously tall stands of pine, barbed wire, and wooden fences. Nearby was a small airstrip from which the lazy, almost drifting Fieslers came and went all day long. The post was normally a quiet, sleepy place, south Austrian rather than German, and even the Anschluss had not changed that.

Eisenbach chafed in such surroundings but he had learned to live with them. His normally brisk gestures had long since been tempered by the prevailing mood. In a way, he was relieved to see that his visitor was as little the typical army type as he himself had become.

Klaus Henkl saluted, introduced himself, and was taken at once into Eisenbach's office. The sun outside splintered from the tops of the tall pines. It was sometimes hard to remember that there was a war brewing not far off and that soon there might be fighting to be done.

"Here at Strassengel," said Eisenbach, spreading his hands in a gesture of mock futility, "things just go on. Outside? Why, there's excitement, of course. But here? More of the usual, which is to say, nothing. I suppose I should not regret it, should I, Captain?"

Henkl did not seem impressed by the major's expansive-

75

ness. He behaved as he always behaved, with a single focus, allowing nothing to intervene, as he did whether listening to music, making love, or doing his job, as was more usually the case.

Henkl came directly to the point. He would need at least three men, possibly more. The best Eisenbach could provide from his intelligence section. They would work, some of them, in civilian clothes. All would report directly to him.

"On whose authority, if I may ask, Captain?" Eisenbach said, hesitantly amused.

Henkl did not reply but, rather, passed across the desk a folded authorization bearing the signature of Colonel Marogna-Redwitz, head of the Abwehr in Vienna.

Eisenbach smiled, then shrugged.

"Three men? Certainly you should take four."

"Four then," said Henkl. "But *good* men."

"Good men? The best. You are in Strassengel now, Captain."

"I'll try to remember."

"And what will these men be required to do?"

"Simply to follow a certain man, day and night. This can be done in shifts, however you care to arrange it. But there must be constant surveillance."

"While you do what?"

"That, Major, remains to be seen."

September 11, 11:00 A.M.: *Graz*

Schanz had spent the morning back in the records room at the Rathaus, this time without Bernkassler. Just before noon he decided to go up to the top of the Schlossberg to clear his head.

The little cog-rail funicular rose smoothly up the side of the hill, while the small white altitude markers went by with astonishing rapidity.

"Sixteen hundred meters," called the motorman, from his wooden perch at the front of the car. Once, the car stopped for a moment. The motorman called down to the engine room on a small telephone, to see what was the matter. While they hung there, halfway up the side of the mountain, Schanz felt

76

completely free of care. The sky was a brilliant blue, the sun warm and comforting. His eyes ached from pouring over the old ledgers but, for the moment at least, what did it matter? He was free of all of it. Just like the time, not too long ago, when he and his wife had gone to Switzerland and climbed a mountain; he could not even remember which one it was now.

The car moved forward again.

A bell rang, and the car came to a halt. Above him rose the walls of the castle, the clock tower with its enormous face, the two spires ransomed from Napoleon. Below spread Graz itself, a swarm of dollhouse white and gray buildings with the bright blue Ufer winding down from the north between them.

He stepped out onto the landing. There were a few other passengers, a soldier with a girl, a mother with two children, a half dozen others. He took no notice, preoccupied once again with thoughts of his morning's work and what he had found.

For a few moments he walked along between the flower beds. Bright gold, deep yellow, red, violet. The thick folder under his arm weighed heavily. Shortly after dawn he had driven Weissblum back to the Reichsfluchtsteuer Bureau where he now lived. He had given his word that nothing would happen to the man. But who could tell? Their final conversation still bothered him.

"Do you think I am a despicable person, Herr Schanz?" Weissblum had asked suddenly just before they arrived at the bureau building.

"Why?"

"Because I have helped you."

"You had no choice."

"You're right, of course. If I had not helped, I would have destroyed myself. Instead, I destroyed someone else. Also a Jew, like myself."

Schanz had not answered.

"You did this to me, don't you see?"

He sat on a bench near a bank of zinnias. The sky overhead was glassy blue, brilliant. Birds wheeled in the distant heights. One of the birds was a glider. From very far away came the hum of motors. The scene seemed to him incredibly peace-

77

ful. And for a moment he felt calm again.

Then he opened the folder.

With the aid of the birth and death registers and the civil marriage records, he had followed the trail of the Frankenberger family that had settled in Graz in 1826. The lines of his genealogical tables spread out like a spider's web through wars, births, deaths, civil upheavals, riots, plagues, and marriages. He had gone back to the ruined synagogue and spent another hour checking the religious marriage records against the civil records he had just examined at the Rathaus. After a time, the civil marriages ceased to be recorded in the Gemeine records. He had lost not a single line. Many had been cut off by deaths, issueless marriages, wars. There were doctors, merchants, even army officers. As the chart moved toward the war, there was little left of the family. Some had moved away to other countries, three even to America. The name itself had died out early in the twentieth century. Only female descendants had survived.

He moved his finger over the lines of the chart as though tracing his way through a labyrinth. Which in fact was exactly what he had constructed. He had needed only a starting point. He had even found that the Frankenberger family firm, whose appearance in the tax ledger had set him on the right course, had been in existence up until a few years before under a different name, under different ownership. He would have to check their records as well. If they had been a client of the Landsbank or any similar old financial institution, there was a chance that the firm's ancient records might also have survived. And who could tell where they might lead?

He had become so fascinated by the search itself that he had almost forgotten how concerned he had been the day before over the reason for that search.

He looked up from his papers. The soldier with the girl on his arm was standing very near to him and for a moment Schanz had the feeling that the boy had been watching him.

No. Impossible. Look at him. A good, cheerful, clean-cut boy, with such a nice young girl. He reminded Schanz of his own son, Helmut, who was about the same age as the soldier. But they were in different branches. The boy with the girl on his arm was a plain infantry *schutze*, while Helmut was a tanker, and a lieutenant at that.

Birds suddenly began to sing in the trees behind him. Schanz rose, stuffed his papers back into the folder, and started down the path.

Why not take a little walk? The beauty of the day had banished his fatigue for the moment. He hardly minded now that he had not slept at all that night. He felt like a young man again. Like Helmut. Like the soldier with the girl on his arm.

September 11, 11:30 A.M.: *Graz*

Of all the possible descendants, linear or otherwise, of the original Craz Frankenberger, only two were left. One, a former doctor, was in "protective custody" at Plotzensee. A telephone call to the prison commandant revealed that the man had died "of natural causes" some months ago and, as the commandant regretted, was therefore "no longer available."

The second person, a schoolteacher who had been taken to Buchenwald on treason charges the day after the *Anschluss*, had been executed. There was no family. The man had been a bachelor.

Which left only one name.

Hermann Jankow. Number 17, Gartnerstrasse.

The apartments of the Jankow family were actually in a little courtyard set a dozen meters back from the street. Gartnerstrasse was a narrow, nondescript sort of place that had at one time obviously been a neighborhood of some gentility but was now going most emphatically to seed.

He rang the bell of the porter's ground-floor apartment.

An old woman came to the door.

"Frau Bergner?"

"Yes? What is it?" She was wearing heavy glasses and squinting badly. Schanz realized that the sun was at his back and the woman could probably see little more than his silhouette.

He held out his papers and his warrant disc. The woman

79

did not respond; it was obvious she was having difficulty seeing.

"Excuse me, sir. This is official . . . of some kind?"

"Security Service," Schanz replied quietly. He had no desire to frighten her.

"You will kindly get the keys for the apartment of Hermann Jankow."

"What's the trouble, sir? Have they done something?"

"You are aware . . . they're Jews . . . of course."

"If they pay the rent, they have the rooms. Unless there is a new law . . . ," she paused, uncertain. "You can't accuse me."

"No one is accusing you of anything. Now, please get the keys and we will have no further conversation about it."

"You don't need any keys. The Jankows aren't here."

Schanz looked surprised. According to the householders' records, the Jankow family was still resident at Number 17 Gartnerstrasse. "There must be some mistake. You say that the family of Hermann Jankow is not here?"

"Gone, sir. The day before yesterday."

Schanz frowned. If exit permits had been issued, they should also have been entered in the record books he had examined. There was no excuse for a lag. He would have to speak to Bernkassler about it. No. Better to go directly to the Reichsfluchtsteuer Bureau. Herr Weissblum could check the records quickly enough.

"We will go up in any event," he said.

Frau Bergner shrugged and led Schanz up the stairs to the third floor. The door to what had until recently been the Jankow apartment was standing open.

There was not a stick of furniture in the place. The grimy walls still showed the outlines of the large bookshelves that had once stood there in the sitting room. There was a litter of scrap paper, ashes, and old newspaper in the corners. Trash, dirt, a few pieces of rag. A child's mitten.

Even the shades had been taken off the windows.

While the porter's wife stood at the threshold looking on disapprovingly, Schanz went from room to empty room. The place had been picked clean.

He grew uneasy. He was used to proceeding according to reasonably scientific procedure, to running his life according to the rules of reason. He did not believe in premonitions or omens. But the stark, empty rooms made him distinctly uncomfortable. It was as though some unseen, unfathomable power had reached down just a few moments ahead of him and had obliterated all traces of just that one piece of evidence he was searching for.

He stalked about the empty apartment, through all of the rooms, up and down the dark brown corridors, turning lights on and off. He opened every door, looked in every closet. There was nothing.

Or almost nothing.

At first he had ignored the scraps of paper on the floor of the bedroom closet. He had been already halfway down the hallway to the front room when something made him go back. He turned on the light again and knelt down for a better look at the scraps he had at first ignored.

Then he realized what it was that had made him so uneasy. The scraps were fragments of a newspaper masthead. The name of the paper was no longer there, only the date: 1931. The scraps were brittle, turning yellow. The newspaper, however, was French, and across the top of one of the strips was written in pencil the letters "WP/CO," and then the word, or name, "Dowling."

He took the scrap, flattened it, and put it in his wallet between his identification card and his notepad.

Returning to the front hall, he confronted Frau Bergner.

"This is impossible. You say that they left only the day before yesterday? Under present regulations they could take practically nothing with them. There have been exceptions, of course, but there is no reason why these people should have been an exception. They are nothing special. So, what happened to their belongings?"

"They were sold," Frau Bergner replied. "A man with a bill of sale came to pick them up right after they left."

"Do you know this man?"

"No. Should I know every junkman in Graz?"

September 11, 12 noon: Graz

"Where is Herr Weissblum? I must speak to Herr Weissblum immediately."

As he waited for the chief clerk's reply, Schanz glanced around the place; it looked like an ordinary enough office, the usual government bureau, a place where tax records were made up or railroad cars routed. File cabinets lined the walls, the furniture was sparse and in bad repair. Some of the employees were obviously Jews, from the look of them; the rest were plain enough. There were only a few uniforms in evidence.

The only thing that distinguished the Reichsfluchtsteuer Bureau from any other government office was the corridor. It was lined with benches and the benches, in turn, were lined with haggard, desperate-looking people. Children slept on the floor on piles of clothing. The smell was strong and unpleasant.

The clerk to whom Schanz had addressed his question gave him an odd look.

"Why, don't you know, Herr Obersturmbannführer?"

"Don't I know what?"

"Your directive has been carried out, perfectly. With no difficulty. Your men took him away less than an hour ago. It was a disgusting scene."

"My men? What are you talking about?"

The clerk produced an envelope. The order was on SD letterhead and was signed, "Ulrich Schanz, Obersturmbannführer, SD, per —", and followed by an illegible scrawl.

Schanz was about to protest that the order certainly was not his, but the clerk was already speaking again.

"They actually had to drag him out. He was screaming—Herr Obersturmführer, can you imagine—screaming that *you* had promised him. . . ." the clerk paused. "As if a promise to such scum—pardon me, Herr Obersturmbannführer, assuming only that you ever said so much as a word to him in the first place—that a promise to such a creature meant anything."

Schanz glared at the man, held out his hand.

"I'll take that."

"The order?"

"Yes, the order."

"As it came in two counterparts, I suppose I can spare you one, Herr Obersturmbannführer, as long as one remains for my records."

Without looking at it further, Schanz thrust the paper into his jacket pocket. Time enough for that later. He still had to get the information he had come for. If Weissblum was no longer there, never mind why, he would have to get it from someone else.

"You have the exit visa records?"

"Of course."

"All of those issued in the past two weeks, if you please. And the exit itineraries." The matter of exit visas for Jews was handled very efficiently. Everything was made as difficult as possible, even after the tax had been paid. It was necessary to file and have approved a detailed route and timetable for the trip out of the country. The slightest deviation could bring about cancellation of the permit.

The clerk went to a nearby file cabinet and came back with a manila folder and a self-satisfied smile.

Schanz took the folder and opened it on the desk.

It was right there on top, the first one.

Hermann and Rosa Jankow, formerly of Number 17, Gartnerstrasse. Two children, boy and girl. Ages. Train route, ticket receipts, stopping places, border crossing point; approximate times according to the published train schedules. Which were never wrong, not in the new Germany.

Schanz glanced at his watch. The train would not be crossing the border at Feldkirch until eight that evening. There was still time to phone Gruner, have the train stopped and the Jankows taken off to await his arrival.

He made the necessary call and then hurried out of the building to his car.

As he turned on the ignition and glanced at the map to determine the best and fastest way to get to the Feldkirch station, he kept wondering why he was doing anything at all. In fact, Kepplinger had given him no instructions whatever as to what to do should he find himself in such a situation. Besides, he had no real proof that this Jankow was even the man he was looking for, and—he reminded himself once again—no idea at all just why he should be looking for him in the first place.

How much easier it would be simply to tell Kepplinger that the Jankows had gotten away. A pure accident, coincidence. There were simply no more clues to follow up. Perhaps then he could even get back to Berlin for the weekend and see Helmut.

Why exert himself? Particularly in view of the fact—increasingly obvious—that he had clearly not been told the entire truth about the investigation. Let Kepplinger go hang.

Why not?

Without having answered any of these questions, he turned the Daimler north and headed toward Bruck, where he could pick up the highway. He felt very annoyed with himself and, for the first time in a long while, completely puzzled by his own behavior.

September 11, 3:00 P.M.: *Graz*

A small green Mercedes pulled up to the curb just ahead of Henkl. The driver was wearing civilian clothes but from the look of his haircut, or the back of his neck at least, he was definitely an army man.

The back door swung open before the car had even stopped.

"Get in, Captain Henkl. Quickly, please."

He hesitated, then did as he had been told; the voice was Major Eisenbach's.

The major was sitting cross-legged in the back seat, a mapboard of Switzerland on his lap.

Henkl asked him what was happening, and why he had made contact in the open like this. It was contrary to the procedures they'd established, and what's more, contrary to common sense.

"It can't be helped. The phones simply aren't safe. I assume that if we can intercept theirs, they can intercept ours. Secondly, we had no real idea where you were. We've been cruising around looking for you for half an hour. And thirdly, we've got to get you to the airstrip at once. Is that enough?"

"Will you be so good as to tell me *why?*"

"Courtesy of Inspector Gruner's carelessness. That's why he's in the Orpo, I suppose. But—to come to the point. Your bird has flown. One of our men followed him out as far as Gratwein but he was driving like a maniac and our fellow simply couldn't keep up."

"He's lost him, then?"

"Not exactly. We know precisely where he's off to—again, courtesy of Gruner. The phone intercepts, you see. He called Gruner and asked him to get hold of the Gripo post at Feldkirch and have the St. Gallen train stopped at the border and a certain family taken off and held. He's gone there now."

Henkl's expression remained severe. "What else?"

"Only the name of the family involved. One Hermann Jankow, his wife, and two children. He was given his exit visa only two days ago. Do you have any idea why. . . ?"

"None whatever, Major. But I expect I'd better find out."

"Precisely why there's a 'Stork' waiting at the airstrip to take you to the Feldkirch station. The Grenzpolizei may be under SD jurisdiction now, but they're still full of our old soldiers. Captain Lugner awaits your instructions, not theirs."

"Can I contact them from the field?"

"The plane carries the necessary radio. It will be safer that way. Impossible to tell where the call comes from if you make it while airborne."

"Very efficient, Major. You should be with us rather than stuck out in the woods as you are."

"Thank you, Captain. I take that as a great compliment. But to be quite honest, I've grown to prefer the woods. There are far fewer wolves there than in the cities."

September 11, 10:00 P.M.: Near Feldkirch

The train carrying Hermann Jankow and his family out of Austria was hardly an express. Jankow had chosen it precisely because it ran along a little-used and sparsely trafficked route, not much more than a spur line, and thus passed through only a few populated towns before reaching the border. There was less chance of anything happening on this route, of a search being conducted or of a family being pulled from the train. Jankow had heard accounts of just such horrors: of people who had paid their fees, gotten their exit permits in order, and had nevertheless been yanked from their trains just before reaching safety. Some had later been released. Most, however, had simply vanished into one of the concentration camps that had sprung up all over Germany.

Jankow kept looking at his watch. It was dark now and a slanting rain battered at the grimy windows of the compartment. The air was foul. It was impossible to get the windows open. The train jolted along through the rain-swept countryside with ominous slowness as though taking a deliberate pleasure in torturing him. Towns loomed up, defined by a few dozen lights, then vanished. Huge forests and mountains swam briefly, phantasmagorically, out of the rain clouds, then were swallowed up whole. Jankow felt that exactly the same thing would happen to him; he was going to be swallowed up whole. He would never make it out. His family would be destroyed, then him. He was sweating terribly, but his skin was ice-cold to the touch.

Jankow's wife sat straight up, afraid to look at anything but the wall of the compartment directly opposite her. The boy, eleven, was asleep, crumpled up on the seat like a bag of laundry. Jankow's little girl, three years younger than the boy, was reading a Wild West story of Karl May's. Now and then the little girl smiled with pleasure; she had only the barest idea of what had happened to them.

Jankow's mouth was painfully dry. He did not dare smoke. So far, the trip had been slow but uneventful. At not one of the stops had a single soldier or policeman boarded the train.

Mountains rose on all sides. They had passed Bludenz at least a half hour before and even at the rate the train was moving it was impossible that they should not arrive at the Feldkirch station within minutes. Jankow squinted at the window. The rain was letting up some. A fog had covered the glass, making it impossible to see out. He leaned carefully over his sleeping son, extended an arm, and began to clear a circle in the fog.

Frau Jankow caught the movement out of the corner of her eye but said nothing. She, too, looked at her watch.

86

A small black circle appeared, through which Jankow could make out some lights and the distant shapes of buildings, indistinct and chimerical in the slowly settling rain.

"Aren't we there yet?" Frau Jankow asked at last, so softly that at first her husband did not hear her.

"I don't know."

Just then the train began to slow down. A bell was heard, clear over the drone of the engines. The sound of footsteps came from the corridor. A blurry shape passed the door-glass.

If it was Feldkirch, they would be across the border within a half hour.

"Hermann. . . ?"

"I know, I know. Be patient, Rosa—almost, almost."

Suddenly they could see the town, the railroad station, the little hotel. Streetlamps surrounded by aureoles of gold in which each drop of rain could be seen slowly moving like a microbe across a microscope slide.

"Why isn't the train stopping? Shouldn't it stop here?"

Jankow didn't understand. His wife was right. The train should have stopped to pick up passengers before going over the border. It would have to stop again at the customs station but it should have stopped there, at Feldkirch. It was the first time on the entire journey something had gone wrong. Hermann Jankow felt that it was an omen. His mouth hung open in astonishment.

The railroad station slid by in a blur of rain and mist. They could see the stationmaster standing under the wooden awning, and a number of people with baggage all waiting along the edge of the platform.

"What's the matter?" Frau Jankow had caught the look of hysteria on her husband's face. She was half up from her seat. The book fell from her daughter's hand. The train was picking up speed.

"I don't know. Leave me alone. *I don't know!*" Jankow shouted.

In the corridor outside the compartment there was an abrupt clatter. The shadows of a number of men were visible. They stopped in front of the Jankows' door. There was a sharp click, then the shadows vanished. Jankow leaped up, almost knocking his son from his seat.

"They've locked us in. Oh, my God!"

The train hurtled forward, kept going. Jankow stood there, pulling at the door, which would not open. How long he stood there frozen with his hand on the lever he did not know—ten minutes, perhaps fifteen. He did not dare move. The train kept going. Another few minutes and they would be over the border. None of it made any sense.

Suddenly there was a great gush of steam past the window and a harsh grinding of brakes. The train lurched to a halt. The Jankow boy pressed his palms against the window and cleared away a large black oval. Now they could see out. Nothing. Only a few lights, a low wooden building with lit windows, and a long, low wire fence divided at intervals by wooden towers.

Again there was movement outside, accompanied this time by a clatter of boot heels. The door to the compartment shuddered, sprang open. A border guard in a long leather coat and boots stood there. Behind him were two young soldiers with rifles.

"The Jew, Jankow?" the officer shouted. He was a big man with a hard slash of a mouth and expressionless eyes. His voice seemed to come from a phonograph in his throat; it had that quality.

"Get your papers out. Quickly."

Jankow's wife clapped her hands over her mouth to keep herself from screaming. Her husband held out his papers. He was thinking, "My God, they've found out about it. They *know*. It's all finished. . . ."

"This is your family? All three of them?"

"Yes, sir."

"Out, all of you. You will come with us."

"I have my permit, sir. See, here, everything is in order. It is signed by the . . . "

"I don't care if it's signed by the Führer himself. Off the train now, or I'll have you dragged off."

The other doors along the corridor remained closed. None of the passengers dared look out to see what had happened. It was enough that they had seen the shadows of steel-helmeted men going by.

"Here, here—" Jankow tried to throw his jacket over his daughter. The officer gave him an odd look but did not intervene.

"Where's your luggage?"

"There's only this." Jankow pointed to the four suitcases on the floor of the compartment. The officer motioned to one of the guards and the suitcases were scooped up.

"Now, you there. Follow me. All of you."

They were led to the end of the car, then down the steps and onto the embankment. The rain was still coming down. Frau Jankow tried to protect her son with her coat. In an instant, her hair had fallen down over her forehead. The make-up she had so carefully applied to cover the pallor of her fear ran, and long red lines and splotches appeared leprously over her face. One of the helmeted guards laughed; the other one seemed embarrassed.

They were led across an open field full of rocks and potholes, to an enclosure defined by the low wooden buildings Jankow had seen from the window of the train. He now realized that this was the customs station.

Stumbling along, trying not to fall and to keep his daughter covered at the same time, he struggled to understand what had happened. The train had not stopped at Feldkirch. No one else had been taken off, though he was certain that there were other refugee Jewish families aboard beside his own. His heart hammered, and he thought that perhaps he would have a heart attack before even reaching the customs outpost and never know why it had all happened or what it meant.

They were thrust inside the low, rough building. The room was like a railroad master's office. A desk, a few chairs, a stove glowing in one corner. On the walls, the obligatory pictures of Hitler hung in the midst of a clutter of the kind of train schedules and maps that could be seen in the waiting room of any railway station.

An elderly customs officer wearing an unbuttoned tunic sat at a table upon which rested a notepad and a telephone. The officer had a wrinkled face, heavy jowls, wore a pince-nez and the pips of a captain on his collar.

"Sit down, all of you. We want to ask you some questions."

Jankow and his wife hesitated.

"Do as he says," demanded the younger officer.

The captain scowled. "Take the children into the guardroom. Let them lie down for a while. The little boy looks half dead."

Jankow shuddered and turned his face away. His wife gave him a frightened look. The older officer behind the table caught the glance and shook his head.

"Nothing's going to happen to you. You won't be harmed. This isn't a police station."

One of the soldiers coughed. He was still carrying the suitcases, one in each hand, another under each arm.

"Put them down over there," the captain ordered. Then he turned again to Jankow. "Let's have the keys."

"What?"

"The keys for the suitcases. All of them. Quickly, please."

Jankow dug into his pockets. The captain had said "please" to him, which made him even more nervous. One of the soldiers lit a cigarette. The other brought the suitcases over to the table, one by one, and opened them. With a practiced hand, the captain dug around in the bags, probed the linings, pulled out the pockets, ripped open the bottoms. Soon the table was covered with underwear, shirts, ties, Jankow's wife's clothing, the childrens' few possessions.

"Which one of them is it that likes Karl May?" asked the elderly captain.

Jankow, taken aback, pointed toward the guardroom to which the children had been taken. He could see them through the partly open door. They were both sitting on the edge of the cot, reading.

"The girl," Jankow said.

"Ah, then she should be discouraged, Herr Jankow. There's too much cruelty in May. 'Old Shatterhand' actually enjoys killing his Indians, did you know that?"

Jankow hadn't known. He felt it best to keep silent.

After a few minutes, the captain rose, sighed, and gestured

to his assistants. "So, Willi, put it all back." He turned to Jankow while the guard stuffed the clothes, helter-skelter, into the suitcases. "There's nothing there. Is that all you brought out?"

"It was all we were allowed to take. Surely you know that."

"Yes, I know." The captain shrugged, annoyed. "Do you have anything else? Let's see your wallet. You, *gnädige Frau*, your handbag, please."

There it was again, that frightening politeness.

Jankow handed over his wallet. One of the guards emptied Frau Jankow's handbag onto the table. The usual litter, a lipstick, pins, a little purse, a folder of family pictures, a timetable, a bottle of pills. From Jankow's wallet, much the same.

The captain seemed puzzled. He sifted through the pile of junk, then thrust it all back at them across the table.

He looked up at the ceiling and rubbed his mustaches. "Willi, they're crazy, absolutely crazy. There isn't a thing here." He turned to the younger officer and took him aside. Jankow sat with his hands clasped in his lap. Outside, the rain had started again.

The officers spoke in low, unhurried voices. Then the younger men went out of the room together. Jankow and his wife were left alone with the older captain.

"You are Jews, yes?"

"We are," said Jankow, in a choking voice. "You have our passports."

"Oh yes, your passports, your permits, all of your papers. Here, take them. We have no use for them."

"Thank you, sir."

"Not at all," the man replied. He stared at them for a long while without saying anything; Jankow, desperate, tried to figure out what was going on behind the distorting lenses of the pince-nez. Finally, the captain rose. He was a tall, corpulent man, a full head taller than Jankow.

"Call the children in here," he said suddenly.

Jankow did as he was told. The children were still dripping wet. The girl was sniffling but trying to hide it; she was afraid that her mother might be angry if she got a cold.

"Do you see that fence over there, that gate? That is the border. You have only to pass through that gate and you are in

91

Switzerland. On the other side, perhaps one hundred meters away, is another little house like this. In it are Swiss customs officers, very much like us. Like myself. Do you understand me?"

"Yes, sir."

"I can see no reason to hold you here. You obviously have taken nothing out with you. My orders were to seize your baggage. You have nothing anyone could conceivably want. A Jew's dirty underwear cannot possibly be of interest, even to the Security Service. I was given no other instructions. I have done exactly as I was told to do, do you understand?"

Jankow held his breath.

"Now, if you please," said the captain, "you will take your children and walk to the gate."

Jankow didn't move.

The captain shook his head. "No one will harm you, you have my word."

Still Jankow hesitated.

"If you stay," said the captain, "there's no telling what may happen to you. I cannot be responsible."

Jankow got up slowly and took his wife by the hand. The children clung tightly to their parents. The suitcases were left where the guards had dropped them.

Jankow opened the door and stepped out into the slanting rain with his family.

"Remember," called the captain. "They should not read any more Karl May."

September 12, 7:00 A.M.: Feldkirch

Schanz stood there in the middle of the little guardroom, dripping wet and exhausted from his drive. His eyes ached. He could hardly believe what he had just heard.

"You did *what*, Captain Lugner?"

"I allowed them to go on their way, Herr Obersturmbannführer."

"You did receive a phone call from Inspector Gruner at Graz, did you not?"

"No, Herr Obersturmbannführer. The call was from a

Sergeant Moedler, if that matters—"

"Yet you ignored . . . "

"I ignored nothing, Herr Obersturmbannführer. I did exactly as I was instructed to do. I took the Jankows off the train, examined their baggage, had them empty their wallets and handbags, and held the entire mess for your arrival."

"But you let them on into Switzerland," Schanz shouted.

"There were no instructions to hold them, Herr Obersturmbannführer. Only to take them off. One must obey instructions exactly as given. Nothing more, nothing less."

"Just so," Schanz replied, oddly relieved. Captain Lugner took a deep breath and pointed toward the pile of suitcases in the corner of the room. He was too old for this sort of thing, he thought. So, for that matter, was this man Schanz. They even looked alike, the two of them. Lugner felt only tired and a little sad. He was not frightened, nor was there any way he was going to be frightened. Schanz understood this and relented. His tone took on a conciliatory quality, a note of resignation and relief.

"This is all?" Schanz prodded the luggage with his toe. "Just this junk? God in heaven, what a smell there is to it."

"What did you expect, Herr Obersturmbannführer? You know the regulations. They could hardly have taken out a grand piano or an oil painting. Just what was it that you were looking for? Graz did not take the trouble to explain. It would have made it a little easier to satisfy you if I'd known what you were looking for. As it was, we simply examined for the usual things. Currency, jewels, objects of value, compromising papers, and so forth."

"What is valuable to one may not seem so to another."

"Quite so," agreed Captain Lugner. "Which is precisely why . . . "

"I understand quite well, Captain."

"That's good, very good, Herr Obersturmbannführer. So, you see, I was only obeying instructions. And had the instructions been more complete, then I could perhaps have done more for you. But the Jankow papers were in perfect order, having just been issued a few days ago. And there were no countermanding orders whatever. Only the instructions from Graz with respect to the baggage which, as you see, I've held for you."

Lugner paused, trying to prevent a smile from developing at the corners of his mouth. "I would have thought, Herr Obersturmbannführer, that the primary thing was to get four more Jews off our Holy German soil, as the Führer says."

"Don't be amusing, Captain."

"I was not intending to be amusing, Herr Obersturmbannführer. I am only explaining to you my motives, my precise attention to duty, and the fact that I have carried out the letter of my orders."

"Spread their things out on the table, Captain. Or shall I do it?"

"As you wish, Herr Obersturmbannführer."

Schanz began rummaging through the Jankows' belongings. He turned pockets inside out, slit linings, emptied bags, cut out the sides and bottoms of suitcases. He examined labels. There was a small packet of travel brochures, which he quickly rifled. Finding nothing, he threw them back. He pulled Jankow's suits apart, wrenched off the heels of the shoes and ripped out the inside panels. Nothing.

When he had finished with the adults' belongings, he spilled out the contents of the childrens' little satchels. He took a penknife and cut open the girl's doll, scattering stuffing all over the floor. He cracked open the china head. There was nothing there. A few coloring books lay on the floor. He went over them, page by page. A paper ship model, unmade, in a brown envelope. Some story books. Cartoons clipped from a newspaper.

He stopped. The cartoons, some of them, were in French. He recalled the scrap he had picked up from the closet, the masthead from an unidentifiable French paper, and carefully folded the cartoons and put them in his wallet.

He continued.

Another object caught his eye: a small, dog-eared stamp album, little more than a notebook. Why he picked it up, he could not have said. By itself it was of no more significance than than the cardboard ship model. Perhaps it was because his own son, Helmut, had collected stamps when he was a boy.

He flipped through the little notebook. Nothing. It was almost empty. There were only a few dozen stamps fastened in.

All the rest of the squares were empty.

Yet . . .

He looked again, aware that Lugner was staring at him.

There were two series of stamps, all recent, all within the last ten years. Nothing older, as is usually the case with a child's album. The stamps fell into two distinct groups. The first, neatly arranged by color, were all Irish Free State; the second, all English. The cancellation marks, with the dates, were visible on many of the stamps.

The Irish group seemed to run from 1931 to 1935. There then followed a gap of about seven months. Then the English stamps began. Most were cancelled out of London.

The last of them bore a clear, hard black mark: "London, June 28, 1938."

He pocketed the album and went over to the window. It was just beginning to grow light. The sun had broken through the low clouds and the rain had stopped. The light had a peculiar translucent quality that made the wildflowers on the slopes particularly vivid.

The mud had dried, the fields were once again passable. The fence and the guard posts now seemed no more than an ordinary cow fence and a few odd towers that served no discernible purpose in such a setting. Schanz thought how fearsome all of this must have looked at night, in the rain, to a family fleeing with two small children. He was both pleased and displeased with what Lugner had done. Pleased because it had been a decent thing to do, the kind of thing he himself would have liked to have done—and there was not the slightest doubt that the misunderstanding had been quite deliberate on Lugner's part—and displeased, too, because he now more than ever had the feeling that somehow, for some reason, the Jankows might have led him to something.

With Lugner behind him, his hands clasped behind his back and his head lowered like an old mountain goat about to butt, Schanz strolled out onto the field between the customs house and the border fence. In the distance he could see a few Swiss soldiers strolling back and forth near their barracks. A trickle of smoke rose high into the air over the guardhouse. He thought he smelled coffee brewing. It was easy to pick out

95

odors. The air was so clean and pure, rain-washed and cool.

"Do you have any idea where they went?" he asked suddenly.

"No, Herr Obersturmbannführer. Only that they went to Switzerland. Where, after that, was no concern of mine."

"Only of mine," muttered Schanz. He kept a strict face and a disapproving tone. But inwardly he was relieved. If he did not know where Jankow had gone, there was no possible way he could pursue him. Besides, he had absolutely no authorization to do any such thing. If there was any chasing into Switzerland to be done, let the Gestapo do it. After all, he was almost sixty years old, and in no shape for such athletics.

He would call Kepplinger, render his report, and ask to be allowed to return to Berlin. There was nothing more to be done here. His wife would be pleased and, if the Reichschancellor's tantrum over the Czechs hadn't gotten in the way, perhaps he might even see his son.

September 12, 9:30 A.M.: Feldkirch

"He's gone. On his way back to Graz, I suppose," said Captain Lugner, handing the field glasses to his visitor.

Henkl lifted the glasses and adjusted the focus. He was just in time to catch a glimpse of the little gray Daimler vanishing around a curve on the mountain road. He handed the glasses back to Lugner and lit a cigarette.

"I don't suppose you have any whiskey around, do you?" Henkl was still chilled from his flight in. The cockpit of the Stork might be glassed in but it was hardly the warmest place in the world, particularly in the kind of miserable weather he had flown through.

"If you don't suppose, Captain, then you would be wrong. Although regulations, of course, are . . . "

" . . . not always observed . . . "

"In spirit, if not in the letter at all times. Our former Emperor would not have wished his officers to catch a chill."

"Just so, Captain."

They each drank a glass of whiskey. Lugner put the bottle

back in the desk drawer and went over to the door to take a deep breath of the crisp autumn morning air. His chest expanded like a barrage balloon.

"What's over there?" asked Henkl.

"Nothing much until you reach St. Gallen."

"And between here and there?"

"Mountains, valleys, fall flowers, goats, a few chamois. Probably a few Jews."

"So that the first place anyone would go from here, assuming they were going into Switzerland, would be. . . ?"

"St. Gallen? Absolutely," Lugner agreed. "Especially if one were travelling with wife and children." He paused to reflect for a moment; then his curiosity got the better of him. "May I ask, Captain, why these people are of such interest to everyone?"

Henkl gave a characteristically rasping snort. "That's precisely what I'm trying to find out, Captain."

"And if I may also ask, Captain, why did Abwehr countermand the order from Graz?" He laughed out loud. "D'you know, I would have let them through anyway, order or no order? Such lovely children. . . ."

Henkl cleared his throat. "So would I. Probably. One never really knows, does one? But I probably would have too," he said, carefully avoiding a direct answer to Lugner's question. There was certainly no point in telling him that Abwehr considered letting the Jankows on into Switzerland by far the safest of their options, especially considering the fact that up until the moment Henkl had spoken to Major Langbein from the cockpit of his plane high above the Styrian Alps, no one in either Vienna or Berlin knew for certain who Jankow was or how he fitted into the complex and delicate negotiations that were even then still going on between the Wehrmacht delegates and the English. Humanitarian considerations had nothing to do with it. They seldom did, even though people like Canaris and Marogna-Redwitz liked to think so.

Henkl turned back into the room and glanced at the pile of ruined clothing that lay on the floor where Schanz had thrown it. He wondered what the good Herr Obersturmbann-

97

führer would have said if he'd known that an Abwehr captain was waiting quietly in the next room all the time he had been cursing over the Jankows' escape and plowing through their underwear.

"He seem interested in anything in particular, Lugner?"

"Nothing. And everything. I don't think he knew just what he was looking for."

"Did he take anything?"

"Only one item. A child's stamp album. A little booklet, really, with almost nothing in it."

"Were you able to see it clearly?"

"As I said, there was almost nothing in it. Only two or three pages of stamps. That was all."

"Stamps?"

"A child's stamp collection," confirmed Lugner.

Henkl looked out of the window, out upon a vast and breathtaking panorama of mountain and sky. Over there, beyond the ridges and the forests, was St. Gallen. The Jankows had gone there, all right. The itinerary filed with the Reichsfluchtsteuer Bureau had confirmed that. Their rail tickets covered passage no farther.

The Swiss authorities would be cooperative. There were always arrangements to be made. A favor for a favor. Canaris had worked such things out before. So had Marogna-Redwitz. Swiss intelligence would be amenable to any reasonable request, provided they did not have to compromise themselves in any way.

The Jankows would be waiting for him, safe in some hotel or Swiss police station in St. Gallen. It would take a few phone calls. Everything would be put right. In an hour or two, he might even find out what was really going on.

Two hours later, Henkl had changed into civilian clothes, sent his pilot down into Feldkirch for the day, and boarded a train at the customs station. Forewarned, the Swiss authorities passed him through the checkpoint on their side of the border without a word and he was on his way into St. Gallen.

The platform was crowded with tourists and vacationers. The first thing that struck Henkl was the conspicuous absence of uniforms. There was not a soldier or a policeman in sight.

He bought a Swiss German-language newspaper and sat down to read it on a bench across from the station. The sun had grown warm and the temptation to daydream was almost overwhelming. A few minutes rest, to clear his head, that was all that he needed.

Just as he was about to rise, his name was called.

"Herr Henkl?"

He looked up, found himself facing a smallish man of indeterminate age with a face like a wrinkled paper bag, eyes almost invisible behind sunglasses of the kind usually worn by skiers, an unpressed suit of no distinction, a hat somewhat too small; the man simply had to be a policeman. Next to him stood a tall, suntanned young man with the amiable good looks of a ski instructor.

"My name is Blaffard," said the smallish man, "and this is Schroeder." The voice was rather hoarse, the accent French, although the man had spoken in German. Henkl noticed that Blaffard's nose was red and that, clearly, he had a cold.

"This will identify me, yes?" said Blaffard, holding out a leather folder. There was a medallion, a card with his photo on it.

Blaffard popped a lozenge into his mouth.

"You *are* Klaus Henkl, are you not?" he asked again.

"I was on my way to see you, Herr Blaffard."

"Then, you see, I've saved you the trouble, Herr Henkl. We try to be good hosts, we Swiss. I admit I was surprised to hear that you were coming to see us. But fortunately we received the call in time. Everything has been attended to, Herr Henkl, and now, please be good enough to come with us."

Henkl nodded and rose. He wondered who it would be this time. Who would be passed across the border in exchange for their cooperation? A rabbi desired by the Americans, a scientist, a banker's cousin, a persecuted Catholic clergyman? There had been so many. He wondered why it was all necessary . . .

In a few moments they had reached a small, unassuming building flying a Swiss flag. Schroeder held open the door. They

99

went into the station house.

"My office is down here, Herr Henkl. A shabby little place, but I hope you won't mind. We have little enough business here, so our quarters are not the most elaborate." Blaffard crunched down on his lozenge. "Now, the question is, what do you want with these people, Captain, or do you prefer the 'Herr'?"

"Whichever you please," said Henkl diffidently. He looked around the room, but it was empty.

"I'm intrigued," Blaffard went on. "Tell me, what's on your mind, Captain? Normally, if you'll forgive me for saying so, you people don't operate quite so openly or quite so precipitously. We have already—how shall I say it?—detained and re-routed two Gestapo agents who seem to have been on the same track as you. Naturally, we cannot tolerate such activities on our soil. But for your good admiral, it is a different matter, isn't it? A gentleman among swine, if you'll pardon my saying so."

"You have them here?"

"The Jankows?" Blaffard's face assumed a hard, cynical expression. "And just who are they, these Jankows of yours? Jews?"

"Yes."

"You force them out. They flee. And then you come chasing after them. How quaint. Tell me more, Captain Henkl."

Henkl ignored the man's sarcasm. He would have liked to smash the smug policeman's face in; well, he could afford to be smug, safe over here in St. Gallen. He would have liked to see how he'd behave in Berlin.

He spoke very quietly, controlling himself only with the greatest difficulty. "I must talk to him. If he is here, *if* you've found him for me, it could be done right here in your office, so that you could assure yourself. . . . "

"I wouldn't consider it any other way," said Blaffard. "These people are our guests, after all. And the man's cousin is a Swiss citizen. A very responsible Swiss citizen." He turned to his assistant. "Schroeder, will you please accommodate the Captain for me? You can see, he's growing impatient. Please."

Schoeder nodded and went out.

* * *

Blaffard sat behind his desk, smoking a bitter-smelling French cigarette, a faintly amused, faintly superior look on his face, while Henkl paced about the room. From the window, he could see out over the city. Above the gabled roofs rose walls of sunlit mountains, soon to be covered with snow. Birds wheeled overhead. Below, in the street, troops of schoolchildren went by, singing.

He struggled not to let Blaffard see how concerned he was. Two Gestapo agents? Not SD? It made no sense. Nothing was fitting together. Schanz had only just left Feldkirch. There had been no time for him to set anyone in St. Gallen after the Jankows. And Blaffard *had* said Gestapo. Not Heydrich's people. He began to doubt for the first time that the whole business had anything at all to do with Kleist-Schmenzin and his mission to London.

By the time Schroeder had returned, the room was full of smoke. Henkl was beginning to sweat. The moment he heard footsteps in the corridor outside, he turned sharply, and saw at once through the green glass door that Schroeder was not alone.

The door opened. A small, pale-faced man in a suit badly in need of pressing came in. His hair was even more disordered than his expression.

Henkl forced himself to remain where he was. Blaffard was talking to Jankow now, rapidly, in a calm, even voice, trying to reassure him. He was not under arrest. Of course not. He was a guest of the Swiss government. His papers were in order; he had nothing to fear. All that was required was that he sit down for a few moments and answer some questions.

Henkl could tell that Jankow didn't believe a word Blaffard was saying. He moved across the room in a somnambulant shuffle, as though he could not believe what was happening to him.

"Herr Jankow," Henkl began, in the softest voice he could manage. "Let me assure you . . . "

"You're from the Gestapo?"

"No. Military Intelligence."

"As if that made any difference," said Jankow almost in-

101

audibly. He sat down in a heap in the chair to which Blaffard had led him. With a look of terminal despair on his face, he turned to the Swiss. "How can this be happening to me? Why are you doing this?"

"Nothing is going to happen to you, Herr Jankow, I promise you. In fifteen minutes you will leave here, alone, and you will never see this man again. You're quite safe. I'll be in the room with you during the entire interview."

Henkl started; he had not expected that. Even after all he had been forced to tell the Swiss, there still were certain questions he could hardly ask in front of anyone. Blaffard caught his glance and answered without being asked.

"It is necessary, Captain Henkl. I promised Herr Jankow. Otherwise he would not have come. And, of course, I could not compel him."

"Understood," conceded Henkl. What choice had he? He turned to Jankow.

"Please, Herr Jankow, be calm. I only want a few words with you."

"I'm through with you people, don't you understand that? Why can't you leave me alone? Why did you have to follow me here? At least promise me that you'll leave my family alone." He paused. "Just who are you and what do you want of me?"

"Abwehr," Henkl replied, "as the inspector has told you. There is no reason why you should be familiar with my name and there will be none, I promise you, for you to remember it."

"Was it on your orders that the train. . . ?"

"No."

"Whose then?"

"I was hoping you could tell me."

Jankow laughed bitterly. "*You* want *me* to help *you*? For what purpose? You must be insane."

Henkl worked hard to control himself. But how could he blame the man? He wanted to tell him that he understood, that it was not Klaus Henkl who was persecuting the Jankows of this world, that as far as he was concerned those who did should be stood up against a wall and shot. This and much else. But he could not. There would have been no point to it. Nor would Jankow have believed anything he could have said. Why should he? A Jew believe a Nazi? What a cosmic joke.

"Sit down. Let's talk, Herr Jankow. Tell me about yourself. Tell me who you are. Perhaps together we can understand this thing."

Jankow sank back into the chair, utterly defeated by Henkl's calm, cold manner. He had seen much of men with just such a manner in the last few months and, Austria or Switzerland, he had gotten used to obeying them.

Without looking up once, as though afraid of Henkl's eyes in the way some animals are afraid to look into a serpent's eyes, Jankow recounted the story of his flight from Graz, of his train trip, and of the incident at the border station.

When he had finished, Henkl said one word, very softly:

"Genealogy."

"What?" Jankow stared at his feet.

"Your parents? Your mother's maiden name? Let's start with those."

"My father—Friedrich Jankow. My mother, Elsa Lustgarten."

"More, if you please. Your grandparents?"

Jankow's voice took on a weary, ruined quality. "My father's father, his name was Max Jankow. He came from Mainz. My father's mother was named, ah, if I can remember, Elisabeth Schwarz. I never knew her, you see. She died before I was born."

"Was she from Leipzig by any chance?"

"No, from Hamburg. Why do you ask?"

Henkl shook his head, foreclosing the question. "Your mother's family, please."

"Father, Moses Lustgarten. A fine man. I remember him as a great, bearded man with an enormous voice. My grandmother, her name was Frieda Frankenberger."

"Where was she born?"

"In Graz."

Henkl's eyes narrowed. He had the feeling that he had touched on something important, but as yet had no idea what it might be.

"Did you have any papers, books, documents of any kind,

that came down to you from any of your grandparents, particularly the one from Graz?"

Jankow looked puzzled. "What does any family have? Old photographs, bundles of letters, things of that sort. Certainly nothing of value." He paused. "What is it you're looking for?" Suddenly, there were tears in his eyes. "If you'll tell me, if I can give it to you, I swear, I will. Before God I will. *Then* will you leave us alone?"

Henkl nodded. There was little he could say. Better to let the man's fear and anger spend itself. He waited patiently. Jankow was now staring directly at him, for the first time.

"What did you do with your belongings when you left Graz?"

"You should know the answer to that. We left them. Everything, every single thing. We brought out only the clothes on our backs and our underwear. Even those we had to leave at the customs station."

Henkl was silent, and deeply ashamed. But he pressed on, as he had to. "It is most important, Herr Jankow. Do you know what became of your belongings?"

"I told you, they were all left right where they stood in our apartment. I didn't have time to even *try* to sell anything."

Henkl sighed. "It's all there, then? You took nothing out at all?"

Jankow's face went dark. He began to tremble. "If you ask me one more time, just once more. . . ." Suddenly, he reached into his pocket. For a second, Henkl thought that he was going to draw a gun, then saw that it was only a wallet.

"Here, here," Jankow was shouting. "Look here. This is all, all of it." He emptied the wallet on the ground. A shower of banknotes and photographs fell out. Henkl, acutely conscious of the man's near hysteria, knelt to pick them up.

There was one photo among all the others that caught his eye; it was incredibly old, yellowed, the edges cracked off. He put the rest of the pictures and the banknotes back into the wallet and handed it back to Jankow. The old photo he retained.

"This? Who are these people?"

"My grandmother, Frankenberger."

"And the others?"

"Her father—"

"Yes? And the other men? There are two of them."

Jankow took the picture, squinted at it.

"This one, I don't know who he is. But the one standing next to my great grandfather was Turnauer, the accountant. He was always spoken of with great respect."

"And this one?" Henkl asked, pointing to a dark-haired, stern-faced woman.

"One of the servants. I have no idea what her name was."

"And when was this taken?"

"You see here—of course, you can't read the Hebrew letters. Excuse me. You see, the picture was taken right after the New Year celebration. A very special event for them, you see. There were very few Jews in Graz at that time. The year, according to the German calendar, was 1836."

"A photograph so early? I did not believe. . . ."

"The process was known, Herr Henkl. A Frenchman, working with Daguerre; he was the assistant, also a friend of Turnauer's and my great grandfather. There was some litigation. Claims that the process had been stolen. At any rate, we have a number of these photographs or whatever they should be called. I imagine they're quite valuable by now." Jankow paused. He looked at the crumbling little picture; his eyes narrowed and then, in a voice which—sometime afterwards—Henkl realized had been very studied in tone, handed the picture to Henkl. "Here, take it. We have others. This may be of value to you later. . . ."

Henkl gave him a puzzled look but took the picture and put it in his breastpocket wallet, behind his identification card.

"Just one more thing, Herr Jankow."

Jankow took a deep breath. There seemed to be something that he wanted to say but could not quite get out.

Henkl waited for a second, then went on.

"Let me promise you this, this one thing. You have been of great help to me. Perhaps even to yourself, who can tell? In return, I want to do something for you. If you have any relatives left in Austria, or in Germany, any friends who need help getting out, to obtain exit permits, to pay their taxes, anything

—I promise you, they will be helped. This, at least, I can do for you."

Henkl waited. He wanted, for some reason quite fervently, for Jankow to say yes, there was someone.

Jankow considered for a long time. Then, in a voice barely audible and controlled only with great difficulty, he said:

"No, it's too late for that, Herr Henkl. There is no one. Not me, not my relatives, not my friends." He paused, as if for breath. They stared hard at one another, Henkl desperate to do something to show that he, Klaus Henkl, was after all a human being, and Hermann Jankow equally desperate now, to be left in peace.

"No one to help," Jankow repeated dully, turning away. "Not even yourself."

For that, Henkl had no response.

Blaffard coughed. "You are finished now?"

"Finished," said Henkl, patting his breastpocket wallet where he had put the odd little daguerreotype. "I will leave at once, Herr Blaffard. You can see me onto the train if you like. Or you may keep me here until our arrangements have been completed."

"For some reason," Blaffard said, "I find myself trusting you. Probably I shouldn't but, then, what is left of life if one cannot now and then have a little trust in one's fellow man?"

September 12, 3:00 P.M.: Nuremberg

For more than an hour they had continued their march by, the Hitler Youth, the Storm Troopers in the dung-brown uniforms, the black-garbed SS, and the Hitler Girls in their white shirts, with flowers in their hair. Zeppelin Meadow echoed to the rhythmic tramp of marching feet. Of all sizes, of all kinds, booted, sneakered, and bare.

Bernhard Michaelis watched all of this with a growing sense of despair. The British Ambassador, Henderson, had sent his regrets. He would be unable to meet with the Herr Reichs-richtsgerat or with Minister Roon. His ceremonial obligations left him no time. He was sure that they would understand, etc.,

etc. Two hours of constant phoning had failed to breach the walls of British obstinacy. Michaelis had in the end gone off to sit in stunned silence while a delegation of judges from the various Federal courts of the land had discussed with Party officials the coming increase in the role to be played by the People's Courts and the dimunition of their own importance. The few aberrations that had been tolerated in the past would no longer be allowed. The swastika armband on the judge's robe now mandated absolute obedience to Party policy. Abstract notions of justice had no place in a judge's deliberations. Decisions must serve not only the interests of the litigants but those of the state as well. If there was a conflict, then the interests of the state would, of necessity, prevail.

Sick at heart, Michaelis had left the hall and gone out to a solitary lunch. Roon, who had come with him to Nuremberg on the train, was still embroiled in a session of the Party's Economic Planning Council.

But what difference did it make? Henderson would not see them.

In the afternoon, Michaelis had dutifully gone out to watch the opening of the Olympic Festival. The weather was perfect. A crisp September day. The sky above Nuremberg was bright, glassy blue, the tiny clouds white as cotton and lined up, as though by military order, like regular formations of dirigibles in the eastern sky.

The vast field was alive with the red and white Party banners. Everywhere one looked, the Hackenkreuz rose up, like a giant black pinwheel about to revolve. The air thrummed with the music of a dozen bands. As far as one could see stretched a solid, never-ending mass of humanity. And all of it cheering, flushed with excitement, stirred by the very spectacle of its own magnificence. Here, certainly, was just the kind of panoply with which the Kaiser had been accustomed to raising the fever of his subjects. All that was lacking was a parade of Imperial Horse Guards.

"They never learn," thought Michaelis sadly, and then wondered *what*, really, it was that they had failed to learn. It seemed to him that, perhaps, they had learned all too well.

After some twenty minutes of desperate searching, he had

finally come upon Roon. The minister had just arrived, fresh from the planning conference, without even a pause for lunch.

"Thus do the faithful demonstrate their faith," Roon reported unhappily. "The Führer goes without eating in order to be out here in the sun and so must we all."

They mounted the reviewing stands, taking their places in the section reserved for lesser members of the government and its various departments. Roon was as depressed as Michaelis; it showed in every glance, in the constant, hardly perceptible shaking of his head and in the grayness of his normally rubicund face.

"It's . . . staggering," was all Roon could say, looking out over the endlessly trooping mass of marchers.

The drums continued to beat. A phalanx of Labor Corps Youth went by, their shovels carried like rifles over their shoulders.

"Portentous," said Michaelis.

Roon corrected him. "No, it's already arrived, it's no longer a question of portent. Magog takes the field."

Their wan attempts at mutual consolation were drowned out by massed marching bands playing "The Watch on the Rhine." Then, with wands, basketballs, and boxing gloves, a troop of gymnasts followed, each group forming itself in turn into a hollow square before the reviewing rostrum.

Michaelis dared not look up. The Reichschancellor was there, his face glowing with fierce pleasure, his arm outflung in salute, rigid and immobile as a tree limb.

"How is it that he never tires?" thought Michaelis. "It is simply inhuman." He wondered, could they ever—no matter what they did—pull down such a man? At that moment he seemed more a force of nature than a human being.

The tidal wave continued unabated. The swastika banners snapped in the breeze. To the left of the stands stood the honor guards of the Elite SS and the Storm Troopers to whom, earlier that day, the Chancellor had presented new banners and ensigns.

Despite himself—and so gradually that at first he hardly noticed it—Michaelis found himself seduced by the pageant. The first thing he noticed was a faint, rhythmic beat echoing through the bones of his body. The music, the tramp of feet. Slowly, his pulse beat began to accelerate. He flushed, his skin began to tingle. He could not help himself; he hated these men from the very depths of his soul but he could not keep from being stirred.

He looked in desperation to Roon, seeking help, a return to sanity. But Roon's eyes were fixed on the moving masses of the SS that were now sweeping out onto the field, crimson banners streaming, their own band out in front. At the corners of Roon's mouth, a faint, cryptic smile suggested itself.

"God help us, it's the same with him," thought Michaelis. "It's the same with *all* of us."

Michaelis stood there in the crisp, golden afternoon, a cold sweat pouring down his forehead. He kept murmuring to himself, "God help all of us."

The evening was no better. Close to the point of exhaustion, Michaelis dragged himself to hear Hitler deliver his closing address to the Party Congress. Roon could stand it no longer. He insisted on remaining in his room at the Grand Hotel. "Call me when it's all over. I suppose I must know what he said. But it's beyond my strength to go there. I simply can't."

And so, Michaelis stood there alone in the swarming hall while the Chancellor of Germany, *his* Germany, ranted and raved like a lunatic. Surely the others in the hall saw this too. How could they not see it?

"The conditions in this so-called nation of Czechoslovakia," Hitler declaimed, "are unbearable. Politically more than 3,500,000 people were robbed in the name of the right of self-determination by a certain Mr. Wilson of their own self-determination and of their right to self-determination. Economically, these people were deliberately ruined and afterward handed over to a slow process of extermination."

Michaelis shivered; yet, at the same time, he could not help but experience a thrill of satisfaction. The more the man raved, the closer he brought the nation to war, the closer was his downfall. The suite at the Charité Hospital was almost ready; Michaelis had spoken to the still-vacillating Dr. Jochmann only that morning, and he had at least confirmed that this small step forward had been taken. There was still the matter of the testimony to be given at the trial, and the certification of insanity. On that point Jochmann still remained vague, but Michaelis sensed that he was moving in the right direction. So much remained yet to be done and there was so little time.

The Chancellor's voice rang out harshly through the hall: "These truths cannot be abolished by phrases. They are testified to by deeds. The misery of the Sudeten Germans is without end. The Czechs want to annihilate them. They are being oppressed in an inhuman and intolerable manner and treated in an undignified way. When 3,500,000 people who belong to a people of almost 80,000,000 are not allowed to sing any song that the Czechs do not like because it does not please the Czechs or are brutally struck for wearing white stockings because the Czechs do not like it and do not want to see them, and are terrorized or maltreated because they greet each other with a form of salutation that is not agreeable to the Czechs, although they are greeting not Czechs but one another. . . ." For the briefest of instants, Hitler paused for breath, gulping down the air as though he were a drowning swimmer just surfaced. Then he shouted out his final denunciation: "When they are pursued like wild beasts for every expression of their national life, this can no longer be tolerated by us. It *will* no longer be tolerated by us. . . ."

For a few moments more, Hitler continued. Then, bringing his fist down splinteringly hard on the rostrum, he stopped suddenly, as though felled by a blow no one could see. Those nearest him on the dais turned, aghast, at the sudden cessation of the torrent. A tense moment passed. Hitler stood there, rigid, staring off into space. Totally absorbed in his own vision and the echoes of his own words.

Michaelis sighed; how horrible it was that he should rejoice to hear such words. But at least, now, the end was in sight. Thank God for some small things, at least.

Then, suddenly, someone gave a signal. The hall thundered with the sound of a thousand voices hoarse from three days' clamoring. They rose to their feet. They sang. They shouted. "Deutschland, Deutschland, über alles . . ."

110

September 13, 6:00 A.M.: *Outside Graz*

The little Arado twoseater came down very close to the treetops, its wheels nearly brushing the upper limbs. Schanz stood there at the end of the field in the chill early morning air, sniffling, his hands in his pockets and his feet wet, wishing that the plane would crash and he would not have to speak to Kepplinger ever again.

The biplane touched down perfectly, rolled along the flattened grasses, and came to a stop less than ten meters from where Schanz was standing.

Kepplinger clambered down and stood by the wingtip, stretching his legs, the skirts of his long leather coat flapping in the stiff breeze that now cut diagonally across the field.

Schanz thought, "If he's waiting for me to go to him, the pig's fart, he can wait until the snow flies. Let him come over here if he wants me."

Why he had ever called Kepplinger he did not know. At the time, it had seemed the proper and cautious thing to do. After all, there was his wife to think of. Now, he realized that his frustration over losing Jankow and the resentment he had felt toward Lugner had clouded his judgment. He would have been much better off if he had simply kept quiet and told Kepplinger that he'd found nothing. Even if it had been Kepplinger who'd ordered Weissblum arrested—and he had no doubt that that was exactly what had happened—Kepplinger could not possibly have found out about Jankow. Weissblum knew nothing except that Schanz had examined fifty years' worth of old records.

Kepplinger was coming toward him, his tall, angular frame moving like an insect through the wind-scoured grass. The pilot, Schanz noticed, had not gotten down. The engine was still idling.

Kepplinger was only a few meters away.

With a snapping gesture, Schanz reached into his pocket and yanked out the folded order.

"*This,*" he barked, thrusting it forward.

111

Kepplinger stopped cold, his face drawn. For a few seconds, he said nothing.

"What about it? Why don't you speak?"

"It was necessary," Kepplinger said finally.

"I promised the man. . . ."

"You had no right to promise him anything. I did what was necessary, that's all. And you are not to ask questions. I didn't come here for that."

"What did you do with him?"

"Protective custody," said Kepplinger, by now visibly agitated.

"Mauthausen or Buchenwald?"

"Schanz!" Kepplinger shouted, going red in the face.

Schanz looked toward the woods. He felt like walking away from the man. If he stayed, it was only for Helmut's sake, for the sake of his wife.

"All right. That's the end of it. As you say, not another word. But let me warn you, if you ever do a thing like that to me again, I will find *a way*, believe me."

"Schanz, control yourself. It was absolutely necessary—you must understand. . . ."

"*Why? Tell me why, Kepplinger?*"

"We were simply cleaning up after you. You are a brilliant man, Schanz, a great researcher. But a messy man. You should have known better than to involve such people. You were told that this is a matter of extreme delicacy, that much caution was required, and yet you involve a Jew, of all people. You let him. . . ."

Schanz cut him off. "He knew absolutely nothing. There was no reason."

Kepplinger began to walk slowly toward the treeline. Schanz, in spite of himself, followed after him.

When they had reached the penumbral region where the forest's shadow blended into the wash of early morning sunlight coming in low through the tall grasses, Kepplinger stopped again and faced Schanz.

He spoke rapidly and in a tone Schanz had never heard him use before.

"Listen to me. This is far worse than you could imagine.

Two of our people went into Switzerland after your Herr Jankow within hours of your call. They were arrested immediately by the Swiss Police. Too quickly, Schanz, which means that someone else knows what we're doing."

"Or else that your men are as sloppy as you say I am."

"They weren't mine. They were Mueller's. Gestapo. Two highly trained agents. So please do not tell me about being sloppy." Kepplinger's face suddenly acquired an expression that was almost comical in its exaggerated anxiety. "Now, out with it, Schanz. What have you found?"

Schanz handed him a sheaf of papers—the family trees, the notes on "Frankenberger Verlag," copies of the records he had taken from the Gemeine archives. Kepplinger glanced at them quickly. There was nothing there he had not already been told. "So. What else?"

Schanz stared at him for a long time before answering. There were certainly many questions that he wanted Kepplinger to answer before he allowed himself to become further involved. Where had the original report come from if not, as was now clear, from the postal authorities or the IVA office, which did not exist? From the other end, in London? If so, who was actually involved? And why had he not been told? What was the purpose of it all, this hunting nonexistent people? Supposing there had been such a correspondence. It was no crime to communicate with the English. There was no war. What had the policeman from Linz been doing in the hall that night at Prinz Albrechtstrasse—old Meinhard?

But Schanz asked none of these questions. Rather, he looked Kepplinger straight in the eye and replied: "Nothing."

"Nothing at all?"

"Nothing."

"You're sure that this Jankow person is the only one?"

"Depending on what we're looking for, it would seem so. There is no Frankenberger in Graz and hasn't been for decades. This man is the only lineal descendant alive and in the Reich. Of course, if your conspirator simply picked the name out of a hat, we might as well forget this line entirely. And to me, it seems perfectly reasonable that this is exactly what has happened."

Kepplinger seemed not to have heard.

"Have you at least confiscated this Jankow's possessions?"

"There was nothing at Feldkirch except dirty underwear."

"And in Graz?"

"The apartment was picked clean. You know how efficient our good German vultures can be."

"Schanz—" Kepplinger snapped. "Enough."

"Yes, I would suppose so. Quite enough. At any rate, there's nothing at all to do about it now."

"Where did it all go? A whole apartment full of furniture and belongings doesn't just vanish like that."

"Sold to the scavengers, as I said."

"Those things must be found."

Schanz was puzzled. It seemed to him at that moment that Kepplinger was more interested in the debris the Jankows had left behind than in the people themselves. And more perplexing still, Kepplinger seemed perfectly convinced, without more information, that it was Jankow they were looking for. No one else.

"I've taken steps," Schanz said quietly.

"All right, Schanz. I will trust your instincts. Stay here and keep on digging. You're doing very well, yes, yes, very well, just as I'd expected. So. Stay in touch with me, do you understand? A report every day now, if you will."

Schanz's bushy eyebrows went up.

Kepplinger continued, "And I must warn you. I have been advised that the Abwehr may have become involved in this matter. Canaris, Oster, that whole pack of miserable degenerates. D'you understand me? The worst thing that could happen is for them to become aware of what we are doing."

"Little chance of that, seeing as how I don't know myself."

Kepplinger went on, ignoring him; he had probably not even heard the remark. "One of their men followed you into Feldkirch. He may be right here now, in Graz, and probably not alone either. We will do what we can to protect you, but you must be careful."

"It would help, really it would, if I knew what I was doing."

114

Dr. Gerhard Jochmann knew perfectly well that he could not read blueprints. If anyone had asked him to explain the lines and markings on the plans he was holding, he would either have had to lie or somehow turn the question aside. All the more puzzling, then, his persistence. As assistant director of the psychiatric division of Berlin's Charité Hospital, he would have been hardpressed to explain the intensity with which he was pretending to study the drawings for the new "treatment" rooms that were being constructed on the second floor of the hospital's east wing.

The space—and it could be called nothing else as it had hardly taken a shape even remotely resembling a room—the space in which he stood was littered with workmen's debris. It looked to Dr. Jochmann as though something was being destroyed rather than being built.

Workmen labored over hoppers in which reeking plaster was being mixed. Huge bags of lime lay about. The place was full of carpenters and lathers, all banging away. The rough outlines of the new compartments were vaguely discernible only with the aid of the first drawing of the set, the sole one that Dr. Jochmann could understand—because it was little more than an architect's rendering; a picture, not a plan.

Jochmann stroked his bald head and adjusted his glasses. He wondered what his wife would say if she could see him; she would have laughed no doubt, and asked him to explain in analytic terms his own behavior. A man was a prophet everywhere but in his own home. That was true enough.

He glanced around him. They might as well have been building a prison. He stepped carefully out of the way of a sweating workman armed with trowel and mixing board. In fact, a prison was exactly what they were building. He wondered if the workmen would work faster if they knew. Probably not. Most of them were as crazy as "he" was.

Out of the corner of his eye, he caught sight of Dr. Kisch, who had just made his appearance at the end of a long, merely framed-out corridor in the company of a large man in a leather jacket far too heavy for the September heat. Kisch was holding some papers and appeared confused.

"Would you mind coming to the yard, Dr. Jochmann? This man—he insists, you must sign."

Dr. Jochmann disliked putting his signature to anything, particularly under the present circumstances, but there was hardly an alternative. The trucker was adamant and perfectly ready to take his shipment back to the warehouse.

Jochmann, Kisch, and the driver went down to the yard, leaving the workmen to their cubicles and plaster. By the loading dock a large van stood, its rear gate open to the platform, its motor still idling. A half dozen men were struggling with a number of flat, head-high crates that looked as though they might contain giant ballroom mirrors or grand pianos. Even on rollers, the crates could be moved only with the greatest difficulty.

Dr. Jochmann signed the papers that the trucker thrust at him, anxious to get away from the man as quickly as possible—the same kind of brute too often seen wearing a uniform these days. Jochmann wondered what the driver would have done if he had understood what the "goods" in the crates were actually for.

Dr. Jochmann thrust the receipts into the pocket of his white hospital jacket. He had signed for a shipment of steel plate, two inches thick. The plates were to be installed in the walls of one particular "treatment" area, a two-room suite consisting of a bedroom and bath, each to be armored sufficiently to withstand the direct fire of a 105mm field gun.

"Do you think we'll need a crane?" asked Dr. Kisch unhappily.

"A crane? None has been ordered."

"Then how are we to get the plate upstairs, Dr. Jochmann?"

"In the elevator, of course."

"It can't possibly take the weight. Besides, the crates are too big to fit through the doors."

"The stairs, then."

"You know that's impossible."

"For God's sake, Kisch, stop telling me how it *can't* be done and go find a way to do it. This is absurd."

Kisch shrugged. "The rooms are nowhere near ready anyhow, so it hardly matters. I suppose the crates can sit here on the dock for a while. The concrete floor slabs haven't even been poured."

Dr. Jochmann gave Kisch a suspicious look. What did he know about floor slabs and concrete?

"Well, then, we'll have the steel taken up a sheet at a time. Surely you can see to that, Kisch?"

It was hardly the best way to do it, but unless events moved more swiftly than anyone had imagined, there would still be enough time. Everything had to appear perfecty natural; the worst thing in the world would be to appear apprehensive. There was nothing unusual about reinforcing the walls of rooms meant for lunatics with steel plate. What the plans did *not* show and what only Jochmann and a few others knew was that all the steel was to be used only for those two special rooms. Once installed between double concrete walls each one foot thick, it would be enough to keep a tank out.

An ambulance entered the yard. Jochmann moved away from the loading dock and went up to his office, leaving Kisch to supervise. Poor Kisch, he had no idea what was going on, yet if anything went wrong he was sure to be implicated. The entire scheme posed many such delicate moral problems. The degree to which they inhibited action depended entirely on the individual. Men like Colonel Oster and Major Heinz of the Abwehr were impetuous, whereas the "philosophers" and the "Christians" among them hung back and considered every possible move with Jesuitical exactitude.

Pray God that the right people got together at the right time.

Jochmann closed and locked the door to his office. Then he shut the Venetian blinds and went to the safe where he kept his case studies. As a matter of ethics, he would let no one else even look at his patients' records. This was well known, so no one thought it odd or in any way suspicious for him to maintain a safe in his office. Dr. Bonhoeffer and a number of the others did the same thing. Nor was the use of pseudonyms for patients considered an unusual practice. If, by chance, an outsider had come into possession of the file marked "Emil," it was unlikely that he would have thought anything of it.

But Jochmann had been working on the study for a long time, assembling and analyzing the information with the greatest of care. It was a terrible picture, no doubt about it. Yet he hesitated still to give his associates the assurances they had asked for, that he and Bonhoeffer would publicly certify "Emil" as insane, that he would stake his reputation as one of Germany's leading psychiatrists on the fact.

They needed his word. He could not even bear to think how much depended on its being given. But in clear conscience he could not yet commit himself. Too much was still uncertain, there were too many unanswered questions. About the man's early childhood, about the sources of his mania. Jochmann had yet to put his finger on the real cause of "Emil's" behavior, of the incredibly violent Jew-hatred that dominated everything he did and often led him to do things clearly against his own best interests.

But Jochmann had no doubt that sooner or later he would find the answer.

He opened the file and began to peruse the baffling basic data:

"Born April 20, 1889, in the village of Braunau-am-Inn, diocese of Linz, fourth of six children. . . ."

September 13, 10:00 A.M.: *Graz*

"The clerks from the Reichsfluchtsteuer Bureau? All of them?" asked Gruner, with a wry smile. "Why, Director Karlbach will have an embolism. He'll have to close for the day."

"It can't be helped," replied Schanz. "I must talk to them, every one of them. And it will be far better here, where they may be frightened into telling the truth. There is something, as you may have noticed, about being asked questions in a police station that tends to promote memory."

Gruner laughed and picked up the phone.

In an hour, the corridor outside the west interrogation room was full. The clerks and secretaries had all been brought in, over the director's violent protests and notwithstanding that there was not a single application to process that day; the Jews of Graz, it seemed, had almost all either left or been thrown into the camps.

To Schanz, it seemed obvious. The only explanation for the miraculous disappearance of the Jankows' belongings literally within hours of their departure was that someone who knew they were going had arranged the disposal of their furniture beforehand.

Schanz had reexamined the Jankow file and was more than ever convinced that he was going in the right direction. Jankow's application for an exit permit had lain there for months, because he had been unable to pay the enormous exit tax. Suddenly, the money had been there, in a draft written on the Landesbank of Graz by the Staatsbank of Zurich. The money had been deposited only the day before that, in French francs, by a forwarding bank in Paris.

But where then was the connection between the Jankows and this "someone" in London? France, yes, but of England there was so far not a trace, apart from the stamps. Nor was there even a hint that the Jankows were involved in anything more than a desperate attempt to get out of the country—which, if they paid for the privilege according to the law, was hardly a crime.

Yet, if all this were as it appeared, why was Kepplinger so concerned? And the Abwehr, what of them? In what way could they possibly be involved?

At a loss, he turned back to his investigations; perhaps, somewhere along the line, a rational answer might suggest itself.

Convinced as he was that it had probably been one of the upper echelon clerks who was responsible for the sale of the Jankows' belongings, he began by questioning the secretaries. A good long wait might do the guilty party a world of good.

He had progressed through six secretaries, two assistants, and one deputy clerk when he came to the first deputy, directly under the chief clerk, Karlbach—a man named Liszewsky.

119

Liszewsky was ushered into the room and sat himself down at once, without even being ordered to do so, coming as close to a parade ground stance as is possible in a chair. He was a small, sallow man of about thirty-five who began the interview by staring fixedly at Schanz and smiling. He did not seem in the slightest bit perturbed, as all of the others had been, and Schanz could only suppose that someone had told him about the subject of the inquiry and that he was, for some reason, completely unconcerned.

He answered in a crisp, high voice, and without any hesitation whatever. Schanz noticed that he did not blink. Not at all.

Schanz took a sip of cider from the bottle he had provided for himself on the table. Then he asked Liszewsky if he knew anything about the purchase of belongings of Jews whose departure had been authorized by his department.

For a split second, Liszewsky seemed to hesitate; he blinked, touched his lips with the tip of his tongue, and then replied with dismaying eagerness:

"Of course, Herr Obersturmbannführer. What do you wish to know?"

"You are informed on the subject?"

Again, for an infinitesimal instant, Liszewsky seemed to hesitate. Then he replied, "Completely, Herr Obersturmbannführer. May I ask why you wish to know? Is there something wrong?"

It had simply not occurred to Schanz that, in fact, there was nothing wrong with what Liszewsky obviously had been doing. There was no law against it, no order, and certainly nothing suspect from a political point of view. He found himself on the defensive, suddenly, to his extreme annoyance.

With visible distaste, Schanz turned on the man. "You have been doing this?"

"It's a privilege of the office, Herr Obersturmbannführer. If I didn't do it, someone else would. Often, in fact, they do. It is not always I. But as I have excellent connections for the disposal of valuable goods, I often take the opportunity. It is all with permission, of course. Director Karlbach . . ."

"So . . . so . . . you've been doing this for some time?"

120

"Yes, sir."

"And does the name Jankow mean anything to you? Were *they* one of yours?"

"Two days ago, Herr Obersturmbannführer, a family by that name left Graz. How could I not recall? Two days ago it was. They left. . . ." He hesitated for a moment as though trying to decide on exactly how to phrase what he had to say. "And, yes, I bought. As always, very cheaply. An excellent purchase."

"Do you still have the things?"

Liszewsky shook his head emphatically.

"Certainly not. Under no circumstances would I retain the belongings of Jews in my own house. Others may, but not I. No indeed. I resold immediately."

"To whom?"

"A dealer here in Graz. A junkman, you might call him, Herr Obersturmbannführer. There was nothing of value, I assure you. Odds and ends, Jew garbage. The sort of thing you might expect. Very shabby things. Nothing that would interest a respectable dealer who sold to respectable people."

"Nevertheless—the name, Herr Liszewsky, the name?"

"It so happens that I have . . . ah, yes, here it is . . . the receipt, right here in my pocket." Liszewsky reached into his jacket with such sudden eagerness that Schanz could not help taking note. He watched the frantic fumbling, the extraction of a soiled, yellow fold of paper on which appeared a pencil scrawl, barely legible: "August Weimathal; received, furniture and miscellaneous goods; 50 marks."

Schanz looked back and forth from the paper to Liszewsky but said nothing for a moment. He noted, however, that Liszewsky was staring straight at him as though measuring his response.

Finally, Schanz spoke.

"Is this all, Herr Liszewsky?"

"Certainly, Herr Obersturmbannführer. If there are any further questions, I should be glad. . . ."

"Not at the moment."

"I remain at your service, Herr Obersturmbannführer. You have only to ask."

*   *   *

121

The storage shed of August Weimathal was located on a narrow street just off the Fröhlichgasse, not far from the railroad station. Behind the shed was a small yard piled high with furniture of every description. A kind of awning made of boards had been erected overhead to keep off the rain. The junkman, Weimathal, was busily at work in his shop refinishing a table. A stocky, powerful man, with a ragged, reddish beard and stern eyes, he took no more notice of Schanz and his warrant disc than if he had been the local health inspector or the man who collected rents.

Weimathal squinted at the yellow receipt that Schanz thrust under his nose, put on his eyeglasses—thick, iron-rimmed affairs heavy as wheel-rims—and grunted as though from indigestion.

"Yes? And so?"

"So—Herr Weimathal. Where is this purchase of yours? You will show me? At once, please."

Weimathal laughed and put down his tools, a heavy wooden mallet and a vicious-looking awl with which one could dispatch a man easily with a single thrust.

"You're joking, you must be. Very funny. Ha, ha, ha . . . you saw what's back there? Look all you want. You're welcome. Spend the day if you like."

"Herr Weimathal, this is no laughing matter. It is essential. . . ."

There was something in Schanz's tone this time, not any trace of menace or command, but rather a muted desperation, that made the junkman look up and reconsider.

"Here now, let me see that again." He took the crumpled yellow slip.

"Where did you get this? That would be a start."

"From a certain Liszewsky from whom you bought the goods. The address was 17 Gartnerstrasse. I imagine you picked them up there."

Weimathal stuck the point of the awl into the workbench.

"Gartnerstrasse, you say?"

"Gartnerstrasse, Herr Weimathal."

"Ah, then you're in luck. The stuff is still on the truck. Come along, and I'll show you."

122

He led Schanz through a slatboard door and into a narrow, dark alley at the end of which stood a small open-backed truck, piled high with pieces of furniture, all roped together.

"That's it. I haven't even had time to unload it. Such junk. I was thinking of just dumping it in the river."

"If you will excuse me?"

"With pleasure," said Weimathal, rubbing his sooty hands on his beard, "take all the time you want," and with that he went back down the alley and into his shop. The renewed banging of the mallet announced the resumption of his labors.

Schanz climbed up on the truck back. There was little room, barely enough for him to stand. He held onto the rough side rails, risking splinters, which he detested.

Bureaus, chairs, a table. A bookcase. Two dismantled beds, complete with headboards. Two night stands and a number of lamps.

Laboriously, he burrowed under the top layers, being careful not to undo the ropes or dislodge the precariously balanced pile.

More of the same.

A child's toy chest, empty. A kitchen table, legs up. Small bookcases, also empty. A half dozen wooden chairs, a stool. Kitchen mops and a bucket with a bent handle.

Schanz continued rooting about in this manner for some time. A packing case yielded no more than a collection of dismally battered pots and pans. There were two boxes of shoes, a bag of shabby women's cloche hats, and another box containing an assortment of mismatched silver.

Schanz clambered down and went back into the shop. Weimathal was still hammering away, jamming reinforcing pegs into the legs of the table he was fixing.

"Herr Weimathal."

The junkman went on pounding.

"*Herr Weimathal!*" Schanz shouted.

Weimathal looked up, annoyed. "What is it you want now? Can't you see I'm busy?"

"Is that all of it? That pile outside?"

"Of course that's all."

"Where are the books, the papers, the paintings?"

"What's there is there. That's all he sold me. There wasn't anything else. I told you, it was a rotten lot."

"You're certain?"

"For fifty marks, you don't get libraries or Rembrandts."

"No, I imagine not, Herr Weimathal."

The junkman went back to his labors. The sweat poured down his cheeks, the mallet rose and fell like a piston.

Schanz, puzzled, walked slowly and thoughtfully out of the gloomy shop and into the dappled sunlight of the Fröhlichgasse.

He went at once to a kiosk and got Gruner on the phone.

"Listen, I need some information. Can you get it for me, right away? This Liszewsky person, can you find out where he banks? Yes? Then get us a copy of his account statement for the last month or so. I want all the figures, particularly the deposits. Yes, I know the bank is closed by now, but this is important. Get the manager out of bed if you have to. If he complains, tell him I will call the Ministry of Finance if necessary. I must know whether Liszewsky's made any large deposits recently. Excellent—in an hour, then. I'll be at my hotel." Schanz took a breath, swallowed, and began again. "Oh yes, and most important, while you're at it, tell your people to have Liszewsky picked up. We have a few more questions to ask that pig's fart before the night is out."

September 13, 9:00 P.M.: Graz

It was a little after nine. Henkl and Major Eisenbach had been sitting in their car across the street from Liszewsky's rooming house for more than an hour, waiting for the man to come out again.

"You're sure that this is the man?" asked Henkl, after a long silence, his tone edgy and vaguely annoyed.

"Absolutely," said Eisenbach. "Our contact at Gruner's office reported that he was held for twenty minutes questioning by your friend Schanz. That was three times as long as anyone else. When he left the Paulisthorgasse, he is also reported to have looked abnormally pale. Shaken, one might almost say."

Henkl considered; he hated waiting. Certainly, what Eisenbach's man said made sense. But if Liszewsky didn't come out soon, he was going to go crazy; he could feel it starting already.

Just then Eisenbach pulled at his sleeve.

Liszewsky appeared at the door to the house, carrying a bunch of flowers wrapped in green paper.

"A woman?" said Henkl, taking note of the flowers. "Good. He'll be gone for a while then."

"He'll be gone for a while, all right. But it's a woman only in a manner of speaking. Certainly not as you meant it. He's going to see his mother. I'm told he has his dinner there twice a week."

"All the same."

"All the same indeed," echoed Eisenbach.

When Liszewsky had at length disappeared down the street, Henkl and Eisenbach, both dressed in civilian clothes, crossed the street and quickly entered the building. There was no one about in the dingy vestibule. The downstairs landing was dark and damp. They were very close to the river, no question about it.

"The third floor," said Eisenbach, consulting the buzzers.

They went up. The door to Liszewsky's apartment was a simple one to open. The first skeleton key Henkl tried did the trick. As they went in, Henkl let his hand drop into his pocket and rest on the squarish butt of his Walther.

The apartment was small and cramped: a hall, a small sitting room, and beyond it, a bedroom. The walls were solidly covered with propaganda pictures of Hitler and other members of the government. Not a book in sight, only a large pile of back issues of *Simplicimus* on a table by the window.

Henkl flicked on a light after first pulling down the window shades.

There was a small desk by the entrance to the bedroom. Henkl headed for it at once. It seemed not only the logical place to look but, given the sparseness of the furnishings and the complete absence of anything else with drawers, the only place.

Eisenbach stood near the door, an amused expression on his face. Henkl's intensity was almost comical.

"He is an orderly man?" Henkl asked, not really needing

125

an answer, as he had already been told that according to his superior, Karlbach, Liszewsky was orderly to the point of mania.

"Yes, yes," said Eisenbach. "So we've been told."

"And if an orderly man does business. . . ."

"He does it at his desk? I would suppose so. You know, Henkl, if I knew what you were looking for, it might help. . . ."

"I'm not sure I know myself. But, in any event. . . ." His words trailed off. He began pulling out drawers. He had never seen anything quite like it. Everything was arranged in perfect order. There were little boxes for clips, for stamps, for rubber erasers; everything was labelled. There was a box for bills, a box for letters, a box for papers. All was as neatly arranged as though Liszewsky had been running a warehouse instead of a life.

Henkl sifted, being careful to put everything right back where he had found it. All right; if Schanz suspected that this Liszewsky had made off with something that belonged to Hermann Jankow, what had he done with it and how was he to find it? For all he knew, he might be holding it in his hand at that very moment and not even realize it.

He opened another drawer. It contained only a long, gray metal box. When he tried to open it, he found that it was locked.

Eisenbach, his curiosity aroused by the clanking, came over.

"Here, let me." The major took out a little knife, the kind called a "Swiss Army" with twenty or more blades of different sizes. In a moment, he had sprung the lock and handed the box back with a superior smile.

Inside the box was a small notebook. Henkl moved over under the lamp and opened the book on the desk.

"Here . . . here . . ." he exclaimed eagerly. "Look at this."

The little book was full of tight, neat entries, all in different-colored inks. Names, addresses, and dates, the amounts of transactions entered in the left-hand column, buyers in the right. It was at once obvious what Liszewsky had been up to. The man had been buying up the belongings of refugee Jews and selling them to dealers all over Europe. There were pages for paintings, for sculpture, for rare books, documents of various kinds, curiosa, silver. Everything. Liszewsky had made a great deal of money over the last two years with his scavengings. Henkl grimaced with disgust.

"Will you take the book?" asked Eisenbach.

"A copy will do. Is the lock broken? I'd like to put everything back just as it was. For obvious reasons."

"It can be managed."

Henkl copied out all of the entries for the last month; there was no telling which of them, if any, involved anything that had been taken from the Jankow apartment. Every dealer would have to be checked out, the most recent first.

"Can we find out in the morning just when Jankow's exit tax was paid? That might help."

"We have that already," Eisenbach replied.

Henkl sighed with relief; that, at least, narrowed things down a little. He would be fully justified in starting with the most recent entries and working back only so far as the date when Jankow had paid his Reichsfluchtsteuer. It was unreasonable to suppose that his apartment had been stripped bare while he was still living in it and before he knew he was going to leave.

"We have some work to do in the morning," Henkl said, pocketing the list while Eisenbach fiddled with the lock on the little box.

"You're sure you have what you want?"

Henkl shrugged. "If I don't, we know where to come, don't we?" But he knew that he had found exactly what he had been looking for. The next step would be up to Major Langbein.

September 13, 10:00 P.M.: Schloss Trcka, The Kahlenberg, Vienna

A fire had been lit in the great stone hearth though the mild advance of September had as yet given no warrant for it. August Trcka, in a purple velvet smoking jacket, his pale face as creased as a ball of discarded writing paper, stared into the flames as though hypnotized. From the phonograph by the opposite wall came the doleful strains of the Adagio of the Bruckner 7th, Furtwängler's latest release. Melitta, to whom that music, by association, was as repellent as the Wagner to which she could now no longer listen at all, stalked about the room in stiletto heels, making a rapid tapping sound on the polished wood floor that at any other time would have driven her husband mad. As it was, he lay back in the embrace of his favorite chair and tried to find some solace in such small physical comforts. Certainly there was little comfort to be had elsewhere. Even his viola was denied him; it was still at Fiebelmann's shop, being repaired.

"For God's sake, August, how much of that medicine did you take?"

Trcka roused himself grudgingly and smiled with an embarrassing gentleness.

"As much as I was told to take. Why should I do otherwise?"

She shrugged and continued walking, now well into her tenth circuit of the room. The music continued, rising, an endless threnody of strings.

"You suppose that I might think to kill myself, is that it?" He waited. She regarded him with a mixture of anger and sadness. "No," he said at last, sure that she was not going to speak. "The thought's crossed my mind. Hasn't it crossed yours? But what's the point? They'll do it for us in time. We needn't budge out of our chairs."

"I never thought I'd hear you talk that way. You, of all people."

"Oh," he said, sitting up with evident effort. "Even I, Melitta, I assure you, can see what's in front of me. We all can. Von Kleist-Schmenzin has returned with his tail between his legs. Our good God-fearing Ewald. Was there ever a man so firm in his belief and so gifted in expressing it? If he could not convince them, who can? Oh, yes, Churchill was responsive, but that was no surprise. It's always easy to speak out when one doesn't have the obligations of power to contend with. I wonder if Churchill would have spoken so plainly if he'd been running things instead of outside criticizing."

"You saw Churchill's letter?"

128

"Oh, yes," Trcka agreed. "Beautifully written. Ringing phrases. But even *he* could make no commitments. He reminds us that he is merely the opposition leader, that it is difficult in any event to commit oneself in advance on the basis of a hypothesis. What can we do with such words? Nothing, of course. From Vansittart we have the promise of a naval manifestation. Now what does that mean? Perhaps the English will send a few punts into Konigsberg Harbor? Good God . . . there was nothing more. Not a word."

The needle of the phonograph was stuck in the groove. For a moment, the clicking noise was all that Melitta heard. She wrenched the arm from the record, almost dislodging it entirely. August paid no attention, which was a powerful indication to her of just how depressed he was. To have handled his phonograph like that at any other time would have been an invitation to violence.

She lit a cigarette and stood by the window. Far below, she could see the Prater wheel, just now lit for the evening, slowly turning against a hazy September sky.

"What is to be done, then? Surely something. . . ."

August smiled faintly and came over to stand by her at the window. "Do you trust me?" he asked gently.

She hesitated. The tone of his voice disturbed her greatly. "Is there any reason I should not?"

He laughed softly. "If there is, I am unaware of it. We should trust one another, shouldn't we? In all things."

She looked away. She knew that he wanted no response to that.

"Well, then," he said. "You do trust me, and I *will* ask you."

"To do what?"

"London, Melitta. Will you go to London for me?"

She turned sharply and stared at him. Had Michaelis been so brazen as to go directly to August with his scheme? Certainly, August knew what was going on between them. He had known for quite a while. But to confront him in such a way? Tactless. Far cruder than she could have even imagined him being.

August seemed not to notice her consternation.

"We are sending another man, Melitta. Not 'we' exactly.

129

It is Canaris's idea. He and Oster have picked the man. God knows why. He's obscure, a military man, not well known."

"But what could *I* do?"

"Open doors for him," Baron Trcka replied. "He will need someone to open a few. Oster has faith in him. He knows much and can express a different point of view from Von Kleist-Schmenzin, perhaps one which the English will find more convincing. That is the plan, at any rate. But he does not know London and has no way of reaching Lord Wilson, with whom he must speak."

"And you want me to do this for him?"

"Among your friends, your relatives, and those who simply owe you favors, there must be one at least—more likely a dozen —who can reach the right people. What do you say?" He was silent for a moment and then, before she could reply, he said with slow, quiet emphasis, "It will give you an opportunity to make a real contribution, Melitta. It is something only you can do for us. And it is something that needs to be done."

She let him know without words that she understood exactly what he was up to. He smiled back, confiding a firm, amused understanding that was entirely beside the point.

"Well? Will you do it?"

She nodded. There was no possible way she could or would refuse.

"There's one more thing. You will be given a message to deliver, later, if it is required. Bernhard will instruct you. You'll have to memorize it. That would be hard for me, but you've always been much more intelligent than I so you should have no trouble. A few words. But, possibly, very, very important." He put his hand on her arm and she felt his fingers tighten as he spoke until she almost cried out from the hurt. "If you receive a cable telling you to come back for your Uncle Casimir's birthday, then you will go at once to Theo Kordt at the Embassy. Bernhard will tell you the rest, what must be done. Pray God it will not be necessary."

"I remember Kordt," she said. "I don't think I like the man."

August Trcka shook his head. "It's the older brother you

130

don't like—Erich. Theo is the good-looking one. They were here once or twice."

She thought for a moment, trying to recall, then gave up. She could not distinguish in her memory between the two men.

"Take my word for it," August said. "Kordt can be trusted. Both of them can, for that matter, but it is Theo you must see."

"And this message—why will it be sent? What will be the reason?"

For a moment, August Trcka did not answer. Then he got up and went over to the fireplace. Only after he had stirred the slumbering blaze into life did he turn, poker in hand, and address his wife.

"It will come, my dear, when the madman has decided to start his war. And it will tell you, so that the information can be passed on to the proper persons, just exactly when that sorry day will be."

September 13, 10:30 P.M.: Graz

Schanz had had his dinner sent up to his hotel room. But he had not as yet touched the food. The bottle of Moselle sat, untouched and uncorked, growing warm on the night table. He had no appetite; now and again he looked at his watch. It had been three hours since he had directed Gruner to have Liszewsky picked up and brought in. But, as yet, the phone had not rung. He was beginning to fear the worst and blamed no one but himself; he should have known the truth the instant Liszewsky had given him the receipt. It was right there on the paper; furniture and miscellaneous goods, 50 marks. And that was all.

He lay on the bed, his head propped up on a pile of pillows as though he were an invalid. Next to him lay a stack of telephone directories and in his hand the little stamp album left by the Jankow child. Bernkassler had obtained the directories from the main telephone exchange where, with untypical efficiency, the authorities had kept stored directories for all the major European capitals going back to the end of the war.

Schanz stared at the album. The run of Irish Free State

stamps stopped in March of 1935. There was a seven-month gap, judging by the cancellation marks, and then the English stamps began, running up to the spring of 1938. The only other information he had to work with were the words "WP/ CO Dowling" that had been scrawled across the fragment of newspaper he had found in the corner of Jankow's closet.

Very carefully, he took the stamps out of the album, arranging them precisely in the order in which they had been entered. Some of the stamps still had pieces of envelope attached to them; the child had not been skillful enough to remove them and had simply stuck the stamps and the fragments of paper in as they were. In a few cases, the stamp had obviously been in the high right-hand corner of the envelope, just below the fold in the paper, and still had affixed to it not only a fragment of the front of the envelope but a bit of the rear flap as well.

On one of these, he found an unmistakable "D," a capital letter, clearly the beginning of a word. It could have been anything, any name in the world, but it gave him the assurance he needed.

Assuming, then, that the words "WP/CO Dowling" and the stamps might somehow be related, it was reasonable to suppose—as he must if he were to avoid having to cross-reference every entry in both the London and the Dublin phone books for the years 1935 and 1936—that the letters had come from a "Dowling" who had lived in Dublin until mid-1935 and had then moved to London. If he could find a listing for that name in the appropriate books and for the right times, he would have something to go on, a hint at least of the direction he was to take.

He was intrigued. Of course, the word "Dowling" might have nothing to do with the letters at all, but the first dates on the Irish stamps did roughly coincide with the date on the newspaper, the year at least. Besides, he was simply too tired to start cross-referencing every entry in both books.

He finally took a sip of wine and opened the two directories on his lap.

There were slightly more than fifty Dowlings in the Dublin directory for 1935.

He began by bracketing the first names. Then he did the same in the London directory, grouping all the same first names both in 1935 and 1936. If the same first name appeared in Dublin in 1935 and in London in 1936, he circled it.

This reduced the list to five groups. Then he checked backward. If the possible London 1936 listing also appeared in the London book for 1935, it was crossed off.

Now the list was down to two sets—a pair of Herbert Dowlings and two Elizabeths.

He paused, took another sip of wine, and turned on the radio on the night table. Mozart. The clarinet concerto. Good enough. He turned the volume low and went back to his directories.

Herbert Dowling also appeared, at the same address, in the Dublin book for 1936. It could be, of course, that he had moved during the middle of the year, too late to be excluded from the printing. He would have to find out in the morning just when the directories went to press.

In the meantime . . .

He drew his finger slowly up the line of Dublin Dowlings. There was no Elizabeth for 1936.

The dates fitted. He went back and checked the London directory again. Even the middle initial was the same.

He leaned back against the pillows, exhausted rather than satisfied.

All right. It was "Elizabeth Dowling." It had to be; it all fitted together too perfectly for there to be any mistake.

Now who the devil was she? What did she have to do with a family of Graz Jews named Jankow, and what did the initials "WP/CO" before her name mean?

His head jerked up before he realized that the phone had rung. He lunged for the receiver, almost knocking the bottle of Moselle from the table.

"Gruner here. Is that you, Schanz?"

"What's happened?" Schanz heard himself demand, hoarse and breathless.

Gruner's voice came back, jovial as ever.

"Come and see for yourself, why don't you? We have a friend of yours down here. He's most anxious to talk to you.

Poor fellow, we had to convince him to leave before dessert. A very slow eater, I'd say, judging by the hour."

Deputy Inspector Gruner wondered how he had come to such a pass.

Once upon a time, he had regarded himself as a decent, even a kindly person. His ability to function as deputy inspector of police had more than once been called into question; he was simply not made of stern enough stuff, they had said. The only reason he had been allowed to remain at his post was that Graz was hardly a hotbed of crime and certainly no center of political agitation. He had little more than routine matters to attend to, and it was not felt that such matters were beyond the capacity of even a man of his genial disposition.

That, however, had been years ago. Since that time, Gruner had been trying. No one could deny that. He had studied the methods used by other police all over Europe. The provincial commissioner had determined to make himself into as efficient a police officer as any Chekist or Gestapo man. It was simply a matter of developing his professional abilities. He had nothing in particular against socialists or communists and certainly not against the average thief or even murderer with whom, now and then, he came in contact. But just as an engineer had to learn to use a slide rule, an artist to mix colors, a ship's captain the rules of navigation, it was expected that a police officer learn to use properly the tools of his trade.

Thus Gruner descended to the interrogations room in the cellar of the Paulisthorgasse building with not only his usual trepidation but also the determination of the dogged student. He did not particularly enjoy taking part in interrogations, yet he had an obligation to learn, a duty as he saw it. And on this particular evening, the obligation ran not only to himself but to his visitor from Berlin as well, an obligation to Schanz as a person, and a distrust of the SD as an institution that had now to be honored by more than mere words.

At the foot of the stairs there was a small corridor that ran between the boiler room and the coal-storage bins. The walls had been painted white and the floor kept spotlessly clean. At the end of the corridor were two small rooms, like a suite of ordinary offices. He went into the outer of the two rooms. Sergeant Wenck and two plainclothes policemen, Prell and Schluter, were waiting for him. Wenck had on a rubber smock of the kind usualy seen on chemical workers.

Schanz was there too, standing by a filing cabinet, turning the bank statements Gruner had procured at his instructions over and over in his hands.

"Are we ready to proceed?" Gruner asked, looking from face to face and finding nothing particularly revealing.

Sergeant Wenck jumped up and reported in a manner more appropriate to the parade ground than a police cellar. Gruner grimaced. He would have preferred everything to be more matter-of-fact. It was bad enough that he had to do these things; there was no need for Wenck to appear enthusiastic about them.

"He's inside, sir," Wenck said. "We've let him sweat for a while."

"He's handcuffed, of course?"

"Yes, sir."

Gruner looked over at Schanz, who wore a stern and disapproving expression and had, thus far, said not a word.

"Well, come on, Schanz. We may as well go in."

Schanz nodded and followed Gruner into the next room. It was fitted out like a doctor's examining room, with a long flat table at one end of which were a set of metal braces like those found in a gynecologist's office. There were also shackles on the cement walls. In the center of the room, handcuffed to a metal chair that was bolted to the floor, sat Liszewsky. One ear was torn, his lips were purple and puffed, and there was blood running from his nose. His normally sallow face looked like a bloody sponge.

Gruner shuddered. How many times had he told Wenck that he preferred less immediately visible methods?

Gruner stood in front of the wretched Liszewsky and turned on an extra floodlight. Liszewsky blinked back at him, trying to make out who it was through swollen, blackened eyes.

Schanz walked up to him and thrust the bank statements under his nose.

"Listen," he said in a stern but not unfriendly tone, "we

know it all, Herr Liszewsky. You see these? Your bank was delighted to let us have them. An excellent record, they said. A fine customer, they said. I should think so. Just look at this. Fifty thousand marks deposited in the last week alone." Schanz waited. Liszewsky groaned but said nothing comprehensible. It was as though he had already felt the edge of the ax on his neck and, considering that he was a dead man, had decided that it was useless to speak.

Schanz, despite his disgust over what had been done to Liszewsky, began to grow impatient.

"The fifty thousand, Herr Liszewsky. Where did you get it and for what? Is it only a coincidence that you sold the Jew's furniture to Herr Weimathal and nothing more? Where did you dispose of the rest of Jankow's belongings? You'd better tell us straight off."

Liszewsky shuddered and looked down. He seemed to be trying to say something now but could not get it past the blood in his mouth. He moaned, and his chest heaved.

"You had no right . . . ," he began, ". . . to do . . . what you did. My mother, you could have killed her. What a terrible thing to do."

"His mother," mimicked Prell. "His *mother* . . . shit!"

"Listen," demanded Schanz, "I want to know where the rest of Jankow's possessions are, the books, the papers. I want names. Speak slowly and distinctly. From whom did you get the fifty thousand and what for? Take your time, speak clearly, and Detective Prell will take everything down."

"My mother, you almost killed her," Liszewsky said again.

"He's been singing that same song all evening," Wenck said.

"It's a lousy song," added Schluter. "I don't like it."

Schanz moved away and whispered to Gruner, "He should not have been beaten like this. Now it will take ten times as long."

"It wasn't by my orders," Gruner replied indignantly. He turned back to Liszewsky and in a quiet and frighteningly ordinary voice said, "All right. Go ahead, Schluter."

Schluter gestured to Wenck.

"Stretch him out on the table, arse up."

Prell and Schluter uncuffed Liszewsky and dragged him over to the table.

"Get his pants off," Wenck said. Liszewsky started to whimper.

Then Wenck went around front to where Liszewsky's bloodied head hung down over the edge of the table. He took something out of a drawer under the table; it had an ordinary electric wire and plug attached to it. He picked up Liszewsky's head by the hair and held the object under his nose.

"Listen, you see this? It's an ordinary soldering iron, the kind plumbers use. It takes five minutes to heat up enough to melt lead. I'm going to ask Schluter here to stick it up your arse. Then we'll plug it in and leave the room. When you decide to talk, please let us know."

He handed the iron to Schluter.

"This is your last chance," Wenck said. "They tell me that even a little of this makes taking a shit an agony for years."

Liszewsky screamed as Schluter did as he'd been told.

"It would be a lot simpler to talk," Gruner said, in a not unkindly way. "Who knows? Whatever you've done, it can't be as bad as all that. We could arrange for leniency if you'd cooperate. We might even let you go entirely."

He waited. Still nothing.

"All right. Plug it in, Wenck."

Wenck plugged the cord into the wall socket. The four men went out of the room, leaving Liszewsky shackled to the table. Prell slammed the door.

Schanz's face was dark. "This is disgusting," he snapped. "I will not be a party to such things."

Gruner gave him a knowing look. "But I notice that you made not a move to stop it," he said unhappily. "You *do* want the answer, don't you?"

They stood there, close to the door. Prell lit a cigarette. Gruner fidgeted. Schluter looked disappointed; he would have preferred to have remained in the room to watch.

Schanz swore and retreated to the stairwell.

"If you get anything, I'll be in your office," he growled.

After a moment, they heard a thumping sound from within the room. Liszewsky was thrashing about on the table, trying to get loose. He began to whimper.

"I hate to hear a grown man doing that," Wenck said.

Gruner glared at him. What the hell did he mean by that?

They all smelled it at the same time—a sour, burning smell.

Liszewsky began to bellow. Even through the heavy door, the sound was unsettling.

"I'll tell you! For Christ's sake . . ."

Gruner nodded to Prell. The plainclothesmen went into the room and removed the iron. Liszewsky was bathed in sweat and crying. His body heaved up and down on the table, making a rhythmic thumping noise like a dying fish on a wharf.

"Prell, take out your notebook, if you please," Gruner said, averting his eyes.

Liszewsky began to speak, a choked, croaking sound. Prell's pencil moved quickly. Gruner was amazed at how fast Liszewsky was talking; he would not have thought it possible in his condition. The blood was gushing out of his mouth. Clearly, he was hemorrhaging.

Wenck took Gruner aside.

"He won't last an hour. He waited too long. I've seen this before."

Gruner shrugged and left the room. An hour would be time enough.

He went upstairs to find Schanz. Prell and Schluter could finish up.

September 14, 11:00 P.M.: *Berlin*

Kepplinger had been preparing for bed when Heydrich's adjutant, Kulsky, and two other men in mufti had begun pounding on his door. There was no time to dress.

"The Obergruppenführer SD gave us explicit instructions. You are to come immediately."

"Well, Kulsky, you could at least give me time to put on a robe."

"A moment only," said Kulsky. It pleased him to see his superiors embarrassed and it pleased him most of all to see the lordly Kepplinger uncomfortable and sweating.

Kepplinger pulled on a robe, told his wife to go to sleep, and went out with Kulsky. The car was waiting at the curb under a stand of elders. The suburb of Schlachtensee was quiet. Nearby, someone was walking a dog, but otherwise there was no one else about.

As the car wound through the sleeping streets, Kulsky maintained a deliberate and infuriating silence. Kepplinger, sitting in his robe between Kulsky and another man whose name he did not know, kept wetting his lips. He was shivering slightly.

Kulsky noticed this. "The night has grown cool, Herr Standartenführer?"

"Cool enough," said Kepplinger, and refused to utter another word. He was not going to give Kulsky the satisfaction of seeing him unstrung.

But what the devil did Heydrich want with him' at such an hour?

It was only after a few minutes driving that Kepplinger realized he was being taken not to Prinz Albrechtstrasse but to Heydrich's residence nearby.

In a few moments he found himself being led through the garden and up to a side entrance, which he knew led to the room Heydrich used for exercise. The sound of violins emerged as the door was opened; Frau Heydrich was probably entertaining. An evening of chamber music. For all he knew, Admiral Canaris was sitting in the living room, sawing away on a violin.

Heydrich was waiting for him in the little gymnasium chamber. He had been working out alone with his foils. Heydrich was known as an excellent fencer and he prided himself on keeping up his skill no matter how pressing his other duties.

"That, and the damned fiddle," thought Kepplinger, stepping into the room and hearing the door slam shut behind him. He knew better than to speak first, and so stood there, waiting for Heydrich to notice him.

Finally, the Obergruppenführer SD turned toward him, his long face gleaming with perspiration. Kepplinger swallowed hard and reported.

"You wish to see me, Herr Obergruppenführer?"

"Obviously, Kepplinger. Why else would you be standing there in your nightclothes?" Heydrich flexed his foil and cut it through the air with a vicious slashing motion.

Kepplinger swallowed hard and waited.

"Things are not going as they should," said Heydrich, after another long pause.

"I was not aware. . . ."

"Then consider yourself 'aware' as of this moment. I'm telling you plainly, Kepplinger, I am not pleased."

"I'm sorry, Herr Obergruppenführer."

"That is hardly an adequate response, Kepplinger. You *know* how important this is to me, don't you?"

Kepplinger nodded; he thought he had said, "Yes, sir," but he heard no sound emerge. Heydrich, meanwhile, had reached behind him to a rack on the wall and plucked out a second foil, which he threw, butt first, to Kepplinger.

Astonished, Kepplinger grabbed hold of it. He had barely time enough to realize what was expected of him before Heydrich lunged. Kepplinger clumsily parried, missing being nicked only by a hair.

"You *do* understand that this matter is, in a manner of speaking, my life?"

"But, Herr Obergruppenführer, I . . ."

Heydrich lunged again. Kepplinger scrambled back awkwardly.

"I hope your work is better than your fencing. Really, Kepplinger, for both of our sakes."

"The hour, Herr Obergruppenführer, I was not expecting. . . ."

"*Watch yourself!*"

The point of the foil shot past Kepplinger's face. In that second, he realized that there was no button on the tip. He had come within an ace of having his face slashed open.

"If we are not successful in this matter . . . ," Heydrich said, his face now beginning to show a distinct strain, his eyes slightly dilated. "If we are not successful, then that pig Himmler will have me exactly where he wants me. I will have no defense against his lies. No possible way to get the better of him, to get the better of the whole lot of them."

"But the accusation is untrue. You've said so yourself. In open court. Twice. It has been proven false."

"If it is said again, at the right time and at the right place, and with new evidence, who knows what will happen? Even if the evidence is false, someone may believe it. I am not willing to take the chance. Are you?"

"Of course not, Herr Obergruppenführer."

Now Kepplinger was working hard, trying to protect himself. He had the distinct feeling that Heydrich was really trying to cut him and it was all he could do, however clumsily, to avoid being stabbed.

"So," said Heydrich, "you must succeed, mustn't you?"

"Please—for God's sake—" Kepplinger let out a sharp, strangled cry. The foil had grazed his hand, cutting in a deep furrow. The blood spurted out, dripping down his fingers onto the floor.

Heydrich went on, as though he had not noticed.

"So, when I tell you that your man Schanz seems to have vanished, you will be as concerned as I am, no?"

"Impossible. I just saw him yesterday, myself."

"Nevertheless, he's gone now. No one knows just where." Heydrich dipped the point of the foil. "Just how unreliable *is* he, Kepplinger?"

"As we said earlier, Herr Obergruppenführer, just unreliable enough so that if it becomes necessary. . . ."

"How unreliable?" Heydrich had finally raised his voice, a most frighteningly unusual thing for him.

Kepplinger was by this time sweating heavily; his hand pained him fiercely and it was all he could do to keep from bringing the wound to his mouth.

"He cannot possibly understand the real purpose of the investigation. He simply doesn't have enough of the pieces."

"No, of course. You assured me that none of the men you're using do. I hope for your sake that you're right."

"I assure you, Herr Obergruppenführer."

"Oh, thank you. I was hoping that you would 'assure' me. Kepplinger, do you realize—?"

"I do, Herr Obergruppenführer."

"Then get out there and find your friend Schanz, bring

him to heel, and make sure that nothing does go wrong, do you hear me?"

"At once, at once," Kepplinger breathed. He leaned heavily against the wall. Heydrich put down his foil, wiped his forehead with a handkerchief, and rubbed his chin.

"Oh, by the way, Kepplinger, when you leave, ask Kulsky to look after that hand. He has a kit in the car. You mustn't let it get infected." Heydrich examined the handkerchief, as though surprised to find it damp. "You really should practice, Kepplinger. You're not very good, did you know that?"

September 15, 12:30 P.M.: Vienna

Baron Trcka had left his interview with Police President Overbeck with a renewed sense of optimism. It had hardly been necessary to say more than a few words. The bluff, granite-faced Overbeck had delivered himself of a few scatological comments concerning gutter brawlers in high places and put himself immediately at Trcka's disposal. Overbeck was one of the few professional police officers who had been left in positions of power after the *Anschluss*. He was a man with a reputation both for ability and for complete loyalty to whatever régime was in power. He had been there since the days of the monarchy and had served with equal vigor Franz Joseph, Dollfuss, and Von Schuschnigg, as well the parade of mayors who had marched in and out of the Rathaus during the past twenty-three years. A careful man, Overbeck had kept his mouth shut. The *Anschluss*, however, had been the last straw.

Pleased with his morning thus far and feeling a little reassured, Baron Trcka walked with what was for him a remarkably springy step along the Schottenring. He was to meet his wife for lunch at Demel's.

He turned briskly at the University and passed in front of the Rathaus. It was a little before noon. The sky was clear, the air full of the smell of apples and of that peculiar fragrance so unique to the Vienna Woods in early fall.

The sight of three huge red swastika banners hanging from the upper windows of the Rathaus caused Trcka a moment's depression. He recovered quickly. In a few weeks the banners would be gone. The whole filthy lot of them would be gone. He himself, he reflected, might also be gone. One could never tell just what might happen. On the other hand, he might himself be up there in the Rathaus, installed as mayor of the city or in some other exalted post. His name was respected, of great antiquity, and it carried with it not only the weight of accumulated centuries of service to Emperor and country but a reputation for moral rectitude that could hardly be equalled among the Austrian aristocracy. He carried his reputation heavily. He had no real claim to it and knew that whatever moral energy he had thus far displayed in the forty-seven years of his life came mostly from his wife. Nevertheless, he would try. He had long since resolved to make a supreme effort to become worthy of his name.

The Rathaus park was full of the usual throng of noontime idlers reading newspapers and feeding the pigeons. A band was playing somewhere not far off. Across the street the hoardings of the Burgtheatre announced a new production of *Der Zerbrochene Krug*. He smiled. A play about judicial corruption struck him, all things considered, as an odd choice indeed.

He had reached that portion of the Rathaus park where a broad pavement bisects the grassy areas and proceeds directly to the front steps of the hall itself when a man he had not noticed at all before suddenly rose from a nearby bench.

At first, it was only the suddenness of the man's movements that attracted Trcka's attention. But as he turned his head toward the man it seemed to him that he recognized the face, although he knew that he had not actually seen it for a long time.

The object of Trcka's attention was an ordinary-looking person of middle age and middling height, wearing steel-rimmed glasses. He had a short, graying beard and his once reasonable coat was now spattered with mud. For a few seconds, the man fixed Trcka with a stare of such sadness and reproach that the baron stopped dead in his tracks.

Still, he could not recall the man's name, although it seemed to him at that moment that the man must have been waiting there especially for him to pass.

Trcka had little time to move and none to reflect further.

The man took a hesitant step forward.

"I *have* paid my taxes, Herr Baron," he complained.

"Sir?"

"The Reichsfluchtsteuer is paid. The relief contribution has been made."

"Please," Trcka stammered. There was a yellow star on the man's arm.

"But you see, Herr Baron, there is still no visa. There is no place to go."

Trcka stepped back, his stomach churning. It had suddenly come to him that the man was Heinrich Fiebelmann, the violin maker, the man who had for years taken care of Trcka's own viola.

"Help me, for God's sake, Herr Baron, help me."

Trcka stood, rooted to the spot. People were turning to stare. He did not dare say a word to the man for fear of being publicly compromised, yet how could he remain silent?

Then, with a motion of what seemed to Trcka a terrible slowness, Fiebelmann took an object from his pocket and held it out. It was a small pistol and for one hallucinatory second, Trcka thought that he would be shot.

The man thrust the barrel of the pistol into his own mouth, tipped back his head, and pulled the trigger. The back of his head flew away. Blood spattered over the bench from which he had just risen. He fell forward so that his knees were the first part of him to hit. Then he pitched over and fell on his face almost at Trcka's feet.

A police officer who had been watching the episode from a few feet away came over. A small crowd quickly gathered around the dead man. Trcka looked at their faces. There was curiosity and displeasure at being disturbed at their noontime leisure. Perhaps even annoyance. Compassion was singularly absent.

Were these then the people with whom he had to deal? God help him. God help them all.

The policeman turned the corpse over with his foot. He prodded the yellow star of David on the man's threadbare coat.

"All right, all right. It's only another shit of a Jew. Clear off now." He gave Trcka a smile and walked off, leaving Fiebel-

144

mann's corpse where it had fallen.

"Good riddance," someone in the crowd said. "It saves us the trouble."

"Someone has to clean up the garbage," came another voice.

Trcka moved away quickly, shaking. If only he had held out his hand to the man, given some sign that he had been ready to help. Even that he had recognized him. Perhaps then Fiebelmann would not have shot himself. But what could he have done?

By the time Trcka reached Demel's, he was trembling all over and could barely control his hands. He could not believe that he had been affected so.

He could see his wife through the tinted glass sitting at a table in front of a silvered mirror with an ornate filigree frame. The service tables were laden with delicacies, deviled eggs, trout in aspic, smoked meats in little curls. A long line had formed by the pastry table, and the dining room was already crowded.

As he pushed the door open, he was overcome by a wave of nausea.

Melitta saw him. For a few seconds she hesitated, unsure what was happening, then got quickly up and came over to help him. He stood there, pale and sweating, unable either to enter or to leave.

"August, what's happened to you? Dear God . . ."

"Help me away from here," he gasped. "Those people, all of them, they are eating—"

"What else should they do here?"

"It's horrible, Melitta, please, at once. They should not see me."

She took him by the arm and pushed him away from the entrance and back out into the street. He hung over the gutter for a moment and thought he was going to be sick.

She put her arm around him for support. He was clammy, sweating and cold. She tried to move him along so that people would not stare. The car was nearby as Fessler had been told to wait for them.

"It is all so dreadful," Trcka muttered.

145

"*What* is so dreadful? Will you tell me or not?"

"Poor Fiebelmann."

"The violin maker?"

"He's dead. He killed himself right in front of me."

She considered for a moment. Where *was* Fessler? The way August was behaving, the situation would become impossible within seconds.

"You simply must get hold of yourself, August. Why should the death of *one* Jew, however it happened . . ."

He cut her off. "But I knew the man. I *knew him.*"

"There have been over eight hundred such suicides in the last two weeks."

"But I *knew* him, don't you understand, Melitta? I knew Fiebelmann."

At that moment Melitta saw Fessler standing in front of a shop window, taking the sun. She hurriedly motioned him over.

Together they managed to get Trcka into the back of his Mercedes.

"Where does the Frau Baronin wish to go? Is a doctor necessary?"

"I'll be all right, Fessler, thank you," Trcka said in a low, distant voice. "Just go home, that's all. Please."

"You're sure?" Melitta asked.

"My God, yes, *yes!*" Trcka cried. Fessler shook his head and guided the car cautiously down the Dorotheergasse and out into the Graben. Head lowered, he avoided looking into the rear view mirror for fear of seeing the baron's ashen, sweating face.

Trcka took his wife's hand and dug his fingernails hard into the palm.

"Don't you see?" he demanded. "I *knew* the man. That's what makes the difference." He paused and shivered. "And that is exactly what is so terrible about it all, that it should make a difference only, *solely*, because I knew him."

September 15, 7:00 P.M.: Berlin

Ribbentrop had gone home early to prepare for a reception at the home of the Portuguese Ambassador. The Foreign

Office was almost empty. It was still light outside, a gray, sultry twilight without a trace of sun, swallowed up by low scudding clouds that pressed down on the city with a threat of late summer rain.

Erich Kordt had remained behind to sift once again through the day's dispatches and prepare the next pouch for London. The sudden tranquility of the Foreign Office, the silence of the long corridors and, most of all, Ribbentrop's absence, contrived to give him a feeling of calm that he had not experienced for some days. He was exhausted, most of all by Ribbentrop's presence—the great stone face, the "glacier," the sphinx. There was one difference; behind the immobility of Ribbentrop's features, there was no secret. Only a monumental, if crafty, stupidity. Trying to deal with such a man on a day-to-day basis, to take his orders and directions and now and then to insinuate as subtly as possible a few common-sense notions, was an exhausting obligation.

Kordt lit a cigarette and leaned back in his chair. His desk was neat for the first time in a number of days. He had tried to avoid his colleagues at the embassies of France, England, and most of all, Czechoslovakia. How could one possibly answer questions prompted by the insane speeches Goering and Hitler had been making during the last few days? Kordt had hoped that the opening of the Party Congress at Nuremberg would have signaled at least a brief interlude of quiet, but the Reichschancellor had simply seized the opportunity of the grand opening to deliver yet another tirade.

Kordt was embarrassed and weary. Something would have to be done, and done soon.

Kordt was concerned about the safety of his brother, Theodor, the counsellor in the German Embassy in London. If it became known that he had revealed to the British Foreign Office Hitler's plans for Operation Green, and war actually came, it would no longer be a question of a perhaps criminal indiscretion but of high treason. In the long run it was no different from what they had all been doing for the last few months, Beck, Oster, Erich Kordt himself, and all the others who were involved in Oster's conspiracy.

At least Theo was safer in London than he would have

147

been in Berlin. Every now and then Kordt toyed with the idea of maneuvering a trip to the London Embassy for himself and simply staying there, but he could not quite bring himself to do it. Not yet.

He began packing his briefcase; he wanted to take the text of Goering's most recent speech home for study. It was just possible that Goering might in some way be used to foil Hitler, just as—for some while—there had been talk of an alliance between the Oster group and Himmler for the same purpose. The intramural warfare, the cutthroat jockeying for power, disgusted Kordt; it was like the bloodletting of the Borgias, or the worst palace intrigues of some Middle Eastern satrapy.

There was a knock on the door. A senior clerk from the communications department entered the room.

"There is a dispatch, Herr Counsellor. You should see it at once."

He held out a folded piece of yellow paper fresh from the radio room. Kordt took it, dismissed the clerk, and for a moment held the dispatch unopened in his hand, almost afraid to read it. His pulse was pounding. Perhaps it was what they had been waiting for, news of a troop movement that would provoke, finally, an English and French response. War. Then Colonel Oster would have the pretext he needed. They had all decided that it was necessary to wait until Hitler had actually forced the issue and started a war; then Von Witzleben would move, the madman would be arrested, confined, and tried. And finally some semblance of normality would be restored.

He unfolded the dispatch and began to read; his hands started to shake. He could not believe what he was reading. He rushed to the phone.

Admiral Canaris's orderly came on the line.

"The Herr Admiral is at dinner, Herr Counsellor."

"Then fetch him. It's of great importance."

"As you say, Herr Counsellor."

In a moment, Canaris was on the phone. He had been dining with Colonel Lahousen and a number of other members of his staff.

"Admiral, I felt you should know at once. We have just received a radiogram."

"Well, what is it?" Canaris's voice betrayed the same tense excitement with which Kordt had first received the telegram. "Has he done it at last?"

Kordt took a deep breath.

"It's not that at all. The radiogram is from London. Chamberlain is coming over to visit the Reichschancellor in order to arrive at a peaceful solution."

There was an astonished gasp at the other end of the line.

"That's impossible," cried Canaris. "*He* is coming to visit *that* man?"

"Yes, Herr Admiral."

"My God," said Canaris. "Then what is the use of it all?"

In the past few weeks, Erich Kordt had become quite used to having questions put to him which he could not answer.

This latest was no exception.

September 15, 8:30 P.M.: Berlin

What a pleasure to be back in Berlin, even if it was only for a few days. The air was crisper, the temperature a good ten degrees lower, and the beer considerably more to his taste. Tieck-Mitringer had had his fill of Strauss waltzes, gypsy violins, and sachertorte, not to mention the sight of squads of Jews on their hands and knees scrubbing out the municipal toilets. Where all of *that* was getting anyone, he was hardpressed to understand; there were far better places the SS could direct its energies. Toward acting like soldiers and getting themselves ready for the slaughter to which their beloved leader was rapidly pushing them, for one thing.

He had gone out to Potsdam the day before, paying his respects both to the General Staff and to his aged mother whom he had earlier installed in a small house in the Teltow suburb. The evening had been spent going over supply requisitions with his liaison to OKW, a light supper, a long bath, and a chapter of a romantic novel before retiring.

In the morning he was fresh and ready. He took lunch at Horcher's alone and satisfied to be alone. The constantly cheerful Major Rudigier had worn him down over the last few weeks and he was pleased to have left him in Vienna. Besides, despite

Rudigier's obvious sympathies, he didn't want him around when he met with General von Witzleben and the others.

Shortly before the dessert, his "contact" with Colonel Oster's group entered the restaurant and sat himself at a nearby table. The man was a lieutenant on Oster's staff and had been used as a go-between many times before. Tieck-Mitringer watched carefully, dawdling over his coffee, until the man's wine order was brought to his table. Red, a good French burgundy. The meeting was on for that evening. He watched with equal attentiveness as the man poured himself three small glasses, establishing thereby the hour that Tieck-Mitringer was expected to arrive. The general ordered another pastry and then departed. Being by disposition plain and blunt, he found it difficult to get used to what he considered the rather childish secrecy measures on which Oster insisted. As far as he was concerned, the simplest thing would be to march a division straight down the Wilhelmstrasse and set things right with a little machine-gun fire in the right places. Just as in the old Freikorps days. He disliked conspiratorial meetings, skulking about, secret contacts, signals and codes. He was sure, moreover, that they fooled no one and that Heydrich, at the very least, knew exactly what they were all up to and simply did not dare do anything about it. He had had it from one of Heydrich's adjutants that on the night before the Court of Honor that was to try General Fritsch on the Gestapo's trumped-up charges of homosexuality was to meet, Heydrich had insisted on being accompanied at all times by a crack pistol shot, fully armed, with his pockets bulging with ammunition. That the army had remained in Potsdam that night had nothing to do with any fear of the SS but simply with their own all too usual squabbling over oaths and loyalty and the "best method" of proceeding.

Toward eight that evening, Tieck-Mitringer put on civilian clothes, took a car, and drove out to Schlachtensee by way of Charlottenberg and then down through the Grunewald. The roads there were sufficiently dark and silent so that it would have been easy to notice if he were being followed. He was reluctant to go at all and unable to see why it was necessary that so many of the "group" gather in one place at one time.

It should have been quite sufficient for him to report through an intermediary that the division under his command in Vienna, together with a substantial portion of the Vienna police, were ready to stand behind the *putsch*. If more was needed, Baron Trcka was the one who should have been asked to come.

A cool September night full of stars turned the Schlachtensee into a pearl-studded mirror. A delightful breeze blew through the chestnut trees. The smell of fall was sharp and unmistakable. Tieck-Mitringer would have much preferred being out hunting.

Which, in a manner of speaking, he was.

He left the car at a distance from Oster's home and walked the rest of the way, smoking a cigar—which was something he never did.

One of Oster's Abwehr people, a certain Captain Leidig, opened the door to the colonel's apartment and hurriedly ushered him inside.

Tieck-Mitringer's first reaction was to try to take in as much of the place as he could, as though he were conducting a reconnaissance for a prospective artillery position. Oster's apartment was certainly in keeping with the man; well furnished, elegant, and suggestive of earlier and better times. A large painting of the Kaiser hung rather ostentatiously on the wall and nearby, with the same recklessness that characterized so many of the man's actions, Oster had hung a photo of his former commander, Major General von Bredow, who had been murdered during the so-called Night of the Long Knives.

Oster, deeply engrossed in conversation with General von Witzleben, barely looked up as Tieck-Mitringer came in. Perhaps he did not even recognize him without his uniform. Certainly there was nothing about his rather ordinary face that merited recognition from someone he had met only twice; Tieck-Mitringer let this seeming lack of courtesy pass.

Captain Leidig stuck with him and introduced him around. Tieck-Mitringer found, to his annoyance, that he was the last to have arrived. Not only had Von Witzleben and Dohnanyi, a judge of the Leipzig Supreme Court and a very important link between the military and their civilian supporters, preceded him, but Oster's entire Abwehr contingent as well: Leidig, who had let him in; Lieutenant Colonel Grosscurth; and the former Stahlhelm* leader, Friedrich Heinz, now wearing a major's collar tabs, were all there ahead of him.

Oster was sitting hunched forward, his elbows on his knees, his face pressed between his hands. He was listening to Von Witzleben, who was speaking openly and brutally of his contempt for the Reichschancellor.

"Is there any doubt," the elder general was saying, "any doubt in your mind whatever, Hans?"

"If there was any, would I have asked you here?"

"Every man under arms in the Berlin Defense District will be at our disposal. I imagine that most of them will agree, once they realize what is going on."

Oster just then noticed Tieck-Mitringer for the first time and greeted him as warmly as could be expected. Somewhat mollified, Tieck-Mitringer sat down next to Von Witzleben and, without being asked, reported that he could say the same for the men under his command. He had similar assurances from the commandant of the Third Medium Division near Salzburg, as well as from the commandants of seven motorized units placed, quite fortuitously, in a hundred-mile arc above Graz.

"Our friend on the Kahlenberg has seen to the civil end of things," Tieck-Mitringer said, pleased to be, if only for a moment, the center of attention. "We have assurances that the police will act correctly, certainly in Vienna."

Oster smiled; it was clear that Vienna was of little importance as far as he was concerned, and that Tieck-Mitringer had been invited more as a courtesy than as a necessity. However, he approached the subject with tact. "Psychologically, it's very important, considering that Vienna is, after all, our friend 'Emil's' hometown."

"No doubt Vienna is important. A broadcast from the steps of the Bundeshaus will be most effective. I trust the Herr Baron can arrange for this?" said Von Witzleben. Tieck-Mitringer nodded, though he had not even considered such a pos-

---

* Ex-servicemen's organization formed after World War I.

sibility before. It would pose no problem; Trcka's influence spread through many sectors of the government and the civil service. Broadcast arrangements could easily be made. Having something to broadcast about was, in his estimation, the far harder proposition. He wondered if he should mention the warning that Major Langbein had conveyed to him some while before. For a moment, while Von Witzleben went on, he considered dropping a few words about discovery, investigation, and plots, then thought better of it. Not only had he heard nothing about the matter since that evening on the Parkring, but if there was anything to it, obviously Oster would know as much if not more about it than he did.

Lieutenant Colonel Grosscurth was speaking: "We have the Twenty-Third Division at Potsdam. . . ."

Von Witzleben nodded, allowing himself a faint smile. He hardly had to be told about the units under his own supervision.

"And Colonel von Hase's Fiftieth Infantry," continued Grosscurth. "General Hoepner's division will be in perfect position, thanks to 'Emil's' own orders. They can easily bar any attempts to relieve Berlin."

"There should be no problem with communications. We'll have the telephone exchange within minutes, the radio broadcasting facilities in the first hour—"

"The telegraph station?"

"That too. The Fiftieth will surround the SS and the SD barracks. Just let the scum stick their heads out, they'll find out what *real* soldiers do for their pay."

Von Witzleben's expression grew stern. He looked about the room, his glance shifting rapidly from man to man, settling finally on Major Heinz.

"And while all of this is going on, what is Major Heinz to do?" he asked, with a suggestion of a smile.

"As we've discussed," said Oster brusquely. "Who is better suited for the job? Isn't that so, Freddi?"

"I might have guessed," said Heinz, with a trace of grim levity. His early reputation for roughneck tactics had clung to him like a burr. When a trigger needed pulling, it was Heinz who was called. Now as always. Tieck-Mitringer remembered him from the early days; another ardent monarchist, a good street-fighter and a man of considerable ruthlessness. He wasn't sure that he liked or trusted Friedrich Wilhelm Heinz, but he could hardly disagree that he was as good a choice as any for the nasty job of going in and actually arresting the Reichschancellor.

"How many men do you think there should be?" Oster asked him.

"Twenty or so. No more," said Heinz quickly. "The fewer the better, as far as I'm concerned. A dozen good men would be enough."

"It may be more difficult than you imagine," Grosscurth interjected. "After all, he is surrounded by fanatics."

Heinz laughed. "And just what do you think *we* are?"

There was a deep silence. Then Oster laughed and slapped Heinz on the shoulder. "That may be, but what if there *is* resistance? Perhaps a larger force?"

"A dozen, twenty at the most. A few really crack shots. . . ."

Von Witzleben gave him a startled, disapproving look. "He must be arrested, do you understand? Not murdered. We've discussed this before. If I am to go along with you—and I can see no other alternative—then it must be done my way."

Heinz took a deep breath. "What do you say, Hans?"

Oster, caught squarely in the middle, looked the old general straight in the eye.

"As far as I'm concerned, we should shoot the swine down at once. With all due respect, Herr General, alive he's worth more than an army corps. Dead, neither he nor any of his gang of bandits are a problem."

"There will be no killing," said Von Witzleben, very slowly, and in a tone that foreclosed further discussion.

Oster nodded unhappily. "Major Heinz will follow the orders of the senior officer in charge. He knows his duty."

"Indeed I do," said Heinz, with a cheerful ambiguity.

It was at this point that Tieck-Mitringer began to realize just how lucky he would be to be in Vienna when Von Witzleben and Major Heinz marched themselves down the Wilhelmstrasse to the Chancellery.

It was also at this point that it occurred to him he had better give some attention to covering his own rear in case something went wrong.

September 16, 12:10 P.M.: Vienna

She remembered well enough how uncomfortable September in London could be and had dressed accordingly. But a woolen suit that was proof against the penetrating damp of early fall in London could be maddeningly uncomfortable on a warm, humid day in Vienna. Tiny rivulets of perspiration worked their way persistently down her neck and into the hollow of her throat. She dabbed angrily at the dampness with a scented handkerchief, feeling a flush of irritation at her own vanity. It was unbecoming, considering the work to which she was committed. Frivolous. She was glad Michaelis could not see her at that moment.

She touched the rim of the broad-brimmed hat she wore, picked up her two suitcases, and entered the courtyard of the little house off the Silbergasse. A small bell tinkled pleasantly as she passed through the wrought-iron gate. Down the street, shaded by a large linden, she could see Michaelis's gray Daimler, the Berliner plates as out of place on the drowsy Grinzing gasse as a British or American license might have been.

"Gnad'ge Frau?" A small, elderly man with Franz Joseph mustaches, carrying a straw broom and wearing a striped apron, came around a corner into the yard. The oak tables were dusty with pollen, some still under canvas cover. The fall crop of grapes was not yet ready to be brought in. A basket of flowers stood on one table, a welter of garden tools was piled on another. The air was warm, rich with the smell of freshly turned earth and flowers. Somewhere a radio was playing, a lazy, odd melody that sounded like a cross between a waltz and an American jazz tune.

"I was told that the proprietor would be expecting me."

"So—I am the proprietor. Alois Gellert, at your service."

"Herr Gellert, then? My pleasure."

She wondered what to do next. The elderly man smiled gently, nodded, and turned, as though to spare her the embarrassment.

155

"This way, please," he said. "Say nothing more, *gnad'ge Frau*. The description given was perfect. Perfect. I would have recognized you anywhere." Then he added, "You should hear how he describes you, *gnad'ge Frau*. How elegant he is. But you do him justice."

He took her suitcases and she followed him across the courtyard and into the house. Just beyond the door was a shaded stairway lit only by the sunlight falling through an octagonal window on the first landing. The light was tawny, the color of good Tokay, the atmosphere of the house warm and lazy.

She felt a nostalgic drowsiness stealing over her. It was almost impossible not to surrender to it. The music seemed a bit stronger inside; the radio was obviously somewhere in the house. She glanced at her watch. It was shortly past noon. Most of the city was at lunch. The London flight would leave in a little more than three hours.

She mounted the stairs. Before she reached the landing she heard Michaelis coming to meet her across the creaking board floor. The house smelled pleasantly of berries and must. The wine press was probably in the shed just behind the garden.

"So, you did come after all," he said.

She laughed. "You promised to drive me to the airport, didn't you? Once I'd let poor Fessler go, what alternative did I have?"

He leaned over the railing at the top of the stairs, looking much younger, somehow, stronger in his shirtsleeves and open collar. Twenty rather than past forty. His pale hair hung damply over his forehead, and he had a distant, bemused look on his face, as though he could hardly believe that she had really managed to get there.

"We haven't much time, you know," she said.

"Time for what?"

"Whatever," she said, with a feigned lightness of tone that deceived neither of them.

"Well, then, if you don't know, you needn't worry. Besides, the Lufthansa captain is a friend of mine. He won't leave without you."

She tried to respond in kind. Despite the drowsy warmth

156

of the afternoon and the smile on Michaelis's face—the first smile she had seen there in weeks—she was apprehensive. The setting was almost too perfect. Clearly, he had planned things very carefully, trying to please her. She could not help wondering if he had ever done anything similar for his wife, though she realized that the thought was totally unfair. Michaelis's wife would never have understood such a gesture, much less the effort it would have cost her stern, uncompromising husband to be that human.

The room was full of fresh flowers. Herr Gellert had cut them especially for her, Michaelis told her. Only a half hour before, so that they would not wilt. He was so accommodating, so romantic. A man of the old school. A man with nineteenth-century sensibilities.

"We could use a little more of that these days, couldn't we?" she said.

He frowned slightly. "Remember, it is precisely those nineteenth-century 'sensibilities' that put us where we are today."

"Oh, Bernhard. Have I spoiled it already? I'm sorry."

"Why should *you* be sorry for what *I* say?"

"I am so often, why not now?"

He laughed. The laugh, too, warm as it seemed, struck her as false, and for a second she felt a terrible chill sweep over her. The room was like the set for a Schnitzler comedy about domestic infidelity. The wallpaper was yellow and patterned. There was a bottle of white wine sitting in a bucket of crushed ice by the bed.

"Do we really need all of this?" she asked irritably, taking off her hat and laying it on a chair near the bed. She pushed the flowers aside, unable to help herself.

He sat down, the expression on his face changing suddenly.

"I had no wish to offend you, Melitta. Quite the contrary. As you see, I wanted everything to be perfect. I did try, perhaps too hard, it seems."

"Poor Bernhard. Don't you understand? Your apartment is what I would have called perfect. The books, the constant litter of ashes, the worn-out spot on the rug, the coffee grounds you

157

spill every morning in the kitchen. Why couldn't we have gone there?"

"It didn't seem right, that's all. Not now. Not any more. The building, you remember, belongs to August."

"So do I, in a manner of speaking."

"Yes, of course, you would remind me of that." He shook his head. For a moment he seemed at a loss what to say. Then the smile returned. He reached for the wine. "Why should we torment each other? We are here. We have only three hours. Nothing will change that fact. So—does the *gnad'ge Frau* care for a glass of Moselle? To toast your departure?"

"Shall I sing 'Adieu, mein kleine garde offizier'? I don't want to go. You know that."

"Nevertheless, you *are* going."

"To please you."

"Yes, yes. If you consider that keeping me from worrying myself to death about your safety is 'pleasing' me, then yes, it is to 'please' me. Somehow, the phrase has a bad ring to it."

"Is that all I'm doing? Saving you the trouble of worrying about me while you insist on risking your own life?"

"Melitta, I didn't want it to be this way. I tried so very hard to arrange everything so that these few hours at least, these few moments. . . ."

"I know, I know," she said. She threw her arms around his neck, not spontaneously and almost with difficulty, but knowing that she had to. "You're right, and I'm being foolish and quarrelsome. By all means, let's have a glass of wine. Let's do all the absurd things that people in our position are supposed to do at a time like this." She drew him down onto the bed, determined not to spoil things. She owed him at least that much.

"Will you make love to me now or shall we drink first?"

He sighed. She noticed that he too was perspiring. His face now looked pale and slightly blotchy, as though he had shaved himself too roughly that morning. He moved with the stiff reluctance of a man tired almost to the limits of his endurance. The instant he sat down beside her on the fresh linen of the bed he seemed to shrink, almost to collapse.

He touched her throat, then kissed her. She tasted wine on

his mouth; he had been drinking before her arrival. It was something she had never known him to do before and a clear measure of the degree of his agitation.

She let her jacket fall on the bed, reached up, and undid her blouse. Then she shrugged off her slip, freeing her small breasts. She waited; it seemed an unusually long time before she felt his fingers circling her nipples. His touch was more irritating than it was arousing. Yet she was determined that they should make love and, to that end, encouraged him in every way she knew.

He responded slowly, almost reluctantly.

Nothing was spontaneous, neither his movements nor hers. Even when he parted her legs. Even when she guided him into her. She lay there as though watching the whole proceeding from a great distance, completely detached, and had the feeling that he was doing the same thing.

A fly buzzed somewhere in the room. Their movements grew slower, subsiding entirely without having brought either of them relief.

She rolled away, lit a cigarette. Her body was running with sweat and glistened in the golden light that glowed behind the drawn curtains.

"We are so civilized," she said, "that we actually pretend passion to please each other. Or is that what we should properly call lying, Bernhard?"

"Compassion," he said. "I think that 'compassion' would be the better word."

She glanced over at the watch she had lain on the night stand. The hands had already crept around to the two o'clock position.

"Will you come to London too?" she asked.

"I doubt it. Unless it should be absolutely necessary. I must stay here, I think."

"Then this may be the last time I shall ever see you?"

"It may also be the last time I ever see *you*."

"We should find something important to say to each other then, shouldn't we? Or at least something tender. It seems only right that we should."

He closed his eyes and did not respond. She knew better

159

than to press him. The fly buzzed closer, circling over the bed, attracted by the two perspiring bodies.

After all, she knew no better than he what to say.

September 16, 8:15 P.M.: London

As she came off the sleek, silver Dornier at Croydon Airport, Melitta experienced a violent, chilling wave of despair. All around her on the rain-swept tarmac she saw nothing but huge, obsolete biplanes overgrown with struts and rigging wires. Next to them the pencil-thin Lufthansa plane looked like a visitor from another, far distant century. How could the British possibly oppose Hitler with weapons such as these? How could Hitler take them seriously if they presumed to do so?

Now, for the first time, she began truly to fear for them all.

By the time the little black cab had deposited her at the Park Lane Hotel, the same hotel where Canaris's emissary Boehm-Tettelbach had taken a room, she was shivering and much in need of a brandy. What she had seen through the gusting rain and fog on her way in from the airport had not improved her disposition—a gray, dismal city full of shabby, seemingly lifeless people. There was no feeling of strength about them at all. Only an air of resignation and of fear.

She had not wanted to leave August; he had been entirely unstrung by Fiebelmann's suicide, and though he had insisted that he would be perfectly all right, she knew better. But there was no arguing with him, especially as Michaelis had added his voice to her husband's. She had to leave as scheduled. There was simply no time to lose, and nothing was more important than that she should get to London.

Michaelis, at the end, had become harsh and withdrawn. He had driven her out to Aspern without saying a word, looking all the while like grim death. They had barely spoken to each other as he put her on board her flight. Their goodbyes were stifled, frighteningly ambiguous.

She wondered if she could bear ever to see him again.

She sat for a moment in the sitting room of her suite, wondering whether to order a whiskey or simply take a hot bath. The strength-sapping damp was so thoroughly in possession of her that her teeth were chattering and she doubted whether she could even manage to dial room service.

From the window she could see a corner of Hyde Park, the full-leafed trees soughing heavily in the persistent wind, the footpaths forlornly empty.

She thought for a moment of ringing up one of her English friends, of possibly even calling Henry Cranwell. She had not wired ahead, but surprise or not, she knew she could count on their immediate hospitality. Just as surely, she knew she would not be able to face a solitary dinner.

She undressed and lay for a long while in a steaming tub, examining her body, a body which seemed to her at that moment insufferably ugly. She had only begun to dry herself, still weak from the heat and her long immersion, when the bedside phone began to jangle.

"Frau Baronin Trcka?"

She waited, silent; the caller took a deep, audible breath.

"Lieutenant Colonel Hans Boehm-Tettelbach, at your service, Frau Baronin. May I have the permission to see you?" His English was odd, crabbed; hers, she knew, was almost perfect.

"Why should you wish to see me?"

"I think you understand the reasons, Frau Baronin."

She paused. "We have not met, you and I. How will I know you?"

"I will find you, Frau Baronin. And you will recognize me. I know that you have been shown my picture."

"Where are you now?"

"As you know, in the same hotel. But it is not wise for us to meet here."

"You could come to my room."

There was a startled intake of breath, then a long pause. "No, I think not." Another pause. "Go to the Marble Arch underground station. Go down and wait for the eastbound train. You will say nothing. Simply get on the train and get off again at the Tottenham Court Road station. Walk down Charing Cross Road to Cecil Court. It is a little street on the left as you descend. Go in, past the store that sells music. There is a small side street. A car will be waiting there. I will join you."

"And then?"

"There is a meeting. It is important that you come with me. You will be known by these people. I am not."

"Where are we going?"

"To the home of Lord Cranwell. You are acquainted, I believe, yes?"

"He lives on Grosvenor Square. Why must we go such a long way about?"

"It is necessary, believe me."

"Yes," she said softly. She would certainly be known there. Cranwell had been an ardent admirer of hers in the years just before she had married August Trcka. Cranwell had even come to live in Budapest for a whole six months for her sake. She smiled grimly; Oster certainly had his information in order. She wondered if Michaelis would have appreciated the humor of the situation.

"Wilson will be there," the voice on the other end of the line said. "It is to him I must speak."

She hung up and dressed, not as quickly as she might have. There had been something in Boehm-Tettelbach's voice that irritated her, a touch of harsh arrogance that she found distinctly offensive. Let him wait on the crowded platform for a while. It would be good for him.

The Marble Arch station was crowded even though it was well past eight and she was not at all sure that the man she thought was Boehm-Tettelbach was actually him.

The crowds did not diminish along Charing Cross Road. The theatres were busy, and despite the chill and the intermittent rain, there were many people on the street. By the time she had reached Cecil Court, her shoes were wet through and her nose had begun to run.

She glanced quickly over her shoulder.

The man was still there, stocky, erect, gray-faced, and harried. A man not at all suited, it would seem, to his task.

The car was waiting right where he had said it would be. She stopped under the awning of a bookshop.

Boehm-Tettelbach stepped up behind her, a ring of keys in his hand.

162

"It is better if we are alone, Frau Baronin," he said.

She nodded, at last certain of his identity. The face she now saw in the yellow streetlight was exactly the face on the photo Michaelis had shown her.

They drove slowly through the side streets, toward Grosvenor Square. Melitta leaned back against the seat, dabbing at her hair with a handkerchief. How absurd it all was. She hadn't seen Henry Cranwell in seven years and now she was to meet him again looking like a drowned rat.

"I thank the Frau Baronin," Boehm-Tettelbach said.

"For what?"

"For the trouble she has taken."

Melitta did not respond; she had not liked the man's voice when she'd first heard him on the phone. Now, in the closeness of the automobile, she liked neither his voice nor the odor of stale cigarette smoke that rose from his damp woolen coat.

"Let us hope that this will all be worth the effort, Colonel, and that we are not on a fool's errand."

She had her doubts. The whole business seemed almost ridiculous. Did her husband's friends really suppose that they could move the English to meaningful action by sending someone like Boehm-Tettelbach to plead their case? She kept thinking of the message Michaelis had had her memorize. It was to be given to Theodor Kordt at the Embassy. If the time came to deliver it, those few words would have more impact than a thousand Colonel Boehm-Tettelbachs.

The rain was still falling when they pulled up alongside Lord Cranwell's house, an elegant four-story structure just off the Square. The door opened at once. A servant had been watching for them. Dripping, they were ushered at once into a ground-floor sitting room.

Melitta had no sooner taken her coat off and was looking for a place to put it when Henry Cranwell came into the vestibule. He had grown stout since she had last seen him and now wore a heavy, graying mustache. He looked, in fact, like a slightly larger, sturdier edition of Boehm-Tettelbach, and she wondered why she had not noticed the resemblance before.

"Melitta—I could hardly believe it when they told me

163

you'd be coming this evening!"

She laughed, not unkindly. "I had no idea myself until just now, Henry. I'm sure that you knew long before I did."

"But how long have you been here? Why didn't you let me know?"

"Three hours, perhaps four, that's all. I've barely had time for a bath."

"Amazing," Cranwell said. "Absolutely amazing. And this gentleman? You are Colonel—what is it?—Tettelbaum, Tettelbach, yes? Excuse me."

"At your service."

"You can vouch for him, Melitta? Of course. I shouldn't ask. Why else would you be here?"

"He is who he says he is," she replied flatly.

Lord Cranwell touched a bellpull. A servant appeared, took an almost silent instruction, and went out again.

"I would have wished to see you again under other circumstances, Melitta," Cranwell began. He got no further. The door to the study opened and the servant admitted a short, wiry man with a nervous smile and an exceedingly large nose.

"Sir Horace Wilson, Frau Baronin Trcka, Lieutenant Colonel Boehm-Tettelbach."

"Madame?" Wilson looked grave, exactly as in his photographs.

Boehm-Tettelbach took a deep breath, snapped his heels together, and gave a sharp, short bow. Cranwell looked flustered. Melitta shook her head in disbelief. Even here . . . such people . . . impossible.

She had seen Lord Wilson's picture many times in the news magazines and the papers. Senior industrial adviser to Chamberlain, he was now the Prime Minister's most trusted confidant. In everything. How Oster's people had ever been able to arrange the meeting, she could not fathom.

Wilson's voice betrayed an equal confusion.

"I'm really not sure that I should be here at all, Colonel. But . . ."

"I assure you," began Boehm-Tettelbach, "that what I have to say is of the utmost importance."

164

"One in my position receives such assurances a dozen times a day. They rarely turn out to be accurate."

Boehm-Tettelbach was silent for a moment, clearly considering his best course. Melitta looked anxiously at Cranwell but saw only a blank, bland face that inspired no confidence at all.

At length Boehm-Tettelbach began to speak. It was absolutely essential that the British government let it be known to Hitler that they would most certainly react with force if he persisted in his demands concerning the Czechs. Only such a direct declaration could prevent a general war. Hitler was determined to smash the Czechs. His hatred for them was almost as great as his hatred for the Jews. The French were irresolute, and Hitler knew it. The Czechs could count on Deladier for nothing.

"The headlines in the Paris papers last week? You saw them, Sir Horace? '*Voulez vous mourir pour la Tchécoslovaquie?*' What can Hitler possibly think? That is the mood of the French; we all know it. And their leaders are even less interested. They will sit behind the Maginot Line and wait, but they will not lift a finger to help. No, no, it is to you English that we must look for strength in this matter."

Wilson, by this time, was sitting back deep in one of Cranwell's leather armchairs, his fingers twined over his knee, his eyes narrowed—whether in concentration or boredom it was impossible to tell. There was not so much as a flicker of agreement to be seen on his face.

Boehm-Tettelbach was sweating; Melitta felt miserable for the man. He was trying, earnestly, even desperately. But he succeeded only in sounding like a provincial schoolmaster, unconvincing and unsure of himself.

"You do understand the Prime Minister's position in this matter, don't you?" Wilson asked.

"We try to understand but, no, to be frank, we find it incomprehensible. What is it he says, that there is nothing that cannot be settled decently between two decent, intelligent men? Hitler is neither decent nor intelligent."

"Would war be preferable?"

"There will be no war if you refuse to give in."

"That, of course, is what Mr. Churchill says. Consider. If we were to adopt your view now, we would be saying that we had been wrong all along and that our bitterest political enemy had been right. Is that what you wish us to say?"

Boehm-Tettelbach looked gray. His eyes closed for a second in despair.

Wilson went on laconically. "Do you wish us to say that our entire economic policy, the policy we have pursued for more than a decade now, the policy of putting Germany back on its feet economically, a policy of which I was one of the prime architects under Baldwin, do you wish us to say that this was wrong too, Colonel?"

Boehm-Tettelbach considered. He licked his lips quickly.

"Perhaps you must."

"Perhaps. But we should need stronger proof than what you bring us. We've heard all of this before, you know."

Boehm-Tettelbach looked surprised. He had not been aware of any such thing. Melitta, who knew of Ewald von Kleist's visit, had kept a discreet silence.

"There are those," Boehm-Tettelbach began, "surely you must know this . . . there are those among us who are only waiting for the word from your government to rise and sweep Hitler into the garbage bin where he belongs."

Wilson smiled palely, for the first time.

"Really? We've heard that before too, you know. And replace him with what? A restored monarchy? A republic? With what aims? We've heard it all before, as I say, and let me be frank with you, Colonel, we find it all hard to believe. Oh, not that you wouldn't be delighted to do away with Hitler, but that any government that might replace him would pursue any different course than he follows. To be frank, it seems to us that it is Herr Hitler's methods rather than his goals with which you disagree. And that hardly seems to be enough to warrant us risking a general war, does it?"

Boehm-Tettelbach's face went ashen and he bit his lip. Cranwell, who had hardly been paying attention, turned sharply and gave Melitta a puzzled look.

"Would anyone care for a whiskey?" he offered.

* * *

What had been accomplished? Nothing. Nothing in fact had been asked of her, only her presence. She had been used simply as a key with which to open a door, and now that door had been slammed hard in her face.

It was demeaning, without doubt, and she burned with a slow anger as she went down the front steps of Cranwell House and walked over to Boehm-Tettelbach's squat black Renault.

The rain had stopped. A faint mist was settling gently through the air. The pavements glistened and the air smelled faintly of turning leaves and autumn.

She shook her head, declining Boehm-Tettelbach's weary invitation to reenter the car.

"I'll walk, thank you. It's not far."

"As the Frau Baronin wishes." He shrugged.

She turned sharply and went off in the direction of Marble Arch, not looking back once after the defeated Boehm-Tettelbach. She knew she would not see him again.

Now all she could do was wait.

September 21, 2:00 P.M.: *Vienna*

Major Langbein had just taken a walk all the way around the Ringstrasse. He had stopped for a few moments by the pavilion next to the Johann Strauss statue to listen to a little music. A string orchestra was playing operetta tunes, but it was impossible to relax at such a time. Hitler was obviously going crazy, ranting at the Czechs, insulting the English, bullying the French. Oster and his group were temporizing, and Von Kleist was back from London with extremely disappointing news. The generals were grumbling among themselves, unsure just what to do.

And now there was this damned business with Kepplinger.

Langbein hadn't heard from Henkl in twenty-four hours. The man was back in Graz. Thank God for that. His stay in Switzerland had caused endless difficulties. The Swiss police had cooperated, but that cooperation had been purchased only at great cost. As a quid pro quo, Abwehr Berlin had promised to deliver a certain rabbi from Cologne whom the Americans wanted very badly out of Germany.

And the worst of it was that Langbein still had no idea what Henkl had gotten in exchange.

If Heydrich was really onto something—if he'd gotten wind of Oster's plotting with General von Witzleben or, worse yet, of the talks Von Kleist-Schmenzin had been having with Churchill—then they were all in for a very nasty time.

"It might even," he thought with some little grim humor, "force the leadbottoms on the General Staff to actually move themselves to do something other than talk."

Langbein had no sooner returned to his office than Lieutenant Rost burst in, as usual without knocking. He was clutching a phonograph disc and a few sheets of typing paper.

"Sir, you should see this."

"If you show it to me, Rost, then I suppose I will."

Rost was unfazed. He routinely ignored Langbein's sarcasm; it was a condition of existence around the office, like cigar smoke and short-wave static.

"Sir, you recall the telephone intercepts you ordered?"

Langbein's eyes narrowed. He lit a cigarette. He felt relaxed—it was reassuring when things were found out according to the tried and true methods rather than by unsettling surprises.

"Yes, Rost," he said slowly.

"Well, sir, we picked up something odd this morning. It may tie in, it may not. But I thought you should know."

"Rost," Langbein said sternly, reaching for the transcript sheets which the lieutenant was still clutching to his chest.

"Sir, do you remember a man named Flom? Andreas Flom?"

Langbein shook his head; he had a dim recollection of the name but it was far simpler to let Rost tell him.

"You recall, sir, he was involved on the edges of the General Blomberg scandal. He had let it out that he had some letters from the whore that the general had married and . . ."

"Rost, *damn* it!"

"Sir, she was a whore, sir. That was certainly true, though what difference it made is another . . ."

Langbein slammed his fist on the table.

"Either give me the transcript or tell me what's on it."

"Flom—" Rost took a deep breath. "The man is a dealer. Rare books and documents. Letters, autographs, and the like. He has a small shop on the Blutgasse, not far from St. Stephen's."

"Yes? *Yes?*"

"Yesterday morning, he received a box of old letters and documents. Postal authorities confirm it, after the fact, of course. Yesterday afternoon, he placed a phone call to a certain Philippe Ledruc, who is resident correspondent for *Le Matin*, offering to sell him some letters which he said would cause a 'tremendous explosion.' That was the exact way he put it, sir."

"More blackmail? Like the last time, I suppose. But why should we be interested in this?"

"I took the liberty of having the package traced, Major. It came from Graz."

"*Graz?*"

"Graz, sir. And as if that wasn't enough, Captain Henkl is back, and the information he brought checks exactly with this. He wants to see you, sir. As soon as he's cleaned up and shaved."

Langbein was not a patient man by nature. Leaving Rost standing in his office, he clattered down the stairs to the washroom. Henkl, stripped to the waist, was bent over the sink, his face covered with lather.

"Rost says you've got something."

"Oh, Major, I was just coming up to talk to you. What time *is* it? I didn't think you'd be here this early."

"I slept here last night," Langbein shot back. "Now, what is it. My God, Klaus, you look a mess."

Henkl's eyes were bloodshot, his complexion even whiter than usual. He was obviously very tired.

As he shaved, he began telling Langbein all that had happened. And all that he had uncovered.

"None of it makes too much sense," he said diffidently, scraping off a wide swath of lather. "I think we may have been on a wild goose chase, Major. How any of this relates to our people or Oster's, I just can't see."

169

"We may have our chance now," replied Langbein, lighting up. "You have the names of the people to whom the Jew's belongings were sent?"

"Yes, of course. I gave them to Rost."

"I know. The question was rhetorical."

"But what then?"

"One of the names was Flom, Andreas Flom. 81 Blutgasse?"

"Yes?"

"Here. Read this," Langbein said, holding out the transcript.

September 22, 3:00 P.M.: London

The envelope had contained a single ticket to a cinema on Oxford Street. The showings were at set times and the seats numbered, just as in a legitimate theatre.

On the back of the ticket were the scrawled initials "B-T."

So the man was still in London. And, obviously, he wanted her for something. She could hardly refuse, even though by now she felt that anything Boehm-Tettelbach was involved in would be bound to fail. The man was totally ineffectual.

Nevertheless, she had gone alone to the theatre and sat dutifully down in the last row with her back to the barrier, waiting. Nothing had happened. The seat next to her remained empty. The usher came by selling programs. She lit a cigarette, put it out, lit another.

Still nothing,

The theatre went dark and the film, a new Russian epic by the famous Eisenstein, began. She tried to pay attention but the dissonant, piercing music gave her a headache. The humid heat of the theatre and the smell of disinfectant made her feel faint. Shapes in violently contrasting lights and darks rushed across the screen. Still the seat next to hers remained empty. A half hour passed. The music poured relentlessly from the loudspeakers, the volume far too high. There were jagged images of Teutonic knights in strange, shovel-visored helmets oddly like those worn by the Wermacht. Troops of horsemen thudded across vast expanses of ice, while Russian knights crashed toward them. The music pounded on as the Teutonic knights chanted in harsh voices, *"Peregrinus, expectavi, pedes meos, in cymbalis. Vincant arma crucifera! Hostis pereat!"*

It was all to much for her. Her temples began to throb and her skin grew unaccountably cold.

The shrill music rose to a crescendo, faded into long-drawn-out chords through which a soft echoing melody threaded itself. Suddenly she felt a touch from behind on her shoulder.

It was Boehm-Tettelbach. He had come up silently and unnoticed to the barrier directly behind her seat.

He nodded; the summons was unmistakable. She rose and followed him across the back of the darkened theatre. On the screen a single figure, a woman, moved among the heaps of dead and wounded.

They passed through a side door and into a corridor that ran along one flank of the theatre, toward the stage and screen.

In the hallway, Boehm-Tettelbach turned with an apologetic, slightly foolish look on his face.

"One feels absurd, Frau Baronin, believe me, for engaging in such childish games. My apologies. But a certain amount of caution was necessary this time and I could think of no other way."

"Who are we going to see now? The King?"

"Please." He seemed deeply offended.

"You could at least have given me some notice, you know. What if I hadn't come back to the hotel in time to receive the ticket?"

"Then, perhaps, the opportunity would have been lost. Or, perhaps, another way would have been found. But as it is, you did return in time and you *are* here."

The back of the theatre was dark and deserted. Melitta had never been behind the screen in a cinema before. It was vast and empty. There were no stage hands visible, no signs of life. Only the persistent crackling of the soundtrack over the giant speakers and a dull, pulsating image on the other side of the screen.

"In there," Boehm-Tettelbach said, as they came to a narrow hallway that had obviously once led to the performers' dressing rooms. It was clear that the theatre had been used as a

171

music hall of some sort before being turned into a cinema. Tattered posters still hung in shreds from the fly-specked walls.

"Who are we going to see?" Melitta demanded. She did not like Boehm-Tettelbach, thinking him a fool, and distrusting him completely. His clumsiness might well lead her into a disaster.

"You, not I," he replied. "I will wait outside where I found you, Frau Baronin. In your seat."

She had no chance to argue with him. He turned and slipped off quickly down the dark hall, leaving her standing before a door slightly ajar. The room beyond was dark, little more than a grimy cubicle. A cot could barely be made out, standing by the wall, a dressing table and a single chair by a crusted window that looked out onto an alley. It was raining again and, for a moment, she found it hard to see.

There was a man sitting in front of the old dressing table. His face, in the half-light, seemed gaunt and harried, his eyes fevered.

"Bernhard—oh, God . . ."

He rose and took her quickly in a hard, almost angry embrace.

"Hush, dearest, don't say a word. Ask nothing. Simply understand that there was no way I could have left things as they were when we were last together." His kisses were searching her face, her eyes.

"Why are you here? How, Bernhard?"

He stopped and smiled grimly down at her. "Our friend Roon was kind enough to put an aircraft of the Gesellschaft at my disposal. With a pilot. He knows how to set the odometer back so that no one will ever know that we have been more than one hundred kilometers out of Bremen. We have just enough range to get here and back to the Baltic coast, where we will refuel. Getting in without being detected was no problem. The English do not watch their coast very carefully. The plane is black and we came before dawn, over the treetops. All in all it was quite an extraordinary experience."

He laughed harshly, but his tone was pained and for a moment she was afraid to say anything. He held her so hard in his arms that it seemed he was deliberately trying to hurt her.

172

"It can only be for a few moments," he murmured. "Thank God he found you. It is a miracle that we have even this little time."

"You still haven't said *why*, Bernhard. It wasn't just because of me. Don't tell me that you came here just to see me. I couldn't bear having put you in such danger."

He hesitated for a long time, his head resting on her neck, then moved almost painfully away and drew a folder from inside his coat.

"Here," he said quietly. "This is for you. So that when the cable comes—and it *will* come, Melitta—you will have these. I will not be able to bring them later."

She took the envelope and looked up at him. Inside it was a small sheaf of papers.

"What are they?"

"You hold in your hands, Frau Baronin Trcka, the proof of our madness. They are the jumping-off schedules for the five armies that are to descend upon the Czechs. Here, do you see? The Second, the Eighth, the Tenth, the Twelfth, the Fourteenth. The times and the concentration points. Also the selection of commanding officers. General Adam in overall command, Beck for the First Army, Von Hammer for the Fourth. The marching orders for chaos. Only the effective date is missing."

"You came all the way here to give me these?"

He did not answer.

"Yes, I think I understand," she said.

"They are from Halder's desk. Oster got them for me. You will show these to Wilson when the time comes and he will have to believe you."

"The love letters of Dr. Bernhard Michaelis to his mistress, the Frau Baronin Trcka." She laughed, not unkindly. "You trust me, then? Finally?"

He tried to take her in his arms again, but she held him away.

"Trust, not love, Bernhard. That was the word I used. The question is, do you finally trust me?"

"Yes, I do trust you. I've always trusted you. What else do you want me to say?"

She looked at him levelly, without blinking.

"Now, if you wish to, you may also say that you love me. Would you please say that now?"

He drew her to him.

"I love you, Melitta, very much. As you know. But to say such things in times like these is—very difficult. Perhaps it is better not to. I don't know any more."

"If only we could have kept things just as they were. For even a little while longer."

"Who knows? Our 'little while' may come again. It may not." He took her hands and she looked up at him, tall, almost a shadow, gazing intently down at her. For a second she was not even certain that it was really him; only the sound of his voice reassured her.

"If we have a good wind and they are ready for us at Bremen, we can make Berlin before dawn."

"Bernhard, couldn't we both stay right here, in London, and be safe? Why not? No, it's impossible, of course. My God, the things you make me think."

"We must be able to dream of such things at least. Otherwise we would surely lose our minds. But we can't act out such thoughts, you and I. That is what I think is called 'moral principle'—the strength *not* to act out such thoughts. Not everyone has it."

"That's true enough," she said.

He seemed to smile uncertainly. "It was considerate of our friend the Colonel to provide us with a bed of sorts, wasn't it? Shall we make use of it?"

She sighed but did not move away, waiting for him. His hands passed with an unaccustomed clumsiness over her body. He began to kiss her all over her face, her neck, and her breast, violently, as though afraid to stop once he had started.

"Bernhard—yes—there may not be another time."

The cot was narrow and cramped. The springs creaked in a way that at any other time would have made her laugh but now brought tears of frustration and anger to her eyes. The air in the room was hot and close and her nakedness brought no relief.

She clung to Michaelis desperately, wishing him to say

174

something to her, anything, but at the same time fearing terribly any break in the silence that would force her, in turn, to speak to him.

There was no pleasure in it and at last, worn and unsatisfied, they moved away from each other as far as the narrowness of the cot would allow. After a few moments, Michaelis got up and began to dress.

She realized that she had never actually watched him do that before and looked away, embarrassed and oddly repelled.

"There's no way even to pretend, is there?" she said. "None, even though we both might wish it."

He shrugged. "I suppose not."

As she too dressed, there ensued a long silence filled with a vast, empty space that seemed to grow and grow like an exploding universe until there was no possible way to reach across it.

"Be careful, Bernhard. You *will* be careful, won't you?"

He laughed then, not sure exactly what she meant.

"I love you," she said, and touched him quickly on the mouth. Then she went out of the room, leaving him still standing there before the cracked dressing room mirror like some despondent old actor who had just heard his cue and suddenly realizes that he has forgotten his lines.

September 23, 6:00 P.M.: *Graz*

Second Under-Counsel Toohey stared past his visitor, past the framed photo of De Valera on the wall of his little office, and out of the window to the street where a magnificent elm was just beginning to show a few touches of fall yellow. He had a week's vacation coming and with the permission of the Vice-Counsel, who was just then himself in Salzburg, he would take it within the fortnight. The plane tickets were already in his bureau drawer. By next Wednesday, he would be in Ireland with his family.

In the meantime he had to contend with the German.

"You have an opportunity to do us a great service," Schanz was saying. "And at no risk or cost to yourself or to your government."

175

"You're sure of that? I wish I were."

"We could obtain the information ourselves, of course. But it would take time. A few days at least. And this is time that I do not have."

"Well, as you say, Herr Schanz, you are asking for nothing that isn't public record anyway." Toohey lit a cigarette. Schanz turned away, sniffling.

Toohey shook his head; he would never have believed the man to be a colonel of the Security Service if he hadn't seen the papers himself. Of course, they could be forgeries. But what would be the point? To obtain something that anyone could freely have, provided he cared to walk into the registry office in Dublin and look for it?

As for himself, Toohey did not like the Germans, and the Nazis even less. True enough, they had been helping the Irish with guns and munitions for a long time. But always to advance their own purposes, that was the first consideration. But hadn't the French done the same thing when the Americans had gotten rid of the British? And no one faulted them for it. Still, he couldn't rid himself of that sneaking dislike. Graz had been a compromise. The Austrians didn't seem quite as bad as the Germans. But he was beginning to think that he'd made a mistake, and that, if anything, they were worse.

Schanz cleared his throat.

"What do you say? Will you do it for us?"

"I'll wire right away. It shouldn't take long. Oh, we'll turn up your missing lady for you, all right, but I do wish you'd tell me why."

Schanz shook his head and said nothing.

"Look here," remonstrated Toohey, "I'm taking a great deal of trouble for you and I may be doing something I shouldn't. It would be better if the Vice-Counsel were here. But of course, he's not, so . . ."

"You won't regret having helped us," Schanz said solemnly, and with just the proper hint of menace in his tone so that Toohey could not tell whether he was being thanked or indirectly threatened. "When will you have the information for me?"

"A week, five days possibly."

Schanz shook his head.

"Tonight."

"That's impossible. If I wired this instant, why . . ."

"In three days, we could get it ourselves. In your position, I could get the information in a day, at most."

Toohey considered, exhaling smoke. "There *is* an outside possibility, you know. We have a pouch coming over tomorrow night. If we were to be lucky, very lucky, it just might be arranged. Would tomorrow night suit you, Herr Schanz?"

Schanz nodded, as if he'd known it all the time.

"It won't be until late, of course. Perhaps ten or even after that. Depending on the Channel weather. Can you come back then?"

"Ten, Under-Counsel? I will be here."

"At the side entrance, please."

"At the side, then."

Toohey showed his visitor out and then went down to the radio room. A single clerk was on duty. As Toohey wrote out the request—God only knew, it seemed innocent enough, but the very source of the question still gave him much pause—he kept wondering why he was doing it at all. But he knew.

It was the damned British again. All his life it had been the damned British. And now, to hurt them—possibly—he was doing favors for butchers.

The lengths to which a man might go to get even . . . why . . . for an idea? A people? Damn it, he didn't even like to think of such things, much less try to articulate them. Much better to think of holiday and home.

He had not even closed the door to the radio room when the cipher clerk began the transmission, in low-priority code.

September 24, 8:00 A.M.: *Vienna*

Henkl was collapsed on the leather couch in Langbein's office, under the stern photograph of General Varela. He read the new transcript rapidly, then slowly, twice, to make sure of every word. The intercept agent hadn't started the machine quite at the beginning of the conversation. There was a little missing but nothing important. Actually, Flom had said little, but what there was was more than enough.

The documents had arrived. They were in hand. He would meet Ledruc at the Prater next afternoon and they would arrange for the transfer. Whatever *that* meant. At the Ferris wheel, where they could be alone in a compartment. The Frenchman insisted that the transfer be arranged immediately. It was too dangerous to wait; there might be war at any minute. The borders would be sealed and there would be no way to get out of the country.

Nevertheless, Flom insisted, he would have to wait. There were important details to be discussed.

The Frenchman was furious. He had paid. The money had been deposited in the Zurich Staatsbank, as promised. And he knew for a fact that it had already been withdrawn.

Flom sighed diplomatically, but insisted.

Finally, the Frenchman gave in. At the Prater then, at one the next day. At the Ferris wheel.

And that was all.

Henkl put the transcript down. Langbein was staring at him.

"You're sure that this is the man?"

"Positive. After we left the clerk's apartment, Major Eisenbach and I checked it all out. We have confirmation at every point, and it all fits together. Our friend Standartenführer Kepplinger sends his man Schanz down to Graz. He roots around for a few days, then goes straight for a Jew named Jankow. But it's too late; Jankow has paid his exit tax and is on his way to Switzerland. Item: the money to pay his tax has miraculously been deposited in an account in Zurich. The funds come from Paris. Item: the chief clerk at the Reichsfluchtsteuer Bureau has been going around picking up the belongings of departing Jews for a song. But—again, Item—this deposit is made two weeks *before* the exit tax is paid. Thus our good clerk, Liszewsky, who normally gets onto his bargains when the exit visas are issued, could not possibly have provided the money. Yet the name of Andreas Flom appears in his records as the person to whom he has been regularly selling rare documents, letters, and curiosa, as he calls it. Item: Flom is also a know trafficker in compromising letters. The last time out, our Herr Flom tried to sell incriminating letters between the whore Eva Gruhn and General Blomberg to the foreign newspapers. And to *what* foreign newspaper exactly? Why, to *Le Matin*, of Paris."

"All of which, of course, suggests . . ."

"That, with all due respect, Major, we had better find out, in the most circumspect way, just what it is that Herr Flom is selling or has sold already to this Ledruc person."

"You look positively delighted, Klaus."

"I do? Well, I've always said, the solution of a difficult puzzle is one of life's most profoundly satisfying experiences."

"It isn't solved yet, Klaus."

"It will be," said Henkl.

"Let's just hope there's still time," said Langbein, thinking of General von Witzleben and what was going on at that moment in Berlin.

"One thing, though," said Henkl, as he picked up the phone to call in Lieutenant Sudermeyer, his lip-reading expert.

"And that is?"

"We still haven't any idea of what's really going on here. Who the 'important personage' is and . . ."

"And?"

"And whether this involves us at all."

Langbein looked disapproving, but he did not disagree. He nodded gravely. "In that, you are absolutely right, Klaus. I've been checking. I've spoken to Oster, to Von Helldorf, to Trcka, and even to Von Kleist-Schmenzin. No one knows who this Jankow is or what, if anything, he has to do with us."

"My impression, Major, was that Jankow was telling me the absolute truth. My instinct is usually good in these things."

"Yet he could have been frightened. He had no idea who you really were, of course. For all he knew, you could have been from IVA, or anyplace, for that matter."

Henkl considered for a moment.

"No. He believed me. And I believe him. Besides, what reason would a person in his position have to do anything to harm *us?* I'm sure he would be under no illusions as to where his best interests, as a Jew, lay."

"*If* he knew."

179

"If," echoed Henkl. "A very big 'if,' I'll grant you."

At that moment, Lieutenant Sudermeyer's voice was heard on the other side of the closed door, asking if he should come in or not.

September 24, 12:50 P.M. Vienna

The afternoon was warm and flooded with sunshine. The distant peak of the Kahlenberg was touched with an opaline haze. The Danube shivered deliciously under the rays of the gentle September sun, darkening almost to its much-vaunted but seldom-achieved blue. The laziness of early fall hung over the surrounding woods. Fashionable women strolled along the Hauptallee, taking pleasure in the shade of the double rows of chestnut trees, just as they had done in the days of Franz Joseph. The bridal paths were in constant use. Workers from the shabbier quarters on the other side of the canal strolled with their wives in an afternoon's holiday. From a considerable distance away came the sound of cheering crowds urging on the racehorses at the Freudenau course. In the Volksprater itself, the concessions and amusement pavilions were very busy; the beer gardens were crowded and the carousel gave forth an unending stream of Strauss, both father and son.

Major Langbein, Henkl, and Sudermeyer had driven as far as the end of the Stubenring by car, parked, and then taken a tram the rest of the way. Each carried a pair of field glasses in a worker's lunchbox. Henkl, in particular, in strict obedience to Langbein's orders, had managed to make his appearance thoroughly seedy. His jacket was stained, his trousers threadbare; he had not taken his regular afternoon shave and the stubble on his cheeks was already beginning to grow quarrelsome. Sudermeyer, a taciturn young man from Danzig, had no idea what was going on and, as a consequence, was even more restrained than usual. He was, in fact, somewhat awed to be accompanying Major Langbein.

Langbein consulted his watch. It was ten before one.

The three men strolled across the amusement park grounds toward the giant ferris wheel that loomed high above everything else like the skeleton of some enormous and oddly circular

180

prehistoric monster. Henkl had remarked that, as far as he was concerned, the wheel looked rather like a giant edition of the one on which Frederick the Great had been in the habit of breaking the bones of his prisoners. Langbein found the comparison neither edifying nor amusing and counseled restraint.

The major's mood was dark, despite the lovely weather. Between eleven—when Henkl had left him—and one—when Henkl had returned with Sudermeyer in tow—Langbein's temper had run the gamut from wild enthusiasm to something approaching despair.

"You may as well know," Langbein had told Henkl just before they left the Abwehr office, "that we have word from Oster that Operation Green is still on. No matter what kind of deal the English propose, our good 'Emil' is still set on invading Czechoslovakia. And, of course, you know what *that* will mean."

Langbein was tormented by a mass of conflicting emotions. As both General Halder and Colonel Oster had long argued—and he did not for a moment disagree—in order for a *putsch* to succeed, the support of the population was necessary. And for that, it was required that there be an overwhelmingly persuasive reason for the generals' rising. If Hitler actually did launch an ill-prepared and under-equipped Wehrmacht against one million Czechs and the combined forces of England and France, the General Staff would have the perfect pretext. Who could fail to support them when their motives were so irreproachable? To prevent a mad, senseless general war and the inevitable slaughter of hundreds of thousands of German youth? In short, to prevent a disaster. The timing was critical. As long as Halder received the promised two days warning of the actual order to strike, all would go smoothly. So far, Hitler was cooperating. But what if he turned secretive, or had a vision, or a hunch? Of a sudden turn to secretiveness, there was little chance; the man loved rostrums, speeches, and floodlights too dearly. But when dealing with a lunatic, one had always to be prepared for the most bizarre turn, the most unexpected reversal. Himmler, it was said, had spent half of the last week closeted with an astrologer.

All of this, however, was not what was really bothering

Langbein. In a moment of idle speculation, he had stumbled upon the one really poisonous question and had posed it to himself before he realized the consequences of putting such a query.

"Suppose," he had asked himself, "suppose the Wehrmacht was actually as powerful as Hitler imagines it to be. Suppose we were assured of success rather than failure. What would your attitude be then?"

And *this* question, Langbein found that he simply could not answer.

Henkl had picked out the perfect spot, a small toolshed roughly fifty meters from the ferris wheel ticket booth. A small window gave a perfect view of both the booth and the wheel itself. With the aid of the field glasses, it was possible to count the gold fillings in a rider's teeth, even when he was at the very top of the wheel's rise. So long as the man did not turn away inside the compartment, everything could be seen.

The shed was suffocatingly hot. The air stank of tar. Langbein threw his coat off and rolled up his sleeves. Henkl noticed that the major's trousers were hitched up very high, giving his already long legs the look of a stork's, the upper part of his body the appearance of being compressed, almost deformed. The short, chunky Sudermeyer took up the front position. Langbein stood behind and looked over his head. Henkl consulted a photo of Flom taken from the files, then kept his eyes on the booth. Sudermeyer held his glasses at the ready, just at the bridge of his nose after the fashion of an artillery observer.

It was now exactly two o'clock.

"Punctual swine. Here he comes."

Flom, dressed in a gray suit with face to match, ambled along the gravel path leading to the wheel. A small, compact man with hardly any neck, he was easy enough to spot. Langbein turned his glasses on him, bringing in a full view of his distinctly unattractive face. Flom's eyes kept moving rapidly from side to side. He was obviously looking for someone.

"Good," thought Langbein. "For a change, everything is going well."

Flom purchased a ticket and went inside the chained en-

182

closure to wait for the wheel to stop and take on its next batch of passengers.

There was a moment of silence. Then Henkl whispered: "Ledruc."

"How d'you know?" Langbein shot back. No one was anywhere near Flom as yet.

"I got his picture from the Reuter's file this morning."

Langbein smiled. His protégé was progressing nicely.

"He's buying a ticket. Sudermeyer, get your glasses on him."

Ledruc, a thin, wiry man of about forty, wearing a suit of a blue somewhat too bright to be accommodated by the prevailing grayness of the surrounding Viennese, discarded his cigarette, ground it underfoot, and bought a ticket. Flom saw him but did not turn in his direction. They stood close, but not too close.

The ferris wheel came at length to a halt and discharged its vertiginous passengers, including one entire communion class that had filled up seven compartments.

The waiting riders began to climb into the empty compartments.

"There. He's managed it. He's alone with Ledruc."

Langbein watched them carefully. So far, neither man had spoken.

"Sudermeyer?"

"I've got them, sir. Please, don't speak. You'll spoil my concentration."

The wheel began to move, carrying Flom and Ledruc high up over the city. Langbein could see Flom's mouth begin to move as the compartment reached the midpoint of its rise. Ledruc did not appear to be listening. He did not turn his head but kept staring straight in front of him.

"What's he saying, damn it?"

"The sun is on the window. It's very difficult," Sudermeyer replied plaintively. "But yes, there—I can—there. . . ."

"They're talking about price, one hundred thousand . . ."

Henkl blinked. He could feel his mouth beginning to dry out.

"What else?"

183

"It's difficult to see, sir."

At that moment the part of the wheel to which Flom's compartment was affixed reached the very top of the rise and hung suspended for a moment before starting down again. The sun danced off the glass and the metal sides of the compartment, making it almost impossible to see.

Then the glare was gone.

Sudermeyer's voice, excited: "I can see—yes—" Henkl could feel his heart hammering away. The sweat poured down into his eyes. Sudermeyer began to speak, repeating slowly what Flom was saying, as much of it as he could make out.

"Grandfather—the father was the bastard son—one hundred thousand marks—a sensation—"

"What?" Langbein was stunned. This was not at all what he had expected.

"The Frenchman is arguing. He says he's already paid. The other man says it's worth much, much more. Considering who is involved. . . ."

Langbein tried to read the lips himself, but got nowhere. It was maddening, having to be at the mercy of Sudermeyer and the sun. His eyes burned. The rims of the glasses had gotten blazing hot.

"There. I've got it. He's telling him now."

Henkl could see nothing. There was a blaze of sun off metal. He blinked, losing sight of both Flom and Ledruc for a second.

Then the wheel had stopped; the compartments were opening up again. People were getting out.

"*Who*, damn it? The rest we know—but the name? Who were they talking about?" Langbein demanded.

"He's going to get more money," Sudermeyer said. "The Frenchman, sir. He says he'll have to wire for it from Paris."

"Sudermeyer, the *name*. The rest of it can wait."

"It was very hard to make out, sir, because of the glare. He doesn't enunciate very clearly, your man, sir. I think he has false teeth or a dental problem. They do that, people with false teeth. I only got the last syllable. It was 'er,' no question about that. The rest—I'm sorry, sir, but there was a glare. I couldn't make it out."

"So it could have been . . . ?"

"Himmler, sir? I don't think so."

"Certainly not Heydrich."

"No sir, nothing like that," Sudermeyer said.

"Who then? Oster?" Langbein drew a breath. "You *did* see his lips clearly, didn't you?"

"Yes, sir."

"Then who was it, damn it all! Who did he say it was?"

"I could only guess, sir. And I'd rather not do that." Sudermeyer's face had gone the color of pipe ash.

Henkl thought he was going to strangle. Suddenly he felt extremely tired and incredibly heavy, as though his blood had been replaced by tar. He flung open the door and took a deep gulp of air.

"Go on outside, both of you. Let me be alone for a moment," Langbein said.

"Are you all right, sir?"

"Go outside. Didn't you hear what I said? Go!"

September 24, 7:00 P.M.: *Berlin*

Oster didn't know whether to feel relieved or to start laughing hysterically. It was inconceivable that Hitler could be so stupid in the face of even greater English stupidity, but there it was. On the table lay a cipher received only an hour before from Dr. Schmidt, the interpreter at the Hitler-Chamberlain talks, advising that no matter what concessions the British were prepared to make, the Reichschancellor had determined to go ahead with Operation Green right on schedule.

"If only they don't back down all the way and simply refuse to fight," Canaris said, pale and agitated before his wall map, trying to concentrate. The cipher had given him a few moments relief, nothing more. Everything seemed to him to be coming apart at the seams. Nothing anyone did made sense any more. Under such conditions, how was it possible to lay orderly, well-thought-out plans? It was like trying to play chess in an insane asylum.

Oster was pacing up and down before the window, looking out over the Landwehr Canal. The sky was deceptively cheerful, bright blue and full of the kind of fleecy white clouds that are more often found in Courbet landscapes than over German cities.

"How is it possible they can behave so foolishly? Don't they have any understanding of what they're up against?"

"Why is that a cause for complaint? Without this stupidity, as you call it, you'd be in a fine position."

"Only because 'Emil' is madder still."

Canaris considered; it was perfectly true. If the British gave in and forced Beneš to cede the Sudetenland, there would be no declaration of war, just another bloodless victory for the Reichschancellor, and no pretext whatsoever for military intervention. Under such conditions, a *putsch* would be out of the question.

"If only Von Witzleben wasn't so stubborn," said Oster, grinding his fist into his hand.

"But he is, and that's that. He may be right, you know. Unless war is actually declared, do you think you'll have any real support from the people?"

"Does it really matter? They'll look away and pretend not to see who murders who, just as they always do."

"If I were that cynical, Hans, if I believed as you do—"

"What?"

"I don't know. I simply don't know."

Oster, growing irritated, examined the dispatch once again. He turned it in his hands as though expecting the words to change even as he stared at the paper.

"Has he left Munich yet? No matter what else, it's not going to work unless we can get our bird back into his cage in Berlin."

"Not yet. Grosscurth phoned me a few minutes before you came up. He's still there."

"It's almost as if he knows."

"Are you losing confidence?"

"In *this*? How can you ask such a question? Are you?"

"There are too many pieces that have to fit perfectly before your puzzle is complete, that's what bothers me. One missing piece—the declaration of war, or if he stays in Munich and does it from there instead of coming back to the Wilhelmstrasse—and it all falls apart."

Oster gave him a desperate look. He knew as well as Canaris did the problems he faced. He also knew the intransigence of the men he was dealing with, the conditions they put on their participation, the price for action. There were a few like Dohnanyi and Michaelis who were participants out of sheer moral indignation. Most, however, were simply out to save their own skins. Oster had often thought of asking Von Witzleben straight out what he would do if the West Wall *was* complete, if he had enough divisions to be sure of overcoming the French, English, and Czechs combined, if he could be sure, in short, of winning. Would he march on the Chancellery then?

"I'm going to fly to Vienna this afternoon," Oster announced. "I want to go over this with Redwitz and make sure that we are covered in the south." He paused, then smiled, knowing what the answer to his question would be. "Is there anything I can bring you?"

"A sachertorte, for Erika. You know her sweet tooth."

"The best, I promise you. If I come back with nothing else."

Canaris looked away. That, too, was perfectly possible.

Sunday, September 25, 11:00 A.M.: Vienna

The Kartnerstrasse was jammed with crowds, all shouting "Ein volk, ein Reich, ein Führer" at the top of their lungs. The proprietors of shops that sold phonograph records and radios had all mounted speakers over their doors and from these issued an incessant blare of martial music. Uniformed Austrian police wearing red and white swastika armbands and slightly confused expressions were earnestly patrolling in front of the old Nazi Party headquarters on Teinfaltstrasse. In front of the Austrian Radio broadcasting building, on the Johannesgasse, long lines of tight-lipped German soldiers in field gray, with bayonets fixed, stood guard. The new Chancellor, Seyss-Inquart, was scheduled to make a speech that evening, just after the finish of Hitler's own broadcast from the Berlin Sportspalast. He was to explain to the country just what was going on in Czecho-

187

slovakia and what would be expected of every loyal citizen of the Reich. Every few minutes a black Mercedes would drive up to the entrance and deposit a minister or an official of the SS. It seemed as though half the Nazi government was in Vienna that night.

As Major Langbein passed the Ravag building, he thought how convenient it would be if the whole place would simply blow sky-high, say just a moment or two after Seyss-Inquart had begun talking.

Disgruntled and perplexed, Langbein drove back to the Abwehr offices and called Roon.

"If a large amount of money, say in French francs, was to be wired into the country," he asked, "would you be able to find out about it before it was released?"

"To what city?"

"Here, to Vienna."

"Have you any idea how much?"

"Say one hundred thousand marks in equivalent French currency, whatever the exchange rate is now. It will probably be coming from *Le Matin* or a connected source."

"It's possible, Langbein. It could be done. With a lot of effort. I would have to go through the Stadtbank clearing-house. The currency control office would be notified. I *could* find out."

"You *can* get the information, then?"

"Of course. How soon do you have to know about it?"

"Before the money is released. That's essential."

"Ah—before? That's another matter entirely."

"But can it be done?"

"With a little luck, yes. I think I can manage it. Listen, you must tell me, how important is this? It will take a few special people to pull it off and it will cost me a few favors I've been saving for a long while."

"It's very, very important—unless I'm completely wrong about this entire business."

"Don't tell me any more. I'll take your word on it. I'd rather not know anything, do you understand?" Roon paused. For a second or two the silence was so heavy that Langbein could hear his own pulse pounding; was Roon thinking twice about it? Then Roon's voice came back on the line. "All right. I'll call you at once, as soon as the money is about to be transferred. You can count on it."

"One more thing."

"Yes?" Roon sounded very tired, and a little vague. It occurred to Langbein that perhaps he had caught Roon still in bed asleep, or making love. He wondered if Roon could be trusted to remember. But he had no other alternative. Clearly, Roon was the only man he could go to. Even the Abwehr was helpless before the intricacies of the German banking system.

"Can you arrange to have notification to the customer of the money's arrival held up until I give you the signal to have it released?" A plan was taking shape somewhere in the back of his mind; he himself was not even sure where it would lead and had only the most general idea of what he was doing. Yet, as he always did, he moved surely ahead, confident of his instincts.

"If I can manage the information to start with," came Roon's weary reply, "then I can manage that, too. There'll be no problem."

Langbein hung up. He went to the window and parted the venetian blinds. A parade was winding its way up the Kartnerstrasse and the thud of drums could be clearly heard even through the closed and bolted double windows. He wondered what was going on in Berlin at that moment. How was the population reacting to "Emil's" latest ravings? His superior, Count Marogna-Redwitz, had circulated a memorandum the day before—while he, Langbein, was still at the Prater—advising all senior Abwehr officers that the mobilization orders had already been drawn and were sitting on General Keitl's desk. October 1, the deadline which the Führer had fixed for Czechoslovakia's capitulation, was approaching inexorably while Chamberlain sat playing with himself in London. The Czech president, Beneš, however, was not sitting still; his fortifications were crammed with troops. The Skoda works were on a twenty-four-hour schedule. In the Sudetenland, Nazi agitation was reaching fever pitch. All of this Langbein had from the circular briefing memoranda that kept piling up on his desk. Henlein's Freikorps were marching in the streets and Beneš was getting ready to crack down.

The empty room seemed suddenly full of shadows. Of events past, present, and future. Langbein paced nervously. He turned on the radio. Hitler was in the middle of another of his ranting speeches. The familiar high-pitched, strident voice cut through him like the pain of a toothache.

> I have taken upon myself sufficient sacrifices in the way of renunciations. But there was a limit beyond which I could not go. How right this was has been proven, first by the plebiscite in Austria; by the entire history of the re-union of Austria with the Reich. A glowing confession of faith was pronounced at that time—a confession such as others certainly had not hoped for. A flaming testimony was given at that time, a declaration such as others surely had not hoped for. . . .

He went on, shouting, cajoling, lowering his voice to a whisper, then suddenly beginning all over again to scream until it seemed as though his voice must crack altogether. The crimes of Beneš, he cried, were inconceivable. . . .

> Whole stretches of land are depopulated. Villages are burned to the ground. An attempt is made to smoke Germans there out with grenades and gas. But Herr Beneš sits in Prague and is convinced, "Nothing can happen to me. Behind me stand England and France."

The crowd roared at every mention of Beneš's name. "Hang him," they shouted. Langbein lit a cigarette, turned off the radio, and went to his wall safe. The cat came over to watch. Good, loyal Lulu. She, at least, had some sense.

He noticed that his hands were trembling. For a moment he stood still, attempting to calm himself. Then he tried again.

As he turned the dial, it struck him that everything he was trying to do was, perhaps, more than a little absurd. Large public events were outpacing his own small maneuverings. Here he was, deeply involved in what at most could be a nasty bit of infighting, while the world was about to come apart at the seams. Under certain circumstances, it could all be useful. A rearrangement of the upper levels of the power structure that might be turned to advantage. But to whose advantage, and for what purpose? He felt he had somehow lost sight of the larger picture, that he no longer had that clear overview that was so essential to the proper implementation of any intelligence operation.

And worse yet, he doubted that anyone else saw it either. Canaris, sitting in Berlin, had held aloof. He had let the impetuous Oster have his head. Generals Halder and Von Witzleben were busy scheming, setting up elaborate plans, deploying brigades and divisions and forming special Kommando squads. But everything they were doing depended, in the end, on there being exactly the right justification for their acts. And at exactly the right time. Wasn't the fact that the country was being run by a paranoid lunatic enough? Apparently not, at least not for the generals. In order to make the wheels of revolution go round, they had first to be made slippery with blood. To stop a war, in short, it was required that one first be started.

The only thing that remained to do was to find out what was really in Kepplinger's files. If the investigation had nothing to do with Halder or Oster, then Schanz could go on his way with Langbein's blessings and the devil take whoever it was with the bastard grandfather.

But the only way to get at Kepplinger's files was to get some of his own men inside Kepplinger's office. To most people, the idea of trying to break into the Prinz Albrechtstrasse would seem the sheerest lunacy; but Langbein knew better. Precisely because it seemed so absurd, the SD itself was not nearly as strict with its own security as it might have been. There were ways that the operation could be pulled off.

Langbein had discussed just such a possibility on a number of occasions with both Redwitz and Von Helldorf. Von Helldorf had made contingency preparations and had even gone so far as to provide Langbein with a map of the sewer systems and the vaults of the old museum buildings next door to SD headquarters. These provided the key to the entire project. Why not, after all? Hadn't the Gestapo done the same thing to the

Abwehr during the Tukaschevsky affair? What a mess they'd left behind. Files scattered all over the place and the building in flames.

Well, turnabout would be fair play. And perhaps something a little bit more.

He would set the operation in motion at once. Actually, he had no choice whatever.

September 25, 8:30 P.M.: Graz

There was something wrong.

Schanz couldn't quite put his finger on it but he was sure it was there.

What had Liszewsky said? "These Jews often sell off everything they have in order to get out of the country."

Yes, that was all well and good, and he could hardly blame them. He'd felt like hitting Liszewsky in the face, his expression and tone had been so sarcastic.

But the dates . . . the timing . . .

Schanz opened the copy of the file he had taken from the Reichsfluchtsteuer Bureau and began to read again.

Then, suddenly, he knew what it was. The landlady at the Jankows' apartment had said that their furniture and belongings had been removed after the Jankows were already on their way to St. Gallen.

After the tax had been paid.

If Liszewsky was working through dealers in half a dozen cities, and would only be paid by them on receipt, which was precisely what his ledgers showed, then how likely was it that a man of Liszewsky's limited means would have advanced such a sizable sum of money to Jankow?

Impossible.

Then where had the money come from? According to the bank records, neat photostats of which were clipped inside the Jankow dossier, the funds had gotten into the Zurich account by way of cable from Paris.

The fragment of old newspaper in the Jankows' closet had been French and on it had been the scrawl "WP/CO Dowling." A connecting link.

192

But connecting what to what?

In the morning he could find out easily enough through the Ministry of Finance whether the deposit had all gone for the Reichsfluchtsteuer or whether any part of it had gone elsewhere.

If it had all been used up, then he would have to acknowledge defeat. Either that or start checking out every name in Liszewsky's ledger.

But if not, if there was a record of other withdrawals—as he now felt sure there would be—he would find himself pointed in exactly the right direction.

He took a glass of wine, a hot bath, and read the newspaper.

The news was bad. More bellicose speeches. Goering was ranting, the Reichschancellor was ranting. And the Czechs were arming. Just what the English and the French were up to, God only knew.

Schanz looked at his watch, sighed, and put down the paper. He was due back at the Irish Free State Consulate in less than two hours.

The sky, he noted as he walked out onto the street before his dingy little hotel, was clear and starry. The flight from Dublin should by all rights be smooth, uneventful, and on time.

September 25, 8:30 P.M.: Berlin

Eight thirty in the evening. A small sewer-repair van stopped one block to the east of the Prinz Albrechtstrasse, just beyond the point where it intersects the Wilhelmstrasse. There the street changes names and becomes the Zimmerstrasse. Three men got out of the van, lifted a manhole cover and began handing down toolboxes. A fourth, the driver, set up two sawhorses to protect the opening from passing cars. Occasional bursts of steam issued from the manhole, further obscuring their movements.

To the north, a small truck entered the intersection of Leipzigerstrasse and Wilhelmstrasse. It was driven by a disguised plainclothesman from the Berlin Orpo, under Count von

Helldorf's personal orders. It paused, then shot forward, slamming head-on into a much larger flatbed truck carrying drums of machine oil loosely fastened with rope. The flatbed was also driven by a plainclothes operative from the Orpo. The impact of the collision turned the flatbed on its side and caused the drums of machine oil to spill into the street. Some of them burst, spreading oil all over the area. Whistles blew, civil police converged, and such traffic as there was at that hour heading into Prinz Albrechtstrasse was cut off.

To the south, at Königgrätzerstrasse, a municipal omnibus full of passengers broke down just as it was making a turn into Anhallstrasse, completely blocking the way in and out of both streets. The passengers got out and stood around in an angry, milling crowd, waiting for another bus to come by and trying to figure out how to get to the theatre or the films, wherever they were going.

A few moments later, at approximately eight forty, the main transformer at the Berlin electrical works on Luisenstrasse, which supplied power to the entire inner city area, suffered a breakdown from unknown causes. The lights went out from Invalidenstrasse on the north to Unter-den-Linden on the south. While frantic technicians tried to locate the source of the trouble, the three sewer workers who had gone into the manhole behind the Albrechtstrasse emerged in a vault directly under and to the rear of the Gestapo headquarters. Under cover of the temporary darkness, they made their way through a ventilating tunnel and into the cellar of the Prinz Albrechtstrasse building on the far side of a concrete wall that separated the interrogation cells from the main heating plant. There, they threw off the overalls that had covered their neat black SS uniforms, stuffed the bundles behind the boiler, and went upstairs by the maintenance passage.

Each man had been provided not only with the papers but also with the appearance of an officer from another city only slightly known at Prinz Albrechtstrasse and who was, at the moment, not only far from Berlin but under Abwehr surveillance as well.

The entire operation had been triggered only an hour before by the news that Colonel Kepplinger had taken the bait and gone off with his wife and two friends to attend what was, for him, a rare evening at the Berlin Philharmonic. The colonel's wife, quite unwittingly, had been maneuvered into purchasing the tickets. There was absolutely nothing to arouse suspicion.

The three men went up, each by a separate route, through the large many-corridored building, directly to the second-floor office complex where Kepplinger's rooms were. The lights were still out all over the area. Sirens sounded outside in the street, not far off; the spilled oildrums down the block had started a fire. One of the trucks was burning. Both drivers had already been taken into custody by the Orpo and hustled away in police cars, to be booked under fictitious names and then released.

The power would stay off for exactly twenty minutes. Then, whether the technicians at the electrical works had found the cause of the problem or not, light would be restored. Rost had little enough time to work, but at least he knew that nothing could possibly happen to throw the lights back on before the twenty-minute period elapsed. Sudermeyer's section had seen to that. Lieutenant Berger, the demolitions expert, had gone off down the corridor to the east stairwell to set his charges. Rost, who had flown up from Vienna that afternoon especially for the occasion, and the third man, a certain Sergeant Guertner, entered the outer secretarial section of Major Kepplinger's offices without difficulty. The door had been left open by Helmut Rost's friend, the typist Ida Sattler. The lock had been jammed simply but effectively by a piece of soft gum eraser such as might easily have gotten there by accident.

While Rost waited at the door to Kepplinger's office, Sergeant Guertner, the best lock expert on Canaris's Berlin staff, went straight to the wall safe where Kepplinger kept his most valuable files. The safe itself was old and not particularly difficult to open. It had never occurred to Kepplinger or anyone else at Prinz Albrechtstrasse that anybody could possibly violate the integrity of their offices. As a result, they took far fewer precautions and were far less concerned with up-to-date security equipment than many another government or military department that had the nocturnal prowlings of the Gestapo to contend with.

Within minutes, Guertner had the safe open. At this point he changed places with Rost and took over the guard position by the door. Through the glass he could see now and then the dark shape of some clerk or SD man stumbling along in the pitch-black corridor. Occasionally a flashlight beam lanced by. No one touched the door.

Rost, meanwhile, went rapidly through the files in Kepplinger's safe, laying them out one at a time on his desk and photographing first the index sheet and then the principal documents in each dossier with a miniature infra-red camera. Rost worked so fast, and in such darkness—to his eye, if not to the camera lens—that he had no real idea of what he was photographing. The only thing he could tell for certain was that the files did not concern either General Halder, Oster, or the Abwehr in general. On the contrary, they appeared to be —just as Helmut had reported weeks before—racial histories of the kind usually maintained by the Rasse Bureau or the Society for Ancestral Heritage.

There was one in particular that he photographed in its entirety. It bore on its cover page the name of Hans Frank, once Hitler's personal attorney and afterwards Minister of Justice for Bavaria. In it were little cards with the names "Weidele," "Schanz," and "Meinhard" typed on them, together with a series of coded remarks. He recognized the cipher at once; it would take less than ten minutes to decode the entries.

Guertner checked the luminous dial of his watch. Seven minutes to go. He heard a soft click, then a metallic spinning sound. Rost had closed the safe again. He grinned. The whole thing, thanks to *his* skill at the tumblers, had taken less than ten minutes. In six and a half minutes more, when the power was turned back on, the electricity coursing suddenly through the wiring which Berger had altered in the east stairwell would start a fire of considerable size. Just as when the Gestapo had damned near burned the Abwehr out of its Tirpitz-ufer offices during the Russian imbroglio.

In the dark, Guertner could just make out Rost coming back through the door to Kepplinger's inner office. He took from his pocket the specially prepared wad of chemically treated ashes and a lipsticked cigarette stub; these he threw into a basket crammed with papers near the unlocked wall files. A drop of water from a tiny ampule and the ashes would at once begin to sizzle and fume. In a moment there would be yet another fire, mostly smoke and little damage, but enough to create total confusion within the building. It would appear, moreover, that the fire had been started by someone accidentally throwing a smoldering cigarette stub into the wastebasket; there would be no way whatever of determining the truth.

Lieutenant Rost clapped Guertner on the shoulder, and the two of them slipped into the still dark corridor. The tiny spool of film was already secreted in the hollow heel of Rost's boot, and the camera discarded down a ventilating shaft after having been broken up into undetectable components.

The lights were still out. Through a window at the end of one long hallway could be seen a night sky trembling with the glow of the nearby oil fire. So much the better. Two fires inside the building, and one, much larger, outside. That would mean that the fire engines would be delayed getting into the Albrechtstrasse—not that it would make much difference, as the Gestapo guards would most likely refuse them entrance unless the fires inside got completely out of control.

Rost felt enormously pleased, not only with the success of the operation itself but with the fact that he had been taken right into the heart of things. Major Langbein had confidence in him; so did Canaris's office. Success could mean promotion; it also would mean constantly working with men whose integrity he respected. The only thing that concerned Rost, really, was where it was all going to lead. The sight of Hans Frank's name on the main file, the one in which Schanz's name also appeared, had given him a distinct start.

Berger, his boiler suit already completely covering his SS uniform, was waiting at the basement entrance to the ventilating tunnel. He breathed a sigh of relief when he recognized his two colleagues and lowered his gun, a heavy military semi-automatic that could have blown them all over the basement wall in less than a second.

"Any trouble down here?" Rost's voice.

"Someone came by to check the main fuse, that's all. He didn't see me. Went right back up."

"Perfect," said Rost, climbing back into his overalls. "Congratulations, gentlemen."

"Less than a minute to go," Berger whispered. "Hurry up."

Rost slipped into the tunnel. Guertner pulled the grating back into place behind them and fastened the hooks just as the lights went back on.

As he wormed his way along the narrow shaft, Rost could not help visualizing the two musicales that were now in progress —Heydrich, his lean, full-lipped face set in a scowl of concentration, sawing away at his violin in Admiral Canaris's living room; and Major and Frau Kepplinger sitting in the Philharmonic Hall, up to their eyebrows in Pfitzner.

It was all Rost could do to keep from whistling. But, after all, what was there in all of Pfitzner that one *could* whistle?

September 25, 10:00 P.M.: *Graz*

Schanz had been waiting in the side vestibule for almost a half an hour when the second Under-Counsel finally appeared, somewhat haggard and clearly a little the worse for alcohol. He held a heavy wax-sealed envelope out before him as though the thing were contaminated—in a way, in fact, that suggested that if the man had had tongs available he would have happily used them.

"Here, take the damned thing and get out of here," Toohey said, the look on his face passing from mere agitation to something approaching panic. "If I hadn't already compromised myself with you, I'd send you packing fast enough."

Schanz took the packet. It was sealed. The second Under-Counsel could not know what was inside. Why then was he so upset?

"You opened it?" Schanz asked quietly, feeling his stomach begin to knot.

Toohey shook his head. "I'm not so damned stupid as all that. But I've got wind of it, oh yes I have, and you can't be up to any good, that's for certain."

Schanz took the packet. It was thick, crammed with papers, and it crinkled.

"I've a good mind to call the police," said Toohey. "But then . . . you *are* the police, aren't you?"

"I might be lying," said Schanz. "My papers might be forged."

"I'm not that stupid, either," replied Toohey, finding his tongue. "I had you checked out, I did. You're the genuine article all right. And now—if you please—with my thanks, you'll clear out, won't you?"

Schanz turned to go, furious; the man had called someone, some office. Probably Prinz Albrechtstrasse, to check on him. Now they knew where he was.

"Thank you, Herr Under-Counsel."

"Oh yes, you're very welcome. And three cheers for Roger Casement and all that."

The door slammed and Schanz went out into the side garden.

For a moment he stood there, thinking that perhaps the best thing to do would be to drop the envelope in the nearest sewer and go back to Berlin.

Instead, he walked down the street to a park, one of those little spots of green that one finds in Graz at almost every turning, sat down on a bench, and opened the envelope.

It was almost midnight. His eyes were tired and he was having difficulty focusing. The light from the overhead lamp wavered and, on top of that, was appallingly dim.

But the contents of the envelope were clear and unmistakable. He felt his heart contract and a nasty cold sweat start down along his forehead. He had felt this way only once before in his life, when he had awakened one morning during the war in a trench and found that his comrade's head had been cut clean off in the night by a shell fragment he hadn't even heard.

He put the envelope hastily back into his pocket, looked around, and after making sure there was no one nearby, walked half a block and hailed a taxi.

When he arrived back at his hotel he immediately placed

a call to his wife in Berlin. While the operator made the connections, he paced up and down, oddly enough growing calmer and calmer.

At least he now had some idea of what he was into, if still far from the whole truth of it. Knowing made it better; he felt his initial panic dissipate and his old instincts reassert themselves. Damn Kepplinger and the lot of them for sucking him into such a mess! Yet there was still a puzzle to solve and he was more than ever determined to get to the bottom of it. The pieces were slowly fitting together, but of the picture that would finally emerge, he still had no clear idea.

The phone rang. It was his wife, sleepy and confused.

He spoke rapidly and deliberately. She, no doubt, had no idea at first what he was saying. It was his tone, cold and even and very unlike him, that finally communicated to her the urgency of what he was saying far more than the actual words.

"I think it's time for you to visit our dear friend Helga. She misses you, liebchen. Yes, you should do it right away," he insisted.

She was puzzled and it took him three repetitions to make her understand.

"We would not want something bad to happen, would we? You know how she gets when you don't visit her."

His wife's tone changed suddenly; her drowsiness deserted her. Her voice became sharp-edged, almost as urgent as his. "Helga" was the mountain they had climbed on holiday the year before. In Switzerland.

Her voice came back to him, clipped and assured. "Yes, yes, of course, Ulrich."

"Tomorrow."

"If you think it's wise."

"I certainly do."

She paused, thinking how best to say it without upsetting him. "Helmut isn't coming home this weekend. What's to be done about him?"

"I'll see to it," Schanz said, but he had no real idea how. "If you have any problem with the arrangements, call Inspector Tenholt or, if necessary, Schmann at Count von Helldorf's office."

They exchanged endearments, said goodbye.

"Give my best to Helga."

"Will you be able to visit her too?"

"We'll see, we'll see."

For a long time after he'd hung up he could not bring himself to open the envelope again. Finally he took the photostat sheets and spread them on the bed.

The first set of entries, from the Dublin register, were in Gaelic, which he could not read. But there was an English translation directly beneath, neatly typed. And below that, stapled to the bottom, was a transcript copy of another entry sheet, this one from the civil register of the City of Liverpool.

There was no mistaking what was written there. The salient information fairly jumped up at him:

> Bridget Elizabeth Dowling, known as Elizabeth Dowling, father's trade, carpenter—profession listed as "actress." Married, June 3, 1910, to one Alois Hitler. Mother of William Patrick Hitler, born—Liverpool, March 12, 1911.

September 25, 10:30 P.M.: London

The cable was waiting for her when she returned from her obligatory thank-you dinner with Henry Cranwell.

The desk porter, a stern, white-whiskered man who would not have been out of place in a Victorian general's uniform, presented the envelope on a little silver tray.

"Is there any response to be made, Madame?"

She shook her head sharply and took the cable at once to her room, opening it only after pouring herself a tumbler of whiskey and downing it in a single swallow. A half hour before, she had been trying as diplomatically as possible to ignore Cranwell's clumsy suggestions and growing more and more agitated from the strain. By the time the rum cake had arrived, she had become completely unstrung.

Now all of that struck her as bordering on the grotesque. How could such petty problems possibly have caused even a moment's real concern?

Her hand trembled slightly. Too much burgundy with

dinner. And now whiskey. Poor August would have thrown up. The cable was direct and exactly what she had expected.

PLEASE REMEMBER TO RETURN IN TIME FOR UNCLE CASIMIR'S BIRTHDAY PARTY. IT IS MOST IMPORTANT YOU ATTEND. HE WOULD BE DISAPPOINTED IF YOU FAIL TO COME. DON'T FORGET TO BRING A PRESENT.

She did have an Uncle Casimir. And his birthday was, in fact, in early October. Michaelis had been most careful on that point. If anyone had reason to check out the message—and there was no telling how far the SD's investigations had gone or just what they had already gotten into—they would find nothing suspicious.

It was not the substance of the message that mattered. The number of words alone told the date of the attack. If less than thirty, then the appropriate day in September was meant; if more than thirty, then one had simply to count on into October.

The message numbered thirty-one words. There could be no question any more. The invasion of Czechoslovakia would begin on October 1. The date, she knew, had come directly from General Halder.

She threw the cable into a wastebasket as she had been told to do. If anyone had been watching her and later searched the room while she was out, he would find only a carelessly discarded message of no apparent importance.

She sat there for a few moments, going over in her mind the message that Michaelis had had her memorize. It was simple enough, and she had not even had to memorize the specific words. An improvisation, Michaelis had said with some humor, would be quite enough.

Only the night staff was on duty at the Embassy building on Carlton House Terrace. The cipher operator answered the phone and at first refused to leave his post to go look for Kordt. The Herr Counsellor was most likely at the reception for the Rumanian Ambassador at the home of Prince Selesescu; would Madame like the number?

Melitta persisted. Counsellor Kordt had assured her that

202

he would remain available at all times. It was a matter of the utmost urgency. At last the man gave in. As she waited for Kordt to come to the phone, she felt a faint tremor steal over her. Why should they trust Kordt? Now, at such a critical time? Kordt's attitude was well known. He was no moralist like Michaelis or her husband. He did not even disagree with Hitler's actual goals but only with his methods.

Perhaps that would be enough. It would have to be.

A moment passed. Then she heard Kordt's voice, harsh and irritated. He had been in his office all the time, working on a report.

Their conversation was brief. She would have to see him at once. A family matter. She could turn only to him.

"Yes, yes," he agreed, growing more and more agitated. He was clearly at the point of exhaustion. "Now it is ten thirty? In half an hour. At Speaker's Corner, yes? An appropriate spot, don't you think? I will come by in a car."

She took off her dinner dress and put on a sturdy woolen suit of the kind English ladies wore in the country. The night had grown cool and, as always, damp. A fog was rolling up from the Thames. From her window she could make out a small crowd gathered at Speaker's Corner listening to a harangue given by a man standing before a banner whose device was obscured by the fog and the darkness.

She waited, then went downstairs, unable to stay any longer in her room alone. Fifteen minutes to go at least. But the Embassy was not far off. Perhaps Kordt would be early.

She stood with her coat-collar pulled up around her ears, the fog condensing in little droplets on her face, listening with increasing fascination to the speaker around whom the crowd had now grown to a considerable size.

He was talking about vivisection. There should be laws to protect animals from experimentation, from pain. It was up to the King—a matter of the gravest importance.

"On no account should animals, animals who are as capable of feeling pain as you and I, on no account should such poor defenseless creatures be subjected to. . . ."

She suppressed a sour laugh.

Behind the speaker the vast bulk of Marble Arch loomed

like a ship unaccountably gone aground on Oxford Street. The grim bars of Cumberland Gate glistened in the thickening fog. The air smelled of diesel fuel, an odor that forever would summon up in Melitta Trcka's mind a picture of that oppressive, magisterial city.

She listened. The speaker continued to rant.

"Of moral significance . . . in times such as these, how can we, how *can* we fail to appreciate the agony, the suffering of the poor cat, of the dog, of the monkey who is butchered in the name of medical science, who dies beseeching us to account for his agony, his poor eyes still wide with trust. . . ."

Something moved just beyond the periphery of her vision. A car had pulled up close to the curb behind her. Traffic flowed on in a sluggish, indistinct stream, headlights mirrored on the rain-glistening pavement.

The car door opened.

"Herr Kordt?"

She moved closer, unsure until she could make out the driver's face. It was Theo Kordt, no question about it.

She got in, hunching low, almost invisible in the folds of her dripping coat. The smell of wet wool was suffocating.

"Is it really important?" Kordt asked sharply.

She could barely make out his features. He was flushed and having trouble steering the car, blinded by the reflected lights, the glassy puddles, the fog, and unused even after so many months in London to driving on what was for him the wrong side of the road.

"I received a cable from Bernhard."

"How do you know it was from him?"

"I know. It was all arranged."

"A signal?"

"Yes."

He turned the car into the darkened park and for a while they drove on in silence between the rain-soaked trees. She tore at her nails, then finally said, "There was a message. I was to give it to you if the cable arrived."

She saw him lick his lips in nervousness. It was always frightening to her to see a good-looking man's face distorted by fear.

204

"Go on." It took him some effort to get even those two words out.

She repeated Michaelis's message, almost word for word, not having to extemporize, and proud as a schoolgirl that she had remembered it all, right down to the last period. She hadn't even rehearsed it, not once.

Kordt suddenly pressed down on the accelerator.

"You're sure? My God, you are absolutely positive?"

"That is exactly the message I was to give you. There is no doubt about it."

Kordt was only forty-five. At that moment he looked ninety. His entire face seemed to have collapsed. His eyes shone with intense points of light, like a cat's.

"We must see Wilson," he said, as though to himself.

"Useless. I was with him little more than a week ago, together with Colonel . . . "

"No." He cut her off. His voice had an added touch of anguish in it. "No names. I don't want to know who went with you. Don't say another word. It must be to Wilson, nevertheless. I'm sure you didn't tell him any of *this*, did you? No, of course not."

"The message hadn't come yet."

"And, of course, you obeyed instructions to the letter, yes?" There was more than a faint trace of sarcasm in his voice.

"Yes, I did." Then, despite his protest, she told him all of it. Except for her companion's name. Kordt was impressed. He had not been aware of the extent of her contacts in London.

When she had finished, he considered for a moment. He took his eyes entirely off the road and stared full at her.

"But you see, it must be Wilson again. And Lord Halifax also. They are the only ones. You will explain, just as you did to me. They *will* listen this time. They must." He paused. The car passed a long bank of chestnut trees and a winding pond. "We shall stop. I will have to make a phone call first, of course. One of those charming red booths will do. Perhaps we will have to wait, perhaps it can be arranged at once. It depends on whether Halifax can be reached. God only knows where he is at the moment. He may not even be in the country."

*   *   *

It had not taken long at all. Kordt had made his call and when he returned, there was a smile of ironic satisfaction on his face.

The car moved slowly along the south side of St. James's Park, past the barracks, and finally off Birdcage Walk and onto Great George Street. There they parked.

"We walk from here. Come, we must go quickly."

She followed him around the corner and down the next street. At a little distance she could see a number of helmeted guards standing rigidly in front of a small brick building. There, she knew, the Prime Minister himself had his offices.

She had no time to contemplate the possibilities. Kordt gestured toward a small garden gate not far from the entrance to Number 10.

She hesitated. The gate opened a little. The guards took no notice. There was someone waiting on the other side, hidden in the shadows of the garden hedges.

"Counsellor Kordt?" The merest whisper.

They were conducted through the garden and into the Prime Minister's office building by a side entrance.

The long-faced Wilson was waiting for them in a small office on the second floor. He squinted sharply in surprise as Melitta came into the room but said nothing. It was clear that he did not care to let it be known that he already knew Kordt's companion.

There was another man with him, older, very handsome in a severe sort of way, infinitely more elegant. Melitta Trcka knew at once who the other man was—the Foreign Secretary, Lord Halifax himself.

Wilson quickly made the introductions.

"The Frau Baronin Trcka . . . it is from her that this extraordinary bit of information comes, I believe." There was a trace of guarded sarcasm in his voice. "Extraordinary information."

"I should be most interested to hear how all of this comes about," said the Foreign Secretary. "Shall we sit down and begin at once? From what I've been told, you seem to feel that there's very little time."

As Melitta turned her attention fully on the Foreign Secretary she was startled to see Wilson hurriedly leave the room. Why? Because he did not care to take the time to listen again? Because he did not, *would* not believe her? Or simply because even if he did believe, it could make no difference?

"Now, shall we begin?" said Halifax, leaning forward in his chair, his long frame hunched and angled like a folded carpenter's rule. His eyes shone with interest. There was in his expression none of the boredom that Melitta had observed two nights before on Wilson's face.

She began, listening to her own voice reciting Michaelis's words once again as though it were someone else entirely speaking. Halifax did not move. His handsome face grew stern, his expression concentrated.

" . . . a prerequisite to any action is a diplomatic defeat for Hitler. The invasion is definitely set for October 1. The troops have already been given their marching orders. If the British government will act, the French will be forced to honor their commitments and Hitler will fail. The army will refuse to move and Hitler will be deposed within hours. But your Prime Minister *must* issue a firm and unequivocal statement. There must be no mistake about his intentions. It must be clear that Great Britain will not stand by and watch Czechoslovakia be destroyed. I am instructed to say this. Give me your word on that and we give you our word that the régime will fall."

When Melitta Treka had finished, Kordt began. He said nothing new, nothing different, but expanded on the message Michaelis had sent with such directness and confidence that it seemed as though he had known the facts for weeks. All of the nervousness he had displayed before had vanished. Either he had found a new source of strength or he was a consummate actor.

Others had probably said the same thing to His Lordship, he had no doubt. But as he did not know who those others were and had his own obligations of conscience to discharge, he hoped that the Foreign Secretary would bear with him. The message brought by the Frau Baronin was, of course, of the utmost importance. Whatever weight of urgency the words of those who had preceded him had borne, surely his words, *now*, must be counted the most urgent. The die was cast. The madman had determined to act. So had others. They needed only a signal, only a word. But that word was critical. Without it, they could do nothing.

Kordt went on at length in this fashion. His eyes flashed. His cheeks darkened with excitement.

The Foreign Secretary betrayed not the faintest emotion. He sat silent and pensive, his legs crossed, toying with a glass paperweight. It was uncertain from the grave cast of his eyes whether he believed Kordt not at all or only too well.

Finally he spoke.

"Well, then, it's all as Sir Horace has told me, isn't it?"

"Is there to be an answer for us? Will you act?"

Halifax looked pained.

"You wouldn't care to hear my own views on this, I'm sure. And as for the Prime Minister, I can only guess what his reaction will be."

"What *could* his reaction be? To know that the order to march has already been given, that it is certain now and only days away? What can he possibly say?" Kordt blurted out.

"Surely . . . ," Melitta added in a stifled voice.

The Foreign Secretary sucked in his cheeks. He chose his words carefully, slowly.

"There is a possibility, of course. There is always a possibility. But the Prime Minister is a man deeply convinced of the need for peace. You must understand that. He sees things broadly, very broadly. England and Germany must come to terms. The only other choice for us, after all, is an alliance with the Soviets, and such a thing he views as plainly impossible."

"What are you telling us?"

There was a long, painful silence.

"Only that I doubt you will get what you want, Counsellor Kordt. I doubt that the Prime Minister will be much moved. Excuse me, Madame, but I doubt that he will even believe what I will tell him—though I have no doubt of it myself." He rose, unfolding his long, elegantly tailored figure, and said in a voice so low that it almost went unheard: "No doubt at all."

Melitta jumped to her feet, her face white with anger.

"No, that will not do. That simply will not do," she exclaimed, in a voice so suddenly loud that Kordt blenched and started back. "You cannot sit there and tell me in that insufferably calm voice of yours that you will do nothing."

"Madame, what *can* I do?"

"You can explain to that . . . that man . . . if he's that at all . . . that his blindness is going to cost millions of lives. That's what you can do." She swept the documents Michaelis had given her off the table and thrust them into the Foreign Secretary's face. "What are these? Do you think they're the outing schedules for the Hitler Jugend? Do you think there won't be bloodshed? Oh, the Czechs will fight, and then you'll have to fight after all. You and the French. Now or later. Is he so stupid, this Prime Minister of yours, that he doesn't see what kind of a maniac he's dealing with? God, he's worse than Hitler, your Chamberlain. Hitler is a wild beast, but your Chamberlain is like the forester with a loaded rifle who can kill that wild beast with one squeeze of the trigger. The beast kills because it's his nature. But the forester has a choice, he can exercise his will. If he doesn't. . . ."

"Madam—enough, please, enough." Halifax's expression was a mixture of chagrin and growing anger. He flushed darkly. Kordt tried to pull Melitta away but she shrugged him off.

"This isn't a game, it doesn't have its own nice rules. There is no such thing as honor here. Not a word that man says can be trusted. He will break the most solemn pledge without a thought. All you need do is utter a few words and he'll slink back."

Halifax rose. Kordt noticed that he deliberately looked away as she spoke, as though he expected that the woman would try to strike him and he would not defend himself.

"If you don't do something it will be on your head, *yours*, Lord Halifax, as much as anyone else's. Oh, only a few fine men will die now. Because, you see, they will try anyhow, even without you. And they will fail without you. They will try, sir, knowing that they will fail. But afterwards, sir, it will be your blood that will be shed, English blood. How will you face *that*, Lord Halifax? With your same diplomat's *sang-froid*? I doubt it, I doubt it very much. . . ."

The Foreign Secretary's hands gripped the arms of his chair so tightly that his knuckles turned white. He seemed completely at a loss as to how to deal with Melitta's outburst.

She was not quite sure what happened after that. She recalled that Wilson came back into the room. Halifax rose to speak with him, his face flushed, his composure shaken. At that moment, Kordt had taken her violently by the arm and pulled her from the room. He was beside himself and began to berate her even as they descended the back stairs.

"Yes, yes, yes. I know. There was no point to it, none at all."

"You have insulted him. And as if that weren't bad enough, it was *unfair* as well. If it was up to Halifax. . . ."

"Oh, of course, that makes all the difference in the world! It isn't really up to him, so it's perfectly all right for him to simply wash his hands of it all."

"I didn't mean that."

"Yes, you did. You meant exactly that. And so did he. That's the trouble. You'll all wash your hands of it."

She covered her face and for a moment seemed to collapse against the wall of the stairwell. When she lowered her hands, her face was streaked with tears and her make-up, so carefully applied earlier that day, had run terribly.

"Oh, my God," she said. "What will we do now? What can we possibly do now?"

September 25, 11:00 P.M.: Berlin

Kepplinger's wife's only pleasure of recent evenings had been the opportunity to dress herself up and have dinner at the Hotel Adlon restaurant. There, with her husband's permission, she could exercise her proficiency in French and English by chatting with the foreign newsmen who often congregated there. They all knew who she was, of course, and lavished upon her precisely the attention which she desired and which her husband supplied only in such desultory and occasional fashion.

Pleased with the evening, but made nervous by Kepplinger's bleak and unattentive mood, she pressed next to him in the back of the taxi as it turned into the Zimmerstrasse. Her eyes closed, she leaned her closely coiffed head on his shoulder and indulged her own mood of reverie, recalling the days of their early marriage when Kepplinger had been a simple lieutenant in a Jager regiment invalided home just before the end of the war. She was all the more unprepared, then, for the sudden tremor that shook Kepplinger's body as the taxi turned the corner.

She opened her eyes abruptly. All she could see was smoke and the flickering of fire in the middle of the street.

Kepplinger shouted wildly at the driver. The taxi bolted down the street toward the Prinz Albrechtstrasse. Frau Kepplinger was thrown against the side of the cab and clutched at her husband for support.

The street was full of fire engines. Helmeted firemen were running about. Police whistles shrilled. The street in front of the Prinz Albrechtstrasse palace seemed alive with Orpo.

The cab stopped before a wall of fire engines. A policeman swung around facing it, about to shout at them to get away. A burning oil slick filled the street. But there were flames coming from inside the building, too. On the second floor, where his offices were.

Kepplinger felt an icy sweat pour down the sides of his neck. He shouted at the policeman to get out of his way, and at the cab driver to take his wife home at once. Not once did he actually address her. She had simply ceased to exist the moment he saw the flames and the smoke.

He could see some of the administrative staff and the clerks running about in the front of the building, trying to draw the hoses in themselves. Armed guards, steel-helmeted and carrying rifles, were forcing the firemen and the curious crowds back together. Kepplinger rushed up the front steps and into the front corridor.

The first person he saw was Kamecke, the chief files clerk for Department V, standing there with smoke marks and a bewildered expression on his face. A collapsed hose ran past him from the steps outside and snaked up the stairwell.

"You've got to let them in," Kepplinger shouted.

"Our orders—the Reichsführer SS gave strict orders," Kamecke protested.

"On my responsibility. Do you want the place to burn down?"

Where the devil was Himmler? Normally, he spent every evening in his office. Just this night, when the entire staff was paralyzed by his strict security measures, the man had to be off someplace—probably with Hitler, if he read the news correctly.

The stairway was black with smoke. Kepplinger bolted upstairs, followed by Kamecke and a half dozen agents who had come up from the interrogation rooms in the cellar. Behind him, he could see that the front doors had been flung open and the firemen were at last bringing in the hoses.

"One man with each fireman. See to it. No one comes in here alone, d'you understand?"

He stopped short at the end of the corridor. His heart sank. A billow of smoke was coming from the anteroom to his own offices. All at once, he was overwhelmed with a feeling of dread. His legs grew heavy and numb as though he were immersed in freezing seawater.

He flung open the door to the secretarial room. The smoke was thick but he could see no fire. Coughing, he ran past the desks, slamming painfully into a corner with his hip.

Himmler wasn't there. Nor was Heydrich. Who the hell was the senior in charge? It couldn't be him, could it? How could such a thing have happened?

He hit the door to his own office with his shoulder; it flew open and he fell heavily onto his knees before his desk. The room was almost clean. No smoke, no fire. He took it all in in one glance. There wasn't a thing on his desk, no folders, no files. He hadn't left anything out after all.

Then he heard the sound of boots, firemen entering the outer suite. Kamecke stuck his head into the room. Kepplinger snapped angrily at him to get out.

The door slammed again.

How could such a thing have happened? Worse yet, who was going to get the blame? Kepplinger could not help thinking that such things did not happen by accident and that it must, in some way, have been connected with the forebodings that had occupied him all the way through the Philharmonic concert. He could hear Himmler's thin, flat voice: "So it occurred to you to go to a concert, did it, Kepplinger? On this night, of

212

all nights? And who, exactly, did you leave in charge of your own offices?"

With a thrill of horror Kepplinger realized that the door to the secretarial suite had been unlocked. So had the door to his office.

Oblivious to the crashing of axes and the spurt of water outside, he knelt before his safe and with barely controllable fingers turned the combination. Thank God, the safe at least was still shut.

He took out the dossiers. They were all there. In the same order as when he had put them away that afternoon. He opened the Frank file. Everything was in place.

As he closed the folder, he noticed that on the title page, just below the code identification and Hans Frank's title, there was a small smudge. He squinted at it. A smudge? He would never have done such a thing himself. He washed his hands at least five times an hour. He could not tolerate dirt, not on himself or any of his subordinates.

Then he looked at his own hands; they were covered with soot. His clothing was black at the shoulders and the sleeves. For a moment he felt a surge of relief.

But how could he be sure?

He put the files back, slammed the safe, and went out into the anteroom. Kamecke was still there, trying to keep the firemen under control and stop them from ruining the files and the typewriters. A helmeted guard had taken his place at the door, an Erma submachine gun in his arms. Kamecke was shouting at the firemen to hurry. They, in turn, looked at him as though he was a madman; what the hell did he think they were trying to do?

Kepplinger shook his head, and with a sinking feeling in the pit of his stomach, walked back into the corridor.

September 26, 7:00 A.M.: Vienna

Lieutenant Rost, exhausted and struggling to stay on his feet, went immediately down to the basement photography laboratory. He found Langbein already pacing about in the semi-darkness.

213

"How long will it take to have them developed and printed?"

"Two hours, sir. An hour and a half if we really press."

"Then press." Langbein started to go out. He paused in the doorway. "Listen, Rost. I know how tired you must be. You're entitled to rest. But I can't let anyone else do it. D'you understand? You must—press."

Although it was strictly forbidden because of the chemicals stored there, Langbein lit up a cigar. In fact, it was obvious that he had been smoking one cigar after another. A tin cup on a table near the darkroom door was full almost to the brim with cigar stubs.

"The minute the prints are ready, bring them up. I'll be in my office. Don't bother to knock. I may be asleep."

Rost let out a sigh and collapsed in a nearby chair.

Langbein trudged up to his room. It was just beginning to get light. The plane carrying Rost and his crew back from Berlin had touched down at Aspern only an hour before.

The day was dreary, full of rain clouds. A storm was brewing over the Kahlenberg and from the amount of light that showed through his office window, it might as well have been four in the morning. He switched on his desk lamp and reached for the phone.

"Roon? I'm sorry to call you so early, but it's critical. Has the consignment we spoke about come through yet?"

"Let me check. I'll call you back in five minutes."

He hung up, lit yet another cigar, and went to the window, swearing quietly to himself. If the money hadn't come through from Paris yet he would have no alternative but to call Trcka and have the transaction counterfeited.

In three minutes, Roon called back. The night clerk had told him that the money had not been wired through as yet. There was no sign of it at the central clearing bank. They would have to wait until normal business hours.

"All right. You tried, that's all I can ask."

"Thank you, Major."

"No thanks for me." He hung up and immediately rang up Trcka.

214

The phone rang for a long time. Then Fessler came on. The Herr Baron was not in, he had gone out with the dogs, as was usual for him at that hour.

"Well, be a good fellow and go out and fetch him, Fessler."

"Is it absolutely necessary, sir? You know how jealous the Herr Baron is of his morning walks."

"Fessler, will you please do as I ask? At once."

The old servant could hardly mistake Langbein's tone. His voice snapped back with a sudden military crispness.

"At once, sir."

Langbein smiled as he remembered; Fessler had once been a sergeant in a Uhlan troop.

Treka finally came on the line, sounding tired and listless.

"You need money?" he said, without waiting for Langbein to ask. "It's all ready. I knew you'd need it. Everything's gotten tangled up, hasn't it? The French are practically on a war footing. To even *think* that a bank draft could be wired in under such circumstances is madness."

Langbein cut him off, trying to keep his tone friendly, appreciative. "You're sure you can manage it?"

"Absolutely. Where do you want the money?"

"If it was coming from *Le Matin*, where would it go?"

"I've checked that for you. They have their accounts at the Zentraleuropaische Landerbank on the Hohenstaufengasse."

"Can you manage it by tomorrow morning? We haven't got much more time. We may be at war in another day or two."

"It will be close, but—yes—it's possible."

"Can we have Herr Ledruc cabled? That the funds are on the way? He should be there at opening, to pick up the money. Tell him that because of the political situation they cannot guarantee that the credit will stand more than an hour. He must draw on it at once."

"Of course. Goodbye now, and good luck."

"Goodbye, and our thanks, all of us."

Langbein hung up. He had to pause for a moment to make sure that everything was clear, that he hadn't gotten anything mixed up. He hadn't been sleeping much for the past two weeks and had spent the last few nights on the cot in his office, tossing and turning, able to doze only with the help of pills.

He rang for Sergeant Drucker, his orderly, and ordered up a pot of hot coffee and some rolls.

Shortly before noon, Rost finally appeared in the doorway.

Langbein struggled up from the cot, glanced at his watch, and glared. "You said two hours, at the outside."

"We had some problems. The chemicals were depleted. We almost ruined one of the rolls."

Langbein gasped. "You didn't, did you?"

"Almost, sir. Here." He held out a mass of still dripping enlargements. "You'll want to see these at once, sir. Wet or not. It's amazing. I never would have dreamed of such a thing."

Langbein swept his desk clean with one violent wave of his arm. Breathing hard, he leaned over the glistening enlargements, now spread out from one side of the desk to the other. Even upside down, Rost could make out the title page, the one that had first caught his eye, the one with the signature and emblem of the Bavarian Minister of Justice, Hans Frank, on the lower corner.

As he read, the color drained from Langbein's face. He shook his head. He could hardly believe what he was seeing. He blinked and rubbed his eyes.

"That's what it says all right," offered Rost, in a very small voice. "You're reading it correctly, sir."

Langbein was stunned. He had been positive that what Rost had brought back from Berlin would prove to be a dossier on Colonel Oster or General Halder, a report on the meetings with Von Witzleben, Beck, and all the others.

Now he knew the truth and he had been as wrong as he could have been.

Langbein looked up, for a moment hardly noticing that Rost was still standing there in front of him. The flush of enthusiasm had faded instantly from Rost's face. He was now the same deathly color as his superior.

"You've read these, Rost?"

216

"Some of them, yes, sir. Last night, and again just now."

"You're mistaken, Rost. You've seen none of them. You haven't read a word. Not one word, d'you understand? You never had these papers in your hands, is that clear?"

Rost by now had begun to shiver. His stomach felt as though it were lined with frost. He meekly nodded his head.

Langbein's voice was stifled, low and shaken.

"Get down to the cipher room and stay there until I tell you to come out. Get your meals sent in. I don't want you to leave this building until I say so. Quick, get moving."

Rost turned on his heels without even a salute and fled.

Langbein stood there gripped by a kind of paralysis he had never experienced in all his life. He caught sight of his reflection in the glass over the photo of General Varela; the superimposition of his own image over the stern features of the Spaniard created a devastating double image, as though he were glimpsing his own ghost. He passed his hand over his sparse hair and fumbled for a cigar. The box was empty. He slammed the lid and hurled it to the floor.

What the hell was he to do now?

The Reichschancellor was ordering a general mobilization along the Czech frontier, Von Witzleben, Halder, and the other generals were playing Hamlet in their offices in Berlin, and he, Ernst Walter Langbein, was standing there with a time bomb on his desk, a bomb bigger than all the bombs the Luftwaffe was preparing to drop on Prague put together.

September 26, 1:30 P.M.: Vienna

Immediately after lunch, Schanz went to a kiosk and called his contact at the Ministry of Finance.

Had they spoken to Zurich? Yes, they had.

Had they obtained the information he'd asked for? Of course; had he doubted for a moment that his orders would be obeyed?

It had been difficult, certainly but, yes, the information was now available.

Schanz held his breath. He knew what he was going to

hear and he heard it in almost the exact words he had imagined.

"Of the hundred thousand marks deposited, Herr Obersturmbannführer, fifty thousand were withdrawn to the order of a man named Hermann Jankow and redeposited with the Reichsfluchtsteuer Bureau, Graz. Of the balance, twenty thousand were drawn to the order of a certain Albert Liszewsky, and the rest to the order of . . ."

"Andreas Flom, Vienna?"

"Exactly, Herr Obersturmbannführer. How did you know that?"

He hung up without answering or even saying thank you.

The sky had cleared; the weather was crisp but certainly not cold. Fleecy, innocent clouds seemed to play over the spire of the Stephanskirche not far off. The Kartnerstrasse was coming to life again, the stores filling up with early afternoon shoppers, the restaurants and coffeehouses emptying out. From a nearby window came the sound of someone—a child probably—practicing on the violin. A Mozart minuet, off key and full of false starts.

For Schanz, however, the time of false starts was over. He knew now exactly what he had to do.

As he crossed the street, he saw out of the corner of his eye a soldier walking along with a girl on his arm. He smiled at first and then, suddenly, the smile froze.

It was the same blond, cherubic-looking young man he had seen in the Schlossberg garden in Graz. And the same girl.

He walked slowly and cautiously, making a few turns, stopping to look in a few shop windows.

A trolley lumbered by, its bell clanging. A horse-cart passed. He turned down the Kohlmarkt and stopped to look at the display of pastries in Demel's window.

In the glass he caught the expected reflection—the young man and the girl were still there.

Kepplinger's people? If so, why? And how had they known where he was? But if not Kepplinger's people, whose then?

He hurried around the corner, onto the Graben, heading toward the church. Perhaps he could lose himself there in the shadows and the alcoves.

Perhaps. And then again, perhaps not.

September 26, 4:30 P.M.: *Vienna*

It had taken Schanz most of the day to shake the two who had been following him. At least twice he'd had the distinct impression that they were not alone, the soldier and his girl, and that there was another one on his trail as well: a face, appearing now and then, disappearing, reappearing with disturbing regularity. But in Vienna there were so many faces that looked the same, it was difficult to be sure.

Now, thanks to yet another rally and a parade down the Kartnerstrasse, he had succeeded in losing them all. No one could possibly have followed him through that mass of screaming, ranting humanity. Faintly disgusted and weary, he had waited in the shadow of a doorway looking back up the Singerstrasse toward the Stephansplatz and the mob. A stand had been set up in front of the church and loudspeakers had been strung up all the way from the archbishop's palace to the Graben. The platz was streaming with torches and red banners, and the shouting was so loud that it was impossible even to hear the martial music blaring from the speakers.

When he was absolutely sure that he was alone and unobserved, he began to edge toward the intersection of the Blutgasse and the Singerstrasse.

Andreas Flom's living quarters were directly above his shop. There was a side entrance and a back stairway. The building was old and dark. There were few if any tenants besides Flom.

He would have no trouble getting up undetected.

He took out his Walther and checked to see if it was loaded, something he had not bothered to do in the last few days.

The clip was full. He stuck the automatic back into its holster and started toward the shop.

September 26, 5:15 P.M.: *Berlin*

Bernhard Michaelis had for some years been taking regular physical examinations twice a year at the Charité. According to

219

his chart, he was already overdue, his scheduled examination having been down for the first week in September. When he announced himself to Dr. Jochmann's nurse in the anteroom of his offices, it was as a regular patient, overdue and certainly expected, for the most ordinary of purposes. Although Jochmann was a psychiatrist, he still practiced as an internist for a number of important, old patients. No one, not even the Gestapo—had they been watching him—would have given Michaelis's appearance there, on that particular day, a second thought.

The attending nurse, Fraulein Gleinicke, smiled attractively and told him that the doctor would be with him in a moment. Michaelis sat down, keeping the slim leather briefcase he had brought with him held tightly on his lap. He had no intention of letting it out of his hands, much less out of his sight. In it were incredible papers, photostats of documents he had just received by courier from Vienna.

A moment later, Dr. Jochmann, looking flustered and worn, appeared at the door of his examining room and motioned Michaelis in.

The room smelled of chemicals. A syringe was boiling in a little stainless steel heater at the end of the table. A diathermy machine stood in one corner, its orange "on" light blinking.

Michaelis started to take his clothes off.

"You haven't come for *that*, have you Bernhard, at this hour?"

"Not really, but even our ox-headed friends would think it strange if they walked in here and found me fully clothed, wouldn't they?"

He folded his shirt and jacket neatly and placed them on a chair. Then he seated himself on the edge of the examining table.

"You've been listening to the radio, of course?"

Dr. Jochmann looked stricken. It was sufficient answer.

Michaelis went on: "You know that there isn't much time left. It may happen tomorrow. Perhaps even sooner."

"I'm a doctor, Bernhard. Politics isn't my field. I simply do not understand."

"The facilities, I know, are ready. I haven't come here to ask you about that."

"What then? What can I possibly do at this point?"

"Your study. Are you finished? Are you ready to give evidence?"

Dr. Jochmann sighed deeply, turned sideways, avoiding Michaelis's level stare. His nervousness betrayed his indecision. Michaelis noted that he looked markedly less healthy than the last time. His complexion was the gray-green of a man with a serious heart condition. Michaelis wondered if they had not made a bad mistake in entrusting Jochmann with such responsibility.

"Only last night," Jochmann said, his voice barely more than a whisper, "I looked again, over everything. I examined my analysis, I checked my facts. I asked myself every question."

"And with what result?"

"You must understand, Bernhard . . . "

"I can understand only one thing, that you're ready. It's essential. We've relied on you and Bonnhoeffer alone. If you fail us in this—"

Jochmann's voice was barely audible.

"I can't. I can come almost to the conclusion you ask me for, but as a doctor, as a professional, I have ethics too, Bernhard, just as you do. I can't give evidence that I do not believe in. My opinion must be based on irrefutable, scientific reasoning."

Michaelis said nothing but reached for the briefcase he had carried into the examining room.

"Look at these. I think that they will supply the missing link in your chain of analysis."

With trembling hands, Dr. Jochmann drew out a slender sheaf of papers, photographic copies of documents on heavy, glossy paper. He stared at them, blinked, his mouth fell open. For a second, Michaelis thought that he might have a seizure then and there.

"This is unbelievable," Jochmann stammered.

"They were taken from the special files of one of Heydrich's most trusted subordinates. Just yesterday. Look at them carefully. Don't answer me yet, just read."

Dr. Jochmann stood there in the middle of the room, in his white coat, the stethoscope dangling, like a noose from his neck. His face turned white, then gray again. The liver spots darkened perceptibly.

"If this is true—" he said, aghast.

"As true as that you and I are standing here, my friend."

"Then I would have no alternative. Yes, yes, Bernhard. I would do as you wish. This seems irrefutable, yet. . . . "

"You must stand up in a courtroom, with the eyes of the entire nation on you, and say, upon your reputation as one of Germany's leading psychiatrists, that he is mad. Will you do it?"

Dr. Jochmann handed back the papers, at the same time nodding almost imperceptibly. "*If* this is all true . . . if there's actual proof. . . ."

Michaelis smiled and put the papers back in the briefcase.

"Now, why don't you go ahead with the examination and see how long I have to live, providing they let me?"

September 26, 9:00 P.M.: Vienna

Andreas Flom had taken dinner at a *weinstube* near the Art Museum. Because of the uproar in the streets it had taken him an unusually long time to get home, so long in fact that the effects of the wine he'd drunk had even begun to wear off a little. Flom disliked eating alone, but tonight there were neither clients nor buyers to provide him with company. The fever in the streets was going to ruin his business, he could see that easily enough. With a war about to break out at any minute, who was interested in rare documents, old letters, autographs, or even blackmail?

If it hadn't been for that fool Liszewsky and that bigger fool, Jankow, he thought blearily as he made his way up the dank stone stairs, he would surely have had a difficult time of it. But now his immediate future at least was assured. He was already quite comfortable and secure, thanks to Jankow. In twenty-four hours or less, he would be a rich man.

He put key to lock and went into the vestibule of his apartment. A cool breeze blew across his face. Curious—he always made sure that the windows were shut before going out. But in times like these, a man grew forgetful. Be more careful in the

222

future, yes, he would definitely have to be more careful.

As he went into his darkened sitting room, a shabby, musty little den that had begun to disgust even him, he noticed that he could still hear the mob shouting and, quite clearly, the strains of "Wacht am Rhein" coming over the loudspeakers. He could see the shadow of the large wing-backed chair by the fireplace and beyond it, an open window.

He flicked on the light and gasped.

"Good evening, Herr Flom," said the man sitting in the chair, a heavy, rather elderly man with large mustaches, who was pointing an automatic at Flom's stomach.

"My God! Who are you? What do you want of me?" Flom's voice stuck in his throat. The police? A robber? He didn't know which was worse.

"We have business, Herr Flom," said Schanz.

Flom drew a breath. Business? Could it be that the man was from Ledruc? Had the Frenchman decided that he wouldn't pay after all, that he'd take what he'd insisted he had already paid for?

Flom hesitated, then took a deep breath and a chance.

"The price still stands."

"Ah, how businesslike, Herr Flom. I admire a man who can be businesslike even when there's a gun pointed at his heart. Now. Sit down." He waved Flom into the chair opposite him.

"A whiskey?" Schanz inquired, now amiable, pouring himself a glass with one hand. "You have excellent taste in schnapps."

Flom was barely able to whisper.

"Who . . . are you? Are you from Ledruc?"

"It really doesn't matter, does it? Particularly as you'll neither see me nor hear from me ever again. Once you've given me what I've come for."

It occurred to Flom that this man could be the agent of any of fifty or more people he had extorted money from over the years. Every one of them would have happily seen him dead or worse. Yet he had always tried to be fair, to be businesslike. He'd set a price, been paid, and then handed over whatever it was he'd had. He'd never been greedy.

This was the first time; but then, the stakes had never been so high before either.

"You're trembling, Herr Flom. Don't tremble, please. I have no intention of harming you. Now or later. As long as you're not stubborn."

"I don't have any idea. . . . "

"Oh yes you do, Herr Flom. Please. We are not children, either of us. Now. The package from Graz, hand it over."

"There's no such thing."

"The papers for which you were paid fifty thousand marks already, Herr Flom. From Paris. You still have them, yes?"

Flom grew pale; it did not occur to him to say that he had already passed the papers on. He had no idea just what this man knew or who he was, and the most important thing just then seemed to be to avoid making the man angry.

"The package, Herr Flom. Now, if you please."

Still, Flom said nothing. His face was ashen; he saw not so much the snout of the Walther pointed at his stomach as the money Ledruc had agreed to pay him flying out the window.

Schanz sighed. He looked around the room. There was an ironing board in a little alcove near the door, with an electric iron sitting, cold, on top of a pile of washing. Flom apparently took care of his own limited needs. Schanz picked up the iron, hefted it, remembering the scene in the basement of Gruner's offices. He sighed again.

"I don't like to do things like this, Herr Flom, but you leave me little alternative. Here. Hold this." He dropped the iron in the startled Flom's lap.

Still holding the gun on Flom, Schanz knelt and plugged the iron in.

"What are you doing to me?" Flom croaked.

"You will hold the iron until you tell me what I want to know. If you move, I promise you, I'll shoot you. First in the leg, then—who knows where? No one will ever hear a thing, not with that racket outside."

Flom could feel the iron starting to grow warm.

"I know nothing," he stammered.

"Perhaps, but perhaps in your safe in the closet? You will tell me the combination? Better yet, you'll unlock it for me. It

224

would be a shame to scorch that fine suit of yours."

Flom started to shift about. The iron was getting hotter. He could smell the heat, the odor of starch. He began to sweat.

"No, no, not a single movement. Sit still or I promise you, a bullet. Listen." Schanz moved toward the open window. The band on the Kartnerstrasse was playing the Horst Wessel song now and the crowd was screaming even louder. He could barely hear himself speak.

Suddenly Flom let out a cry and pointed.

"All right—the safe, there."

Schanz shrugged, very much relieved. He doubted whether he could have seen it through; it just wasn't his style.

Flom dropped the iron, pulled the cord out of the wall, and went to the closet. He knelt and began turning the dial.

"There is no gun in there, is there, Herr Flom? I hope not. A crime against the state, to own such a thing. If I were you. . . ."

"There's no gun. I swear it."

Kneeling in the dark closet, Flom quickly opened the safe. For a few seconds his fingertips rested on the inner ledge.

"Are you—from Ledruc?"

"Sicherheitsdienst," said Schanz very quietly, matter-of-factly. Flom groaned. He seemed paralyzed.

"The papers," said Schanz.

Flom didn't move.

"I promise you, you will not see me again. Or any of us. If you give me the papers." He could see the packet, just inside the safe, on the upper shelf. There was nothing else there.

Flom seemed unable to move. His face was running with sweat.

"In there, on the top shelf. Take them . . . my God, look at my hands . . . look how I'm shaking. You, *you've* done this to me."

Schanz reached past the man. As he touched the edge of the envelope, he realized what a terrible mistake he'd made. Just as he knew he would, Flom suddenly threw himself against the safe door, slamming it against Schanz's arm. The gun flew from his hand. He cried out and fell over, jerked off balance.

Flom went careening across the room, knocking down

furniture and lamps. He had just reached the door to the corridor when Schanz managed to retrieve his Walther. He lay on the floor, waves of pain shooting up his arm—he was sure his wrist was broken.

Flom slammed against the door, wrenched it open, and rushed into the landing.

Schanz got off one shot. He heard a yelp—at most he had hit Flom in the leg. Certainly nothing serious.

He struggled up, cursing. He was too old for this kind of thing, too slow. Too careless.

Then he heard a crash out in the hallway. He ran out. Flom was nowhere to be seen. There was a long dribble of blood across the landing, leading right to the top of the stairs.

He looked down.

Flom lay at the bottom of the long flight of stone steps, face up, his body twisted like a discarded puppet. His eyes were wide open and there was blood both on his leg, where the bullet from the Walther had hit him, and all over his head.

Slowly, Schanz went down after him. By the time he had reached the bottom it was clear that Flom was dead. From the look of him, his neck was broken. The shot had hit him in the foot and he'd tripped going down the stairs.

So that was that.

In the dim hall light, Schanz took the papers out of the envelope. There were three sheets, each in the same clumsy hand. The paper was very old, yellowed and almost crumbling. On one of the sheets there was a date, clumsily but clearly written: March 15, 1838.

He read quickly. They were almost the same, all three of the notes. Thank you for the money, honored sir. Little Alois is well. We are doing our best. He will be educated, he will have enough food to eat, thanks to your generosity. Thank you, honored sir. Again and again. Bitter, but restrained.

He was not surprised, either, when he came to the signature, the same on all three letters.

Now, at last, he knew for certain what the entries "MAS and Son" in the ancient Frankenberger Verlag bank records had meant—all fifteen years of them.

Schanz stuck the envelope back into his pocket and went

to the doorway where he stood for a moment, listening. The crowd was still roaring, the band still playing.

Then he went out. He felt calm for the first time in a very long while.

September 26, 10:15 P.M.: London

She lay exhausted on the bed, the curtains of her hotel room window drawn tight against the insistently damp London night. The radio on the washstand crackled and spat like a logfire, the voice of the BBC announcer barely audible. He was paraphrasing—in English—the news she had just heard by direct transmission from Nuremberg in German, the harsh, hysterical voice of Adolf Hitler inveighing against both his real and his imaginary enemies.

Midway through the speech she had become vaguely aware of another voice. It was a moment more before she realized that it was her own.

"My God, my God, my God," she had muttered, over and over.

Too much. How was she to bear it all? It seemed at that moment as though all the terrible events of the past few days had been directed against her personally. None of it had had anything to do with politics, with the Czechs, or the Sudeten Germans, or even with men named Heinlein, or Hitler or Halifax or Himmler . . .

How odd—all those H's. A sinister letter, she thought. Shaped like a guillotine frame.

She reached for the silver water bottle on the night stand and for the aspirin in the little enameled Hungarian pill box her grandmother had left her.

Suddenly, the phone began to ring. She recoiled, then reached out for it.

"Yes?"

"Frau Trcka?" It was a bland, disconcertingly affable voice with a profoundly British accent. "Frau Trcka there, please?"

"Yes, the Frau Baronin Trcka is speaking. Who is this, please?"

"Ah yes, Frau Ter-ska. Have I got it properly? An unusual

227

name, you know. Well then, of course you don't know me. My name is Mullberry, Doctor Herbert Mullberry. You see, I was asked to call. A friend of yours, I beieve."

"Who is it who told you to do this? His name?"

"You *do* know a Dr. Gerhard Jochmann, don't you?"

She grew instantly suspicious. Jochmann was a friend of Michaelis. Bernhard had often spoken of him and she had no doubt that he, too, was involved in the conspiracy.

"What have you to do with this Dr. Jochmann, please?"

"My, my—no one's told you then, have they? I feel rather the fool, you know."

"Please go on."

"I'm to tell you that all the arrangements have been made, you see. But of course you have no idea what I'm talking about, do you? Dr. Jochmann was so insistent—he asked specifically that I call you personally, as soon as a bed was available."

"Pardon? A bed?"

"At the Mullberry Sanitorium, of course. At my sanitorium, Madame. A few miles south of Chelmsford. I must say, you *do* sound surprised . . . I hope. . . ."

"And what am I to do at this—sanitorium? Please continue."

The frighteningly matter-of-fact voice at the other end of the line went on.

"Why, rest, of course. No more than two weeks, Madame. I'm afraid we simply can't manage more than that. We're full up, you see. But we'll certainly take good care of you while you're with us. I can assure you of that. I promised Dr. Jochmann. We have a great deal of respect for him here. A fine gentleman and a fine doctor. Naturally, when he asked us to make room, no matter what the inconvenience. . . ."

"You needn't worry," she snapped.

"I beg your pardon, Madame?"

"I won't be troubling you."

She slammed the phone down so hard that the entire mechanism almost fell from the stand.

Did they take her for a complete fool? Could they possibly assume that she would believe such a fantastic story? She had never thought the SD would be so clumsy—or perhaps it was the Gestapo or even Amt VI.* It was so absurd. She began to laugh hysterically. Did they really suppose it would be necessary to lure her to some out-of-the-way place, to take her back by force or to kill her in secret? If anything had happened, and she had no doubt now that it had, she would be at the airport within an hour and on the first plane back. Whatever else she might have been during her life, she had never been a coward, and she had no intention of letting August or Michaelis go to the block alone.

Besides, if they had failed, what else was there for her, for any of them?

It took her over twenty minutes to get through to the Vienna operator and another five to reach Schloss Trcka.

The voice on the other end, quite distinct, was not that of old Fessler who usually took all phone calls. Rather, it belonged to no one she knew—a cold, grating, rather aloof voice that sent a tight knot of panic slamming into her stomach.

"Yes? I can't hear you. Who *is* this?"

"Who are *you?* Where is Fessler?"

"This is Dr. Stozl. Who is calling, please? You must identify yourself."

"This is the Frau Baronin Trcka. I wish to speak to my husband. At once."

"That is not possible."

"And why is it not possible?"

"Because he is resting, Frau Baronin. He cannot come to the phone." There was a long pause. "And where are you calling from, Frau Baronin?"

"Never mind that. Why can't he come to the phone?"

"He is resting. I told you that." The man's voice grew irritated, imperious. "We had to give him a sedative."

"*What* is the matter with him?"

"There is no need to worry."

"What is the matter?" She was almost shouting now.

The doctor paused. She could almost hear him thinking, trying to decide just what to tell her.

Whatever he said, it would be a lie.

---

* The Foreign Intelligence Section of the Reich Central Security Office.

"Nervous exhaustion, Frau Baronin. One could call it that. It is not serious, I assure you. When are you coming back, Frau Baronin?"

She remained quite silent for a moment and then, with quiet deliberation, said:

"Do you hear me, Dr. Stozl? Are you there? Operator, there is something the matter with the connection. . . . Operator, can you hear me?"

Then she pressed the disconnect and hung up the phone.

For a long time she simply sat there on the bed, her hands folded together in her lap to still the trembling.

She did not want to seem afraid. Even to herself.

September 27, 10:00 A.M.: Vienna

Sudermeyer took off the headphones that were attached to the telephone intercept system in the basement of the building where Philippe Ledruc had his apartment. A pot of coffee bubbled on a spirit burner. A glass dish at his elbow was full of cigarette stubs and half a dozen paperback books and magazines lay around on the cellar floor. He had been there, waiting for the call from the Landsbank, for almost nineteen hours.

He picked up the phone and rang Major Langbein's special number.

Finally, someone picked up.

Sudermeyer recognized Langbein's characteristically exasperated breathing on the other end before the major spoke even a single syllable.

"The Landsbank has just called, sir. The money is in."

"Ledruc?"

"The Frenchman's on his way. I saw him go out less than a minute ago." There was a small window at the upper edge of the cellar wall that gave a good view of the front steps. Sudermeyer had seen Ledruc's brightly polished, pointed French shoes go by just as he had taken the earphones off.

"Anything for me to do here, sir?"

"Pack up and don't leave a trace."

"Understood, sir."

"Now, follow him over to the Landsbank, then out to the

Prater after him. With your glasses again, just as before. His meeting is at noon. This time we want to know every word."

"Understood, sir."

Langbein hung up.

Sudermeyer packed his equipment. He could stow it in the back of the little Opel he'd used coming over. It would be safe enough there. He worried about that equipment. He didn't want to be paying for it for the next five years out of his monthly paycheck. That had happened to someone he knew, a sergeant in the 23rd, who'd lost a howitzer up a telephone pole when the pintel pin had come loose going around a curve. He couldn't afford anything like that, and who could tell, the electronic equipment he'd drawn out was probably at least as costly as a howitzer. He drew little enough as it was.

But enough to buy some cigarettes. That was what he needed most. He'd just realized that he was down to his last two.

He went back upstairs, feeling pleased with himself. So pleased that he decided to splurge; he'd buy two packs of English. "Sailors," if he could find them.

September 27, 1:00 P.M.: Vienna

"Apparently no one feels like being amused today," Henkl said sourly. "Amazing. Our good Viennese are showing some common sense at last. War actually threatens to make the ferris wheel obsolete. The next thing you know, they'll even stop eating five meals a day."

He was fooling no one with this kind of talk; his face was drawn, his eyes red and feverish. Langbein had shown him the enlargements from the Kepplinger files. He had seen the reports, the letter from London, all of it.

He glanced at Langbein. The major gave no evidence of having heard him. He was looking around. The Prater was almost deserted. The weather had helped; great gusts of abnormally cold wind were rolling in from the east over the mountains. A frost the night before had killed all of the fall flowers and the leaves were already turning gray, weeks ahead of schedule. In a little while, the foliage of the city would be as bleak as the complexion of its inhabitants.

A few lone equestrians cantered along the bridal paths, absurd and incongruous in their formal riding attire. The circus rides kept at it, pumping music into the air, but hardly anyone came. The three coffeehouses were empty; a few gloomy citizens sat in corners, reading their newspapers for the fourth or fifth time that day, hoping that somehow the news would change on the next reading.

The giant ferris wheel revolved slowly, as though it were dying, carrying hardly half a dozen passengers each cycle. From where Langbein and Henkl stood, they could see a long convoy of covered army trucks going by on the Hauptallee, just outside the park. The soldiers in the back weren't singing. They were just sitting there, looking stunned and sullen. No one had really believed that it was going to happen. Not again.

Langbein looked at his watch. It was almost time. The toolshed was a good place to be on a day like this, a shelter from the nasty wind instead of the oven it had been on the last go round.

The ticket seller for the ferris wheel was an Abwehr man. So was the attendant who sat the riders in their compartments. Altogether, in addition to Langbein and Henkl, there were six more operatives stationed around the wheel. The Abwehr was, in fact, the wheel's most aggressive patron that day. Ever since Langbein had seen the photostats, he had tripled his forces. If he'd had more men available, he would have put them there too. If he could have filled the entire Prater with his staff, he would have done it. The skin on the back of his neck puckered every time he thought of the file and how bad the truth really was. And now that he knew, he and the rest of his people were far too deep into it to extricate themselves.

There had been no question of simply sending a squad out and arresting Flom. That way he would have gotten the man but probably not the papers. With Operation Green about to break around their heads, he had no time for interrogations, searches, even torture. He had to have the documents at once, and the only way to get them was to flush Flom out with the papers in his hands; allowing him to go ahead with his transaction was the only sure way of doing it.

232

He'd told Henkl the truth. He owed him that much. Henkl hadn't batted an eye. He'd remained silent for a moment, then simply shaken his head. He'd made no comment since then, but Langbein had noticed how carefully he'd checked his weapons, how he'd loaded up not the Walther PK he usually carried but a heavy-duty Luger P.08, which would not only knock a man down but throw him against a wall five meters away.

Just what was he to do now? Suppose they did catch Flom? Suppose that the papers Ledruc was willing to pay 100,000 marks for did in fact provide the final proofs missing from the Kepplinger file? What the devil would he do with them? He doubted that even Canaris would have the answer for that one.

From the carousel not far down the walk came the strains of "The Count of Luxembourg Waltz," the prearranged signal that announced Ledruc's appearance. Hartmann would be right behind him now and Wolff not far to his left, herding him toward the ticket booth.

"I still don't see why we didn't go for Flom directly," said Henkl, fingering his Luger.

"Because unless the timing was absolutely perfect, there's no telling what he might have done with the documents. Sixty seconds and we might lose them. Or they might be hidden somewhere. It could take us days to get the information out of him."

"Not if we turned him over to Kepplinger," Henkl said. Langbein refused to respond.

Henkl shook his head and checked the gun again.

"You're not going to shoot him, so stop fooling with that."

"It might be the better way, for all of us," replied Henkl.

"It might be, but you're not going to do it."

"No, I'm not," said Henkl, but his tone was far from reassuring.

"That's an order. Unless he fires first, which he won't."

Just then Ledruc came into sight at the end of the pathway. He was walking warily, and with a slight limp. He stopped to blow his nose and looked behind him once. Hartmann kept right on walking and went past him, then sat down on a bench to tie his shoe. Of Flom there was no sign as yet.

233

Ledruc stopped. He seemed to sense that something was wrong. He moved back a few paces, then forward, then back again, as though trying to make up his mind.

Henkl whispered harshly, "The last time, he waited until Flom had gone into the enclosure. It's the same thing again. He won't move until Flom shows himself."

"Where the devil is Flom? He should have been here by now."

Ledruc was getting more and more nervous. He was looking around, from side to side. The area around the Reisenrad was empty, exposed. There was only one person beyond the enclosure waiting to get on.

"Where *is* the man," Langbein complained, looking at his watch. The sweat was rolling down his long face in spite of the chill in the air, and he looked almost comically unhappy.

Ledruc, by this time, was pacing around the ticket booth and, like Langbein, looking constantly at his watch. The gate closed and the ferris wheel started to move. Ledruc kept patting his jacket pocket. The money, of course.

The shed was cold. Henkl shuddered. Sudermeyer had his glasses trained on the Frenchman but was picking up nothing except a great deal of nervous lip licking and swallowing.

Ten minutes passed and still no trace of Flom.

Suddenly, Ledruc turned about sharply, as though he had come all at once to the conclusion that he was better out of the affair entirely. He started to walk away, very quickly.

"Don't move," Langbein warned. Henkl leaned against the door of the shed—a little too heavily. Suddenly it gave way and he fell out headlong, sprawling onto the ground, the Luger flying from his hand.

Ledruc, startled by the sudden movement and the noise, whirled around, a look of horror on his face. Hartmann jumped up from the bench and ran toward him while Wolff moved in from behind.

"Damn you, you did that on purpose," Langbein shouted, rushing out of the shed and past Henkl, who had by now retrieved the Luger but was still on his knees.

Langbein was astonished at how fast the Frenchman moved; he had taken him for a man of about fifty and assumed that he would be no match for a young man like Hartmann or even Henkl. But Ledruc was off and running down the path like a rabbit. Hartmann was making no progress at all. The gap between them lengthened.

"I can bring him down. I've got a clear shot," Henkl cried.

Langbein stopped in his tracks, whirled, and knocked the gun from Henkl's hand.

"That would be the worst, the *worst* thing."

But there was no question of a clear shot or of any shot. A crowd of children, the first of the day, had just turned the corner by the carousel. Ledruc crashed through them and was gone around the other side of the building in a twinkling.

"It just isn't possible," said Wolff, coming up behind them, breathless and panting. "How could the man move so fast?"

"He wants to stay alive," Langbein said. "And if we feel the same way, Sergeant, I suggest we all start running a little harder too."

Just at that moment there was a furious braying of horns and another convoy of military wagons with motorcycle outriders whirled by along the Austellung-allee, completely blocking the way. Military policemen with white gloves shouted and waved. The trucks rolled on by, sending up a cloud of dust and autumn leaves.

Langbein stood there, his mouth hanging open. Even if he had been in uniform, he could not have stopped the convoy to get across.

But Ledruc had made it across, just ahead of the lead truck and the first wave of motorcycles. There was not a trace of him to be seen.

Langbein stood there for a second, then whirled angrily on Henkl.

"All right, you know what's next. Damn it, you wanted it this way. Now we've got to go for Flom, haven't we?"

From the head of the Blutgasse, Langbein could see that a small crowd had gathered in front of the entrance to Flom's shop. A number of helmeted Orpo were trying to push a small but intensely curious crowd back away from the building. One of the policemen was standing by the door to the building, holding it open. A man carrying a black medical bag was just emerging. A lazarette wagon stood, two tires up on the pavement, its rear door yawning open a few meters away.

Across the street, standing back at a respectful distance, was one of Major Eisenbach's men, a young fellow dressed in the uniform of a lance-corporal. With him was a girl who, a week before, had been a typist in the communications section at the Strassengel cantonment. The lance-corporal saw Henkl and signalled with a brief wave of his hand that he should stay where he was.

Henkl took Langbein's arm and dug his fingers in hard.

"We wait here, sir."

"Klaus? What is this?"

"Wait. There's the lookout, the one we had in the building opposite the shop."

A man in a blue boiler suit was standing a little way apart from the lance-corporal and his woman, just at the entrance to a small coffeehouse. Henkl led Langbein over to him. The major seemed dazed by what they had both seen, frightened without knowing why. He was sweating and looking constantly at the door where the Orpo was nervously waiting.

Just then, two men came out carrying a stretcher with a sheet over it.

The man in the boiler suit pulled Henkl into a doorway.

"It's the owner of the shop over there, the one we were watching. The mail carrier found him this morning at the foot of the stairs. He'd fallen and broken his neck, they say."

Langbein watched intently, with an ever-increasing feeling of dread, as the stretcher was loaded onto the lazarette wagon. The part of the sheet along the leg was saturated with blood. It was obvious that Flom had done more than break his neck. He'd been cut or shot, and badly too.

"You heard nothing?" Langbein demanded.

The lookout shook his head. "All last night there was a rally up there in the Stephansplatz. You couldn't hear yourself fart, sir. If you'll pardon me, sir."

Henkl gave him a sour look but said nothing.

"But," the man went on, "we did get something."

"Yes?"

236

"About seven this morning, someone came out of the building. We hadn't seen anyone go in because of the rally and the parade. The street was very crowded, sir, and it could have happened any time. But this man we saw come out, it could have been the man from Graz. Heavy-set, old-looking, wearing a rumpled coat."

"Kaiser Wilhelms?"

"Yes sir, as fine a pair as you'd want to see."

"Schanz, damn him," Henkl exclaimed, smashing a fist into his palm.

"Captain, we thought it was peculiar. He stood around as though he knew someone was watching him and he wanted to be seen."

"So, of course, you let him go?" Langbein said; he was looking beyond, to the Orpo and the wagon. They had just closed the doors and the crowd was beginning to disperse.

"No, sir, he's being followed. We know exactly where he is. Upstairs, there's a radio, if you want to make contact with the car. It seems he's headed back to Graz."

The wagon pulled down off the curb and the siren began its up-down, up-down whooping.

"And, sir," said the lookout, "there's one more thing. I heard one of the Orpo say so. . . ."

"What's that?"

"They think a burglary was involved. The safe in the dead man's apartment was open. But they say it was very odd. The money wasn't touched."

Langbein nodded to Henkl, but not a word was needed. Henkl was already clattering upstairs to the radio set.

September 27, 4:00 P.M.: Berlin

All afternoon the skies above Berlin had been threatening rain, but not a drop had fallen. The air was hot and dry and difficult to breathe.

General von Witzleben sat fuming in the rear of an open Mercedes staff car at the head of the Second Motorized Division as it proceeded slowly down the Wilhelmstrasse. They had already passed through the workers' quarters where they had met

237

only sullen faces and threatening gestures. The soldiers, themselves frightened and confused, had tried to ignore their reception and had marched on, straight ahead, toward the Wilhelmstrasse and the Chancellery where Hitler was waiting to review them.

The Twenty-Second Infantry Division, under General Count von Brockdorff, followed the armored cars and motorcycles of Von Witzleben's division in strict step and full pack.

To those watching from the sidewalk, it appeared as though the troops were heading for the railroad station to entrain. Why else, on such a stifling day, would they be marching with full battle gear and equipment?

Von Witzleben stared straight ahead, his eyes barely visible under the peak of his cap.

"If this is what that lump of horse-shit wants, then this is what he shall have," Von Witzleben thought. His adjutant, sitting next to him, scowled at the sullen onlookers and at the sky as well. "If only it would open up and give us a little lightning and thunder. Our good German people always go for a little spectacle. If you want an omen, what's better than thunder and lightning?"

The steady tramp of men, the rumble of trucks, and the hornet's buzz of motorcycles continued. The staff car moved forward. Once, Von Witzleben turned slightly. Directly behind him came an honor guard of horsemen, then a contingent of artillery, drawn by trucks.

That afternoon, Von Witzleben had been in touch with General Hoepner in Thuringia. Hoepner had command of the First Light Division and had been given orders earlier that day to turn his troops toward the Czech border. What a bitter irony. Now, without need for subterfuge of any kind, Hoepner would be in perfect position to bar any attempt by the *Leibstandarte Adolf Hitler* to fight its way into Berlin to relieve the Chancellery. General Halder was ready, and Von Stuelpnagel had been acting as liaison all week, working out the final details.

The parade swept past the Ministry of Justice. Von Witzleben smiled. There would be "justice" soon enough.

Major Heinz's men were waiting for the order to go to the Chancellery and arrest the maniac, and it would be no surprise if the rest of their preparations—confinement in the Charité, then trial—were rendered unnecessary. Major Heinz still had the attitudes of a Freikorpskampfer. If he was left to his own devices, it would all be over in two minutes. And who was there to stop him? He, Von Witzleben, had protested; there was to be no killing. But after the events of the last few days, he had determined not to lift a finger to stop Heinz.

Von Witzleben's car came within sight of the Reichschancellery. He could just make out Hitler's figure up on the balcony, surrounded by his staff. It would be so simple to stop the march right in front of that balcony, unlimber a few guns, and blow the bastard out of everyone's lives. He swore angrily to himself; he was beginning to think like Heinz.

Time enough. First the German people had to see, *really see*, once and for all, just what a maniac the man was. It was obvious from the long faces, the empty sidewalks, the closed windows that had greeted them all along the line of march, that bellicose speeches in sports arenas were one thing and actual war quite another. The issuance of ration cards the week before had certainly thrown cold water on the festive mood in which the Führer's speeches had been received during the past six weeks.

It was one thing to bully the Czechs. It was another to take on not only President Beneš but France and England as well. At first, Von Witzleben had been afraid that Chamberlain and his conciliatory attitude would ruin everything. But the Führer, true to form, had at the last moment delivered an impossible ultimatum. There was no way in the world even a Chamberlain could give in now. Without the slightest doubt, there would be war this time. Within twenty-four hours.

Von Witzleben cocked his head to one side and looked up.

He could see the Chancellor clearly now, up there on the balcony. Hitler's head was lowered, his right shoulder visibly jerking. He was obviously agitated, deeply disturbed by what he saw.

Von Witzleben turned to his ADC, Major Stroessner.

239

"What d'you think, Rudi? Are they ready yet?"

The major's gaze swept the almost empty Wilhelmstrasse. The only real movement was the endless line of troops, the tanks, the motorcycles, and the trucks. And the flapping swastika banners over Hitler's balcony.

"It's time, Herr General. They're ready, all right."

The parade moved on, passing directly under the balcony. Von Witzleben refused to look up.

He was still thinking how easy it would be to unhitch a few howitzers and end it all right then and there.

September 27, 5:00 P.M.*: Aspern Airfield, Vienna*

The airport was crowded with transports. The clumsy, corrugated JU-52s came and went like giant armored insects. The sleek, immensely long Condors waited, like the birds of prey for which they were named, dark and menacing on the side runways, loaded with supplies and lacking only their bombs and crews.

Because of the jam-up, it had been almost impossible to get out of Aspern. Henkl and his pilot had been waiting on the runway for over an hour.

"You can't smoke here, Captain," the pilot kept reminding him.

"The devil I can't. If we blow up, we blow up. It's God's will and that's that."

The pilot sighed and kept looking up at the sky. It was dark although it was only late afternoon. The smudgy gray clouds dropped lower by the minute, and a relentless wind swept a cold mist over the field from end to end. The drops glistened on the Stork's greenhouse.

"When, damn it? When?" thought Henkl. He knew exactly what was going on and why he couldn't get off the ground, but that hardly made it any better. In fact, it made it considerably worse. A mobilization; the Wehrmacht was on full alert. Operation Green was actually only hours away. General von Witzleben was massing his troops outside of Berlin and

240

Christ only knew what Oster and the others were getting ready to do.

It had all happened so fast. Henkl could still see the stretcher covered by the bloody sheet and hear the whoop-whoop of the siren as the body was carried away. He'd known it. He'd felt it in his bones that something like that would happen. Only death stopped avaricious swine like Flom. He could have told Langbein that if he'd only asked.

And what stopped a man like Schanz?

What made him do the things he did? Henkl ached with frustration. How was he possibly to know, to understand? He had never even met the man, spoken to him, had time to study him.

A man as clever as Schanz was supposed to be simply didn't allow himself to be followed like that without a reason. Eisenbach's man reported that he had followed him out of the city to the road to Neustadt, heading south from Vienna. There was no question in anyone's mind. It was as they'd thought. Schanz was going back to Graz.

He had been followed as far as Murzzuschlag by the first team and picked up just south of the town by the second car, brought up from Graz by radio.

But why? Why so obvious? It rankled Henkl that he simply could not fathom the man's motives. It would have made far more sense had he headed back to Berlin.

Henkl lit another cigarette and began to hum a Bach passacaglia. What difference did it all make? Another six hours and it would all be over.

The sky suddenly opened up and a freezing rain doused his cigarette. He swore. Water sluiced down his collar. He pulled his cap tight over his forehead.

The radio began to spit. The control tower was trying to make itself heard.

"Sixteen nine, are you prepared for take-off? We have clearance. You are clear on runway seven. You have six minutes, sixteen nine. Please proceed at once."

The pilot shrugged and climbed up into the greenhouse, beckoning Henkl after him.

For a moment Henkl just stood there in the pelting rain, as though he hadn't heard. Then he climbed up.

Another flight of "Iron Annies" was just coming in from the west.

Loaded with troops.

September 27, 7:00 P.M.: Graz

Schanz stood for a moment in the basement of the Rathaus, a puddle of water forming around his feet. His coat was sodden, his hat a shapeless mass. He shivered, shifted the ring of iron keys from one hand to another, and approached the vault door with the same dignified deliberateness that a man mounting a scaffold might hope to achieve.

There had been but one sleepy night guard on duty, the same man who had been there on his earlier visit—one of Gruner's people. Fine. Not only had the man recognized him and let him pass without so much as a question, but he would be useful later on. Schanz knew exactly what to do.

He had seen the soldier and the girl across the street when he had left Flom's shop; there again, just as they had been the day before. And a man in the window opposite as well, with field glasses. He had made sure they had seen him, backing the little Daimler around so that all three of them could get a good clear view of the license plate. And he had moved very slowly going out of Vienna, so as to give whoever might be following ample time to pick him up.

He had seen no one until he was well out onto the southbound autobahn. A small car had appeared, far behind him, and had hung there, just barely visible, all the way to Murzzuschlag. Then another had appeared and tailed him to Graz. Once into the city, he had managed to elude the man, but had parked his car right in front of the Rathaus where it was sure to be seen. He needed time, at the right intervals, that was all.

It was the first time in his life he had ever trusted Kepplinger. If he'd been wrong, or had been deliberately lying and it was not the Abwehr that was trailing him, then he was a dead man.

He refused even to think about it.

242

He turned the key and the heavy doors swung open, revealing the long, dusty stone chambers. He felt almost comfortable there, among the shelves of old ledgers, the ancient birth and death registers, the bank records and land transfer books. It was, after all, among just such books that he had spent most of his life.

He glanced at his watch and went in. The whole process should not take more than a half hour at most.

He surveyed the ranks of ledgers, astonished all over again at how far back they went. There were the records, laboriously inscribed by armies of faceless clerks and scriveners, the records of every withdrawal and deposit by every customer of every bank in Graz from 1780 until the fall of the Emperor, when the banking system had been reorganized under the new republic.

He knew exactly where to look, even without Bernkassler's assistance; his memory was at least that good. He smiled. He had been there before, seen the same thing. Only now he knew what it meant.

The records were perfectly ordered. For each year, the bank's account books were entered alphabetically, by depositor, with every transaction listed neatly below.

He had only to locate the "F" volume and turn to "Frankenberger Verlag."

He had seen the cryptic entries for the first time in the 1836 volume, but according to the information he now had, they should start some time earlier. Why not start at the beginning?

He took down the required volume and spread it on the table, turning pages with a keen anticipation.

It was there, neatly written in a tight, precise hand. "Frankenberger Verlag, Graz," and below the name, in smaller, even more precise entries, three pages of transactions. Every deposit, every withdrawal.

He took out his notepad and a pencil and began to read.

Purchases, routine commercial transactions, regular deposits, all showing a general increase in the firm's fortunes. Nothing at all unusual. He began to grow uneasy. Had he been wrong? Was it possible? Or had he simply gone back too far?

243

He took down the next volume and then the next. Still nothing. Bales of yard goods, dyes, thread, machinery, needles, payments to vendors, receipts from all kind of commercial establishments.

1835: nothing.

1836: nothing.

1837: nothing.

Then he found it, a simple entry, not really unusual in itself, but odd simply because it was different from the others in three almost unnoticeable respects.

First, the entry was clearly an acronym: "MAS and Son."

Second, it was the first of a series of regular monthly withdrawals in favor of the same "firm." And third, each withdrawal was for exactly the same amount.

He set the ledger aside and took down the next year's volume. The entries continued, regular as a quartermaster's monthly requisitions. He put the book on the pile and took the next.

The entries went on, continued in fact for fifteen years, finally stopping in 1852. He noted them all down, making a list of his own in his notepad, each month, each withdrawal. At the beginning, the clerks had not entered addresses for creditors in whose favor withdrawals were made; but by 1840, most of the entries carried an identifying location, a city or town, as well as the name of the firm or agent and the amount.

It all fitted now. Meinhard—the man whom he had seen on the stairs that night at Kepplinger's office—Meinhard was from Linz. That was why Kepplinger had summoned him. And God only knew what *he* had found.

"MAS and Son" seemed to be located in Strones, near Linz.

Schanz noted it down. He knew his history well enough, and also his geography. In the mid-1800s, Strones was still little more than a post stop. What business could there have been in such a place as might have had regular transactions for fifteen years with a large and successful firm in Graz—a firm like Frankenberger Verlag? No, MAS and Son stood for exactly what he thought it stood for.

The payments were not commercial transactions at all but

support payments to the mother of the younger Franken-berger's bastard son.

And the initials stood, unquestionably, for Maria Anna Schicklgruber. . . .

From a window on the second floor of the Rathaus, over the stair landing, Schanz looked out into the rain-streaked night. The downpour had let up again. Vast puddles filled the street, dappled by the lighter rain that was now falling, soft and soundless as a mist.

The car was there once more, parked well up the street, almost invisible behind a line of elder trees. Ther was only one man in the car. He had no way of knowing just who it was. He had to believe in what Kepplinger had said, he had no other choice. If it was his own people, or IVA agents, he was a dead man. If it was the Abwehr, as Kepplinger had warned, then he had a chance.

On the way out, lugging the heavy suitcase stuffed with ledgers, he spoke hastily to the night guard. The man was to call Inspector Gruner at once and tell him to go with a few men to the top of the Schlossberg and wait, by the funicular landing. In an hour, there would be something for them there, very important.

The guard saluted and Schanz left the building. The rain had let up and for a moment a pale, cold moon became visible through a rent in the clouds. Schanz thought of his son, out in some sodden field along the Czech border, waiting, as he was, for what was to come.

Pray God he was still there and that he stayed there for at least the rest of the night.

He got into his car and switched on the lights. The car at the end of the street did the same.

He looked at his watch. Gruner would need a half hour at least. Fine; it was a nice night for a drive.

September 27, 7:30 P.M.: Vienna

Count Marogna-Redwitz looked grim and exhausted. He sat behind his desk, as rigidly as if posing for a photograph.

In full colonel's uniform, a plate of sandwiches by his elbow barely touched, he was twisting a pencil between his thumb and index finger, a sure sign that he was having difficulty controlling himself.

From the screened window of his office, he could see the searchlights scything over Vienna, touching the spire of the Stephanskirche, the Rathaus, even the ferris wheel way off in the Prater. So far, no sirens at least. No French bombing planes.

"You hardly need *me* to point out the implications of this . . . this *thing*." Redwitz said, touching the photostats of the Kepplinger file. He drew his fingers quickly away, as though the paper were burning hot.

"Hardly," agreed Langbein. He was on his fourth cigar since entering.

"If this is true—if it can actually be proven—it will mean the end of that lunatic once and for all. No one will lift a finger to help him." Redwitz looked stricken, as though the weight of the world's insanity and brutality had settled all at once on his shoulders alone. He sighed. "It would explain so much, particularly if he knew, if he even feared for it. Can you imagine the thought eating away at him, making him into what he is today?"

"Just like Torquemada," replied Langbein, touching the file tab which carried the same title that Heydrich had given the dossier. "How ironic, how terrible it would be, if everything, all of this, has been merely the ranting of a paranoid consumed with self-hate."

Redwitz looked out of the window. A flight of planes was passing high over the spire of the Stephanskirche.

"Will Captain Henkl be able to find the proof?"

"We know where Kepplinger's man is. He seems to be running . . . perhaps he's realized his own position at last. The Greeks weren't the only ones who slaughtered bringers of evil tidings. A few hours and we'll have him and whatever he's found besides."

"And Heydrich? Why did he do this? What did he intend?"

"We can only assume," said Langbein thoughtfully, "but the assumption would seem borne out by the facts that we now

246

have. If I had to commit myself, I'd say that he's done it in order to give himself some protection against Himmler. As you know, Himmler has tried to play the same grotesque joke on Heydrich before. We know he was behind it the last time and, surely, Heydrich does too. For years now, he's used the threat, the rumor, to keep Heydrich in line. The lie about the step-father named Süss, the possible truth about the mother whose name, according to the headstone, was—after all—Sarah. Who can tell? Insurance? What better insurance could he have than to possess real proof of the same thing with respect to the Reichschancellor himself?"

Redwitz looked at his watch.

"Six hours to go, Ernst. No more than that, Von Witzleben is ready. Major Heinz is ready. All it lacks is for that madman to actually declare war. Then, like Wallenstein, he falls. Damn him, he falls."

"And if it is proven," thought Langbein, "if this insane thing is actually true, he will never, ever rise again."

September 27, 9.00 P.M.: Graz

It had started raining again.

The Daimler was right where Eisenbach's man had said it would be, parked on the Sackstrasse, a little way short of the landing stage for the cog-railway that ran up the side of the Schlossberg to the castle gardens at the top.

Henkl waited under cover of some trees, hoping that the downpour would let up. But the rain continued to beat down relentlessly.

Finally, he gave up. There was nothing for it but to get drenched again. It would be possible to approach the car along the treeline, partially under cover. He squinted into the driving rain, hoping to catch sight of Kepplinger's man. But thus far there was only the car. Empty. Just standing there.

"The son of a bitch, where is he hiding?" Henkl checked for his gun. He still had the Luger, on full automatic. Good. The Walther would have been a liability in such weather.

He approached the car, painfully aware that Kepplinger's man could be almost anyplace, hidden, watching him.

"But why here? What does he want here?"

The car was empty, he could see that from a fair distance. No, the man wasn't on the floor, and the trunk was far too small. He had to be around somewhere, doing something, but where?

None of it made sense. There was no reason for Schanz to be back in Graz. If he had the documents, whatever it was that Flom had been trying to sell to the now vanished Ledruc, why had he come back to Graz? The lookout had picked him up again coming out of the Rathaus, carrying a large satchel. Why hadn't he gone straight back to Kepplinger? Why come here, to the Schlossberg, in a driving rain?

Only if the man was running from his own masters did it even begin to make sense . . .

Henkl moved cautiously up the path toward the funicular staging. The little ticket booth and the landing platform were empty. It was the only direction in which Schanz could have gone.

He noticed something on the ground, floating in a puddle —a leather strap, the kind used on old-fashioned satchels. Schanz had had just such a satchel coming out of the Rathaus, no?

All right. But be very careful. Keep to the trees.

He loosened the Luger in his holster, let his hand rest on the butt. Ahead of him, the little cog-railway began its tortuous ascent to the top of the Schlossberg. The chain in front of the landing stage was down.

Curious.

He stepped out into the open. There was nothing else to do. And why not? Kepplinger's man had no idea who *he* was. He could not possibly be recognized.

Again, something curious—the sliding door of the funicular's cab was open. It should have been closed, locked up for the night. The rain was sweeping into the passenger cab, forming pools around the seat where the motorman normally sat.

Then he saw it.

On a seat inside the cab, on the opposite side from the door, was a large brown satchel.

He looked around carefully, slowly. No one. He was sure

248

that Kepplinger's man must be watching him. He had to be there. Very well. He knew he was being set up. He was no fool. He knew he was the mouse going for the cheese; but he had no choice.

He went over to the cab. The satchel lay on its side, dry, well away from the door. He could see that it was full of heavy, very old ledger books.

From the Rathaus? If so, what were they?

Henkl hesitated, then ducked quickly into the empty cab, crouching low. His free hand went out for the satchel.

Suddenly the cab gave a violent lurch and the door slid shut with a crash. The motor barked and the cab shot forward up the tracks.

Henkl was thrown against the seat, hitting his shoulder. The Luger skittered across the floor.

The cab continued to climb—too fast, much too fast. Henkl swayed from side to side. The ascent was steep, unnerving under the best of circumstances. Henkl was sure that the car would jolt from the tracks at any second and plummet down the steep incline. Already he could see the little landing stage far below, like a pale gray postage stamp. Trees swept by. The cab, exposed on the open side of the incline, took the wind with little grace, swaying perilously and threatening at any moment to topple from its tracks.

Henkl cursed. It was plain enough now. Kepplinger's man had been in the control room, watching him—probably through field glasses—and he had deliberately walked right into it.

Just then the cab ground to a stop as precipitously as it had started.

The little emergency phone by the motorman's seat began to ring. Henkl stared. He was trapped, hung halfway up the side of the mountain.

He picked up the phone, knowing what he would hear.

"Good evening," said a calm, almost merry voice on the other end.

"Nicely done. I walked right into it."

"You knew. You wanted to walk."

"How else was I to find you?"

"And so you have, after a fashion." There was a pause. "I

can see you clearly through my glasses, so don't try anything unwise. The door is locked. It would take a crowbar, which you don't have, to get out. And I warn you, don't try to shoot the lock off. The ricochet could kill you in there. The whole thing is lined with steel plate. For the protection of the riders, of course."

Henkl drew a breath. He looked out, grew dizzy. The rain continued smashing at the cab.

"All right. What do you want? Why didn't you just shoot me?"

Schanz laughed mirthlessly. "First of all—exactly who are you?"

"As I can't see why it should hurt to tell you, Klaus Henkl, Captain, Abwehr, Department Nine, Vienna."

"As I suspected. You're not, of course, from IVA, are you?"

"No. You must have the papers that were in my car by now. Why do you ask?"

"Not yet I haven't. But you're right, I could check in a minute, and if you were lying . . ."

"You'd kill me?"

"Exactly."

"I've told you the truth."

"You'd better have," replied Schanz. "Now, listen to me. Do just as I say. First, look in the satchel. There you will find everything that I've found. A packet of letters which I took from a man named Flom—you've heard of him?"

"Yes," cried Henkl, growing exasperated and, for one of the few times in his life, genuinely frightened.

"The letters are thank-you's from a lady named Maria Anna Schicklgruber—the name may be familiar to you—to a Jew named Frankenberger who lived in Graz a long, long time ago. In 1838, to be precise. She is thanking this man, this Jew, for sending money to help her support the bastard son of Frankenberger's own son. This Maria Anna Schicklgruber, you see, had been a servant in their home and, after the fashion of the times. . . ."

Henkl let out a soft groan, barely more than an exhalation. It *was* true then—the suspicions, the threats that had been made in the letter they had found in Kepplinger's file, the letter

250

written by the son of Hitler's half brother. He stared at the satchel as though it were about to explode.

The voice on the other end continued, slowly and deliberately:

"You will also find fifteen years' worth of records from the Landsbank of Graz, which I have taken the liberty of borrowing from the archives. If you look under 'Frankenberger Verlag,' you will find regular monthly payments made to something described as 'MAS and Son,' which is, of course . . ."

"Maria Anna Schicklgruber and her son . . ."

"Who was, of course, at first just Alois Schicklgruber, later Alois Hüttler, later Alois Hitler. The father of the current Reichschancellor."

There was a long silence, broken only by the incessant drumming of the rain on the steel roof of the cab. In a fury, Henkl began wrenching at the door. No use. It would not budge. The lock had obviously been tampered with.

Schanz's voice came over the dangling receiver, harsh and urgent.

"Don't do that, Captain Henkl. You can't get out. It's impossible."

Sweating and cold in every part of his body, Henkl retrieved the phone.

"What do you want? Why have you got me locked up in here, with these . . . things?"

"Because I want to exchange favors with you."

"Favors?"

"Obviously, you are interested in these 'things,' as you call them. Otherwise why would you have been following me all this time?"

"We didn't know. It's funny, almost . . . we thought that you were onto something else altogether. We didn't know about—this—until yesterday."

"But you are still interested?"

"More than before. These 'things' can be very, very useful to us."

"I assumed so, Captain. Well, then, I propose to make you a present of them, for whatever use you may want to make of them. I can only assume what that use might be, knowing

Admiral Canaris's attitude and that of Von Helldorf."

"Yes, yes, go on."

"And in return, I want only one thing."

"And if I should refuse?"

Schanz laughed. "You won't. You see, at the top of the railway a certain deputy inspector named Gruner is waiting with some of his men. I took the precaution of having him called before leaving the Rathaus. He is expecting a 'present'— he doesn't know quite what, but I promised him he'd be very interested. One push of the lever down here and you are in his arms, satchel, documents, and all. I imagine that he will know what is to be done with someone who suddenly appears with such incriminating material. Exactly, I'm afraid, what Colonel Kepplinger had in mind for me. And, by the way, don't think you can throw them out the window. The windows won't open. I suppose you could eat them, if you think you could manage it, but aside from that . . . So, what's your answer?"

"I hardly have a choice, do I? What do you want in return?"

"Only this. I have a son, Helmut Schanz, who is a lieutenant in the third tank division with General Hoepner. They happen to be out on night maneuvers at the moment, so I assume that he's reasonably safe. I also assume that inasmuch as Heydrich will be looking for me shortly, he will also be looking for my son. That's what kind of a swine he is. I want my son safe and out of the country. Promise me he will be delivered across the Swiss border, to St. Gallen where my wife is already waiting, and you go back down the Schlossberg, satchel and all, and to your car."

"We would have done that for you without all of this. You know what Canaris thinks of Heydrich."

"I have your word?"

"You have my word, the word of us all. I promise you that you'll have your son within twenty-four hours, at St. Gallen, as you ask. And what about you?"

"I can manage for myself, thank you. One favor is enough."

"Done then," said Henkl.

"Done," echoed Schanz. "And by the way, when you get down to the landing stage, you'll want to get out, of course.

The door is built to stay locked so that passengers won't accidentally be thrown out. Look under the motorman's seat; there's a little box and in it you'll find the key."

Henkl could not suppress a smile. The man had had it all worked out perfectly. He glanced up through the rain-spattered front window. The top of the Schlossberg was lost in a mass of low, rushing clouds.

Too bad. He would never get to meet Deputy Inspector Gruner.

September 27, 12:00 P.M.: Berlin

Kepplinger was in a cold sweat. He had been kept waiting in the anteroom of Heydrich's office for over an hour. During all that time neither of the adjutants at work behind the low railing that separated their desks from the waiting area had looked at him once. Kulsky, in particular, seemed to be deliberately avoiding him, as though to even glance at him might mean permanent contamination.

Kepplinger's mouth was dry. He did not dare light a cigarette. Unaccountably, he found that he could not remember whether Heydrich smoked or whether, on the contrary, he could not stand the smell of tobacco. He found it difficult, in fact, to focus on anything other than the fact that once more he had been routed out of bed by two surly SD lieutenants and this time driven direct to Prinz Albrechtstrasse in the middle of the night. It was the kind of treatment usually reserved for criminals and traitors; he knew that well enough.

He sat there, twisting the signet ring on his left hand until the flesh went raw beneath, trying to think of what could have happened. What could have gone so horribly wrong as to cause—this?

Earlier that evening, just before dinner, he had heard all about the march-by of Von Witzleben's troops along the Wilhelmstrasse and the disastrous impression it had made. The Reichschancellor was in a rage, denouncing the army, the entire country, for a pack of spineless fools. What kind of a mood must Heydrich be in, then?

He did not even hear it the first time his name was called.

He looked up only when the chief adjutant called a second time in a nasal, annoyed voice: "The Obergruppenführer SD will see you now."

Kepplinger jumped up. The door to Heydrich's office was open.

He went in, in a state of panic.

Heydrich was seated behind his desk, going through some papers. He did not even look up as Kepplinger came into the room and gave a shaky Party salute.

Heydrich went on reading, marking and underlining things with a red pencil. Finally he spoke, his lips hardly moving.

"Sit down—at once, Kepplinger. No, wait. Remain standing. You won't be here that long."

Why didn't the man look up? He couldn't see his eyes; that was the worst of it. Even Himmler always looked at you and you could tell at once what he was thinking from the way his eyes moved behind his pince-nez. Heydrich was another case entirely. He would often conduct entire interviews without once looking at the man to whom he was talking.

Heydrich's long hands skimmed over the papers before him, the slender, almost delicate fingers searching for something. Suddenly, he looked up. Kepplinger blanched. Heydrich gave him a look of such hatred and contempt that Kepplinger felt his sphincter muscles move.

Then, all at once, he recovered his self-control. He straightened to a sharp, military stance and confronted Heydrich without moving a muscle. "Let him do his worst, the bastard. He will anyway, so there's nothing to be afraid of."

"This," Heydrich began in his high, gnawing voice. He prodded a folder from the pile of papers before him. It was his duplicate of the file that had been in Kepplinger's safe, the "Torquemada" folder.

Heydrich's long, equine face took on a faintly bemused expression. The small eyes narrowed until they almost vanished. Kepplinger noticed for the first time that Heydrich, too, seemed to be highly agitated. His thick lips trembled slightly, his high forehead glistened with perspiration.

"Do you still have your copy, Kepplinger?"

"Of course, Herr Obergruppenführer. It's in my safe."

"Have you had it out during the last few days?"

"Your orders, Herr Obergruppenführer, were . . ."

"I know what my orders were. Nevertheless, are you certain . . . ?"

"Absolutely."

Heydrich's lips barely moved:

"Then how do you explain the fact that a copy of the letter of the nephew, William Patrick, has turned up in Vienna, in the office of Count Marogna-Redwitz?"

"That's impossible!"

"Precisely what I thought. It *is* impossible. There are only two copies of that letter in the world. The one in my file, and the one in your file. Of course, there is also the original, but I don't suppose that the Führer sent it down to Redwitz to have the spelling checked, do you?"

Kepplinger began to stammer. "It is simply not possible . . . how can such a thing . . . ?"

Heydrich cut him off. "I have it from an unimpeachable source. One of our men in the photo section. He saw the negatives."

"A photograph? No, no, no—how could it be?"

"But it is, Kepplinger. It is, believe me." Heydrich began tapping his desk in a slow, steady rhythm. Kepplinger, for one wild moment, thought that Heydrich was actually beating out the rhythm of some piece of music or other. "And so, will you tell me, please, how did they manage to come by such a thing? It seems to me that there are only two possibilities. Either you have deliberately betrayed me, or else you've been criminally negligent, which comes down to the same thing."

All at once, Kepplinger saw exactly what had happened. The fire the night before last—it had been too much a carbon copy of the Tukaschevsky affair for him to have believed it to have been for the same purpose.

But—obviously—it had been.

Kepplinger began to stammer explanations. Heydrich cut him off.

"Exactly as I said. Criminal negligence. And so. One other

question which, you may understand, is not unrelated." Heydrich's voice rose suddenly, almost to a scream. "Where is Schanz?"

Kepplinger stared straight ahead. Heydrich's face was a blur. How was he to answer? He'd had his people searching high and low for the man for the last three days with no success.

"Well, then, I can tell you if you don't know, Kepplinger. Your man Schanz is in Switzerland, that's where he is. He went over the border less than an hour ago. We almost caught him, but he slipped by us at the last moment. It doesn't matter, though." He tapped another file on his desk. "We'll have the son in custody within an hour. Then, I can assure you, he'll be back."

Kepplinger was having trouble staying upright. His palms were ice-cold and he could hardly focus his eyes.

"In the meantime," Heydrich went on, "now that you have ruined this entire affair and compromised us all by your stupidity, let me ask you, what do you think I should do with you?"

"I swear to you, Herr Obergruppenführer . . ."

Heydrich suddenly got up from behind his desk. "Enough. Kulsky will show you into the next room. I do not expect to see you again." He leaned over and pushed a button. "Goodbye, Kepplinger."

Heydrich's aide came into the room.

"You will escort this man into the next office. Everything is prepared?"

The adjutant barely nodded. Instead of the look of nasty triumph Kepplinger had expected to see on the man's face, there was an expression—almost—of horror. Kulsky had seen his own fate all too clearly and all too suddenly for his liking.

He took Kepplinger shakily by the arm and led him out into the corridor.

"There is a paper and pen. You may write to your wife. The Obergruppenführer has given his permission. Anything you write will be read . . . so . . . ," Kulsky's voice sank to a whisper, "for God's sake, don't write anything foolish."

He opened another, smaller door.

Kepplinger found himself in a small room containing only a table, a chair, and a cot on which lay a bare mattress with blue and white ticking.

On the table, just as Kulsky had said, was paper, a pen, and a bottle of ink.

Next to the pen was a glass of water and a small phial.

September 28, 3:30 A.M.:
Near Passau, Germany

A column of tanks was moving through the dark field just beyond the edge of the woods. The air smelled of recent rain, the soil was fresh and pungent. Especially where it had been churned up by tank treads. "Like a plow," Rost thought, "in a way."

He strained to see but could make out the shapes of the tanks in only the vaguest way. The night was swarming with troops on the move. Transports and trucks streamed down the road toward the Czech border, only ten kilometers away. Overhead, reconnaissance planes shuttled in and out of the tattered clouds like darning needles trying to stitch the sky together. Rost had never seen anything like it before in his life.

Hitler was actually going to do it.

He still could not believe it. Something had to happen to stop it. But for the moment, at least, that was not his affair. He had been there on the Czech border, between Passa and Rosenheim, for only two hours, and more than half that time had been spent following the two SD men who had appeared almost at exactly the same moment as he had.

He could just barely see them through his night field glasses, about three hundred meters away, standing by themselves just at the edge of the treeline. There was not the slightest doubt in Rost's mind; they were after the same thing he was —Lieutenant Helmut Schanz.

He turned and spoke in a whisper to the Panzer major who had accompanied him—Helmut Schanz's commander. They were standing at the rendezvous point where the lieutenant and his group were shortly due. Everything had been worked out. Quickly and efficiently and without questions. The Panzer commander had followed Rost's orders without hesitation. Rost was acting on the direct authority of Count Marogna-Redwitz and, for Major Meischner, that was more than enough. Besides, Abwehr Vienna had been in direct contact with General Hoepner and the order had come down: Do whatever the lieutenant from Vienna asks.

That order had been meant to apply only to the removal of Lieutenant Schanz. Now it had even more serious implications. Murderous, in fact, but it could hardly be helped. Rost had always known that sooner or later in his line of work he would have to kill someone. He had scarcely expected, however, that his first would be two of his own countrymen.

Rost licked his lips. It was the first time in his life he'd ever done anything like this. He hoped he would be spared the duty of viewing the results.

"The swine," said Major Meischner. Rost hardly heard him. He had the glasses up again.

"You're sure that's the exact spot, sir?"

"You'll see in just," he consulted his watch, "it should be exactly two minutes from now."

The SD men were growing fidgety. Rost could see that. They heard the same noises that he did, saw the same dark and indefinable shapes moving heavily through the night. The forest and fields were full of sounds, yet nothing could be seen. Not a single vehicle had its lights on. Full security was in effect.

The SD men stood at exactly the coordinates they had been given by Meischner's adjutant, waiting there for Lieutenant Schanz's unit to arrive. Everything was exactly according to the book. No one could be faulted. They had been given entirely correct information. There was only one thing they had not been told.

That Lieutenant Schanz's unit was to rendezvous from an attack formation, at full speed.

At that moment, exactly as the sweep hand of the major's watch touched the twelve, the edge of the forest where the two SD men were standing erupted with an enormous roar. The tanks, which had been moving slowly in column along the forest road, had suddenly fanned out and were heading the last fifty meters through the treeline at full speed, smashing everything in their way, to burst out into the open field in battle formation before wheeling around to the rendezvous point at the opposite side of the meadow where Rost and Major Meischner waited.

Rost watched, horrified—though the whole thing had been arranged at his request.

The tanks came crashing out of the forest, almost on top of the two SD men. There were no lights. Dust flew. The air was full of branches, churned-up dirt, leaves, and grass. For a few seconds, Rost could make out the two figures trying desperately to scramble out of the way. He could hear nothing except the clamor of engines.

Then the front had passed over the spot where the two SD men had been standing, leaving nothing in its wake but churned-up earth and a tangle of broken tree limbs.

Of the two men there was not a trace. In the morning, their remains might be found, mixed with the earth. A few scraps of black uniform. Perhaps a shred of their identification papers, a warrant disk or a belt buckle.

"An accident," said Major Meischner, shaking his head. "Regrettable, but in wartime it is the business of soldiers to be killed, no?" Major Meischner lowered his voice. "A pity we can't oblige all of them in the same manner."

Rost lowered his glasses.

The major smiled. The tanks had come to a halt on the opposite side of the field.

"Now, Lieutenant Rost, shall we go and collect young Schanz? I shall be very sorry to lose him, but I suppose you people know best."

September 28, 6:30 A.M.:
The Kahlenberg, Vienna

"What d'you mean, you *can't* get through?" Tieck-Mitringer demanded. The young lieutenant of the signal section pulled off his headphones and stared at his commander, his face appearing even more flushed than it was because of the rosy dawn light streaming in over the Kahlenberg.

The lieutenant opened his mouth, trying to think what he could possibly say other than to repeat himself. If he did, as he well knew, he would bring on a shouting rage, and General Tieck-Mitringer's shouting rages were well known. As were their consequences.

"Well, have you lost your tongue, Brenner?" Tieck-Mitringer demanded. The signal lieutenant had never seen his general quite so agitated. Even so, Brenner was astonished at how close Tieck-Mitringer seemed to be to losing control of himself. The general's habit of stalking about during the worst of the winter with no coat on had given rise to all sorts of myths and legends about his toughness and self-discipline. In reality, as his ADC knew all too well, Tieck-Mitringer was a very unpredictable man and certainly anything but well balanced.

Lieutenant Brenner continued to struggle in silence with the apparatus at his feet, trying desperately to elicit some sort of response from the special phone line that had been patched into the closed circuit to OKW in Berlin.

"The trouble," the young man said at last, "is on the other end, sir. There's absolutely nothing wrong here. General Halder's end simply doesn't pick up."

Tieck-Mitringer stared, considered a tirade, and then thought better of it. He crushed his *feldmütze* down on his head as far as it would go and stalked off through the crisp autumn leaves, leaving the signal lieutenant crouching there in the bushes over his crackling but otherwise useless apparatus, looking for all the world like Laocoön doing battle with the serpents.

From the forward slope just below the treeline, Tieck-Mitringer could see units of his division moving spectrally through the forest in full battle gear. Far below, on the road, and barely visible along the edge of the woods that ran directly to the highway, tanks, armored cars, and motorcycles mounting machine guns waited. Everything was hidden; if one did not know where to look, it would have been impossible to have spotted any of them. Tieck-Mitringer's camouflage section was one of the best in the Wehrmacht. It was said, only partly in jest, that the entire Twenty-Seventh could vanish completely in the space of half an hour and that it would take bloodhounds to find them again.

The whole operation had been laid on with the utmost of care. The maneuvers had been planned weeks before as a preparatory exercise for the support of Operation Green. No one could possibly be suspicious. No one could possibly ask why, on this particular day of all days, half of the Twenty-Seventh Division was fanned out in an arc that entirely encircled Vienna's southern perimeter and, coincidentally, formed a solid wall of tanks, mountain troopers, and armored cars around the slopes dominated by the Schloss Trcka.

There were only two problems, and they were problems that were driving Tieck-Mitringer crazy. First, he had not yet been able to find an escape hatch for himself, a way out if things should go wrong. Second, and even worse, now he could not get through to Berlin to find out what was happening.

He unbuttoned his tunic, unconsciously undid the flap of the holster that held his Luger, and looked around for Major Rudigier.

Overhead, a swarm of midges buzzed. The air was rich with the smell of apples and wine, the sky a bright blue. Perfect for bird watching and for the Luftwaffe. But the sky was still, as though both bird and man knew instinctively that it was hardly the time to be buzzing about where anyone could see them. And then there was the mist, which stubbornly refused to burn off. Those on the ground could see up, but a pilot passing overhead would have seen nothing. That much, at least, was to the good.

"Rudigier, where the devil are you?" the general shouted suddenly.

In response there was a nearby thrashing of branches.

"Sir?" called the major, appearing in a camouflage of brush and leaves that struck Tieck-Mitringer as absurdly amusing.

"You see our phone station over there?"

"Yes, sir."

"Well, it doesn't work, Major. You, *you* are now responsible for seeing to it that it *does* work. The minute you

261

are through to General Halder, I want to know about it. No—
the *second* you are through!"

"Where will you be, sir? With all of this camouflage, it's
hard . . ."

Tieck-Mitringer cut him off.

"It's not important that you know where I am. As long
as *I* know where *you* are, and *you* will be with Brenner by the
phones, yes?"

"Yes, sir," Rudigier snapped, knowing better than to argue
when Tieck-Mitringer was in *that* kind of mood.

"If anyone asks you where I am, I've gone hunting, d'you
understand?"

"Perfectly, sir."

"You'd better."

With that, Tieck-Mitringer pulled the forage cap from
his head. With a heavy, long-legged stride that made it look as
though at every step he was intent on crushing something underfoot, he marched up the slope and into the deep forests, which
were still there only due to the genius of God in cutting short
the life and landscaping ambitions of Gustav Eugen Trcka.

Tieck-Mitringer had the uneasy feeling that, after all, it
might have been far easier to have dealt with the old man than
with the son.

Fessler had oiled, loaded, and laid out all of Baron Trcka's
hunting guns. The huge oak table in the dining hall looked like
the workroom of a museum during inventory. For himself,
Fessler had chosen a prewar English shotgun, which he had
polished to mirror brightness. Thus armed, he had stationed
himself in the east tower, from which he could keep watch
over the slopes on the approach to the castle, the Kahlenberg
itself to the west, and the vast, misty panorama of Vienna
below, cut through by the dim, undulating Danube, gray and
dreary in the half-light of early morning.

Although the baron had been officially confined to bed by
Michaelis's friend Dr. Stozl, with what he was pleased to refer
to as a "nervous imbalance," Trcka insisted on stalking about
the halls of the castle like an unlaid ghost, his expression
vacant, his face the color of bleached muslin, his hands trem-

bling uncontrollably. Stozl had long since given up trying to enforce his instructions and had gone back to Vienna muttering obscenities about the degenerate nobility. "One can administer only just so much opium, after all."

Shortly before dawn, old Fessler came rushing down to the main hall, carrying his loaded English birdgun and crying the alarm.

He found Trcka sitting morosely by a dying fire, a brandy snifter in his hands, a mohair lap-robe over his knees, fragments of his viola on a nearby table. Fessler himself had reclaimed the instrument—or what was left of it—from the vandalized remains of the suicide's shop the day after Fiebelmann had shot himself.

Major Langbein was striding up and down the long room as though pacing off a new parade ground. Michaelis, who had arrived only the night before from Berlin, lay in exhausted sleep on a sofa near the window.

Fessler hesitated, startled by Langbein's presence; he had no idea how or when the man had gotten there. Trcka barely looked up.

"If the Herr Baron pleases . . . ?"

"What? Oh, it's you, Fessler, is it? Haven't you gone to bed yet?" The baron looked puzzled. "What time *is* it, Fessler?"

"If the Herr Baron pleases, there are . . . troops in the woods directly below the garden. Tanks, if the Herr Baron pleases. . . ."

Langbein hardly took notice. Michaelis sat up, rubbed his eyes, and looked around. Trcka, as though half remembering something, simply nodded.

"It's really quite all right. I know all about it."

"But *tanks*, Herr Baron."

"I know, I know, Fessler."

When Fessler had finally been convinced to leave, Langbein allowed a pale flicker of a smile to turn the corners of his mouth; it was, all in all, an unpleasant expression.

"Tieck-Mitringer's men, of course," he said.

"You're sure?" Michaelis asked.

A pause.

"No, in fact I'm not sure at all. But they'd better be."

263

Langbein looked at his watch; it was a little past seven. Two hours before, he'd gotten a message from Henkl that he thought he had found what they'd all been looking for in Flom's shop and would be right up. Why, then, was it taking them so long? Certainly at night the trip up to Trcka's estate should have taken no more than an hour by plane.

All sorts of terrible thoughts began circulating through Langbein's mind. What if Henkl had really found "it" and had suddenly suffered one of his periodic crises of conscience? At a time of such stress, with everything about to come crashing down on their heads at once, who could tell how even a man of Henkl's normally manic insistence on logic might behave?

Suppose that he'd decided that the catastrophe that would be caused by revealing the "evidence" would, in the end, be even greater than the catastrophe that would ensue if it were concealed? Suppose he had decided that there was .more to gain for Klaus Henkl if he took whatever it was directly to Heydrich than by taking it to his own chief? Suppose . . .

There were a hundred possibilities, each one worse than the one before.

"For God's sake, Ernst, stop that pacing, can't you?" Trcka cried suddenly, unable to stand it one second longer. He put the snifter to his lips, found the glass empty, and with a violent gesture of exasperation hurled it against the fireplace mantel. Langbein thought that he saw traces of tears in the man's eyes. Dr. Stozl was right; it had gotten "that bad."

Michaelis turned sharply.

"Perhaps you should go back upstairs, go to sleep, eh, August? Shall I call Fessler back? There is really no need for you. . . ."

"No, no, *no*," Trcka insisted, jumping up. "Why should I be shut out, now, of all times? Is that what you want to do, to shut me out? It won't make the slightest difference to *them* that I was upstairs in bed when it all happened. If it goes wrong, they'll chop off my head too, just the same as yours."

Langbein exchanged appalled glances with Michaelis. Michaelis finally overcame his disgust and said in his most cheerful, matter-of-fact voice, "We may as well at least have some coffee."

Trcka smiled sheepishly and called for Fessler. Michaelis fled to the leaded window and breathed in the damp dawn air as deeply as he could. The mist was still rising from the forests, thick and glowing now with morning sunlight.

The dark shapes of the fir and chestnut and also of the tanks and armored cars of Tieck-Mitringer's Twenty-Seventh Division were just then becoming visible.

Below the point on the road up to Schloss Trcka where it climbed through a particularly thick pine wood, some two hundred meters short of the lower edge of the baron's formal gardens, a roadblock had been set up. Two motorcycles with sidecars mounting machine guns stood obstinately in the way, backed up by a small armored car parked just to the side of the road, the muzzles of its guns covering the approaches with chastening thoroughness. The woods on either side were full of soldiers. Telephone wires snaked every which way.

Henkl's Opel had been sitting in the middle of that road, brought to an abrupt halt by the combined threat of machine guns and cannon, for over a half an hour now. Henkl, beside himself with frustration, was storming back and forth, shouting and waving his arms. Rost, to whom this would, under other circumstances, have seemed amusing, stood white-faced and silent by the side of the car, ready to dive for cover if the sergeant in the closest motorcycle sidecar should decide that he'd had enough of Henkl's raving, all of which had not suc-ceeded in moving the roadblock one centimeter.

"Herr Hauptmann, understand, I wouldn't care if you were Himmler himself," the sergeant had observed with infuriating calm, "you wouldn't get by unless the General said so."

"Well, damn it, find the General then!"

"I can't leave my post. The Herr Hauptmann must realize that."

The conversation had gone on in this vein for fully a quarter of an hour. Henkl had finally threatened to have them all shot.

"Shot is just what we'd be if I let you through. Orders are

265

orders, as the Herr Hauptmann realizes, I'm sure. Besides, you're not even from this division, so how should I know *who* you are?"

Henkl, still clutching the satchel into which Schanz had crammed the fifteen iron-bound bank ledgers, was desperate. He had never before been in a position where superior rank was not honored. In the past, the Abwehr cuff-title and tabs had always been sufficient to ensure immediate passage anywhere. He was beginning to realize that his present predicament might be no more than a distinctly unpleasant preview of things to come.

Just then, General Tieck-Mitringer came out of the woods, boots muddy, his tunic open and flapping, his *feldmütze* mashed down onto his heavy boned forehead, and his holster flap undone. Behind him came his ADC, Major Rudigier, and three grim-looking but sharply turned out lieutenants, all of them carrying submachine guns. The contrast between the appearance of the general and his subordinates was striking and, to Henkl, rather ominous. He instinctively distrusted people who could not manage to button their jackets properly—a reaction, Langbein had once cautioned him, that only someone who had never been in a trench could afford.

"What's this, Gruber?" Tieck-Mitringer shouted. "What've you got here?"

"As you see, Herr General."

"I see, but I'm in no mood for guessing games, Gruber. Let's have it."

Henkl flushed. Why the devil was he asking the sergeant rather than addressing him, Henkl, directly? Not only sloppy but a boor as well.

"Claims to be Abwehr, Herr General," said Gruber.

Henkl had had enough.

"Listen here, this is a disgrace. If the Herr General pleases, I am Captain Henkl, Abwehr, as you see, under Major Langbein's section. You know Major Langbein, I believe, sir. I report directly to the Colonel, Count Redwitz. It is imperative that I . . ."

"It is imperative that you stop shouting," Tieck-Mitringer cut in. "Now, calm yourself and let's have it all."

Tieck-Mitringer stumped over, at the same time waving the three lieutenants back. It was obvious that he had at least a vague idea why Henkl was there; his whole expression had changed when Major Langbein's name was mentioned.

"Gruber," he shouted, "pull off the road, you idiot."

Sergeant Gruber saluted smartly, gunned his motorcycle, and withdrew to the side of the road.

Tieck-Mitringer's voice was low and confidential.

"You've gotten yourself in the middle of a . . . ," he paused as though unsure of just how to express himself, ". . . a maneuver," he said finally. "They're all on a combat basis, and my orders were . . ."

"Herr General, I'm sure you will understand that Major Langbein . . . "

"That troublemaker?"

"Major Langbein is waiting for me at the Schloss Trcka. I know," Henkl said, while Rost blanched an even lighter shade. "I *know* that the Herr General understands exactly what is going on. I beg you, don't delay me any longer. I have urgent information for the Major."

Tieck-Mitringer gazed up toward the schloss. The outlines of its grave stone turrets were clearly visible, but the lower bulk of the castle itself was still shrouded in mist.

He turned suddenly and shouted past Henkl into the woods.

"Brenner—damn it, Brenner—is the line clear yet?"

In a few seconds, a lieutenant wearing a leather apron crammed with wire snippers, cables, and screwdrivers came running out of the woods.

"Not yet, sir. We're doing our best, but it's . . . "

"On the *other* end Yes, yes, I know all about it. It's always on the other end." Tieck-Mitringer spat and ground the spittle under his boot.

"You get a phone line up to the castle at once, d'you understand, Lieutenant Brenner? At once; if you have to lay the wire yourself. And when you get through to General Halder, you will ring up to me, also *at once*. Do you understand that?"

The general turned on Henkl as though he were about to strike him.

"All right, you two. We may as well go up there now. I'm coming with you."

"Sir?" Henkl's mouth dropped open. This he had hardly expected.

"And move over," Tieck-Mitringer commanded "I'll drive. You don't think I'd trust my life on a road like *that* to an intelligence officer, do you? Intelligence, my arse. It's lucky you had intelligence enough to keep yourself alive back there. Only barely, as far as I could see. Sergeant Gruber would have enjoyed letting you have a few rounds. Well, then, come on. You were in such a hurry before and *now* look at you."

Henkl slammed the car door so violently that he almost caught his fingers.

September 28, 8:00 A.M.: Berlin

Most of Major Heinz's Commando squad had slept that night in the Abwehr offices on the Tirpitz-ufer. Some had slept on cots, some on the floor, still others in unused offices or in the basement storage rooms.

Until late at night they had congregated near and around the radio room, waiting for the latest word, waiting for yet another zigzag of policy that might require a change in their plans. None had come. London had at last declared unequivocally that if Czechoslovakia were attacked, England would fight. France had joined in the declaration. The lines were clearly drawn. At twelve noon the previous day, the Reichschancellor had issued orders mobilizing nineteen divisions and naming 3:00 P.M., September 28, as the hour for the first wave of attacks. The stage was now set and everything, so far as Friedrich Wilhelm Heinz knew, was ready.

His squad began to assemble. He had chosen twenty-three men, some of them Abwehr, some regular army. All of them could be counted on to act bravely and with decisiveness when the time came.

The door opened and Lieutenant Dachstein, a slender, blond Bavarian, came in carrying two submachine guns. He laid them on a table by the window, next to a line of Lugers that had been cleaned, oiled, checked, and loaded.

268

Heinz himself had a Luger in his holster and a smaller Walther automatic in each coat pocket. In his boot top he had stuck a dagger that had been sharpened to a razor's edge. Some of the men were carrying grenades as well as small arms.

Only a few minutes earlier, Colonel Oster had stopped by to tell Heinz that everything had been arranged; the big double doors behind the guard at the Chancellery entrance would be unlocked. Heinz and his men could walk right in and there would be none but the customary ceremonial sentries to stop them.

General von Witzleben was waiting at Defense District Headquarters on the Hohenzollerndarm, together with General Halder.

"General Brauchitsch has gone to the Chancellery to hear Hitler's final decision. Then he will give the order. Certainly by noon."

Heinz smiled. He and Oster understood each other perfectly. Although an ambulance was standing by to convey the arrested Reichschancellor to Charité Hospital and the special, steel-lined suite of rooms that had been prepared for him, there would be little need for it except as a hearse. Heinz had no intention of letting Hitler leave the Chancellery alive.

A second squad was poised in the vicinity of the Berlin Radio station building. One of Germany's leading psychiatrists was ready to go on the air the moment the station had been secured and announce to the country that their leader was certifiably insane. There had been word of extraordinary developments in Vienna, where additional material of considerable importance had been discovered. A direct line to the Marogna-Redwitz office was to be kept open at all times.

Heinz's twenty-three men stood about the large, empty room, grinning and cracking jokes. Heinz liked that; there was no sign of tension whatever. He had chosen wisely. His men were all thoroughly committed, thoroughly professional. The whole action would take less than fifteen minutes. Five, perhaps, to drive over to the Wilhelmstrasse and another ten to execute the bastard.

"Cigarette, Major?" It was Lieutenant Dachstein, who did not smoke himself but always seemed to be carrying cigarettes, which he unfailingly offered to others.

Heinz shook his head and took out a cigar. It was the kind of heavy, ropy black cigar with which once, years ago, he had lit the fuses of hand-bombs before heaving them out of the trenches.

"Dachstein, tell me. What are you going to do with yourself when this is all over?"

"Why, Major, I haven't given that a thought. Have you?"

"No," thought Heinz, "I haven't either."

September 28, 9:00 A.M.: St. Gallen, Switzerland

From where he stood, Schanz could easily see his wife and son at breakfast on the little terrace of the Hotel Grunewald. The morning had dawned fresh and beautiful only moments after he had come into sight of St. Gallen. Earlier that night, the accommodating Captain Lugner had busied himself and his men looking for a break in the fence-wire two kilometers to the north.

He had not yet had a chance to wash, to shave, or to sleep. But despite the fact that he had been up and on his feet for over thirty-six hours without rest, he felt invigorated and refreshed. The sight of his son, puzzled but safe, sitting in the hotel room with his mother, was all that he had needed to banish his fatigue.

There had been a bouquet of flowers on the table, waiting for him, arranged in the old Imperial German colors. No card. There was no need to ask where they had come from. He had heard of such things happening before.

Schanz had excused himself and gone down to the garden to be alone for a while, to gather his thoughts and his emotions. He had almost begun to weep when he had seen his son. Not that he had thought that Captain Henkl and his superiors would go back on their word, but with the situation worsening and the war about to break out at any moment, he had had grave doubts whether even the Abwehr could find Helmut and deliver him out of the middle of a general mobilization.

Yet there they all were.

And there too, in the same hotel, in the very same garden, was someone else, a someone else with whom he wanted desperately to speak. Captain Lugner had given him the message just before he had gone across the border and Feldkirch.

"A friend of yours thought that you might like to know; he says that he appreciates how difficult it is for a man with an inquiring mind like your own to live with unanswered questions."

Schanz could see them, sitting all together in a row on a bench on the other side of the little garden. Behind them, a bank of fall flowers was in full bloom. A small, inconspicuous man, his equally inconspicuous wife, and two small children.

He went up to them, slowly and casually, so as not to alarm them. He spoke with the utmost gentleness.

"Herr Jankow? Permit me to introduce myself—a refugee like yourself—my name is Ulrich Schanz, formerly Obersturmbannführer of the Sicherheitsdienst."

Jankow looked up. He neither blanched nor showed any expression whatever. It was almost as though he had not heard at all. Schanz saw that Frau Jankow had grabbed hold of her husband's arm. The boy went on reading and the girl did not look up from playing with her doll.

"There must be some mistake. What could you possibly want with me, Herr Schanz?"

"A certain Klaus Henkl has suggested that we should talk."

"Ah—Henkl. But you? You are not . . . ?"

"No, I'm not. We've never met, you and I, but in a way we have been far closer than you and this certain Herr Henkl whom we both know."

"Hermann," breathed his wife. Precautionary.

"No, no, let him go on. We're perfectly safe here."

Schanz nodded. "I too am a fugitive. I crossed less than two hours ago. My wife and son are up there." He pointed to the terrace on which mother and son could be plainly seen, having their coffee. Schanz's wife saw him point and called down to him.

"Ulrich, when are you coming up? You simply must rest."

"A moment, a moment." Schanz turned back to Jankow, who was now staring at him with a look of intense interest.

Schanz began to speak, very slowly, very softly. The chil-

271

dren did not even look up once. He explained all that he had done, all that had happened.

And when he had finished, he said, "There are still questions. I can only guess at the answers. Will you at least tell me if I'm right?"

"It can harm no one now," Jankow said. He took his wife's hand. "It can harm no one now."

"So," said Schanz. "The end I can understand. It is the beginning that eludes me. The scrap of newspaper with the name Dowling on it."

"You found *that*? I thought I'd thrown it out years ago. *Paris-Soir*? Yes, of course. You see, the Reichschancellor's nephew, or rather the son of his half brother, had written an article. It was called to my attention because this nephew mentioned that the Chancellor's grandmother was reputed to have worked as a servant in the house of a Jewish family in Graz. There were almost no Jews in Graz at the time besides our families. I became curious. What a terrible joke it would have been if. . . ."

"And so, you got in touch with him, this William Patrick Hitler, this nephew of our Führer?"

"Yes," said Jankow. "At first he answered from Dublin where he had been living with his mother. She had grown up and married there. When her husband, Alois, had deserted her and gone back to Berlin, she had moved to Liverpool where the boy, William Patrick, had been born. Later she had gone back to Dublin and in thirty-five, after the article, they had moved to London."

"Of course. That explains the Irish stamps."

"You saw them, too? Ah, the boy's stamp book. Yes, yes."

"Go on."

"And then, from London, which you must also know, he continued the correspondence. The stamps from those letters were in the album too, of course. The letters, after the very first, were always addressed in the mother's maiden name, Dowling. As you must also know. And his letters, to me, were sent to 'Frankenberger,' *poste-restante*, in Graz. Rather ironic under the circumstances, don't you think?"

"All of this is clear," said Schanz. "But what happened

next? The letters, the money, *my* involvement? This is what I do not understand."

"We wrote to each other for a long time. We asked each other questions, tried to answer them. I think that he had in mind writing another article and was looking for more information. I began to search everywhere. Nothing had been thrown away. For generations, the Jankows and the Frankenbergers had been like packrats. Every scrap of paper any of us had ever laid pen to was still there. We had so much. Both families had lived in Graz for over a hundred years. There were boxes, suitcases, trunks full of all kinds of things. Letters, documents, photos." Jankow looked straight at Schanz. "If it hadn't been for the letters, the three ancient letters from Maria Anna Schicklgruber, I wouldn't be here now."

"It was *you* then, from the start?"

"At first, after I'd found them, I had no idea of selling them. I was afraid even to touch them. Believe me, Herr Schanz, there were nights when I wished I had never started to look for such things. But by then everything had begun to change. I was terrified, just as you must have been when you first held them in your hands. I did nothing. For years. It was all going to get better, I said. The madness could not last. But it did. The new laws, the book burnings, the beatings, the killings, the camps. At last we decided that we would have to leave. But by then it was too late."

"The Reichsfluchtsteuer?"

Jankow nodded. "Where was I to get so much money? They demanded of us one-quarter of my worth, but at the same time forbade us to sell off our stocks and bonds on the exchange. I could sell them privately for only a fraction of their value. There was simply no way to raise the money. I have relatives here in Switzerland, but they did not have the money either. Then I thought of the letters. There was a man in Vienna who could arrange such things. I learned of him through that vampire, Liszewsky, at the Tax Bureau. The arrangements were made with my cousin's help—William Patrick, his suggestion at least—who to contact for the best terms. A man at the French paper for which he had once written his article." Jankow paused. His wife looked away. "It was done, all arranged. A letter of credit was deposited in Zurich and the tax paid. I sent the letters on to Vienna through Liszewsky. He never really knew what was in them, only that they were to be used to blackmail someone important. For this, he took a fat fee for himself. And for his silence. And so." Jankow cleared his throat. "What more is there to tell? We got our exit permit and came here. An odd incident at the border, though—we were afraid that at the last minute we weren't going to be let through."

Schanz said nothing, simply nodded.

Jankow went on; it was coming out like a flood now. "The next day your Captain Henkl arrived. Obviously something had gone wrong. But I didn't know what it was. And I don't care. We're here, Rosa and the children. I have relatives in Lausanne who will take care of us until we are able to manage for ourselves."

Schanz looked long and very hard at the man, waiting for his question—what had happened to the letters, where were they now? Who had them?

But Jankow asked nothing. He reached out and patted his son on the head, then shook his own head as though he had read Schanz's mind.

"I don't want to know. What difference could it really make? Who would have believed it? It's enough that we are safe and you, you seem a decent man in spite of it all, it is also enough that you are safe, you and your family."

"For the time being," said Schanz.

"In this world," replied Jankow, "it is always for the time being, is it not? What more can one ask?"

September 28, 9:45 A.M.: London

Melitta Trcka had often wondered why it was that bright, beautiful days which caused others to feel elated, hopeful and happy, inspired in her only a dark and bottomless despair. Perhaps it was the heightened sense of just how much there was to be lost. Perhaps it was only the perversity of a nature that sought to affirm its own individuality and independence by opposing almost everything and everybody. She had never been entirely sure just which it was—and now it hardly mattered.

The beauty of the day, all warm September sunlight and soft blue skies above the Victorian chimney pots and gabled roofs of London, was almost unbearable. The rains had finally ceased but there was still a faint hint of mist in the air which gently, almost imperceptibly, blurred contours, softened colors, and gave everything a distant, dreamlike quality and, to her, a poignant fragility that perfectly matched her mood.

Cranwell had been unexpectedly sensitive and solicitous. He had offered his help but had not tried to impose it. He had gently tried to dissuade her from returning to Vienna. It wasn't quite the time, he had suggested. "Wait a week or two, Mel, perhaps things will, ah . . . settle down. A bit chancy at the moment, I'd say." He had not come right out with a direct warning; he knew her too well for that. But he had been as gently persistent in his own way as Michaelis had been strident and August plaintive. But to no avail.

She had refused to remain in London. Her mind was made up. Her bags had already been taken to the airport, her ticket was purchased and waiting to be picked up. Her flight would leave in less than five hours. By the next morning she would be back in Vienna.

Twice more she had tried to call through to Schloss Trcka. Once Dr. Stozl had come gruffly to the phone, once she had been disconnected. She had been able to speak neither to her husband nor to old Fessler. What else could she do but go back? There was only one more thing she might try, one more person from whom she might possibly find out what had happened before irrevocably committing herself.

Now she stood for a moment like a forlorn child in front of Number 9, Carlton House Terrace. A fragrance of late-blooming roses filled the air. Inside the Embassy building, through the ground-floor windows, she could see crisply uniformed figures moving about. One window allowed a glimpse of scarlet, the edge of a huge swastika banner that hung in the anteroom.

She hesitated. Would Kordt know anything? If he did, would he tell her? Bernhard had always insisted that the man was an opportunist, nothing more. If the direction of the wind had changed, could he be trusted?

A hum of traffic rose from the Mall. Strollers and nannies pushing prams could be seen parading placidly along the periphery of St. James's Park. Perhaps Cranwell was right. What was the point of going back? What could she accomplish other than to throw her own life away? By now, surely August, Michaelis, and the others must be in prison or dead. There had been not even a hint of a coup in the papers or on the radio. Hitler continued to rant and Chamberlain to temporize. Nothing had changed.

She went inside.

A clerk in naval uniform rose instantly from behind the reception desk at the end of the foyer. On the wall over his head hung a picture of Hitler dressed in silver armor.

"I wish to speak to Counsellor Kordt, if you please."

"You are expected, *gnadige Frau?*"

"He will see me."

"Impossible, *gnadige Frau*. Counsellor Kordt is not here."

She held herself in check. Had Kordt, too, been arrested? Right there in London? Had it all moved that fast, that silently?

"When will he return?"

"I have no information on that subject, *gnadige Frau*," the clerk said sharply, as though astonished and a little annoyed that he should have been asked a question the answer to which he so obviously could not be expected to know.

"Is he out for a walk? Has he gone visiting for the weekend? Has he been posted to India? Or perhaps he has simply gone to the bathroom?"

The clerk's stare turned icy.

"If you wish an inquiry to be made, you will have to state your business, please. Name, first of all . . . " He had already taken out a pale green pad of forms.

She turned instantly on her heel and walked quickly across the shallow marble foyer.

"*Gnadige Frau*," the clerk called sharply after her. Two other functionaries, attracted by the shout, looked in from adjoining rooms.

She did not turn back until she had reached the Mall.

There was no fear; there was nothing for her to be afraid

276

of. She knew exactly what she was going to do and why, and it had nothing to do with either love or loyalty for Michaelis or her husband or anyone else besides herself and the needs of her own conscience.

She stood for a few minutes at the head of the steps leading down to St. James's Park. Above her, the slender column topped by a bronze statue of the Duke of York rose like a needle pointed into the heart of the achingly beautiful blue September sky.

She turned and hailed a cab.

"Croydon Airport, please. You do go that far, don't you?"

"In a hurry, mum? Got a plane to catch?"

"I've all the time in the world," she said, settling back against the cool leather seat and beginning to shiver slightly. "Drive as slowly as you like. It doesn't matter to me at all."

September 28, 10:30 A.M.:
The Kahlenberg, Vienna

The entire proceeding had about it a distinctly ceremonial, almost sacerdotal air. Major Langbein sat in a high-backed chair on one side of the baron's elegant writing table, the photographs of the Kepplinger dossier in a morocco folder before him; opposite, on the other side of the table, and arranged quite by accident in an almost perfect semicircle, were Michaelis, Rost, Henkl, Trcka, and Tieck-Mitringer.

Only a moment before, Tieck-Mitringer had been told for the first time of the contents of Langbein's stolen folder. He stood, rooted to the spot and just barely beginning to recover his normal truculence. In one corner of the room, surrounded by wires that led off into the corridor, was a solitary field-gray telephone in a canvas cover. Lieutenant Brenner and Major Rudigier, both carrying submachine guns, had just been dismissed after completing the installation.

Henkl, now in the center of the arc, held his briefcase, as yet unopened, in exactly the same manner as one might, on another and more appropriate occasion, hold a votive offering.

With lowered eyes, Langbein slowly advanced his right hand. His fingers hesitated at the edge of the morocco folder.

277

"I think," said the major slowly, as though by ritualizing his speech he could somehow put off the inevitable, "I think that we had better go through it all, item by item. Then we will see what Henkl has brought us."

"That's ridiculous," exploded Tieck-Mitringer, wrenching his cigar from his mouth. "Let's see what the man's got. You there, Hauptmann, what've you got?"

"An orderly procedure," interrupted Michaelis, adopting his most judicial expression. "We should be patient, take things one at a time."

"You take them as you like, Herr Michaelis. I want to know what your man's got. If it clinches this incredible business. . . ." Tieck-Mitringer could still hardly believe what he had heard; the whole thing sounded to him unbelievable. His mind, preoccupied as it had been for days with maneuvers and troop dispositions, was just beginning to focus on the real significance of Langbein's discoveries.

Henkl, flushed with excitement, needed no further urging. He had, after all, just been given a direct order by the senior officer in the room.

He placed the satchel on the table.

Langbein reached out for it with all the delicacy and caution one would exercise in disarming a boobytrap.

"It's in there, sir," said Henkl. "Naturally I didn't touch it myself. I haven't even seen any of it yet."

Major Langbein appeared confused for a second. Then he upended the satchel. The ledgers slid out one after the other onto the table. The little manila envelope containing the letters fell out neatly, right on top, where it could hardly be missed.

"It's all there, sir," said Henkl, savoring in what even he recognized as a nasty sort of way his superior's bafflement.

Langbein opened the first of the "F" ledgers.

"Turn to the entries for 'Frankenberger Verlag'," said Henkl. "You see the notation 'MAS and Son'?" And he began to explain.

Langbein put his cigar into a glass dish and leaned over the ledger, tracing the entries with an unsteady fingertip. Baron Trcka looked on from his elbow. Tieck-Mitringer mumbled something and his face grew dark. Henkl went on, explaining as best he could, telling all that Schanz had told him while he was trapped in the funicular halfway up the Schlossberg.

"All of this proves nothing," Tieck-Mitringer broke in. " 'MAS and Son'? Why, that could mean almost anything."

Henkl nodded. "Under ordinary circumstances, sir, I would agree. 'MAS and Son' by itself could mean almost anything. But now, when we have these as well. . . ."

He took the envelope from the table and handed it to Langbein. Tieck-Mitringer scowled; obviously he thought that the papers, whatever they were, should have been given to him.

"Read them, Major," said Henkl. "I think when they are read, there will be no questions whatever."

Langbein extracted the three folded pieces of rag-paper, yellow and crenellated at the edges. With the delicacy of a lepidopterist, he opened the papers and spread them out on the table. Then he took out his glasses and as everyone else came around behind him, began to read.

The letters were all addressed to a "Herr Frankenberger" of Graz, thanking him for the gift of money that he had sent and for his promise to continue sending such money to help in the support and education of "the child." The letter continued in script large and laboriously incised in the intense manner peculiar to persons barely literate and fiercely proud.

"If you wish to see your grandson, or if his father wishes to see him, then you have only to ask. I am so sorry to have caused so much trouble, but it wasn't my fault. Even so, I am grateful to you that you understand that it was also not little Alois's fault."

The letters were signed "Maria Anna Schicklgruber." There were no envelopes; the letters consisted, after the fashion of the time, only of a fold of paper closed with a pin.

There was a long silence. No one looked at anyone else.

"Well, gentlemen?" said Langbein at last, in an exhausted voice. "What have you to say?"

Michaelis was the first to take up the challenge.

"Before we come to any conclusions, let us see what we have . . . all together."

"You have a doubt still?" Langbein scowled. "Why you, of all people?"

279

"Major, I am trained to have doubts about everything. Even after a conviction, I often still have doubts. If you will—there must have been hundreds of Schicklgrubers in Austria in 1837. And the name Maria Anna? While certainly suggestive, it does not actually prove anything. In the early 1800s, every other female in the Empire was named Maria Anna or Anna Maria."

Henkl stepped back as Langbein, with a long sigh, spread the "Torquemada" dossier before him. There was the letter from William Patrick Hitler, the copies of the Linz birth registries that Meinhard had obtained, the police residence photo of Maria Anna Schicklgruber dated 1852, the death certificates of the witnesses to the change of name on Alois "Hüttler's" birth registration; all of it.

Langbein stared at the documents. He paused, mumbled, "Klaus, I must thank you. What an excellent piece of work. This is, in fact. . . ."

"Get on with it," growled Tieck-Mitringer, his earlier manner now returning. "You're stalling, Major. Let's hear the worst."

"Or the best," suggested Trcka.

Langbein sighed and bent over the papers. "First we have the letter of the Reichschancellor's nephew, which threatens to reveal the 'dark secrets' of his birth. Second, we have the fact that Alois Schicklgruber, later Alois Hüttler, later Alois Hitler, was born in Strones in 1837, to a woman named Maria Anna Schicklgruber, an illegitimate child. Thirdly, we know that the acknowledgment of his paternity as it appears in the register of the Linz Diocese in 1867 was made years and years after his birth and that the signature of the witnesses who vouched for the putative father's recognition of paternity were probably total forgeries at worst and half forgeries at best. One of the men was twenty years dead at the time, as was the alleged father, and the other was a total stranger. Next. . . ." Langbein drew a breath. "Really, Herr Reichsgerichtsrat, is this necessary? You, of all people. . . ."

"Go on, Major," snapped Tieck-Mitringer. Behind them, in the corner of the room, the phone had begun to emit vague crackling noises. Sunlight streamed in through the huge windows of the living room. The sky behind Major Langbein was already an oppressively cheerful blue.

Langbein drew a deep breath again and went on.

"As Captain Henkl has already shown us—and here are the documents to prove it—for almost fifteen years, substantial payments were made by this Frankenberger, this Jew of Graz, to a certain Maria Anna Schicklgruber of Strones who," he emphasized his words, glaring now at Michaelis, "who we can most certainly assume is the same Maria Anna Schicklgruber who signed these letters, and later. . . . Do we really need more than this? How could anyone doubt it? With all of this evidence?"

Bernhard Michaelis simply shook his head.

"There is still the basic problem of identity, Ernst. As a judge, I am accustomed to listening to proofs, to weighing them, to examining them closely, and to evaluating them according to what they *are*, not what I would *like* them to be. I have developed a certain caution regarding 'facts'."

"What's the matter with you?" exploded Tieck-Mitringer. "If you're not convinced, well, I am. The bastard, the swine, the maniac!"

"As I was saying, Herr General, the question still remains, *Is* this the same Maria Anna Schicklgruber as the grandmother of our Führer? You will admit that neither Schicklgruber nor Maria nor Anna were or are today uncommon names in the region?"

"That's true. I admit that."

"You see?"

"Herr Reichsgerichtsrat, I must say, you sound to me as if you want this to fall through," Langbein cried with sudden formality.

"Not at all. But we must be sure. Absolutely sure."

Henkl, who had been standing in the center of the group, stone silent since he had handed over the book, took a step forward. As he did so, the field telephone by the archway entrance began to ring. Rost, being junior, went to answer it just as Major Rudigier and Lieutenant Brenner made their appearance, still armed, and were waved quickly away.

"Major, may I see those papers there? *Those*," Henkl said.

He seemed to be pointing at the photographs of Maria Anna Schicklgruber's Imperial Police residence reports.

"This?"

"No, next to it. The picture of the woman herself."

Rost, from the far corner of the room, called out: "General, you're wanted on the line."

Tieck-Mitringer swore and stamped over, almost wrenching the phone from Rost. He began talking quickly and inaudibly into the mouthpiece.

Henkl took no notice. He picked up the faded little picture. It showed a stern-faced woman, not unattractive, with a strong jaw and sad, deep-set eyes. Henkl squinted at it, turned it to the light.

"Well?" questioned Langbein.

Henkl took a deep breath.

"It could be . . . yes, it just could be . . ."

"It could be *what*, for God's sake?"

Henkl reached into his tunic pocket and pulled out an envelope.

"Here, look at this and then tell me—you, Herr Reichs-gerichtsrat—tell me what you see . . . "

Michaelis came over, took both the daguerreotype and the envelope.

"What's in there?" demanded Langbein. "You didn't tell me."

"I forgot all about it until just now. It's an old picture—I took it from Jankow. Old, but clear, Major. One of the first of its kind, I imagine. Even earlier that that one there."

Michaelis was by now examining the picture himself.

Henkl went on: "It shows a family group, as you see. Jankow's maternal great grandparents. The Frankenbergers. The very same family."

"But what. . . ?"

"Do you see the woman in the rear, at the left? Jankow didn't know her name. He thought that she was a servant in his great-grandmother's house, which she seems to be, judging by the way she's dressed." Henkl waited for a few seconds. Michaelis lowered the picture and stared.

282

"Can you get me a glass, a magnifier of some sort? I can't see the face that clearly."

"Look, look closely," urged Henkl. "I'm sure . . . "

"It doesn't look like the same face to me," said Langbein guardedly.

"Wait . . . wait," said Michaelis. "Here, let me put the glass on it." But though he held the magnifier close over the tiny image, he did not look down. Rather, he spoke directly to Henkl as though there were no one else in the room. "If it is . . . *if* . . . can you imagine the impact it will have? It would be the final, absolute explanation for his madness. He must have known all along or at the very least *suspected*, long before he received the letter from his nephew. That letter, gentlemen, reads as though the writer believes that Hitler *did* know all about it, that it was a *known* secret he was threatening to reveal. Oh yes. He has known and the German nation has allowed itself to be led by a man whose every act is the result of this one thing, this hatred of the Jews that is nothing but self-hatred, a consuming insanity of precisely the same kind that drove the mad Torquemada whose name graces this file. Consider, gentlemen that the racial laws are so drawn, by *him*, that a one eighth Jew is not a Jew at all if he does not consider himself as such. Thus Hitler has insured that he will not suffer what he makes others suffer. Yet for him, inside, even the *idea* that it might be true has been enough to make him . . . "

Michaelis got no further. All at once everyone became aware of Tieck-Mitringer who now stood halfway between the archway and the table. His face was dark, his eyes wide, staring and slate-colored like those of a drug addict. For a second, Henkl thought that he had been shot. He stood there, swaying slightly, the field telephone still in his hand. He was shouting at the top of his lungs for Major Rudigier and Lieutenant Brenner.

In an instant the pair had appeared in the doorway.

"Cover them. See that no one moves a step," Tieck-Mitringer cried.

Without understanding but without hesitating either, both Rudigier and Brenner swung the muzzles of their submachine guns around until they were pointed directly at the group by the table.

Then, suddenly, Tieck-Mitringer began to laugh—a long, loud, almost hysterical guffaw that seemed to come right from his bootsoles.

"It's all over. Finished, done with. You can put all of that shit away. It doesn't matter any more."

Langbein froze. His hand dropped to his waist and only the fact that his holster was visibly empty prevented Brenner from pulling the trigger.

Tieck-Mitringer stood there, his chest heaving, the tears rolling down his face. When he had finally gotten control of himself, he began to speak in a hushed voice from which all inflection, all emotion had been suddenly and completely drained.

"I have just spoken to General Halder, gentlemen. And do you know what he has told me? No, of course you don't know. You couldn't possibly imagine such an idiotic, impossible thing. General Halder has just told me this, gentlemen . . ." He was now speaking in short, disconnected spurts. "They were all ready to move, Von Witzleben and Heinz, all ready to go over to the Chancellery and arrest *him*. But General Brauschitsch wanted to make sure. 'Wait,' he said, and he went over himself, first, to be certain that Hitler was really there. And no sooner had he arrived than your friend Kordt got hold of him. Mussolini had just been on the phone from Rome, proposing himself as mediator, at the instance of the British and the French. As mediator, gentlemen. As an *arbitrator*. And the Führer has accepted his offer. D'you understand what that means, gentlemen? That word 'accepted'? There will be no Operation Green, no war, no British and French intervention. Chamberlain is already on his way to Munich to settle things. The deal's been worked out. There will be cheering crowds in the streets of Germany, gentlemen, cheering crowds . . . by the weekend . . . cheering the genius of our Leader. The Führer has won again. Without shedding a drop of blood."

"Then," whispered Trcka, "There is no possibility now of a putsch . . . my God . . . none whatsoever."

"Exactly what Von Witzleben has said. Even Oster agrees."

Michaelis looked as though he had been struck with an

284

axe. Rost instinctively grabbed for his arm, afraid that the man would fall. Langbein slumped in his chair, aghast.

"Major Rudigier, you, Brenner—hold it steady. Gentlemen, no one move, please." Tieck-Mitringer stepped briskly over to the table.

"Under the circumstances, Major Langbein, to keep these documents would constitute an act of treason to the head of state and to the country."

He reached out and snatched up both the letters and the faded picture that Henkl had produced. Then, as everyone watched, frozen, unable to offer even the slightest resistance, he took out his cigarette lighter and touched the flame to the papers. He held the scraps in his huge hands as they smoked and curled, oblivious to the little flame that was burning at his flesh as well.

Then, very slowly, he opened his fingers and a few flakes of gray ash floated to the floor.

Trcka moaned. Not even Langbein dared speak. Henkl's eyes were red and the vein on his temple was throbbing intolerably.

Tieck-Mitringer gathered himself up, coming almost to attention.

"And now, if you will excuse me, I have work to do. Major Rudigier will issue the necessary orders. It's back to barracks for us. It would seem that the army won't be needed for a long time to come."

He turned about sharply and strode from the room.

Just as he reached the archway, he stopped, did an about-face, and with a fierce and thoroughly ambiguous violence, flung out his arm in a rigid salute.

"*Heil Hitler*," he said and, turning, left the room.

Epilogue

HALDER, FRANZ: Chief of General Staff, 1938–42. Arrested after the failure of the July 1944 plot against Hitler's life. Imprisoned at Neiderdorf, freed April 1945. Still living.

OSTER, HANS: Chief of Staff of the Abwehr to 1944. Arrested after the failure of the July plot. Executed at Flossenberg concentration camp, April 1945.

CANARIS, WILHELM: Director of the Abwehr to 1944. Arrested after the failure of the July plot. Executed at Flossenberg concentration camp, April 1945.

MICHAELIS, BERNHARD: Judge of the Supreme Court to 1944. Arrested after the failure of the July plot. Beaten to death at Plotzensee Prison, April 1945.

LANGBEIN, ERNST WALTER: Chief of Operations, Abwehr, Vienna, to 1945. Captured by Russian troops. Last heard of in Danzig, 1953.

HENKL, KLAUS: Iron Cross, second class, Stalingrad, 1942. Killed in action during the Russian occupation of Vienna, 1945.

SCHANZ, ULRICH: 1940 to 1949, proprietor of Schanz's Dry Goods, St. Gallen, Switzerland. Retired in 1950. Memoirs published by Kaltenborn Verlag, limited edition, 1957. Died of natural causes, 1961.

TRCKA, AUGUST: Voluntarily confined to Bitterberg Sanitarium, Linz, 1938–43; said to have been working on a history of the Thirty Years' War. Died of natural causes, 1952.

TRCKA, MELITTA: Managed Trcka estates to 1945. From 1945 to date, consultant, vice-chairman, later chairman of the board, Presner Export-Import—watches, miscellaneous optical parts, Vienna, Paris, London.

TIECK-MITRINGER, HUGO: Assistant Chief of Staff to General Field Marshal Keitl to 1944. Killed in action, Krivoi Rog, The Ukraine, February 1944.

ROON, HERBERT: Board member, I. G. Farben, 1941–44. Tried Nuremburg, 1947, sentenced to eight years' imprisonment; sentence commuted, 1949. Elected Deputy to the Bundestag, 1950–55. Retired to family estates near Darmstadt, 1956.

JOCHMANN, GERHARD, M.D.: Director of Psychiatry, Charité Hospital, Berlin, 1939–45. Cleared by de-Nazification panel, 1946. From 1948 to date, private psychiatric practice, West Berlin; lecturer in abnormal psychology, Frankfurt, Cologne, Edinburgh, and elsewhere.

Finis